A trembling had begun deep inside me as the old sense of spinning started in my brain. I was whirling, whirling into oblivion. It was as though I could hear the amplified explosion of a gun going off in this room, echoing down through time. I could hear the dreadful impact of a bullet on flesh, see the dazzle of light on the gun. And the blood—spurting.

A voice belonging to the present reached me from the doorway. It was Gail. "You remember now, don't you, Laurie? Why not pick up that deringer? Pick it up and hold it the way you did that other time. Put your finger on the trigger and pull. Go ahead—fire it. You want to, don't you. . . ."

DOMINO

Phyllis A. Whitney

FAWCETT CREST • NEW YORK

DOMINO

This book contains the complete text of the original hard-cover edition.

Published by Fawcett Crest Books, a unit of CBS Publications, the Consumer Publishing Division of CBS Inc., by arrangement with Doubleday & Company, Inc.

ISBN: 0-449-24350-8

Printed in the United States of America

First Fawcett Crest printing: December 1980

10   9   8   7   6   5   4   3   2   1

My thanks to those who helped to make *Domino* possible. To Marlys Millhiser and Lucinda Baker, who know the West, and whose books I admire. To David Clemens of the Huntington Public Library, who found all that wonderful material about deringers for me. And especially to Sara Courant of the Patchogue Public Library, who never fails me, no matter what peculiar roads of research I choose to follow.

THE FIRST MOVE

The old woman sat by the bedroom window looking out upon the town her father had built. Since there had never been room for more than a few streets running in narrow file along the ledge beneath the mountain, it wasn't a large town. Now its false fronts were crumbling and the gallows frames that had topped the mines were long gone to dust. Once every house had been occupied and the bustle of furious activity had spelled riches for all. Once she had been young and handsome and vigorously alive. Wealth and power had been hers to do with as she pleased.

Today, while the wealth remained, both real and potential, the power lay dormant in her own weary body, and no one thought of her as a woman anymore. When there was no one left to help her with the fight, how was she ever again to rouse herself to battle? Wasn't it easier to close her eyes and let it all go away, give in to the Enemy? Not merely the enemy of time and age, but her real enemy—that man who strode the streets of Jasper with all the force and energy at his command. Not waiting for her to die, as he might have done more kindly, but ordering her out of his way. Threatening her.

His offer of money she could resist. She didn't need any more money. What frightened her most was his hinting that if she would not give way, there were stronger weapons he might use. He had even mentioned a name— "Noah"—and that had sent old pain, old horror and despair striking through her, shriveling her very flesh. It was a name she had tried not to think of for years. One she couldn't bear to remember now in her weakness and desperation.

Though it cost her painful effort, she had attempted to warn Caleb Hawes, her cold, sometimes intimidating family lawyer, that the man out there was dangerous. Caleb had said there was nothing anyone could do at this late date. He wanted her to let the horrible past keep its secrets; wanted her to give way, give in. Once there had been a time when Caleb would never have dared to urge her in any direction she didn't choose to take. These days she wasn't sure she could trust him. Certainly she wouldn't do as he wanted.

Never would she give in, despite the moments of wavering. Not as long as there was breath left in her aging body. Eighty-four years of life, and she wasn't done yet. Not quite yet. If only she could be the woman she had once been. Or was that woman still here inside, wearing this frail disguise?

The man she feared couldn't yet command her fully. He couldn't bring Noah back to haunt her. Not as long as she chose to stay in this house and block everything he wanted, not while the last remnants of her strength remained. On mornings like this, with sun pouring in the windows and the mountains blazing with light, she always felt more valiant, more willing and able to fight. But when the early dusks came and light vanished in long mountain shadows, her courage slackened. She couldn't go on like this forever. He would wear her down, defeat her in the end, wipe out all that she held dear. In a sense, he would wipe out history.

Unless.

Unless she sent for the child. That dreadful, destroying child whom she had never wanted to see again. The child who had brought her life down in ruins about her, and who still lived out there far away to the east. Of course she was a child no longer. All that had happened twenty years ago. She had been no more than eight when she and her mother had fled from this house. She was a woman grown now—and totally unknown. Nevertheless, she was alive. The aunt was still there. She had written from time to time, and she could be reached. The child could be reached.

8

Not a child. She must try to remember that. A girl, a young woman. A woman who might be persuaded to help her grandmother. It was time to decide.

She would write to the aunt now. She would make her plea. After all, that girl owed her something—owed her for everything she had done, everything she had destroyed.

Across the room, on a desk she seldom used anymore, writing paper and pen awaited her. The old woman reached for her cane and drew herself painfully to her feet, hating her own frailty. She turned for one last look out the window upon the town that *he* was taking from her, and then moved purposefully toward her desk.

I

Because it was crucially necessary for me to escape New York, I had come to Connecticut as the one haven to which I could turn.

Sitting here on a bench in the peaceful little park that surrounded Dillon's summer theater, I tried to let apprehension flow away from me. My setter, whose obvious name was Red, leaned at my knee watching ducks paddling in the pond, now and then tugging reproachfully at his leash.

I was grateful for maple branches overhead shielding me from bright June sunshine. Light was a part of what troubled me. It needn't matter here. I could let the thing happen—if it must—and gain my release for a time. But this was no way to live for the rest of my life, and I had to find a way out. I *must* find a way.

Only a week ago in New York I'd heard them talking in the office of the university press where I worked as an assistant editor. "It's her husband's death, you know. He was much older than Laurie, but it was a very close marriage, and she's still devastated, even after two years." The words warned me that my rising tensions had begun to show. There was no way to stop this, and I knew what the humiliating, frightening outcome would be, knew no way to avoid it. Doctors had never helped, and I was through with tranquilizers. Nor would I go to a psychiatrist.

After all, Peter Waldron, my husband, had been a psychiatrist and the author of several much consulted books on emotional disturbances. I could grow angry even now when I thought of how he had used me. My office friends knew nothing about the facts of my marriage, and their judgments were utterly false. Now at last something new was happening inside me. Some strength of will too long submerged, perhaps suppressed, was rising in me. I meant to let it rise.

In the warm June morning the park was quiet all around me, innocent and dreaming. Last night I'd come here alone to the summer theater to test myself. The lights and crowds had not disturbed me, and I'd been quite taken by the vital young actor who had played the lead. No one had noticed me, and that had been reassuring because it meant that I was doing nothing as yet to make myself conspicuous.

Yet this morning, when all about me was peaceful in the sunlight, the familiar tension was rising again and beginning to vibrate, almost in tune with the bees. When a dragonfly darted near me, I ducked nervously. In a little while that frightening top in my head would begin its spinning—faster and faster.

Well, let it come! Let it come, and for once face it through, I told myself.

The red setter whined plaintively and looked up at me, pleading until I gave in. "All right, Red, have your fun." I let him off his leash and he bounded joyfully away to investigate strange territory, as unaware as I that he was shortly to become a messenger of destiny. My thoughts turned inward, as they did too often nowadays.

It wasn't, as they thought at the office, that I still missed Peter with the same sense of fright and loss that I'd felt at his death two years ago. I had married him when I was twenty-one, a few months after my mother had died, and we'd had five years together. Not very quiet years, as it proved. I had even turned up in one of Peter's serious tomes. The woman in the case he had recorded had short brown hair and was small, while I was tall and piled my long fair hair on top of my head. Nevertheless, the disguise was thin, and it was me he was writing about. My "aberration" that had so fascinated him was all there, and I'd recognized myself at once with a sense of deep hurt and betrayal. I had hated being examined in print in such meticulous detail by my own husband.

Yet I still missed him—most of all at night. I missed the comfort of arms to hold and protect me, and the pillow talks we used to have. How empty a bed could be when you slept alone.

My feelings toward Peter had always been ambivalent. He had been my protector, counselor, lover—even something of the father I couldn't remember. And he had loved me in his own way, despite the fact that he was so much older and wiser than I, just as I had loved him in mine. Even though he hadn't proved to be the source of all the answers I longed for, he was truly a nurturer. Just as my mother had been. And I was too much of a leaner.

How often I had wondered if everything might have been different if my professor father had lived. But he had died of pneumonia when I was two, and my mother must have suffered deeply, for she could never bear to talk about him. I had seen pictures of her when she was the young wife, Marybeth Morgan, and quite beautiful, with huge eyes, a tremulous mouth, and a lovely figure. Though in life I could only remember her fading, her giving up, and the way she stared at me sometimes with a despairing watchfulness. As though she waited in dread for something to surface in me. At least, through an inheritance my father had left her, there had been enough to live on, and we hadn't suffered on that score.

Such memories had been surfacing more than ever lately. At the office my editor had said, "For God's sake, Laurie, you're twanging like a harp. Take your two weeks and get away. See if you can get those nerves in hand and some color back in your face."

My aunt's house in Connecticut had always been a storm port in need. I telephoned Ruth Thorne, and as always, she said, "Come." She had never protected or nurtured. She had never approved of the fearful way my gentle, sad mother raised me. Perhaps it was Ruth's vinegar and spice that really fed my spirit when I needed it and grew tired of the diet of milk toast and hot lemonade my mother fed me so protectively.

At my aunt's invitation, I packed a suitcase, shut up the house in Long Island that I'd shared with Peter, and put Red beside me in the front seat of Peter's decorous blue sedan. Ruth took one look at me when I arrived and pushed me out of the house.

"Get outdoors, get some exercise. Come back when you're good and tired. And no picky eating. You'll take what I put on the table or back to New York you go!"

I laughed and hugged her and went out for a walk with Red at my heels. But not even her doses of vinegar caused the spinning in my head to subside.

I used to warn Peter when it started, when it might be coming on, and he would follow its progress as though I were indeed a bug on a slide. Afterward, shaken by what had happened, I would be quiet for a while. Until it began to build up all over again, winding like some terrible child's top, forever spinning and reflecting a light that dazzled and frightened me. Peter had wanted to take me to a confrere who would hypnotize me, but I'd flatly refused. I needed to be cured of whatever disturbed me, threatening my very sanity, yet at the same time I had always been afraid to face whatever I might learn. Far deeper than the desire to know, there had been in me a fear of knowing. It was that fear that I must somehow find the courage to defeat. Fear in particular of that name which sometimes returned to haunt me. *Noah.* Who was Noah, and why did the sound of his name bring terror with it?

Now as I sat drowsing on my bench in this pleasant park, Red came bounding back to put his paws on my knees and look lovingly into my face. He seemed to sense my moods, and I sometimes felt that his utter devotion helped me more than Peter ever had. Red might coax me at times, but he never required anything more of me than the love I gave him back.

When I'd petted him sufficiently, he bounded away again, ears flopping, red plumes flying—straight for the open door of the theater, not far away. I called him back, but he paid no attention, so I got up, not hurrying particularly, never dreaming what awaited me, and went after him. The doors were open, so there must be someone inside.

13

The building was a converted barn, and a lobby had been partitioned off beyond the main entrance. Other doors opened into the theater itself, and of course it was through one of these that Red went rushing. I didn't care for the idea of chasing him vainly through the seats of the orchestra section, but there was no help for it. At least it would give me some exercise, and I hoped we wouldn't be disturbing anyone. This hope was dashed immediately. Up on the bare lighted stage the actors of the summer stock company sat around a long table, with blue-bound scripts before them. An electrician was testing lights, and on the table a large coffeepot offered sustenance. An undistinguished aluminum coffeepot—so prosaic an object to change one's entire life.

Red of course made a great commotion as he galloped down the aisle, heading directly for the stage, sensing friendly humans. Humans were always friendly to Red. Up the steps he bounded, making his choice at once in the actor-director of the company. I slowed my steps, hating to be conspicuous. I didn't belong here at all, interrupting a rehearsal, and dressed as I was, so much more formally than the actors on the stage in their jeans and shorts. My pale blue linen suit and wide-brimmed straw hat set me off as a city dweller. Though the hat wasn't so much for fashion's sake as because it shaded my face. As Peter had often pointed out, I was all too often given to hiding.

There could, however, be nothing inconspicuous about my approach in the wake of my uninhibited dog. It was as though I were the play and the actors the audience. They stared at me, some of them smiling, and the man whom I had seen in the lead role the night before stood up with a pat for Red and came to the edge of the stage to watch my approach.

"Rescue is at hand," he said over his shoulder to the company, and flashed me the brilliant smile I remembered from his performance last night.

I tried again to summon Red, who was by this time garnering so much attention that he had no time for me.

Helpless to do anything but walk toward the stage, I could only look up at the man who waited for me.

At first glance I would never have called Hillary Lange my ideal for lead material in a play. He wasn't handsome, though his rather rugged features added up to something not easily forgotten. His height barely topped that of his leading lady, but his body was sturdy and well muscled. His hair grew thick and brown above his forehead, and there was a dark flash to his eyes that could surprise with its intensity—so that one's attention was compelled. When he moved, I had noted that it was with the grace of a dancer, or of some lithe, prowling creature that had never been wholly tamed. On stage I had recognized him as unique. He had presence, electricity. Something I didn't know how to name. Perhaps it was that dark, half-threatening intensity that the female in me responded to, whether I liked it or not. Up there on the boards he certainly commanded—as he was commanding me now. I was just below him by this time, murmuring embarrassed apologies, when he stopped me.

"Never mind all that. Will you help us out?"

His words surprised me and I stood still, startled into my old impulse to flee any unfamiliar situation. His voice went on, its sonorous quality soothing, taking for granted my response.

"One of our cast seems to have been delayed. Will you come up and help us out—read the part of Maggie for our next production?"

Inside me the old voice was crying, "No, no—I'd be frightened to death! I couldn't possibly . . ." But my feet had better sense. They took me directly up the steps, and he came to give me a hand, bringing me to the empty place at the table next to his own. Standing beside him, I was aware of being tall and too thin, and somehow too pale and blond beside all his dark vitality.

Red jumped at me in joyous approval and I patted him down, clipped on his leash, and looped it around the leg of a chair at the back of the stage.

"Stay," I told him sternly, and for once he decided to obey.

15

Hillary Lange reached for my broad-brimmed hat with assurance and removed it. At once I could feel hairpins slipping, and a fair tendril fell over my nose. He laughed, lifting it back from my face with one finger—and it was as though some current had touched me.

"Tell me your name," he said.

I answered without hesitation, "Laurie Morgan," and wondered why I hadn't said "Waldron." True, I no longer wore Peter's ring, though I wasn't sure why I'd wanted to put it aside since I didn't think I would ever marry again. And now I had put aside his name as well. Yet I didn't feel especially disloyal. I'd given Peter everything I could. He was gone, but I was alive, and I had to find a new way for myself.

"Laurie Morgan," Hillary Lange repeated, an odd note that was almost wonderment in his voice. As though in his quick way he already sensed something I would grope my way toward more slowly—that we were going to mean a great deal to one another.

He introduced me to the company and then handed me the blue-bound side for my speeches. "It's a very small part—you won't have any trouble. It's just that it's a key role and we need it to go through the reading. Run through it yourself, if you like. We'll give you time." Nonchalantly he dropped my hat upon an empty chair and waited. Everyone else waited too, perhaps not as sure as their director that this amateur should be invited to participate.

I noted the name of the play and looked into the dark flash of his eyes. "I've seen it in New York. I remember the part."

Somehow I thrust back a self-consciousness that wanted to envelope and smother me, and read my opening lines. Not too badly. Only a falter here and there. I was scared but I was doing it, and lightning hadn't struck me down, nor was anyone roaring with laughter. With this new tension perhaps the other was fading a little.

Hillary's eyes were upon me and I could tell that he was pleased, perhaps even a little surprised, and the tiny kernel of courage began to grow. I read on with more confidence.

16

The spotlights were still being turned off and on, as the stage crew experimented with them. They made me uneasy, as lights often did. But at least they weren't being focused on the table—and they had nothing to do with me. I could hear my voice growing in strength with my growing assurance.

Then, without warning, one blinding beam of the big spot turned suddenly and fell directly upon me, fell also upon the chrome plating of the coffeepot, striking from its sides a silver dazzle. And I knew that the moment I always feared had come. My voice broke in the middle of a word, and my eyes stared. My body froze into a state that was almost catatonic, though I knew, as if from a distance, what was going on around me. Vaguely I heard voices raised in alarm, heard someone speaking my name. But there was nothing I could do except stare in utmost terror at that silver flash of light. Then the spot was turned off, in response to Hillary's shouted command. I was aware of what was happening, but I couldn't move. Red was alternately whining and barking wildly. Red *knew*.

Hillary came behind my chair and put his hands on my shoulders, shaking me gently. Someone whispered, and I heard him stop the whisper curtly. With the light turned off the nightmare broke its spell, releasing me, and I could look about in shame and dismay.

I was trembling and my body was bathed in sweat, but the spinning was gone, the tension released. The moment of frightful revelation had once more been postponed.

Hillary pulled back my chair and helped me up. "We'll take a break," he told the others, and I went with him blindly to a side door that opened upon the June morning, leaving the whispering behind.

We sat on the grass beside the pond, not bothering with a bench. Inside the theater someone had released Red, and he came dashing out to frolic around us, making friends with Hillary at once. At least I had stopped shivering.

"I'm sorry," I said. "I'm all right now. I really am," but my voice broke as I spoke the words.

17

He was studying me with a sympathy that was as welcome as it was unexpected. I needed someone to cling to, if only for this passing moment.

"Has this happened to you before?" he asked.

"Not for a long time. I'm so awfully sorry—"

"Stop apologizing," he told me. "I shouldn't have drawn you into something you didn't want to do."

I liked his saying that. Usually men considered very little what I wanted, but were given to instructing me in what they thought I ought to do.

"Do you know what causes it?" he went on.

"No, not really. Yet it seems to happen when there are strong lights around. Perhaps they hypnotize me in some way. I'm not unconscious. I know what's happening, but I just freeze."

"I see," he said quietly. "I'd like to understand."

With complete naturalness he took my hand in his and held it gently.

"You're very pretty," he said, "and much too frightened. What can I do to help?"

For the first time since Peter's death I wanted to let myself go, to respond to a touch, to accept anything that might be offered. Hillary Lange was even more compelling up close than he was on a stage, and I felt all my resistance weakening.

"Try to talk about it," he said. "Talking may help."

That was what Peter had always said, and sometimes I had tried. Now I tried again, haltingly, putting my few memories into words, finding it almost easier to talk to a stranger than to my husband.

Mostly, I remembered mountains. Not the gentle mountains of the eastern coastline, but the tall, fierce mountains of the West. Sometimes I could close my eyes and glimpse a rugged cone-shaped outline that stood up alone against the sky.

Over the years I'd had a strange half-waking dream in which I seemed to be on a horse riding wildly toward the high, dominant mountain, driven by the desperate knowledge that I must help someone. Someone I loved who was in terrible danger. In my dream I could feel a

18

cold wind stinging my face, and hear the sound of hooves pounding after me in frightening pursuit. But I never followed through to any conclusion, and when I was fully awake the dream had no meaning.

All this I poured out in a tumble of words to Hillary Lange, and he listened gravely, considerately.

There was something more that I had never told anyone, and that I couldn't put into words even now. I could almost remember the face of a young boy, perhaps a few years older than I. A face that could appear stubborn and rebellious, yet always kind when he looked at me. I had no name to attach to the memory, but only a sense of warmth and comfort. The memory of a time of frantic fear, when young arms had held me awkwardly, young hands had soothed me as they might have soothed a lost kitten.

Perhaps I'd never told Peter because he would have analyzed a precious feeling out of existence. He would have told me that I was looking for a protector and this was my sexual fantasy, my fantasy man. Whether that was true or not, I didn't want to tell any of this to the stranger beside me. But there was something else that I could speak of.

"I remember a mountain town with one main street and false fronts that made it look like a movie set. Except that these were the real thing. And there was a house. My grandmother's house, I think. The house of my father's mother."

"Take me into your house," Hillary said. I could sense the electric urgency in him, and knew that he had the actor's ability to empathize, to almost become *me*.

But not even in response to so intense an interest could I open the door of that house.

I had tried before, at Peter's instigation, but I could never force mind and memory beyond the closed door. Sometimes there were flashes that came without warning. Glimpses in my mind's eye of an enormous shadowy room, of a flat box of some dark wood that sat on a table. A box I was forbidden to touch. Vaguely, too, I remembered my grandmother. Grandmother Persis of Morgan

19

House. Her first husband's name had been Morgan, like mine. The "silver Morgans" of Jasper, Colorado. This I knew from my mother's tales. But I couldn't remember my grandfather—if I'd ever known him. And there had been another man. That man named Noah. But here my thoughts flinched away, not wanting to remember.

I went on aloud to Hillary. "Something must have happened in that house when I was about eight years old. Something so terrible that it made me dangerously ill. Afterward my mother brought me home to the East, where she had grown up, and I was in a hospital for a long while. When I was well again, I couldn't remember anything about that time in Colorado. What was more, my mother didn't want me to remember. I never saw my grandmother again. So much is gone."

Gone except for those disturbing glimpses that came like flashes of light, and those times when the feeling of tension began to build and I grew horribly afraid. It was as though something in me knew that once I remembered I would be annihilated. My reason—everything—would go! Peter said that was ridiculous, but he could never convince me of anything else.

I spoke abruptly to Hillary. "Let's go back. Tell them to keep those lights off, and I'll try again."

He looked approving. "Good for you. I like courage. Come along then."

Courage? The thing Peter had always told me I had too little of? I stiffened my spine and my will, and went back with an inner quaking that I didn't allow anyone to suspect. And I read my lines straight through, coming in properly on the cues. When the reading was over the actors crowded around me, and some of them even patted me demonstratively, as people were often given to doing. As though I were a child who had fallen and been hurt and was recovering, much to everyone's relief. It was a role I was very tired of playing.

Hillary stood aside and said nothing, offered me no soothing words or pats, but there seemed something truly concerned in his watchfulness that reached me. When the company broke for lunch, he led Red and me out to his bright yellow car and drove us to Aunt Ruth's. She came to the door with a raised eyebrow when I brought Hillary up the porch steps, but she greeted him guardedly and invited him in.

His refusal was graceful enough, and I expected him to vanish out of my life and never be seen again. Instead he held my hand for just a moment.

"Will you have dinner with me tonight, Laurie? This is our night off at the theater."

It was my new self who answered, "I'd love to."

"Then I'll pick you up around six-thirty. There's a good place out on the highway."

I wondered if there was a tiny edge of triumph in the laughing look he turned on Aunt Ruth, as though he guessed that she didn't wholly approve. Then he was gone, driving off in that yellow car, and I followed her inside.

"That was fast," she said. "Where did you find him?"

She knew very well about those spells I'd had most of my life, and I told her just what had happened, perhaps sounding a little pleased with myself.

"Watch out with that one," she said when I was through. "He's pretty overwhelming."

"I know," I said, and she let it go.

She had tried to bring me down to earth, but I was too keyed up, too newly intoxicated. I ran past her up the stairs to my room—the room that always waited for me. It wasn't necessary—or possible—to explain to anyone about Hillary Lange. There was something I had glimpsed in him out there beside the pond when he had been concerned about me and trying to help. Like my mother, like Peter, Hillary Lange might be another "nurturer." And did I really want that?

"Here we go again," I said to Red, and he barked his approval. Red had liked Hillary too.

I tried to reassure myself. An interesting event had happened in my life, and I didn't mean to turn away from it. I needn't ever again be as dependent as I had in the past—of that I was sure—but I wanted a friend. Even as

21

unlikely a friend as Hillary Lange, and I wasn't going to let Aunt Ruth's prejudice stop me.

Falling in love was something else. That wasn't for me right now. I closed my eyes, determinedly foolish, and began to think about the coming dinner tonight.

II

In mid-July, Hillary's dressing room backstage at the Dillon Theater was warm and close. The small fan turning listlessly on his makeup shelf didn't help a great deal as I sat waiting for the curtain to ring down on the evening performance. The telegram that had brought me here lay folded in my purse, and I didn't need to read it again until Hillary was with me.

What a lovely few weeks these had been. Nearly over now, leaving me still unsure of what lay ahead. From the first, Hillary had sensed the troubled ground on which I walked, sensed my readiness to draw back in the face of even the slightest coercion. So there had been no pressure on his part, but simply an alert waiting.

In a way that puzzled me. Why Laurie Morgan for Hillary Lange? He could have almost any woman he wanted. It was a little like Peter all over again, and I was by turns happy and doubtful, and still terribly unsure—of myself. I wasn't ready for any irrevocable step, and he seemed to be willing to wait. Bit by bit he had drawn me out—"discovering" me, as he put it. Mostly, wonderfully, we liked the same things. We liked Tennessee Williams and Paul Zindel and Neil Simon. We enjoyed the novels of Jorge Luis Borges—and Agatha Christie. We adored Alec Guinness and Paul Newman and the Marx Brothers, and we were in thorough agreement as to the excellence of Jean Stapleton and Maureen of the same name. We

22

agreed about Laurence Olivier and argued over Richard Burton, finding it as much fun to argue as to agree. We were fervently for peace and wanted to do something about world hunger—though what, we weren't entirely sure.

We were, I suppose, entirely self-absorbed. I managed a leave of absence from my job, and felt only a slight pang when it was so easily granted. Aunt Ruth was a good sport. Though she spoke her mind from time to time, she let me stay with her until Hillary's season ended. This was to happen in a week or so because the stock company run had not been an unmitigated success and a summer play boasting name actors was coming to fill out the rest of July and August.

Occasionally, when Hillary had the time, we drove to a nearby stable, since we both loved horses and riding. A residue for me from the days when I'd visited my grandmother in Colorado and learned to ride by the time I was six. Hillary had done some work in Hollywood and ridden in a few cowboy pictures, among other things, so he was at home in a saddle.

Probably by this time he knew more about me than I did about him. I knew that his father, whom he'd loved, had walked out when he was quite young, though father and son had been reunited later. Other than that he told me very little. I sensed that he was a man who enjoyed possessing, but that it was hard for him to give himself away to another human being. In spite of his open manner there was a reserve in him, a privacy, that I respected. If he had to allow me time, I had to make the same gift to him. So to some extent we moved warily with each other. He could be moody at times, turning touchy and remote.

I knew that he remembered unhappiness and was afraid of total commitment, of marriage, of permanent ties. So we left each other free—and I liked that best too. Yet I sensed that with the season's ending there must be a change. Either a strengthening of our relationship or its dissolving. I had a feeling of waiting, of marking time, of something about to happen. I was not entirely sure of what it was that I really wanted.

There was one trait of Hillary's that disturbed me. He was, I discovered, capable of exploding into terrible rage. I saw this happen one morning when I was watching a rehearsal, and I knew that everyone on the stage was alarmed by him in that moment. He went off by himself afterward for a few hours of recovery and we left him alone. When I next saw him, he seemed himself again, but the explosion had frightened me. There was an uncertainty that lay behind my affection, and I knew that nothing was firmly settled between us yet.

Now as I sat in his dressing room, laughter rang out from the stage. The play was nearing its end, and in a little while the applause would sound. After the curtain calls Hillary would come rushing in, keyed to that high that actors reach after a good performance. The company and the players might not have been remarkably successful, but audiences came to see Hillary Lange, and the applause was for him, no matter what role he played.

Often I had the feeling that while Hillary was enormously talented, he had yet to find himself. He had written an unsuccessful play or two, tried his hand at directing—yet had always fallen back on acting for his bread and butter. Not so much because he was especially gifted as an actor, but because of that mesmerizing spell he could cast upon an audience, and that made him valuable in any play. He had only to be himself. Already I knew that he wanted a great deal more than that, but exactly what I had no idea, and perhaps he didn't know either. Not yet.

Just once he had alarmed me by his talk of writing another play—about me. About amnesia. My sudden anger had surprised us both. I knew it stemmed from what Peter had done. I meant never to be anyone's guinea pig again, and when he saw my reaction Hillary told me to forget it. Of course he would write nothing that might hurt and upset me. Yet a certain damage had been done, and I moved uneasily with him for a time after that. We weren't quite sure of each other yet, and we both held

24

back, sensing perhaps that this might be a greater commitment than any casual affair. A greater commitment than either of us was as yet ready to make.

One of the things that most disturbed me was a sense of his watching, observing, questioning. As though I were a puzzle he must unravel. Yet he was always gentle with me, never demanding. Actors were like that, I began to realize. It was necessary for them to study the raw material at hand. How else could they transfer reality to the make-believe world they inhabited? So I mustn't mind his watching.

Then today everything had changed. The telegram had come. I had taken it to Aunt Ruth at once, and she had told me the one thing I'd never dreamed. During all these years she had felt duty-bound to report from time to time to my grandmother in Jasper, whether the old lady showed any interest in me or not. For a year or two there had been a lapse into silence, and then, a few weeks ago, Persis Morgan had written asking for my address. Something she had never done before. Without consulting me, Aunt Ruth had told her I was spending the summer in her house.

After all these years of deliberate silence the telegram had been sent directly to me, and it had thrown me into a state of quivering uncertainty. It was as if quicksand had opened beneath my feet, dragging me under, as though there were no safe step I could take in any direction.

"You don't have to go," Aunt Ruth said flatly when I showed her the wire.

But perhaps I did have to. That was what frightened me.

"Persis Morgan," she signed herself, so she, too, had taken back the Morgan name—the name of John Morgan, her first husband and my grandfather. Once I had loved her, as a very small girl. I seemed to remember that. And then in my growing years I'd come to hate her as an unknown ogre who had abandoned me and hurt my mother. For all that time there had never been any letters, never a Christmas or birthday card, and when I asked Mother about her, she had wept so bitterly that I learned

25

not to question. So I had thrust back my resentment toward a heartless grandmother and put her out of my mind.

Nevertheless, over the years, because of my pleading, Mother had told me a little of the past. Grandmother Persis' father had been an Englishman with the romantic name of Malcolm Tremayne. He was a younger son left nearly penniless by the system of entailing that allowed only the eldest son to inherit title and property. He had come, like a good many young Englishmen of that day, as an adventurer to Colorado. With his partner, Tyler Morgan, he had been lucky enough to strike silver in the side of a mountain, and they had named the mine the Old Desolate, after the mountain itself. Malcolm had married a pretty dance hall girl named Sissy Farrar, who was playing the "Silver Circuit," and brought her to live in the town of Domino, which sprang up below the mine. Thus my grandmother was born in Domino and grew up there to marry Tyler Morgan's son, Johnny.

I had never known my grandfather because he was already dead when we visited Jasper. Persis had married again, but about my grandmother's second husband my mother would never speak.

Now after all these years, when I hadn't known whether she was dead or alive, there had come this peremptory wire from Persis Morgan. She must be in her eighties now, and I couldn't understand why she had suddenly chosen to send for me. Interesting that she, too, had taken back the name of Morgan.

Through the open door of the dressing room where I waited, I could hear the sound of applause rising in enthusiasm as Hillary took his last bows. How they loved him! Not just the women. He was thoroughly masculine, and men liked him too. I savored their approval, but still wanted him to hurry.

He came in on that whoosh of air that always seemed to stir in his whirlwind passage, even across a room—his own personal wake. I had never seen him move with anything but a spring in his step and a swiftness of motion. What a beautiful man he was. What a sometimes outra-

26

geous, entirely beautiful man! And I was close to falling hopelessly in love with him. Dangerous—dangerous. But it could happen.

"Darling!" His pleased surprise was evident. I almost never went to the theater. But his antennae were as sensitive as ever. He came over to me, smelling warmly of makeup and sweat, and tilted my chin in his hand. "Something's happened?"

I took out the telegram and handed it to him silently. He read the words aloud: " 'I need you desperately. You must come. Letter follows. Persis Morgan.' "

I burst into words the moment he finished. "What arrogance! What an impossible old woman! All these years when she's never so much as noticed my existence—and now, to summon me like this!"

"She knew where to find you. She must have been very much aware of your existence."

"It turns out that Aunt Ruth has been writing to her all this time. And I never knew." I was feeling betrayed on all sides. Especially betrayed by some strong governing emotion rising in me. I spoke against it angrily, denying. "Of course I wouldn't think of going, no matter what she may say in her letter."

Hillary sat down before his mirror and began to work on the removal of makeup. In the glass his eyes avoided mine, but he spoke quietly enough.

"That's right—you don't have to go if you don't want to. But are you *sure* you don't want to?"

I stared at him, feeling still further betrayed, and he laughed.

"Don't look like that, Laurie. You must do what you please. I just wonder if you can know so quickly what that should be."

"What would you do?" I demanded.

His eyes flashed in the mirror. "I'd go, of course! Think of the adventure! Think of the possibilities! How can you pass them up?"

"What possibilities?"

"Answers, Laurie. Don't you want to know what hap-

27

pened out there? Don't you want to free yourself of the past once and for all?"

He was beginning to sound like Peter.

"No," I said flatly, "I don't," and left it at that.

Often after the show Hillary would come to Aunt Ruth's for me, and we would drive out for a late supper somewhere. But tonight, when he was dressed, he said, "I'll take you home. You're upset and you'll need to sleep on it. Don't worry any more tonight. We'll talk again tomorrow."

I nodded and wished that this feeling in my solar plexus like a knotted fist would go away. Tonight I would have liked to stay with Hillary and listen to him tell me that I need pay no attention to that woman in Colorado, or to her sudden arrogant pleas. But he wasn't telling me these things. For once he seemed not to sense my need, and he left me with a quick kiss and drove away before I could find any words to explain.

I didn't go into the house right away, but sat on the veranda steps, with the summer night humming about me. How lonely a summer night could seem. Frogs in a pond somewhere were harrumphing, and tree creatures added their chorus. The air was still warm from the day's hot sun. Yet—unwillingly—I thought of mountains. Cool, high mountains. Of one mountain in particular. A strange cone-like shape that had often risen in my dreams to haunt me with a meaning I'd never been able to fathom. That mountain was part of the mystery. The mystery of me. Had Peter been right? Was Hillary right now? Unless I saw it again, stood on its slopes, I would never know and the haunting could go on forever. I would always be afraid of sudden dazzling light and what inevitably followed the flash. Must it be like that for the rest of my life?

Something told me that not to know was the best way, the wise way. Aunt Ruth, too, though my mother had always refused to tell her what had happened in Colorado, urged me not to go. Today, after the telegram had come, we sat together over coffee cups in her bright old-fashioned kitchen and she talked a little about her younger sister, my mother.

"Marybeth was afraid of what might happen to you, Laurie. I think she worried too much. Even though I loved her as my little sister, I never thought she had enough guts. You do, Laurie, and someday you'll find that out. But I'm not sure that going to Colorado is the way."

Aunt Ruth was the only person who had ever accused me of having guts.

"I don't know," I said. "I just don't know."

Now I sat on the veranda steps and pushed all these things futilely around in my mind, still coming to no decision. In the end, I swallowed hard upon questions I couldn't bear to face and went to bed.

I needed Peter, I needed Hillary—I needed anyone at all who would hold and comfort and reassure me. Love me. But part of me resented a need that made me helpless and unable to decide for myself. A woman needed a man's arms, but not only to shield and protect. And I was no longer certain exactly what I wanted from Hillary. I wasn't even sure what he wanted from me.

Two days later the letter from Persis Morgan came. There were only a few paragraphs, the handwriting sometimes vigorous, sometimes wavering—as though the writer had forced herself to be assertive without complete success. The notepaper was heavy, the engraved address merely *Morgan House, Jasper, Colorado,* which in itself had a certain ring of arrogance about it.

I phoned Hillary and he met me in the park after Saturday matinee.

"I thought you told me the town was called Domino," he said when he'd read the letter.

I was impatient with irrelevant remarks. "No, no! That's where the first mine was dug—on Old Desolate. When Persis' father became rich, he built a mansion in Jasper." I closed my eyes against a flash of memory. "That was a bigger mining town, built by all that silver. Jasper is still on the maps. I looked it up once, years ago. I suppose Domino has long since blown away."

29

"She doesn't really say why she wants you," Hillary puzzled.

"She sounds hysterical. Melodramatic. Hinting that someone is trying to destroy her. And it's no affair of mine."

"Are you sure of that? Have you written to say you won't go?"

I stared at him, feeling oddly antagonized. "Not yet. There hasn't been time."

"What's going on in that funny little head of yours, Laurie?"

I felt increasingly impatient. With myself as well as with Hillary. I didn't have a "funny little head." I couldn't possibly go to Colorado—and that was that.

"If you don't go, you'll never know what happened," he repeated.

"That's right. I'll never know what horrible thing I may have done out there."

"You were eight years old. Whatever they are, a child's acts are to be forgiven."

"How can I forgive myself when I don't know what there is to forgive?"

"Isn't that the point?" he asked gently.

We were sitting on the same bench by the pond where I'd sat that first day when Red had wandered into the theater. I remembered what had followed when I'd gone up on that stage. I remembered the light, the dazzle. And I remembered another time since then, when the top in my head had begun to spin. We'd had a date to go riding, but when Hillary came for me I was sitting in my room upstairs at Aunt Ruth's with a mirror in my hands and the sun striking from it. I had blanked out. It had taken both Hillary and my aunt to bring me back into the real world.

Restlessly I jumped up from the park bench, leaving the circle of his arm, and walked to the edge of the pond. A frog sat looking at me from the bank.

"I suppose I could go," I said over my shoulder. "I could at least go and see what is happening and why she wants me there. I could find out that much."

Speaking the words seemed to release something in me.

30

It was as though giving up began to dissolve that knot inside me. Hillary said nothing, but when I turned and walked back to him he was smiling his approval.

"It won't be easy," I said. "But I'm tired of being helpless and leaning on other people. I'd better go, no matter how scared I am."

He made one of those swift decisions that were characteristic of him. "What if I go with you? We could face the old dragon together."

I went into the arms he held out to me, and my relief was enormous. I had never expected this, yet apparently it could be managed very easily.

The company was dispersing after next week, and Hillary wasn't sure what he wanted to do next. It was already too late for a fall play, and he was willing to take some time off. Perhaps he'd try writing again, and a change of scene might furnish just the inspiration he needed. Besides, he meant to keep an eye on me—so he'd better be there in case I needed him.

I had never loved him more. I gave myself willingly into his hands, agreeing to all the preparations he suggested, trying not to see Aunt Ruth's pained disapproval, thrusting back my own treacherous fears that never quite subsided. One small part of me still held back with Hillary, not altogether sure—though wanting to be sure. It was just that I never wanted to give all of myself away again. There had to be something at the core that was still mine alone—and it was that core that was guiding me now, sending me out to Colorado, even though I was letting Hillary plot my course.

Not that we left for Jasper immediately. First there was correspondence, although not with my grandmother. A somewhat stiff letter came from a man named Caleb Hawes, who was apparently the Morgan attorney. He referred to her as "Mrs. Morgan," and not by the name of her second husband, which I couldn't even remember. His letter, addressed to me as "Mrs. Waldron," was polite and noncommittal, and he let nothing of himself come through. He was an instrument carrying out Persis Morgan's wishes. There were no more words of desperate

31

need. My grandmother was very old, he explained, and she wanted to see me. A visit would be greatly appreciated and all my expenses would be taken care of. I would, of course, be a guest in her house. I accepted as coolly—though I didn't feel cool. I was growing more excited by the moment, with an excitement that overrode my deepest fears and drove me relentlessly in the direction I had chosen. And I signed myself "Laurie Morgan."

In a way this excitement and exhilaration resembled my feeling about heights. It was something dangerous, but not to be resisted. Something I could not stop myself from experiencing.

I didn't mention in my reply to my grandmother that I would arrive with both a companion and a dog. Best to handle that once we got there, Hillary said. He would stay at a motel, if there was a motel, and out in that country dogs were probably acceptable. Aunt Ruth didn't want to keep Red, and I didn't want to part with him anyway. He practically died whenever I put him in a kennel.

So it was arranged. And so we went to Jasper, Colorado—Hillary, Red, and I.

All the while, out there at the foot of a mountain called Old Desolate, the dry bones of a town named Domino waited for me. Waited as though destiny had planned my coming for nearly a hundred years.

III

All the way to Denver by plane the emotion in me grew, part excitement, anticipation—part plain fright. The thought of an autocratic grandmother I had never seen and had no reason to like would alarm me if I let it. And so would the thought of whatever it was that I might learn about myself once I was there. At the same time, counteracting my fears, was a new and rising sense of being in control of my life for the first time. I was going at last to meet whatever it was necessary for me to meet, and that knowledge helped me to bluff and to achieve a brave front for Hillary.

Nothing had begun to spin in my head to alarm me, and that I managed this surface calm must have surprised him. From time to time I caught him watching me as though I had suddenly emerged as a woman he had never seen before.

My poor Red suffered the incarceration of plane travel with no grace at all, and his reunion with me at Stapleton Airport was ecstatic. I had to apologize to him and return the fervency of his affection before he could be calmed.

Persis Morgan's attorney, Caleb Hawes, met our plane, and my first glimpse of him did nothing to reassure me. He was tall and poker-straight, with a chilly manner. A man of great dignity, probably in his late fifties, with a long face creased down each cheek by a vertical line that added to his look of unsmiling austerity. Dark hair clung to his skull, conservatively short. As conservative as his correct gray business suit and plain tie. Hardly a western type, I thought. But then my grown-up experience of the West had been mainly through old movies.

His companion better fitted my expectations, if I had any. He was young, perhaps in his early thirties, tall, thin, wiry, and sunbaked. His Levi's, faded denim jacket, and scuffed leather boots were for real, not for style, and the beat-up cowboy hat he wore with jaunty confidence suited him. When he took off his hat, I saw that thick black hair curled tight to his head and grew a little long at the back. His name was Jonathan Maddocks, and the sound of it roused a faint memory in me, as though I might have heard it before. He regarded me with frank interest out of smoky gray eyes that seemed to see a great deal, but were not entirely friendly.

"Jon works for Mrs. Morgan," Caleb Hawes added to his introduction.

As the young man bent to pick up our bags, I was aware of his continued oddly appraising look, and I had

33

the increasing feeling that Jon Maddocks was more than a hired hand, and that he did not altogether approve of me and my coming.

Caleb Hawes showed no surprise when I introduced my friend, Hillary Lange, and my dog, Red, but I suspected this was simply because he was not one to display emotion of any kind. His stiff courtesy told me without words that he was performing a duty for which he had little enthusiasm. And I guessed that he might have opposed my coming.

Jon Maddocks went ahead with our bags, and on the way to the car Mr. Hawes explained that we would drive to Boulder, and then to Nederland, where we would turn west into the mountains. He had of course brought the jeep from the ranch, since the side road to Jasper was rough going. This was no tourist trail, he said, and we must be prepared for a tiring trip. I suspected that he meant this would serve me right. There would be no friendship whatever with this man.

Hillary was placed in front beside Jon, who was driving, while the attorney, Red, I, and our bags were sorted into the rear. The man beside me was not given to chitchat, though Jon and Hillary were talking casually enough up in front—mainly because Hillary was asking questions that the younger man appeared to answer laconically.

Red put his head on my knee, forgiving me for my recent abandonment, and I stroked him absently.

When we'd left Denver behind on the road to Boulder, I made my first comment to Caleb Hawes' cold profile. "I didn't know that my grandmother owned a ranch."

"It's still called that," he told me. "Though it hasn't been a working ranch, except for a cow and a few horses, for a good many years. But you must remember it. You came here often enough as a child."

So he knew about that. "I remember riding," I said. "And I remember mountains. Not much else."

His silence had a ruminative quality, as though he were turning my reply over in his mind.

34

A few miles went by without conversation before he finally offered a faintly reproachful remark of his own.

"We didn't expect Mr. Lange. While the house is a large one, of course, much of it is closed up, and there has been no preparation for another guest. I'm not sure Mrs. Morgan—" He floundered, and I knew the proprieties were worrying him.

Hillary heard and turned in the front seat. "Don't worry about me. If there's a motel or a boardinghouse, that's where I'll plan to stay. I don't want to inconvenience anyone."

There was relief in Caleb Hawes' response. "There's the Timberline Hotel, though I'm not sure Mrs. Morgan will approve of your staying there. It's the only place in town, so perhaps thay can put you up until we—uh—have told her about your being here."

In other words, break the news that Persis' granddaughter had arrived accompanied by a man, I thought.

"What's wrong with the Timberline?" I asked.

"Nothing. Nothing at all. It's running, and it has been recently renovated. A man named Mark Ingram has taken over and opened up the hotel."

Again he paused, and I sensed something hesitant in his manner, though I'd have said Caleb Hawes was hardly a hesitant man.

In the front seat Hillary turned again to fix him with a look that seemed almost challenging. I hoped he wouldn't take to baiting the people I must make my peace with.

"Is this the man Laurie's grandmother hinted about in her letter?" he asked. "The one who is supposed to be trying to—what was the word she used?—to destroy her?"

"An unfortunate choice of expression," Caleb Hawes said. "He's hardly attempting that."

"Just the same, he's as good as bought up most of the town," Jon Maddocks said unexpectedly. Until now he had been mostly silent, giving his attention to his driving. "Ingram would like to buy Mrs. Morgan out too, but she has gumption enough to resist him."

Caleb Hawes cleared his throat with a sound that

seemed to carry cold disapproval for our driver. "We can discuss all this at some more suitable time. The point is that the Timberline is available and almost empty."

"That sounds fine to me," Hillary said, and I heard a certain relish in his voice. All this was an adventure to him, and I suspected that he might enjoy tilting at a few windmills. There were times when I wasn't sure he understood my own predicament as fully as I'd have liked.

By this time we had passed through the town of Broomfield. There was an open stretch as we followed the mesa, with a spectacular view of Boulder and its environs, before the road dipped down into Boulder Valley—that great bowl at the base of the Flatirons.

Caleb Hawes broke the long silence during which I'd watched the mountains hungrily, and moved for the first time into a more personal area. "What is your work, Mr. Lange? What brings you to Colorado?"

"At the moment Laurie brings me," Hillary told him cheerfully. "She didn't want to face an unknown situation alone, so I came along. To fend off Indians, or whatever. As for my work—I'm an actor."

"A very good one," I put in, sounding too eager to convince.

The lawyer decided to ignore Hillary for the moment, and went on to address me. "Mrs. Morgan did not consult me about your coming. If she had, I'd have advised against it." He looked away, out the window at the mountains that were coming a little closer all the time as we drove. "For the moment I'm staying at the house myself, since your grandmother's state of mind and health have grown precarious."

"Can you tell me what's wrong?" I asked. "I mean why she sent for me now?"

"She'll tell you herself. Though she may not see you until tomorrow. She was in bed when I left this morning, and it seemed likely she would stay there."

"Is she ill then?"

"I suppose you could call it that. Ill of old age. Do you remember her at all from your visits as a child?"

"Only a little," I said cautiously.

"I was surprised that you were willing to return, Miss Morgan. I remember the state you were in when your mother took you away."

"You—remember?"

"Yes, of course. After all, I was there in the house when—that is, at the time you left. My father was head of our Denver law firm, but he was ill and I had come up to Jasper to take care of some business for Mrs. Armand."

He was going too fast for me. I felt suddenly cold in spite of the bright day and the western sun still flowing over the tops of the mountain range we followed.

"Mrs. Armand?" I repeated.

"Yes—surely you remember that your grandmother was Mrs. Noah Armand at that time. It was only after Noah—went away—that she took back the name of her first husband—Morgan. It's a respected name out here."

Armand. That was the last name I hadn't been able to remember. And Noah was the name that sometimes came into my mind carrying some frightening connotation that I always turned away from.

I spoke hurriedly, hating the tension in my voice, "I'd better tell you—I don't remember anything about the time when I last visited my grandmother. I was ill when my mother brought me East and I was in a hospital for a while. Afterward there was a gap in my memory. So it's all gone."

I was aware of the half-turn of Jon Maddocks' head before he attended again to his driving, but he didn't speak. At my side Caleb Hawes' straight mouth tightened.

"Perhaps it's wiser not to remember. Your grandmother will be just as glad. She doesn't want to recall that time either."

It was hard not to shiver. How long could I remain outwardly calm in the company of those who remembered every detail of what I had so completely forgotten? I tried to remind myself that this was the reason for my coming—to know, to find out. Only I mustn't go too fast. I must take this a step at a time, so that I could learn how to deal with it in a way that wouldn't overpower me and send me over the precipice I feared.

In the front seat Hillary had turned to watch me, his look intent, and I knew that he half expected me to crack, to fall apart in terror, sooner or later. But that I was determined not to do, and I managed a smile.

"We're missing the mountains," I said. "Let's not talk. Let's just watch."

We were driving through Boulder now, and I could see the thousand-foot-high Flatirons, with their jagged peaks slicing the sky. Then the road took us up Boulder Canyon to Nederland, and on west.

I recognized nothing of what I saw. I could look at the spectacular scenery with the eyes of a stranger seeing it for the first time. With a sense of awe, yet without recognition. I only knew I loved the mountains—any mountains. Before long I found myself breathing more quickly as the air thinned to a mixture I wasn't accustomed to, and Caleb Hawes noticed my puffing.

"It may give you a sort of euphoria at first. You'll think you're full of all kinds of energy—so watch it. You'll tire quickly until you get used to the altitude. Just breathe faster for a while."

At my knees Red yawned widely, and Hillary looked around and grinned, following suit.

"Tell me about Jasper," I said to Caleb. "I've seen pictures of Central City. Is it like that?"

"It's hardly a Central City, or a Leadville, or Durango. Not room enough to spread. Your great-grandfather, Malcolm Tremayne, found a rich vein of purple quartz over on Old Desolate that assayed high in silver. It pinched out after a while, but there were other strikes. Enough to make him one of the silver kings. So Jasper was born."

"I'd like to have seen it in the old days." Jon Maddocks' voice carried a deep timbre. When he spoke, I noticed that we all listened—though he had said so little that his words always seemed to come as a surprise. He continued, with his eyes on the road ahead. "I've heard my grandfather talk about it. The way those little camps like Domino sprang up all over the place. The way thousands poured in, crazy for gold and silver. He used to say it wasn't just the notion of wealth that kept them going. It was treasure fever—the strike that could be made just over the next hill, or in the next riverbed."

His words brought pictures to my mind that Caleb Hawes' dry facts had not done. I wanted to hear more.

"Was your grandfather a miner?"

"My great-grandfather was a Cornishman. He was one of the tinners who came to America when the bad times hit the tin mines in Cornwall. He worked in Domino along with Malcolm Tremayne and Tyler Morgan, and he's buried in the Jasper cemetery. He died of lung cancer from the rock dust, I gather. Your grandmother remembers him. It's strange to think of that whole silver boom over so suddenly."

"Why? Why was it over?"

"It's a complicated political story. But to put it simply, the bottom dropped out of silver when Congress removed the price support back in 1893. A lot of the camps disappeared into dust almost overnight when that happened."

"Not everyone left," Caleb Hawes said. "The Tremaynes and the Morgans stayed on. They were rich enough by that time to do as they pleased, and they'd made sound investments. So that's where they raised their families, right in Jasper, and sent them off to school in Boulder and Denver."

"Until my father went to school in the East," I said quietly. "And met my mother there."

There was a momentary silence before Caleb Hawes spoke coolly. "Something your grandmother has always regretted."

I turned to him with a sudden appeal I hadn't meant to make. "I have a feeling I'm not welcome here. I won't stay long. Perhaps only for a few days. Long enough to find out why my grandmother wanted me to come. I don't belong here, and there's nothing I can do for her—so I'll leave as soon as I can."

"Once you belonged here," Jon Maddocks said.

The deep tones of his voice seemed to probe something dangerous in my memory, as if sleeping terrors stirred and grew ready to waken.

Hillary came to my rescue. "Laurie's a New York girl

now. I can't see her putting down roots in these mountains."

"She can't help her roots," Jon said, his eyes always on the winding mountain road, so that I saw only the back of his head, the battered rim of his hat. I couldn't place him, pigeonhole him, and I was beginning to suspect that no pigeonhole would ever accept that lanky, sinewy body. Had I known him when I was little? It was possible, since he was only a few years older than I. Yet I had no sense of recognition. Surely I would have known him at once if he had been the young boy who sometimes came into my dream.

"What I can't understand," Hillary went on, "is why Mrs. Morgan would want to stay in so remote and broken-down a place at her age."

"It's her home." Caleb sounded curt. "She doesn't mean to be put out of it, no matter what anyone else advises. She is a determined woman. At least she used to be."

"Used to be?" I repeated.

"She's changed," he said, and was silent.

Hillary put another question of his own. "Why does she disapprove of the Timberline?"

Apparently it was the wrong question, and the attorney closed his lips tightly on four words. "You'd better ask her."

I didn't mind the silence that followed. The mountains were awesomely beautiful, and I longed to be out where I could climb them, get to the very top, where I could command the earth below me. I gave myself over to watching whatever offered—tall spruce and hemlock, aspens with their quivering leaves like "silver dollars"—I remembered that phrase. Occasional outcroppings of red rock raised eerie pinnacles beside the road, and a mountain stream tumbled down the canyon toward the plains. Now that we were long away from Boulder there were fewer signs of habitation, but it was clear that cars had come this way, because of the pitiful animal bodies left on the pavement.

"Hold tight," Caleb said. "This is where we turn off on the road to Jasper."

40

It was a rough gravel road—very rough—and I could see the need for a jeep. Wind came whining around craggy peaks that were etched now in gold from the lowering afternoon sun, so that mauve shadows fell across our way. Already it was cooler, and I was glad of my suede jacket and warm pants. Red whined uncertainly, and I knew that strange scents from the deep woods were reaching him. He responded to my hand and snuggled closer for reassurance. He was not a very brave dog, and all this was unknown territory.

Once, looking down between aspens on the hillside below, I saw the main road we had left winding off in hairpin turns below us, with a car following its looped ribbon like a tiny bug. The sense of height was exciting, and the sense as well of moving out of touch with a world I knew—the world of cities and living towns. This was still wilderness. Forest and cold mountain streams, the steep-pitched sides of slope and canyon, hadn't yet been reached into destructively by man. I began to experience a bit of that euphoria Caleb Hawes had mentioned, and I knew that once I had loved all of this.

For the first time in some miles Jon Maddocks spoke. "Look ahead!"

I stared through the windshield at snow peaks lifting gloriously against a cornflower sky where the sun still shone.

"The Continental Divide," Caleb informed us, sounding like a textbook. "Running all the way from Canada's northwest territories to Mexico. The backbone of North America."

Yet the Rockies were beginning to seem more like a jumble of mountains to me, spreading beyond and beyond forever, and not at all like a thin backbone. They were indeed rocky, and not like the gentler mountains of the East.

Now it was my turn to cry, "Look!" as I pointed toward broken ties and rusted rails running below the road we followed. "Did trains come up here?"

"Of course," Caleb said. "That's the old narrow gauge that took out the ore from Jasper when it was mined.

41

Wherever there was enough silver or gold, the railroads came. That track hasn't been used since early in the century. We're nearly there now."

For a little while the lonely mountains had calmed me, but now I braced myself, waiting for my first glimpse of the town I could vaguely remember.

There had been a sign on the highway we had left announcing that the Pass was open. A reminder of what could happen when the snows came. Now we seemed to be traveling through a narrow cut between high peaks, and here the shadows were thick, almost as though night had begun, though it was still late afternoon.

"Jasper can be cut off completely in the winter months," Caleb said. "The road gets cleared out eventually, but there are sometimes snowslides that take days for the road crews to cut through. Electricity is the first thing to go, of course, and the telephone. Though we have shortwave radio now for emergencies."

"Mrs. Morgan doesn't stay up here through all that snow, does she?" Hillary asked.

"Sure she does," Jon said. "I've been here with her for the last few winters. That's when you find out what you're made of."

Caleb's laugh was dry. "Not for me! I'll take Denver in the winter anytime. But the Morgans have always stayed here in the mountains, along with a few other hardy souls who dislike civilization. They have oil for heat and propane gas for cooking. And some extra generators. The old oil lamps come out, and the candles. Of course food supplies are stocked well ahead of the first snow, and there's even one last store in town that operates. Jasper was never completely abandoned, so it hasn't deteriorated as badly as most old campsites in the mountains. Now it's having its first real face-lift."

There was something in his tone, part denigration, part admiration, that caught my attention. "In what way?"

"Ingram's taking charge. He's done over the Timberline, and as I told you, he owns most of the town by now. He wants to turn Jasper into a ski resort, get the access road paved, open up ski slopes. And during the summer bring tourists in for a taste of the old West."

"He doesn't own Persis Morgan," Jon Maddocks said.

Caleb went on, ignoring him. "Your grandmother holds the land outside Jasper that Ingram needs for his project. So you've arrived in the middle of a war, so to speak."

I exchanged a look with Hillary and saw that his eyes were bright with anticipation. If I had been brought here to fortify my grandmother's opposition, Hillary would be ready for a fight. But would I? What could I possibly do?

"How do you stand on this?" Hillary asked Caleb.

"I work for Mrs. Morgan. Her interests are of course the interests of my firm. But Mark Ingram is pretty powerful, and it might be better for her to sell and get out. More sensible. She's grown too old for this sort of fight. And Ingram could be a ruthless opponent."

Before I had time to wonder about his words, I saw that the road had opened and we were descending from the Pass. The mountain dropped off precipitously to a stream far below. Along the narrow expanse of ledge between mountain and canyon stretched the town of Jasper, Colorado, and something stirred in me. Recognition? I wasn't sure.

I knew only that suddenly I wanted to turn and run, wanted only to escape what was coming up so surely ahead of us as the road dropped to the level of the town. But I sat hunched in my seat, knowing that I could not run, knowing that I wouldn't even if I could, and that a knot of stubborn determination was gathering in me that would have to substitute for courage.

So this was Jasper, and possibly my fate? All right then—I would meet it as well as I could, and that was all I need ever ask of myself.

IV

The way we followed was clearly the main street, with another running parallel below and two or three other streets on the hill above. Still higher were the ruined structures of old mines and the bare mounds of tailing dumps left behind to scar the land forever.

To my surprise, the main street was far from empty. Many of the false fronts had been repaired and refurbished with new paint. Men on ladders and scaffolding were working on buildings that were still shabby and dilapidated. The pounding of hammers, the ring of metal on wood sounded everywhere. If I'd hoped we would enter a lonely, empty street that would evoke the past so that a feeling of familiarity would stir in me, I was to be disappointed.

Freshly painted signs announced a blacksmith's shop, a barber's, where a pole was being newly striped, and even a livery stable. The latter was operating, since horses stood in the stalls and repairs were being made on a buckboard. On ahead a small white church raised a new steeple above its lower neighbors.

Cars and trucks had been parked on the side streets, above and below, obviously belonging to the influx of workmen from the outside world. Some of these houses seemed to be occupied, probably being used as living quarters for this army of help.

Somehow all this effort to spruce up everything took away the appeal for me. The Jasper I remembered was gray and weathered and growing shabby—like an old friend who had lived for a very long time. This new Jasper meant nothing to me, and I felt recognition only for those buildings that still showed the signs of age, whose windows were broken and siding splintered.

Farther on along the street an impressive building with thin posts holding up its extended roof indicated by a new sign that it was the Opera House. Next door was a post office and general store, and then an empty jail. The town was noisy with hammering and pounding and the voices of workmen.

Across from the Opera House the Timberline Hotel stood out because it was the largest building in sight, and had been painted a dazzling white.

"We'd better stop and unload Mr. Lange here," Caleb said to Jon Maddocks.

I must have made some involuntary sound of protest because Hillary reached back to touch my knee. "I'll be fine, Laurie, and so will you. I'll see you early tomorrow. It's better not to spring me on your grandmother until you've had a chance to get acquainted with her."

"I'll come in with you for a moment," I said as Jon got out to help Hillary with his bags. "I'd like to see the hotel."

Caleb came with us. A board sidewalk in good repair fronted the building, which was set slightly above the street, with three steps to mount. There was even a narrow porch, painted white like the rest, and for the moment empty of chairs. Wide double doors stood open, and when Caleb motioned to us I stepped into an older world.

Outside there was still considerable dilapidation and neglect, for all the effort that was being made, but here the good-sized lobby was perfect in its restoration. Furnishings of Victorian sofas and pedestal tables had been installed, and the carpet wore large cabbage roses in its pattern. If the red velvet draperies at every long window were modern synthetics, one would never know. The gold cords that tied them back were untarnished, and again undoubtedly synthetic. On the wall had been hung prints of Remington paintings and photographs of famous Colorado mining towns—Telluride and Cripple Creek in their past glory. Mark Ingram, whatever else he was, had renovated well.

A room opened off the lobby, and I glimpsed the long mahogany bar with the picture of a reclining and scantily dressed lady above it, and a brass spittoon at each end. Small tables were set about the room, and a few patrons from among the workers in the town had wandered in, to be served by a florid gentleman in shirt sleeves, vest, and flowing mustache, who moved with assurance against a background of mirrors and bottle-filled shelves. This, too, was authentic. And at the same time synthetic and only make-believe. Was this the way to recover the past? I didn't know.

At the far end of the room was a small stage, empty now, with its crimson curtains looped back in folds at either side. All was ready for the performance that would begin whenever a tourist audience appeared. Or a movie company with attendant crews and actors.

Behind me Jon Maddocks set down Hillary's bags and as I turned I caught his sardonic look and sensed that he liked the refurbishing no better than I did. But when I gave him an uncertain smile, he merely looked past me and followed Caleb and Hillary toward the handsome black walnut desk in the lobby. There a middle-aged woman with unlikely red hair greeted us, nodded to Jon, and then regarded me with frank interest as I moved to join the men.

She, at least, had not yet been renovated to match the period furnishings. Her well-worn jeans made no attempt to hide generous proportions, and a red sweater with snagged sleeves fitted her snugly.

"Mr. Lange," Caleb said, "this is Mrs. Durant. Belle, Mr. Lange is here from New York. He may move over to Mrs. Morgan's later, but he will stay here for tonight. Miss Morgan, this is Mrs. Durant."

"Belle," she corrected, giving me the full regard of warm brown eyes that seemed naturally cheerful. "Nobody calls me anything but Belle."

Her voice was oddly harsh and unmusical, a little hoarse, as though she might be more accustomed to shouting across a field than to speaking decorously indoors.

46

"So you're the long-lost granddaughter?" she added.

Since women usually forgot me once they'd seen Hillary, I knew it was only burning curiosity that made her look at me so intently.

"I didn't know I was lost, but I'm Laurie Morgan," I said.

"Morgan used to be a big name around here. How do you feel about coming back after all this time?"

"Morgan is still an important name," Caleb corrected, saving me the need of answering. "Miss Morgan was a small child when she left, so she doesn't remember Jasper very well."

Belle Durant smiled at him—a rather knowing smile, as though she didn't especially care for him. Then she turned to Hillary.

"You want to look at the room before you move in, Mr. Lange? There's only one other guest right now, so you can have your pick. Mr. Ingram hasn't got things going yet."

"Whatever you have will be fine," Hillary said, and turned upon her the same look of smiling interest that he gave everyone he met. I could almost see her melt.

"Come along," she said. "I'll take you up."

Jon Maddocks had moved to the door, his back to us indifferently, though I had again the curious sense that he missed nothing.

For a moment I clung to Hillary's arm, suddenly aware that I was losing an anchor. He kissed me warmly and unselfconsciously. "You'll be all right, honey. Don't forget that you're the one who is doing your grandmother a favor by coming here. I'll see if I can storm the palace early tomorrow."

"Early" might not be before noon, I knew, since Hillary had the actor's habit of rising late. A long stretch of hours without him lay ahead of me, but I managed to smile with make-believe confidence. I had to learn to lean on myself and no one else. I'd better get on with it.

Hillary carried his bags toward the stairs at the rear of the lobby and went up them in Belle's wake. When they'd gone, I followed Caleb out to the jeep. Jon was already in

47

the driver's seat, and Caleb and I got in back again. Once more overjoyed that I had reappeared, Red waited for me.

"Do you remember anything at all about the town?" Caleb asked as we bumped along the narrow street, slowing to let a man with a ladder cross ahead of us.

I shook my head. "Some of the fronts seem familiar."

Behind the buildings on our left the next parallel street dropped to a lower level, and beyond that the mountain pitched off into the steep cliffs of the canyon. I seemed aware of the general topography without any clear view out the windows. Above on the right the mountain rose a thousand feet, with only two more parallel streets carved along its side. The town was stretched thinly along this narrow ledge between mountain height and the drop-off to the stream below, which undoubtedly accounted for the fact that it hadn't sprawled out like other boom towns.

We drove slowly over ruts in broken pavement. At least the road had been paved at one time and wasn't covered by the original mud. I tried to still a rising sense of anxiety as we neared my grandmother's house, reminding myself that I was no longer the child who had left here twenty years ago and there was no reason to be engulfed by fears I should long since have outgrown. There was nothing real to worry about—yet I went right on worrying.

"There's Morgan House ahead," Caleb said. "People around here used to call it the Silver Castle. In honor of the mines, of course. But after her father died, your grandmother took over, and she would allow no other name but Morgan House. It's still pretty impressive."

It didn't look quite as overwhelming to me as it had when I was small, yet I was immediately and irrationally terrified of every inch of it.

"Please stop," I called to Jon Maddocks. "Could we wait just a moment before we go on? I want to—to get used to this again."

He braked the jeep on a street that had emptied of activity at this end.

Caleb glanced at me uneasily. "Are you all right?"

48

I wasn't all right, but I couldn't explain. I sat staring at that intimidating house rising ahead of us out of long mountain shadows. This was no frame house, but a mansion built solidly of red brick. Wooden posts ran around a wide porch that surrounded two sides and the front of the house, holding up the extended roof of the porch. Above, set back from the porch, all the windows of the two upper stories were arched with brick horseshoe frames. Wide brick steps rose to the porch, and an arched glass door stood closed and unrevealing at the top. The house sat at right angles to the street, arrogantly blocking any access from the town to whatever land lay beyond. From four round windows its central tower looked commandingly out upon Jasper and the mountains. Across the front of the property, and disappearing around the sides, ran a chain link fence, astonishing in this setting, and obviously intended to repulse intruders.

By today's standards perhaps it was an ordinary house, four-square and without much grace or beauty, yet it demanded respect. Occupying a place where the land narrowed, it dominated Jasper to a greater degree than the larger Timberline or Opera House, and to me it gave no welcome. Its staring windows seemed to focus upon me, rejecting, blaming. Blaming for what?

"You can see Ingram's problem," Caleb said.

That wasn't what I'd been considering, and I gave myself an inward shake back into reality.

"Yes," I said. "I begin to understand."

"As things are now, the town can't grow an inch," he went on. "It never could because of the Morgans. It has gone up and down as far as possible, while all the remaining desirable land lies beyond your grandmother's house —thousands of acres, owned by her. Ingram wants to commercialize Jasper, turn it into a tourist attraction, and only your grandmother stands in his way. She's rich enough to fight him. But too old. Right now he's trying to scare her out—and maybe he'll succeed."

"I don't see why she wants to fight," I pondered. "Why would anyone want to stay in a place like this?"

In the front seat Jon Maddocks made a sound of dis-

49

agreement, a derisive sound. I seemed to be endearing myself to him less and less.

"Let's go on," Caleb said curtly. "You'll have to ask your grandmother yourself, Miss Morgan. I've done my best to persuade her to move out. It's pointless to stay."

"Why should she move out if she wants to stay?" Jon Maddocks demanded, and I wondered again about him. Who was he? What role did he play in the Morgan scheme of things? A hired ranch hand who told off the family attorney?

Caleb gave me a thoughtful look. "Ingram's not a man to cross swords with. He's enormously powerful, wealthy, and he does what he sets out to do. One sick old woman isn't going to stand in his way for long. I'm sure he could be vindictive if she gives him cause. Sometimes it's better not to fight, and I've so advised her."

Some feeling I didn't understand seemed to motivate this rather unemotional man. It showed in the sudden movement of one hand—a spasmodic, dismissing gesture. It showed in the tightening of his straight mouth, and seemed to etch more deeply the long creases in his cheeks. He really did want my grandmother out of her house, and I wondered if he had stated his true reason.

"Is that why she sent for me?" I asked. "Because nobody else will stand by her?"

"We all want what is best for your grandmother."

"Of course," I said smoothly. "But I can't help her either. It seems obvious that she should pack up and leave."

He nodded his agreement and I went on to another question. "What kind of staff can she find to help her with such a house, up here in the mountains?"

"Jon takes care of the outdoors, with the aid of a boy from town. Years ago Jon's mother used to keep house for Mrs. Morgan. After she died, the blacksmith's daughter, Edna, came in to do the housework, and she still manages, with some part-time help when it's possible to get it. The cook, Bitsy, is growing old and cranky, but she, too, has been in the house for years. Since Mrs. Morgan's strength has failed, Dr. Burton has sent in a nurse

50

from Denver—Gail Cullen. She seems capable enough."
His voice chilled slightly.

"You don't like her?" I said.

Caleb hesitated. "She has made herself useful. The house is better run since she's come."

His doubts about the nurse were clear, but it wasn't for me to persist in questioning at this point.

Jon braked the jeep as we reached a gate in the uncompromising fence that cut rudely across the end of Jasper's main street. A link fence in good repair that had been painted a glossy green.

"We'll let you out here," Caleb said. "Jon can drive the jeep around the house, and we'll bring your bags in the back way. What do you want to do about the dog?"

"He can come with me for now," I said firmly.

Caleb opened the door to help me out with stiff courtesy, while Red leaped and thrashed until I snapped on his leash and quieted him.

After he had opened the double gates, Jon Maddocks returned silently to the wheel. Again I felt that he missed nothing, and I wondered why he seemed to listen so intently.

"I'll close the gates after you go through," I said, and he nodded.

"Be with you in a few minutes," Caleb told me. "I need to talk to Jon. Just go up and ring the bell. She's seen us anyway."

He was looking up at the tall central façade of the house and I followed the direction of his eyes. Someone was sitting in a chair drawn before a window on the top floor, just under the tower. A woman in a dark robe, half lost in shadows.

I stood frozen, staring up at the window. It wasn't possible to see her face, or for her to see mine clearly at this distance, yet it was as though our eyes locked in challenge. Intuitively I sensed power in that seated figure, and my own determination faltered. She wouldn't be easy to deal with, that old woman in the window, even though she had asked me to come.

51

"She'll send Gail down," Caleb assured me, and Jon started the jeep.

When they'd driven through to follow a road around the house, I pulled the gates shut and latched them in place. These iron gates came from an older time, and didn't match the expensive modern fence. Cold metal curlicues seemed familiar to my fingers. Strange that hands could remember what the brain had lost. With Red at my side I walked slowly toward the house, not looking up. Not for anything would I raise my eyes again to the old woman who watched me from high above. There was pride in my ignoring her, and I held to it, though I knew my own uncertainty as well.

A cement path led toward the steps, with brown grass on either side. No shrubbery hid the bare brick of the foundation, though a few pine trees and hemlocks grew here and there in desultory fashion. More than ever it seemed a bleak and arrogant house, with few graces but great authority. I slowed still more as I approached, still reluctant to mount the steps.

I had come here for a purpose, and I must not let apprehension defeat me. Once I had stepped inside this house that purpose would be set and my determination must not falter. Yet something in me that was still craven seemed to whisper, "Let it not come too soon! Let it not be too sudden!"

As I hesitated, the glass-topped door opened and a young woman of about my own age came to stand above me, waiting. She wore a well-cut white nylon uniform, but no cap. Her long brown hair had a shine to it and was drawn back loosely and caught with a black ribbon at the nape of her neck. She was perhaps more striking than pretty, but obviously a vibrant, attractive woman, and one with that cheerful self-assurance the nursing profession often conveyed.

"Good afternoon, Miss Morgan," she said. "I'm Gail Cullen."

She held out a hand in greeting, and I went up the steps to take it.

"Mr. Hawes has gone around with the jeep," I said.

"Of course. They'll bring in your bags shortly. You must be tired after a long trip, and over that awful road. We'll all be pleased when Mr. Ingram manages to get it paved." She smiled. "All except Mrs. Morgan."

I remained noncommittal. "I'm glad to be out of the car."

"Of course you are. What a beautiful dog!" She bent to Red and he gave her his immediate love, as he was likely to do with anyone who so much as looked at him. Sometimes I wished that I'd been blessed with a one-woman dog.

"Do come in," she invited. "I expect you remember the house? You visited here as a little girl, I understand."

Was there something faintly sly in her words, or was I becoming overly sensitive? Why should I have the feeling that this ostensibly cheerful young woman was ready to dislike me, that she didn't want me here?

I followed her through the open front door and saw that a long hall carpeted in Turkey red stretched ahead of me, with narrow stairs rising on my left. There was a prickling at the back of my neck, as though my senses recognized what my eyes did not remember.

"No, I don't recall much about the house," I said quickly.

The words came out sounding more defiant than I intended, and Gail Cullen turned about at the parlor door and stared at me, her dark eyes widening. "How very strange. I can remember a great many things from when I was a small girl. Especially about visits I made."

"I don't think I've wanted to remember," I told her.

She was still staring at me, her eyes bright and curious, as that woman's at the hotel had been. "Perhaps that's a good thing. I'm sure it's all best forgotten, and your grandmother will be terribly relieved. She really hasn't been sure how she was going to face you."

So this woman knew also. I felt suddenly closed in and claustrophobic. All about me were those who were aware of the terrible truth—whatever it was—that I had blanked out of my memory. Inevitably one of them would let something slip, would tell me before I was ready to

53

know. I had come here to learn everything—that was true. But first I must get used to the odd terror this house roused in me and that I seemed to feel especially here in this hallway. One step at a time, I reminded myself. Nothing too quick, nothing too soon.

Gail Cullen had sensed my uneasiness, and she spoke lightly. "You'll get used to the house. I have, more or less. It's a spooky old place. It's a house where things walk at night—if you let your imagination run away with you. Come in and sit down in the parlor for a moment. You're looking pale. When they bring in your bags, I'll take you up to your room. Can I get you something to drink?"

I shook my head, not liking this woman any better than Caleb did, for all her apparent sympathy.

A door stood open on our right, and she led the way, waving me into a chair. I was glad not to linger in the hallway. This room, at least, didn't frighten me. It was as Victorian as the Timberline's lobby, but these were genuine antiques and they had lived in this house for a long while. I had a relieved feeling that I must have loved this room as a child.

Patterned in small, faded flowers, the rug picked up the hint of rose in the wallpaper. Wing-backed Queen Anne chairs were drawn before a fireplace with a black marble mantel, on which sat two cut-glass vases, empty of flowers. A tall English case clock stood proudly in one corner, its hands stilled at some long-ago hour. There was a red plush sofa, several Hepplewhite chairs with shield backs, and a table that must have been descended from an Adam design, with its rosettes and delicate acanthus scrolling. On a table lay several magazines, with an ancient copy of *Atlantic Monthly* half exposed, surprisingly under a more recent issue of *Ms.* The last would be Gail Cullen's choice, I suspected. The books between carved bookends were all old. Thomas Mann, Hemingway, Fitzgerald, rubbing elbows with Zane Grey.

At least it was a warm and reassuring room, for all that it must date back to a day when parlors were kept for

54

special occasions. A room not often in use even now, I judged.

Only one thing about it seemed disturbing. At the very back were two closed sliding doors of dark mahogany, and I wondered about the room that lay beyond. Perhaps a dining room? But why should I think of a dining room as faintly ominous?

"If this were my house, how I'd love to do it over," Gail said. "It could be made modern and much more comfortable, but of course Mrs. Morgan won't hear of anyone touching it."

I checked an impulse to exclaim in dismay over this woman's idea of change, and bent to my dog. "Stay, Red. Be quiet now." Then I looked up at the nurse. "When will I meet my grandmother?"

"She's impatient to see you. So it can be as soon as you've had time to settle into your room and refresh yourself from the trip."

"How is she? Mr. Hawes said—"

The nurse, who appeared to be more than a nurse, just as Jon Maddocks was more than a ranch hand, shook her head. "She's still holding on. Perhaps because she's waiting to see what you are like."

Her words were far from reassuring. I didn't want anyone's life hanging by a thread connected to me, and I hoped she was exaggerating.

When Jon appeared in the hall with my suitcase and carryall and Caleb looked into the parlor, I felt only relief. Gail Cullen made me more than a little uneasy.

"Hello, Caleb," she said. "Miss Morgan is tired from her trip. Perhaps you can take her bags up now?"

Caleb regarded her coolly, and I sensed his instant and probably justified resentment. "Jon will take them up. But I'm not sure about a dog in the house."

Jon moved toward the stairs with my bags. "The dog can stay with me," he said as he started up.

I followed him, and both Caleb and Gail Cullen came after me. On the second floor Gail moved ahead of us. The hall above was dark, but she moved with a sure step toward the back. As she opened a door, light cut through the gloom and I was aware of a second flight of stairs, equally narrow and forbidding, mounting into more darkness above. The upper floor seemed utterly still, as though someone up there held her breath, listening. I shook off the notion. I mustn't be influenced by Gail's words about the house being spooky.

Jon set my bags down just inside the open door and turned to me, ignoring the other two.

"Red will be fine down at my place," he said. "Dogs usually like me."

Which meant that he liked dogs. I thanked him, and he gave me a strange, long look before he turned away and ran lightly down the stairs to where Red awaited him eagerly at the foot. It was a look I had no way to read, though I felt that it asked something of me.

"I thought you might like a view," Gail said, crossing the room to pull up a plain green shade. The view she offered drew me at once, and I went to the window.

This time recognition struck me like a blow that I had no chance to avoid. The vista was of an open valley in which the buildings and fences of my grandmother's ranch formed a nearby cluster on the right.

Ahead a high mountain meadow stretched away, with elevations rising on either side—gentle slopes thickly wooded with aspen and pine that might do very well for skiing. But it was the peak at the far end of the valley that arrested and held my attention.

It was like nothing else nearby, but stood alone, a single cone rising high enough so that its top caught the last full sunlight, though its lower slopes were lost in shadow. A perfect cone with a bare, rocky head that pierced the bluest sky I had ever seen. I knew about Colorado skies. Somehow I knew. And I knew they could cloud over in the afternoon, though now this peak stood clear at its top, with the sky that pure, deep cornflower above and behind it.

"I know that mountain," I said softly. "It means something to me, but I'm not sure I remember what."

Behind me Gail was laughing as though I'd said something funny, but Caleb came to stand beside me at the window.

"That's where Malcolm Tremayne and Tyler Morgan struck silver," he told me. "It's up there that the mine was located. That's Old Desolate."

V

The name was part of my childhood, but not entirely a hurtful part. One of those strange flashes went through me and was instantly gone: a child with her hand in that of a tall, kindly man as they climbed the trail up Old Desolate. Not the boy I sometimes dreamed of—this memory was of a grown man.

"I've been there," I said. "I know I've climbed that mountain."

"More likely you went up on your pony." Gail spoke behind me. "Your grandmother says you had one when you visited here. Suppose we leave you to get settled now. The bath is two doors down the hall."

Caleb remained at the door. "I'll come for you in half an hour, Miss Morgan. Then I can take you to your grandmother."

I nodded, aware that the two of them still hesitated, watching me. Perhaps they could see that something had left me faintly dazed.

"Are you all right, Miss Morgan?" Caleb asked again.

"I'm fine," I said quickly. "Thank you for meeting us in Denver."

Gail Cullen, poised to leave, turned back, her attention caught. "Us?"

"A friend has come with me," I explained. "An actor from New York—Hillary Lange. He's staying at the Timberline for now."

"The Timberline—well!" Gail said. "That may upset your grandmother. Why didn't you bring him here?"

Again I wondered how she dared to be so forward.

"I suggested that we tell Mrs. Morgan about him first," Caleb said, still cool, and I sensed the antagonism between these two. "However, I doubt that Mrs. Morgan will want Mr. Lange to stay permanently in the enemy camp. Not that I feel Mark Ingram is an enemy. He's being a benefactor to Jasper, God knows."

I thrust back a growing feeling of irritation with them both and looked out toward the mountain. "Was there a town over there—a town named Domino?"

"It's hardly a town anymore," Caleb said. "It was never much more than a small mining camp on the far side of Old Desolate, below the mine. There's not much left of it now."

Both the mountain and the thought of a town almost gone drew me. "I'd like to visit Domino," I said.

"That's not a good idea." Caleb spoke firmly. "The whole place is rotting and dangerous. The mine especially."

"Except that house in Domino where Malcolm Tremayne took Sissy as his bride," Gail countered. "If I have to listen to that story one more time, I'll go up the wall. But Caleb, I don't see why I can't take Miss Morgan over there if she can ride a horse. I can keep her out of trouble. The place fascinates me too."

Behind the cold shield of reserve Caleb Hawes wore, there seemed to burn a suppressed anger.

"I'll be back for you in half an hour," he told me, and went away.

Gail laughed softly. "Oh dear, I do get under his skin. He wants so much to take charge, and no one ever lets him. I'll see you later. Let me know if you need anything."

When I was alone, I stood by the window for a moment longer, wondering about these two. Caleb Hawes, I was beginning to feel, was a conserver of secrets, while Gail appeared to be stepping far beyond her duties as a nurse. There was something altogether wrong here,

58

though I probably wouldn't stay long enough to find out what it was.

Now I must get ready for the meeting with Persis Morgan. First, however, I moved about, examining the room. It was spacious and informal, with rag rugs on the floor, a patchwork quilt covering the walnut four-poster bed, a small dressing table with a ruffled flounce, and several comfortable chairs, one of them a rocker. A round marble-topped table offered a few worn and shabby books, and there was a huge mahogany armoire for my clothes, in lieu of a closet.

I had stepped into a world that was closer to the past than to the New York I had flown out of this morning. The sharp change left me feeling a little disoriented, as though I couldn't be quite sure of who I was in this mountain setting.

Quickly I began to unpack. I hadn't brought much with me. Just assorted slacks and jeans, blouses and sweaters, with one short dress and one long, in case I needed to dress up, which seemed unlikely.

When my clothes were on hangers in the armoire, I went down the hall for a shower in an old-fashioned bathroom with cracked linoleum on the floor and fixtures that were wearing down to the brass. Back in my room I put on navy slacks, a pink blouse with a dark blue vest over it, and brushed out my hair, repinning it on top of my head with blond tortoiseshell combs. At least *I* looked familiar in the mirror.

Nevertheless, I still felt uncertain about what might await me upstairs. The brief, almost psychical encounter I had experienced outside had shaken me. I wasn't ready to think of her as my grandmother, yet she was my father's mother, and she was the one who must tell me what I had come here to learn. I might turn away from letting anyone else speak the words, and tell myself that I need take only one step at a time. But now I had taken all the steps, and the time for the truth was almost upon me.

When Caleb tapped on my door, I was outwardly ready. Inwardly my heart had begun to thump and my palms were damp. It did no good to tell myself that what-

59

ever had occurred when I was a child had no real power to affect me now, and that once the amnesia cleared I would have the strength to face whatever must be faced. I knew better.

Drawing a deep breath, I opened the door for Caleb.

Had I noticed before how thoroughly forbidding he could seem? Those creases down his cheeks gave him a harsh, unrelenting look, and I wondered if he ever smiled. Certainly he was not a man who was happy with his world, and I wondered why. Gail's flip words about his wanting to take charge didn't seem to be a full answer.

"Mrs. Morgan wants to see you at once," he told me.

"I'm ready," I said. "I think I'm ready." He started away from me and I added, "Wait, please," and he turned back.

I had surprised myself a little with my sudden appeal, and knew I was trying to mark time.

"Is there anything I should know before I see her?" I asked. "I feel so—so unprepared."

"You shouldn't have come. But since you are here, you must see her and then take your leave as quickly as you can. I mean you must leave Jasper. Your presence can do nothing but disturb her. You aren't needed here."

Strangely, his open opposition braced me a little, and I went ahead of him toward the stairs, walking briskly.

On the top floor a narrowness of hallways again prevailed. Sissy and Malcolm had bothered little with such furbelows as gracious hall and stair space, but they had built generous rooms. A single light burned above the stairwell, and the rest of the hall stretched into shadow, with closed doors on either hand.

"Does she stay up here all the time?" I asked, pausing at the top of the stairs.

"These have become her royal chambers." He seemed openly sardonic. "Of course that wasn't the case in the past. Her rooms were below, and those long legs of hers took her all over the house—and the ranch. She used to ride the mountains as well as anyone I ever knew. I can remember her when she was strong and active, and believe me, she ruled Jasper when there was something here

60

to rule." The sardonic note was gone as he remembered the woman Persis Morgan had been.

When I still hesitated, he spoke impatiently, as though I, too, had turned into someone he remembered—a child.

"Go on, Laurie. She's waiting for you. Your grand-mother's room is at the front of the house."

Reluctantly I moved to the door. Caleb stood beside me, his knuckles raised to the wood. A voice so faint I could scarcely hear it answered from beyond, and Gail Cullen came to open the door, her white uniform a patch of light in the gloom.

I stood on the threshold of a room that was large and dim. Floor-to-ceiling windows ran along the far side and around one corner, filtering in what little daylight was left. The old woman had returned to a bed that stood half concealed behind the door.

When Gail moved ahead to lead us in, the view of Jasper the room commanded assaulted me from the windows. A view that was nearly overpowering. The house looked straight down Main Street and took in the upper and lower streets as well, where lights were already coming on. Above, the mountains crowded in, looming dark against the sky, clear to the high pass through which we had come earlier this afternoon. Only their crests were still etched in a shimmer of gold, the massive slopes turned dull gray in the fading light.

I could understand that Persis Morgan might prefer this room to any other in the house. If she couldn't move around easily anymore, then such a view might lift her spirits.

"No lights, Gail?" Caleb asked curtly, and the nurse raised her shoulder in a shrug, gesturing toward the bed.

"You know I don't like to be looked at, but turn on the lights if you must!" The voice from the bed quivered with impatience. "And you can leave us, Gail. I'll ring if I want anything."

Gail Cullen bent over the bed for a moment, smoothing the coverlet, then slipped softly past us out the door. I wondered if it was only fancy that she looked at me slyly again, seeming to know so much more than I knew.

61

Caleb touched a switch and led me toward the bed. "Mrs. Morgan"—he spoke formally, as though he addressed royalty—"this is your granddaughter, Laurie. As she told us in her letters, she prefers the name Morgan to Waldron."

A faint sucking in of breath reached me from the woman in the bed, but she said nothing, and even in lamplight little of her was visible. The bed was wide and plain—a four-poster of dark wood, with no canopy, and the woman lay beneath quilts on this warm day, with only her head visible, propped against a huge pillow. Gray hair framed her face, drawn from a center part into two long braids that lay upon the quilt. Her face was pale and cross-hatched with lines. Strong lines, I thought. The face of a woman who had known life and probably lived it to the hilt, even though she might now be approaching death. Slight movement beneath the covers brought forth a long-fingered, bony hand that she held out to me.

"Come here, Laurie Morgan."

I went to her hesitantly, wanting to feel no pity. I wanted to think of her only as a stranger. But her hand was there, held out to me and quivering slightly. I took it and felt the cold shape of her bones in my own warm fingers. The touch repelled me.

"Go away, Caleb," said the voice from the bed, speaking more strongly now.

He had no choice but to obey the command, and I didn't look around as he went quietly from the room.

In the lamplight the old woman's eyes had seemed mere slits, set deep in shadowed sockets, the lids drooping with age at the outer corners. Eyes in a death's-head, I thought. But now she opened them widely, and I was startled by the dark, snapping life that looked out at me. Above them, in accent, thick brows had resisted the graying and were still dark.

She drew her hand from mine and pointed. "On the table over there—that framed picture. Bring it to me."

I turned to look about the room, seeking a distraction that would calm me, enable me to get through this interview. I hadn't forgotten my purpose in coming to this room, but something traitorous in me was once more eager to postpone the answers that I sought.

The furnishings were good. Again American Chippendale and Hepplewhite—perhaps brought long ago over the plains from the East. The carpet looked like an Aubusson, with faded tapestry roses against a deeper red. On the round walnut table to which she directed me stood a gilt-framed picture, and I picked it up. A young woman's face, aureoled with bright gold hair—the likeness tinted—looked out at me, smiling. The photograph was old, and it had been made long before color photography.

"Do you recognize her?" the voice from the bed demanded.

I knew what she meant, and I stared in fascination. It was my own face that looked back at me. The same nose, the lips shaped into a smile in the picture, the curly fair hair that wanted to tumble in ringlets and that she, too, had worn pinned on top of her head.

"It's uncanny," my grandmother said. "That is the first Persis—my mother, Sissy Tremayne. I didn't resemble her. I was dark like my father, and I was never soft and round like Sissy. But you look like her. Except that she was small. You have her fine bones, but you're tall—with my long legs. Well? What do you think?"

I had no idea what I thought. I had no feeling in me except one of confusion and dread.

"Never mind," she said. "Put it away, and come here and sit down."

Clearly it was natural for her to speak in commands. When I'd returned the picture to the table, I drew up a chair beside the bed. I had nothing to say to this woman, I had only questions to ask. She had summoned me and she would have to talk. But for the moment all I wanted was to conceal from her how badly this meeting had shaken me. She mustn't suspect this mindless quivering that went on inside me.

"I thought I could never bear to look at you again," she said. "But I have nowhere else to turn. I have an enemy out there. You must help me to defeat him."

Various retorts came to mind, but I could make none

of them in the face of this old woman's weakness. Only her amazing eyes seemed fully alive. In a sense I could understand why she spoke in commands. She had no strength to waste on amenities. Perhaps she had never bothered with them anyway.

"Caleb says you've forgotten what happened in this house. Is that true?"

Somehow I managed to speak. "I can remember coming here when I was small. I can remember the house a little. But everything else has been lost in an amnesia I suffered when I was ill. I didn't want to come here now because I've been afraid of remembering."

"It's better not to remember. Let it go. We'll both start from this moment. It's all I have, anyway."

This was the time. This very moment was the time, and I could allow myself no further delay. I gathered my last shreds of courage and spoke to her directly.

"That won't do. Letting it go, I mean. I don't want to endure the rest of my life with something I'm afraid of buried in the past. I have to *know*. No matter what it is, I have to know."

Before my eyes she seemed to shrink still more into herself. "I'll tell you nothing. You don't know how lucky you are not to remember. I only wish I could forget."

The deeply sunken eyes were veiled from me, and I saw that her lashes were white and thick above the lined cheeks. Her lips pressed tightly together in silence against me.

I stood up. "Then I might as well leave as soon as Mr. Hawes can take me back to Denver. I came here only because I need to know the truth."

Her eyes flashed open, and suddenly I was aware of the woman inside the failing body. A woman of strength and character—a woman who must have been a power in her day. Probably handsome and fascinating as well. Age made it too easy for those of us who were young to forget, and my sudden insight made me soften toward her just a little.

"No!" Her voice carried its full tone, compelling me to

listen. "I brought you here to help *me*. First you must do that. Then you can go."

She could almost be frightening in her intensity, and I tried to back away. "I don't know what you want. I don't think there's anything I can do."

"When I'm ready, I will tell you what to do."

I tried to bargain with her. "If I can help you, then will you tell me what I want to know?"

"We'll see. I'm not sure what you're made of yet. I don't know whether you can stand the truth."

Neither did I, and that in itself was unsettling. But she was becoming more real to me now—not just a figure lying in a bed.

Again she issued an order. "Go to the window over there. The middle one. Look above the town on your left. There's a clear grassy slope high up where the mountain was never honeycombed with mines. That's where he means to build his house. They've already been blasting up there, clearing the rock. He will be able to look down on the whole town. Look down on me! And when it's built—unless I stop him—he will put a bulldozer on this house and tear down every brick, clear it out of his way. He'll destroy the valley, clear the trees from the slopes all the way to Old Desolate."

Jasper had faded into gloom, except for a few lights. At the far end of Main Street the mountains rose sharply to the timberline, rocky-bare at their crests, with crevices of snow still showing white here and there against the evening gray. Closer in, above the town, the mines had left their debris and ghostly, tumbledown shacks were visible in silhouette. Above and beyond the tailing mounds lay a space of rocky meadow. I could barely make it out in the dimming light, but I could understand that a house built up there would command everything below it, looking down triumphantly upon Persis Morgan's chimneys.

I returned to the bed. "What does it matter? What can it really matter, whatever he does?"

Her mouth tightened, and I saw how age had narrowed the upper lip to a thin line, while the lower had remained full and willful, conceding nothing to the years. Her jaw

65

was still strong, and her chin hadn't vanished into neck folds, but pointed out at the world as arrogantly as it must have when she was a young and fascinating woman.

"You are a stupid child, after all." She turned her face away from me on the pillow.

Perhaps I had some of her own stubbornness in me. "You might as well explain," I said. "You might tell me why you've brought me here and why you think there's anything I can do. Mr. Hawes said that man—Mark Ingram—was trying to frighten you out. What did he mean by that?"

She remained silent for so long that I began to think she had dozed off. I was moving toward the door when she opened her eyes.

"Mark Ingram could be made to fear *you*," she said. "After all, you're a Morgan, and a Tremayne as well. There ought to be some loyalty in you."

"I don't want to be used to make anyone afraid."

Indignation rose in her voice. "Then go away! Just go away. You're no good to me at all."

"I'll leave as soon as I can," I promised her. "But first I want to ride up the valley to Old Desolate. I want to see Domino—and then I'll go."

"No!" The word seemed torn from her. "I won't have you going out there! You have no right. I can see now that it was a mistake to bring you to Jasper. You're useless to me!"

"I agree. I'm certainly of no use to you when I'm blind and ignorant of the past. I can't care the way you do about family and old traditions that I know nothing about. If you wanted me to be loyal, as you call it, that should have been shown me when I was a child. Why did you send me away—my mother and me?"

"How could I do anything else?" Her words carried the sound of old anguish in them. "Don't you think I'd rather turn to anyone else in the world than you? If only there were someone who could meet my need!"

I had opened the door to escape, but she spoke again, halting me. "Why do you want to go to Domino?"

"I'm not sure," I said. "The mountain pulls me. I want

to see it before I leave. There's something back there in my childhood that I'd like to recover."

"You're not to go," she said, and closed her eyes.

I went into the hall. Caleb had waited, sitting on a Shaker bench near the stairs. He saw my face, and led me to the bench and helped me to sit down.

"Has she told you?" he asked. "Has she made you face it?"

"No. I asked her, but she wouldn't tell me anything."

"I knew nothing good would come of bringing you here."

"I suppose I've known that all along too. But I had to come. I don't know what she wants of me, but I can't give her anything. Will you tell me what I need to know? Then I can leave."

He was shaking his head, regarding me sternly. "No, certainly not. Your grandmother has asked us to say nothing to you about the past."

Persis' voice, strong enough when she chose to raise it, called from the bedroom. "Caleb! Are you there? Come here to me, please."

He left me with a curt nod, and I sat on for a few minutes, trying to relax my tension, trying to shake off a reaction that seemed senseless and made me angry with myself. Why had I let that poor old dying woman devastate me like this? There was nothing I could do for her, and in some inchoate way I knew she meant danger to me. Now, with Caleb's further refusal, I could leave in good conscience and never need to know anything more about myself. Couldn't I?

One thing I was sure of. I couldn't endure this repressive house for a moment longer. I rose and went downstairs, straight out the glass front door.

It was twilight now in the long shadows cast by the mountains, though Old Desolate still held its head high in a last touch of sunlight. Standing on the porch, looking out toward the narrow street that led through Jasper in the opposite direction, I found it not as long as it had seemed during our slow approach. No more than four or five blocks in all. The lights of the Timberline were bright, and I longed to go down there and look for Hillary. But it was better to work out these few hours on my own.

At least the thing I most dreaded hadn't happened. In spite of so many uneasy moments no tension had started to spin inside me, to build pressure that could be released only in one frightening way. Not even the meeting with my grandmother had started it up again.

I walked down the steps and around the house within the compound formed by the link fence. Lights shone in windows just above me, and I could hear a clatter of dishes as a table was being set in the dining room. I wondered where Red was, and if I could find him and take him for a quick walk before dinner. It was chilly outside with the sun gone, and I had no jacket, but I would walk briskly and keep warm.

The fence stretched away in a large enclosure, as though Persis Morgan meant to have one cut through on the way up the valley. A narrow cement path circled the house, ending beside a dirt road that pointed off toward the ranch buildings, where a few lights burned.

One structure appeared to be a barn, and I could hear the mooing of a cow, the stamp of horses' hooves. Vaguely I could recall rides when I was little. Again the flash of memory. Not alone. With a man who rode beside me on a horse much larger than my pony. Could he have been my father? But my father had died when I was only two. He was buried in Denver, my mother had told me. I surely wouldn't remember him even if I could have ridden when I was so small. And yet I had always harbored fantasies about him as being loving and considerate, and always interested in *me*. How often I had made up stories about him to fill in that empty place in my life. I couldn't go away until Persis had given something of him back to me.

Drawn by a wish to find Red and see the animals, I followed the road toward the barn. The building had been painted a traditional red, now faded, and its wide doors stood open on a lighted area, allowing warm, pungent barn odors to surge out upon the air. Off to the right were several other buildings—a small cabin, a garage, a long structure that was probably an old bunkhouse.

As I approached, I heard music. Someone must be playing a radio, or perhaps a record player. Then I saw the man who sat on a stool in the wide doorway, light shining behind him. He held a guitar upon his knees, and I knew this was no canned music. He was singing an old song—"My Rose of San Antone"—and I stood still to listen. When the words came softly to an end, he drifted without a break into "Somewhere in Monterrey." These were the old lonesome songs of the West, sung in a voice that lifted to the mountains and belonged to them. Songs the rock-and-rollers had forgotten—those sentimental tunes that made something prickle at the back of my neck.

This was a feeling not unfamiliar. Over the years I had found that so much as a few bars of "Springtime in the Rockies" would start tears in my eyes, and I remembered Peter saying, "Oh, come now, Laurie! How corny can you get?"

I didn't care. It was *feeling*. A yearning. I had responded to it then, and I responded to it now even more, because something in me belonged here. No matter how much my coming to Jasper had frightened me, or how firmly I'd denied any ties with my grandmother, I belonged.

The singer had slipped into the lonely sound of "Tumbleweed" when Red, who was dozing at his feet, sensed my presence and leaped up to come dashing toward me. The music stopped as Jon Maddocks set his guitar aside and stood up.

That was when I *knew*. This man had been the boy who held and soothed me so long ago in those moments of terrible fear. With a flood of emotion memory poured over me, only this time I knew for certain that it had been reality. For me it had been the one reality that for so long comforted and sustained me—even in a dream.

The years fell away, and I ran toward him with the joy of recognition surging through me.

"Now I know!" I cried. "Now I remember!" And it

was only with last-moment restraint that I kept from flinging myself upon him in the delight of discovery. That and the fact that he stepped back from my rush in some alarm.

I tried to collect myself. "I'm sorry. It—it just hit me all at once who you are." I tried to backtrack, to deny emotion. "It—it was good of you to take Red. I hope he won't be too much trouble."

With the lights behind him I couldn't see his face clearly, but his tall silhouette had the lean, wiry look I'd noted earlier, and black curls lay close to his head, faintly exotic and foreign. Yet when he spoke, the flavor of the West in his speech seemed easy and familiar to my ear.

He ignored my outburst. Perhaps he didn't even remember. "We're already friends, Red and me. I get along with most animals."

"I wish you hadn't stopped singing." I felt wistful about that, and ashamed of my behavior.

"I sing for myself, not to entertain anybody."

How touchy he was. How far removed from that kind young boy I remembered.

"I thought I'd take Red for a quick run before I go in for dinner," I told him.

"Better not in the dark. The ground's pretty rough since we don't run to manicured lawns." The words had a curt sound to them, and I sensed the same antagonism that I'd felt in him earlier. Why he wore a chip on his shoulder toward me I didn't know, but it was plainly there, and if I had remembered him as a friend, he certainly wasn't reciprocating.

I agreed without rancor, however. "All right. Then it can wait until morning. I needed to walk around a bit after the interview with my grandmother. It was—unsettling."

His next words startled me. "It took you long enough to come back to Jasper."

I hadn't imagined the antagonism. For some reason Jon Maddocks resented me and was thoroughly prepared to dislike me, yet I didn't want to take offense.

"Why should you say that? My grandmother never wanted me here in the past. From the time my mother

70

and I left Jasper until now, I've never heard one word from her. Then suddenly, without warning, she writes me to come. Just like that."

"And you came running," he said.

In spite of my good intentions I began to resent this persistent baiting. "Not because of her. Because of things you can't possibly understand."

"Try me." He had turned a little so that three quarters of his face was illumined and I could see the straight set of his mouth and the shine of gray eyes. Smoky, they'd seemed in an earlier light. It wasn't possible to be easy with him, and I was growing increasingly uncomfortable. His words carried a sting that got past my guard.

"Why should I try to make you understand?" I asked. "You don't sound in the least as though you wanted to listen."

I told Red to stay and turned back toward the house, but before I had taken two steps he was beside me, his hand on my arm.

"You listen to *me* now! She needs you. To *them* I'm a hired hand and shouldn't be bothering her. But you'll be able to talk with her often. And I only hope you're half the woman your grandmother is."

His words left me feeling suddenly desperate.

"I don't know why she sent for me, or what I can possibly do for her, now that I'm here. She wouldn't even tell me why she wanted me to come. There's nothing to do but leave as soon as possible, and then I won't be seeing her at all."

He spoke directly, without equivocation. "They think you've come to grab whatever you can when she dies."

I didn't know what he was talking about. "Who do you mean by 'they'?"

"Caleb Hawes. And perhaps that nurse who's turned up and seems to be taking over the house."

"But why should they think I—"

He stepped back from me, and as light from the barn touched his dark head, the anger went out of his face.

"I'm sorry," he said. "I shouldn't have spoken to you

71

the way I did. I don't know what I expected of you, or why I should think you'd be any different."

"Different from what?"

"Laurie!" His voice was gentler now, softer. "I do remember, but that was a long time ago."

I continued to stare at him. The mountain wind was cold and everything was growing darker, making me shiver. When I closed my eyes I was on a horse again—the pony I'd ridden as a child—and I was tearing up the valley toward Old Desolate, with hooves pounding hard in pursuit and this same cold wind in my face. Terror, awful terror, lay in the house behind me. A goal pulled me ahead toward the mountain. Something I had to reach. I mustn't stop, because if I didn't get there . . . !

When I began to shiver in the wind, Jon put his hands on my arms, steadying me.

"You're cold." He reached toward a hook near the barn door. "Here, put on my sweater."

It was a woolly beige cardigan, and I slipped into its generous warmth gratefully, aware of a barn and outdoor scent that was somehow comforting.

"What do you remember?" he asked.

"Only a little. There was a boy who was kind to me when I was frightened. But I still can't recall what frightened me. My grandmother wouldn't tell me."

"Perhaps that's for the best. She's the only one who would know the whole story. Don't listen to anyone else."

I hugged his big sweater around me as though his arms held me again. "But I have to know. It's what I came out here for. I can't leave without learning the truth. Will *you* tell me?"

He seemed to change before my eyes—to stiffen and draw back from me. "I was only a kid when it happened. I could only guess at a lot of it. I don't know *facts*. In any case maybe you have to earn the right to know."

What a strange thing to say. No one else had ever told me anything like that. I'd been told by Peter that I *must* find a way back. Hillary had thought I should open those doors. And Grandmother Persis had said to let it go. But never before had anyone said I must *earn* the right to understand my own past. Why hadn't I that right automatically when I was the one person most concerned? His words made me angry. He had no right to judge me, as he was clearly doing.

I fondled Red again, thanked Jon coolly for the loan of his sweater, and started back toward the house. This time he let me go, and no sound of singing followed me. I felt a strange sense of loss. The comforting part of my dream would never come again. My mysterious, loving young friend had disappeared into the reality of the stern, reproving man he had become. Nor was I any longer that small girl for whom a boy had felt a protective affection. We were indeed antagonists now. His momentary relenting was only for an incident long ago that he, too, had remembered. It was foolish to feel the wetness of tears on my cheeks.

Behind me as I walked away, Red made soft whining sounds, but I didn't turn back. I followed the rough road to the house, stumbling once or twice in the dark, and ran up the porch steps. I wanted only to put the barn and that man with a guitar behind me as quickly as possible.

VI

When I entered the hall, a bell upstairs was clanging furiously. It sounded like an old-fashioned cowbell, and at the sound a woman came rushing out of the kitchen at the back of the house, a laden tray in her hands. She ducked her head at me in greeting and hurried up the stairs, carrying Persis Morgan's meal.

I found myself alone in the hallway, with the Turkey-red runner stretching past closed doors at the back, and once more I experienced the same uneasiness I had felt earlier in this spot. As though something unhappy might have taken place here that the unconscious part of me still remembered.

I saw that the dining room door stood open on my left, opposite the parlor I had already visited. So the dining room wasn't the room at the back that made me uneasy. I hung Jon's sweater on a rack near the door and walked into the dining room to escape the hall.

No one was here as yet. My feeling of distress subsided a little as I once more stepped back in time. Not in memory, but in history. This room, I suspected, hadn't been changed in years, though I couldn't recall it clearly. It was a dark, rather oppressive room, heavy with handsome walnut paneling.

Somehow I seemed to remember as I looked about that my grandmother's husband—the man who was not my grandfather—hadn't cared for children at the table. So I had been given my meals earlier in the kitchen. A place that I must surely have preferred to this room that was so dark and repressive.

From over the fireplace an antlered elk's head looked down at me with a familiar stare, and this at least I recalled. I was returning its glassy look when Gail Cullen walked into the room. She no longer wore her uniform, but had changed to a swirly green dress that became her. Brown hair had been loosened from its bow and its dark gloss hung past her shoulders in a thick mass, making her look very feminine and pretty and unstarched. Yet my instinct to feel doubtful about her remained.

When I turned to look once more at the elk's head, she nodded. "I do agree. But I understand that Johnny Morgan, Mrs. Morgan's first husband, was quite a hunter, and we're lucky those heads don't look down at us in every room. She wouldn't think of moving it, though it doesn't help the digestion. Lately I've been sitting with my back to it in Mrs. Morgan's place. She doesn't come downstairs for meals these days, and I'm let off for supper. Edna takes care of that."

"Isn't it hard on the rest of the house to have her way up there on the third floor? With all that running up and down stairs whenever she rings?"

74

"She won't hear of being anywhere else, and the servants are devoted to her. It may not be for long, anyway. She seems to fail visibly from day to day."

"Caleb didn't tell me what is wrong with her."

"The doctor doesn't really know. She won't go into a hospital for tests. Mainly it's old age, deterioration. Mr. Hawes says she's about eighty-four, though she's absurdly vain and won't tell."

"Do you know why she sent for me?" I asked.

"Didn't she tell you?"

"Not exactly. Only that I am supposed to help her in some way."

Gail dismissed that with a flick of her hand. "Let's go over to the parlor. We can at least have a drink in a more cheerful atmosphere before supper. Mr. Hawes should be joining us soon. We dine early here because it gets dark so quickly, and because early dining has always been the custom. Heaven forbid that we break with tradition."

I followed her across the hall, where a fire had been lighted beneath the black marble mantelpiece to warm air that was growing chill. The elaborate chandelier was dark, but sconces on the walls gave electric light, and there was a lamp on a reading table. I sat in a winged-back chair near the fire and watched the flames until they soothed me a little.

Gail brought me bourbon and water without asking. "Our stocks are low, since Mrs. Morgan doesn't approve. Johnny Morgan used to drink as well as hunt, I understand, and I expect she often had her hands full with him."

I took the glass she handed me and sipped, aware that her dark eyes were watching me with curious intent.

"Don't you really remember anything?" she asked softly. "Doesn't the word 'murder' recall anything to you?"

The sound of that word, flung at me without warning, went surging through my mind in echoing waves. She had spoken deliberately, clearly meaning to cut through whatever defenses I had. I suspected that she was eager to tell me anything I might ask, but I shrank from her malice. If what I must learn was almost too horrible to be borne, it must not come to me from this woman. Jon was right. Only my grandmother could tell me the facts truthfully.

"If you'd like to ask any questions," she went on in that soft, cheerful voice that I so distrusted, "I do know quite a bit of the story. Mr. Hawes felt that I ought to know about it, once we learned that you were coming. This must seem a haunted house to you, and there's only one way to stop the haunting."

"If there's anything to tell, I'd rather hear it from my grandmother," I said quickly.

"Who will never tell you anything," Gail shrugged. "As you please. Though I can't believe that it's healthy to go through your life without ever facing up to the past."

Caleb came into the room in time to hear her last words. "Stop that, Gail. Mrs. Morgan is enormously relieved that Laurie can't remember what happened here. If you try to tell her the story, she will be very angry."

Again Gail shrugged, but I suspected that she had no wish to make Persis Morgan angry at this point.

Caleb came over to the fire and stood near my chair. "Your grandmother asked me to tell you that she's grateful to you for coming. She feels that she didn't make that clear, and she hopes you won't go away at once." He paused, and I knew he was repeating a sentiment that was not his own. "There's still a great deal she wants to talk with you about," he added.

None of this reassured me. As always, he was coldly remote, disapproving of my presence. But at least Persis Morgan had reconsidered to some extent.

"I don't know," I said. "Have you mentioned Hillary Lange to her?"

"Yes, naturally. Mr. Lange is to stay at the Timberline for now. That didn't upset her as much as I thought it might. Your dog is to come upstairs with you tomorrow morning when you next visit your grandmother. She's always had dogs herself until lately—outdoor dogs. Now that she no longer rides and can't be out with them, she has never replaced the last one that died." His words still seemed to be repeated by rote, and I wondered what he was really thinking.

I had drunk very little and was ready to set my glass aside when Edna summoned us to the dining room.

"We follow what used to be the custom when this was a working ranch," Gail said, "and have our main meal at noon. This is merely a light supper."

The long table, set with linen and heavy silver, had a formal look, even for supper. More tradition, undoubtedly. Draperies had been pulled across the windows, closing the room in with a heavy dark green that seemed oppressive. My chair felt stiff behind me, and the glass eyes of the elk watched in disapproval from over the mantel. I had a feeling that he had taken a special dislike to me.

Cold ham, hot creamed potatoes, pickled beets and eggs, cucumber and tomato salad, were all appetizing, but I was no longer hungry.

The terrible word that Gail had planted in my mind still chilled me, and the questions I wanted only to suppress were flowing in. Who had been murdered, and by whom? Was this the terrible thing that I had witnessed and that had so shocked me that I'd had to suppress it ever since? I had the feeling that at any moment something would trigger full memory and disaster would fall on my head.

Well, let it! I told myself. *Let it come!*—and was not comforted.

Conversation between Gail and Caleb held off the silence, though neither was particularly cordial to the other. Perhaps by this effort they at least closed ranks against me, and that might be their chief purpose.

There was one person, however, whom I wanted to know more about, and when an opening came I asked about Jon Maddocks. "He doesn't seem to fit his role as ranch hand," I said. "Though I'm not sure why I feel that way."

"You'd better not tell him that," Gail said. "He fits it all right. A ranch hand is all he wants to be. He's made his choice."

77

"Oh, come now," Caleb chided. "You know Mrs. Morgan regards him as one of the family."

"Because he gets around her. He always has. Have you been talking to him, Laurie?"

I told them about hearing his guitar and going out to the barn, looking for Red. But I was careful to say nothing about Jon's warning to me against those in this house, or of the fact that I'd remembered him from my childhood.

"Who is he?" I asked idly. "Where does he come from?"

Caleb answered me. "His grandfather worked for Malcolm Tremayne and Tyler Morgan in the mine on Old Desolate. Later on his father worked on Mrs. Morgan's ranch and married a Spanish girl from Mexico City."

So that explained the look about Jon Maddocks that was not altogether Cornwall—that dark, romantic look.

"His parents died when he was young," Caleb went on. "Mrs. Morgan helped him, sent him to an engineering college in Michigan. When he got out of school he worked in the East for a few years. For a big oil company. Then he threw it all over and came back to Colorado."

"Why? Why did he come back?"

Caleb shook his head. "Who knows? He's not especially communicative. A lack of ambition, I suppose."

"Except with Mrs. Morgan," Gail put in. "He seems to know how to butter his bread there. I suppose he's looking for something in her will."

I bit back my resentment of her words. She didn't know Jon . . . but did I?

"Is she that close to death?" I asked. "That everyone seems to be—waiting?"

They both looked at me as though they disliked what they saw.

"May I remind you," Caleb said, "that I have been Mrs. Morgan's trusted friend for most of my life, as my father was before me. This isn't a gathering of vultures. Your grandmother *is* our great concern."

"And I've been told that her will was made years ago,"

78

Gail added, her tone light and faintly amused at my hint of suspicion. "Nothing anyone does or doesn't do is going to matter very much now. She's too weak and in no proper mind to make changes."

"I wonder if that's true," I said boldly. "I thought her very alert mentally."

Gail nodded. "Of course your coming would furnish a certain stimulation, but don't count on its lasting."

"I'm afraid that's true," Caleb said.

I wanted to listen to no more. There was just one thing to do. I would talk to Hillary at once and see what he could make of what seemed to be happening in this house.

The meal was over. I would walk to the Timberline, I told Caleb as I left the table.

"I'll drive you there in the jeep," he offered, but I shook my head.

"I'd rather walk. I've been sitting since morning."

I left the table and went upstairs for a jacket, but when I came down Caleb was waiting for me with a flashlight.

"It will be dark and the going is rough. If you must walk, I'll go with you. Then perhaps your friend Lange will bring you back."

I had to accept, and we left the house together. By the moment I was growing more eager to see Hillary, to talk with him. He would get me through. He would understand and never condemn me, as others were so ready to do, and he would back me in solving the puzzles that still resisted me. I was trying my best to reassure myself.

Outside, the night seemed intensely dark, the crowding mountains only massive shapes above us. Far up on my left as we walked into Jasper, the ruins of mine structures stood black against a lighter sky. Here in the mountains the stars were closer, more visible than I'd ever seen before.

Since the board sidewalks were broken in places, except where repairs were being made, we walked in the street. Activity had ceased as workmen went off to their temporary shelters or invaded the Timberline bar. The hotel lights were our beacon, and Caleb saw me to the porch steps.

"I'll leave you here. Phone if you want me to take you home."

I thanked him and went into the bright lobby that I'd visited earlier that day. Belle Durant was not behind the desk, but there was a bell I could tap for assistance if I wished. First, however, I walked about the lobby, looking into the now well-populated bar, moving on to the empty dining room, where only a few tables had been set. It was a large room, darkened by rich walnut paneling, with two impressive chandeliers down its length. Heavy red velour draperies framed long windows, and a dark red carpet to match covered the floor. I imagined the room as it could be—glittering and luxurious, with linen and silver shining for the tourists to come, and perhaps flowers on every table.

Just as I turned from the door, a deep voice spoke behind me. "You're Mrs. Morgan's granddaughter."

It was a statement, not a question, and I swung about to face a man who was large and decidedly magnificent. Probably in his sixties, and dressed rather impressively in gray, from doeskin jacket to well-cut cord trousers. A gray that matched thick pewter hair and eyes that were picturesque in themselves, and his skin had a ruddy, well-tanned look, with lines raying out from the corners of his eyes. I had no doubt at all that this was the Mark Ingram who was besieging my grandmother's castle.

"Yes, I'm Laurie Morgan," I said.

He nodded, and I thought, *This is what a poker face is like*. He was a man who would give little away, and his manner neither welcomed nor rejected me, though his strange, almost colorless eyes were alert and watchful, studying my face intently as he spoke.

"I'm Mark Ingram. Welcome to Jasper, Miss Morgan. May I offer you something to drink? I think we ought to get acquainted."

I didn't want that until I knew more about where this easy familiarity would lead. "No, thank you. I'm here only to find Mr. Lange."

80

"Your friend went for a walk. At least you can sit down for a few moments here in the lobby, so we can talk."

I could hardly escape without seeming rude, and I went to one of the velvet upholstered chairs Ingram had indicated. He followed more slowly, and I noticed that he leaned on a silver-headed cane and sat down carefully, easing his right leg.

"Have you seen your grandmother yet?" he asked.

"Yes. I paid her a visit this afternoon."

"It's too bad that she doesn't make things easier for herself. She could sell the house and ranch land to me for a generous sum, you know, and then go where she would be more comfortable and have better care."

Ingram was certainly nothing if not direct.

"I don't know anything about it," I said.

"She's an old woman, and Caleb Hawes tells me she's not well. Another winter in Jasper is likely to finish her off. I can't figure out why she holds on so stubbornly."

"How long have you known my grandmother?" I asked.

The full, rather sensual lips above the well-trimmed beard moved into a sardonic smile. "I've seen her just once. Since then I've petitioned the great lady for an audience, but so far she's refused to see me again. She sends word that Caleb Hawes is her spokesman and I can talk to him."

I didn't like this man. "Why don't you leave her alone?" I asked. "They tell me that she grows weaker every day. If you wait a little while, perhaps you can deal with her heirs."

"Yourself among them?" he asked quietly.

I stared at him. "I hardly fit into the category of heir when she has had nothing to do with me for twenty years. I'm sure she has already made her will, and there's no reason why I should be mentioned."

He let that go. "How about letting me show you the Jasper valley while you're here? We can get around that fence of your grandmother's."

It was a surprising invitation, and I wondered if I was

in the line of cultivation because he considered me an heir.

"I don't expect to stay very long," I told him. "In any case my grandmother's nurse, Miss Cullen, has offered to ride with me to see the old mine and visit what's left of Domino before I leave."

"At least," he went on, "you'll be here for the Forty-niners' Ball I'm planning?"

"A ball? In Jasper?"

"Why not? It's the perfect place for a big shindig. We can use the old Opera House, and I'll bring in guests from all around. To celebrate the reopening of the town."

I had a feeling that he was baiting me as Persis Morgan's granddaughter, but before I could respond, Hillary came breezing through the door, fairly sparkling with enthusiasm. He kissed me warmly and then spoke to Mark Ingram.

"I went over to have a look at your Opera House. Laurie, wait until you see it! The proportions are perfect, and when it's done over in fresh red and gold it will be a little beauty."

To watch Hillary's excitement had always kindled a response in me, but now I held back, dismayed and uncertain. It seemed a little too extreme, and I didn't want him to be enthusiastic about anything that belonged to Mark Ingram.

Ingram nodded benignly. "I thought you'd like it."

"Hillary," I said, "I do want to talk with you. Please."

He gave me his direct look that could always penetrate any smoke screen I might put up, and saw my need.

"Let's go up to my room," he said, and to Ingram, "You'll excuse us?"

He led the way toward stairs that were far wider and more gracious than those in Persis Morgan's house, and as we climbed he put an arm about me.

"Was it very bad, Laurie? I hated to let you go alone, but it seemed better for you to see it through on your own in the beginning. My presence would only complicate matters."

Down the hall he opened a door that had been left unlocked, and when I followed him in, he put both arms about me. It was good to lean into his comforting support, but after a moment I stepped back, lest I turn weak and all too submissive again. I needed desperately to find my own way. Right now I needed to talk more than I needed to be held.

"Has something gone wrong?" he asked. "Have you met your grandmother?"

"Yes, I've met her. I don't think we like each other very much, and she wouldn't even tell me why she wanted me here. Except that I'm expected to help her oppose Mark Ingram. Which is foolish, to say the least."

"It may take a little time. You can't rush anyone that old."

"It's she who has been rushing me." I moved away from him. "This room is like something out of a western movie. I'd have expected more luxury from Mark Ingram."

The brass bedstead was covered by red and green patchwork, and a large oval braided rag rug lay aslant across the floor. There was an oak bureau, rocker, armchair, and plain deal table. A closet had been hung with cretonne, and I could imagine a hidden gunman stepping out from behind the curtain.

Hillary grinned. "Look out the window. You'll probably find John Wayne or Gary Cooper down there right now."

I stepped to the glass and saw that a flat roof extended over the porch—that same roof where somebody always got shot and rolled over the edge. I smiled, and Hillary looked relieved.

"That's better. You've been forgetting how to smile lately. I was told that there are more luxurious suites, but I thought I might as well play out the fantasy. Try the Morris rocker, Laurie. You'll find it more comfortable than it looks. Sit down and tell me everything."

This was what I wanted. While Hillary sat on the edge of the bed, I rocked gently, relating a slightly edited version of what there was to tell. I mentioned briefly the meeting at the barn with Jon Maddocks. But I didn't want to repeat all that he had said, or bring up the fact that I'd remembered him from my childhood. Nor did I mention that ominous word, "murder," which Gail had flung at me. For some reason I was holding back.

"What about me?" Hillary asked when I stopped. "Am I to be accepted by your grandmother?"

"Caleb has told her that I've brought a friend, and she thinks you should stay at the Timberline for now. I don't know whether you'll be summoned to the house. For all that she's supposed to be so ill, everyone seems to snap to attention at her orders."

"I may not wait to be summoned. What else?"

"There's a nurse who appears to be taking charge— Gail Cullen. She and Caleb Hawes don't like each other, and I think she's trying to ingratiate herself with my grandmother."

"Is that so bad?"

"I don't know. The entire atmosphere is a bit creepy and peculiar. It's as if they're waiting for her to die. And neither of them wants me there."

"Why do you think that?"

"Gail—the nurse—seems almost malicious at times. And Caleb says openly that I shouldn't have come. Then there's Mark Ingram. When we spoke just now, he was hinting that I might become my grandmother's heir."

"That's possible, isn't it?"

"I don't want that!" The words came out with a vehemence that startled me. I hadn't thought about inheriting, so why should I react with such repugnance to the idea?

"All right. Don't get excited. Is there anything special you'd like me to do?"

"I think you should come to the house and meet my grandmother as soon as possible. Whether she asks for you or not. I'll see if I can pave the way. And if I ride over to Domino with Gail Cullen tomorrow, will you come with us, please? She makes me uncomfortable."

"Why is that? What is really happening that has upset you so badly, Laurie?"

I couldn't hold back any longer. "Gail asked me if the word 'murder' meant anything to me in connection with the past. I don't know whether it does or not, but it terrifies me."

Hillary drew me out of the chair and into his arms. "Darling, don't let them throw you like this. If it all gets too much for you, whistle and I'll come. If I have to break down the door."

It felt wonderful to cling to him and be comforted, to be held and kissed so that I could pretend that nightmares didn't exist. Yet something in me wasn't responding with the old fervor.

"Of course I'll come with you tomorrow if you ride up the valley," Hillary went on. "Don't worry about the nurse or Hawes. I'll be there. Have you remembered anything, Laurie?"

I felt a little steadier now, and I went back to my chair. Somehow the moment was wrong for being held too closely.

"Not really," I told him. "Except for a flash of recognition now and then, nothing has come back. But they all watch me as though something may happen at any moment, and they all know whatever it is I've blacked out. I think Gail would tell me at the slightest encouragement."

"So? Isn't that what you've come for?"

"I don't want to hear it from her." Hillary moved restlessly about the room, and I hurried on. "Whatever there is to tell must come from my grandmother. She's the only one who knows the truth. Mostly, though, I just want to leave as soon as we can get away. That's what I wanted to tell you."

He paused in his restless prowl. I knew he wasn't pleased with me, and I hoped that one of his moody spells wouldn't take over. I supposed that all high-keyed, creative people must have these highs and lows, but sometimes I didn't know how to deal with them.

It was a relief when he thrust back his annoyance and spoke persuasively—though I didn't want to be persuaded.

"Laurie, honey, you've come here to get over being frightened. Isn't that the whole idea? I think you should stay awhile."

"No. Nothing is the way I thought it might be. I'm going home."

He came to a stop before my chair. "Shall I walk you back to the house? You're tired and upset. Things will look better in the morning. They really will, you know."

For the first time I felt that Hillary had failed me. As perhaps I had failed him. We didn't truly understand each other in this matter. But at least he made no further effort to keep me there, and as we went downstairs I could sense a coolness between us. Even though I resisted the idea, he reminded me a little of Peter. Perhaps the man didn't live who liked to be opposed on anything.

When we reached the lobby we found Mark Ingram at the desk talking to Belle Durant, who had returned to her place. There had been a transformation in her.

Tonight she wore a wig as red as her unnatural hair, but puffed into a nineties hairdo, with a coiled pat on top held in place with jeweled combs. Her yellow gown flowed to her toes, showing a good deal of décolletage and a revealing slit from the knee down. The costume looked better on her than jeans and a shabby sweater, and for the first time I realized that she was a handsome and rather arresting woman. Her interest in me seemed not to have abated, and I was aware of her frank, not unfriendly, stare as we crossed the lobby.

Mark Ingram turned to smile expansively. He must have cut a dashing figure in his youth, I thought. In fact, he still did, in spite of his years and the slight limp he revealed as he came toward us leaning on his silver-headed cane.

"There you are! Hoped I'd catch you before Miss Morgan left. I wonder if you'll both have dinner with me here tomorrow night. I'd like to talk with you about my theater project, Lange. And it would be a pleasure to see Miss Morgan again. We don't have many visitors coming to Jasper yet. But we will, we will."

At Ingram's words excitement seemed to come alive in Hillary again, and he pressed my arm in warning, lest I offer an objection.

86

"Thank you. We'd enjoy that. I'd like to hear more about your plans."

I said nothing until we were outside. Caleb had left his flashlight for us, and Hillary flicked it on to guide our steps. For a few moments I tried to restrain myself, but when we were a short distance from the hotel I burst into words.

"I don't want to go to dinner with that man tomorrow night! You shouldn't have committed me to that. You can go if you like, but I don't think I should. My grandmother—"

He squeezed my arm a little too tightly against his body, silencing me. "Since I'm neither a Hatfield nor a McCoy, I'm not on any side. So I'll be there myself."

"Of course. You do as you please, Hillary. But don't ask me to come and be nice to that man."

We had reached the incongruous iron gate in the even more out-of-character link fence around the Morgan house, and he flicked off the flash.

"Don't upset yourself, darling. Nobody's forcing you into anything. But it might be a good idea for you to have a toe in the enemy camp, as it were. It might even be useful to that old woman up there. So I think you might reconsider."

I couldn't promise, and I still resented his lack of support. We walked in silence through the gate, and at the porch steps he said a quick good night and turned back toward the hotel.

He had left the flashlight with me, and its beam led up the steps. Just as the light reached the door, someone moved to one side, out of its direct path. The man was Jon Maddocks.

"Hello," I said, trying to sound casual, though he had startled me. I remembered Gail's remark about a house where things walked at night. "Isn't it a beautiful evening?"

"The mountains are always beautiful." He spoke softly, and I could catch a hint of that cadence in his voice that might have come from his Spanish mother.

He opened the door for me, gave me a softly mocking

87

"Adios," then went quickly down the steps and around the side of the house. I stood for a moment looking into the darkness after him, wishing that he would stop being so prickly toward me. I could remember him as a friend, and I needed a friend.

Now why did I think of that when I had Hillary? So instinctive a disloyalty troubled me.

No one seemed to be about when I went inside the house, though it wasn't very late. Lights still burned in the front parlor, and I stood in the doorway for a moment, looking about the beautiful, empty room. The *front* parlor. Why did that phrase spring to mind? If there was a front parlor, as used to be the custom, there must also be a back parlor. Those sliding doors at the rear of the room would open upon it. I walked toward them slowly, following an urge that seemed to well up inside me and have nothing to do with reason. But when I tried to slide the doors apart they resisted my effort, and I knew they were locked. That was odd in a house like this, where no one seemed to lock anything. Not even the front door.

The need to enter that room was strong in me, and almost mindless. I went into the narrow hallway with its long Turkey-red runner and walked purposefully back to the hall door of the rear parlor. That door, too, was locked. For a moment I stood with my hand on the knob, and I could feel the old tension beginning to rise in me—that faint spinning sensation. If it weren't stopped I would soon be trembling uncontrollably, and after that might come . . .

All desire to enter the room evaporated and I fled toward the stairs and ran up them, pulling myself along by the banister. *Craven, craven,* I told myself. But I couldn't wait now to reach the safety of my room. With all my senses alerted, I knew that back parlor was a dangerous place for me—a place of threat to my well-being, perhaps to my sanity. How could I have imagined that I could carry through my purpose in coming here when I was so easily thrown into the fears of childhood that still threatened me?

When I reached my door I stopped because something

large and dark had been hung over the doorknob—something round and dry and prickly. It was a wreath—a very old funeral wreath!

But why? Why here at my door? I lifted it from the crystal knob with both hands and saw that a lettered white card had been slipped between its dry leaves. With hands that shook I carried the wreath into my room and sat down in a chair, turning on the reading lamp.

Black-lettered words seemed to leap out at me from the card in my hand.

RICHARD MORGAN

REST IN PEACE

(IF YOU CAN)

VII

I don't know how long I sat with that dry and dusty wreath on my knees and the small white card in my hand. Strangely enough, this wasn't one of those times when I blanked out. Movement was perfectly possible, but my heart was racing, my palms wet.

The card in my hand had brought my father close with a strange clarity. My fantasies about him were always so real that I often forgot that it was I who made them up. From snapshots I had seen, I knew he had been tall and very handsome. He had worn glasses for reading. I knew that because I had come across a pair among the few things of his my mother had kept. But I never pictured him wearing them. In my imagination he was altogether too dashing for that. A hero figure whom my mother had never stopped loving. About whom she seldom talked because the pain was so great. All her life she had been true to his memory, turning away from any man who wanted to be her friend. Even when her beauty began to fade, she still had been lovely and appealing, yet she had lived out a sterile life.

With an effort I shook myself from this dreaming, knowing very well that my vision of them both was based on no real understanding of what they had been like as human beings. Even my mother, who had been with me so much longer, I had seen only through a daughter's eyes. She had never existed for me in her own right until I started to grow up, and then it was quickly too late for me to know her.

Now, though the reason wasn't clear, this wreath and card seemed to threaten the very dreams I had clung to over the years. And if these fantasies of my parents were destroyed, what would I have left?

The dusty wreath on my knees seemed suddenly repugnant to my touch, speaking only of death. I jumped up and carried it to an unscreened window. When I raised the sash, cold night air and a wind from the mountains blew in, funneling through the valley. I held back the card and flung the wreath out into darkness, heard it clatter dryly somewhere below.

But there was no reassurance to be found in flinging it away from me. A message had been delivered. Not merely one of malice, but of warning as well. For the first time I sensed danger around me. It wasn't just that there were those who did not welcome my coming. Looking out into darkness and the mountain stillness, I could feel the almost palpable threat that had been made, the attempt to frighten me into mindless terror.

That I wouldn't allow.

There had been terror for me here once before. Far away at the end of the valley I could make out the dark cone shape of Old Desolate standing against a starry sky. The wind chilled me, but I stayed for a moment longer, lost in a memory of galloping up that valley on my pony, with terror at my heels, and a desperate goal to be reached. Then I slammed down the window and turned back to the room, where ugly questions still remained to be answered.

Why should my father's name be written on that card when he had died so long ago that I couldn't really remember him?

I knew I would not sleep easily tonight. I wrote a quick note to Aunt Ruth, to be mailed tomorrow, and then I looked at the books on the marble-topped table. One title caught my eye: *The Morgan Mines of Colorado,* and I picked up the old, rather fragile volume. The print was small and the yellowing pages had a tendency to stick together. The author's name meant nothing to me, but there was an engraving as a frontispiece to the book—a representation of the mountain I had just seen out my window. Old Desolate. Had the book been placed here for me to see?

I sat down, determined to read myself sleepy and learn something about the Tremaynes, and the Morgans as well. The mother lode that Malcolm Tremayne and his partner, Tyler Morgan, had discovered on the mountain had made them both wealthy, but there had been other strikes besides in more important mines, with ore that hadn't played out so quickly. The pages dealt particularly with the men and women involved, and I found the book fascinating in spite of its flowery and slightly stilted style.

An old fellow whose nickname was "Dominoes" had first cut into the mountain and found silver ore. Tremayne and Morgan, working with slightly more sophisticated methods, had tunneled in from another direction, and had bought the old man out for the little he wanted.

Sissy Farrar, my great-grandmother, had been the beautiful toast of the Silver Circuit in her late teens, singing and dancing her way into the miners' hearts, under the strict chaperonage of her mother. Her father had been a "hard rocker," coming out in the first spate of the Gold Rush, but never succeeding. When the handsome young Englishman, Malcolm Tremayne, appeared on the scene, Sissy had eyes for no one else. It had been a dashing courtship, and she had given up without a qualm her life as an entertainer. With never a whimper she had settled down to the early privations of Domino, and in the end, apparently, she had become as fine a lady as anyone could wish.

A certain aura of danger seemed to have hung about Malcolm Tremayne. In a day when they had almost gone out of use, he sported two silver-mounted deringers that he learned to use well, and legend had it that he'd once killed a man who was annoying Sissy. It was agreed by all that Tremayne was not a man to trifle with.

I could smile a little as I read. This was a tale out of the old West, and I loved every word of it. Perhaps before I left I could ask Grandmother Persis what she remembered of her father and mother.

I read on. The mine on Old Desolate had "pinched out," and Domino was abandoned. There was still silver in Jasper—if ever silver became valuable enough again to justify the expense of getting it out. The Tremayne and Morgan fortunes were secure and not dependent on mining, so when the silver boom ended they were not destroyed. However, when Malcolm died, there were no Tremaynes left in Jasper, whereas the Morgans were still around. So it was mainly the Morgan name that was remembered.

The narrative closed with Persis a powerful figure in her own right. She had married Tyler Morgan's son, Johnny, who had died when Richard Morgan, my father, was still a small boy.

There was nothing to give me a clue to more recent history concerning my grandmother's second marriage to the man named Noah Armand. Or anything about what my father's life had been like as he grew up. I knew that we had lived in Denver for a time, and that my father had taught English literature in college. But I wanted to know much more.

I felt a deep and growing need to substitute reality for the fantasies I had clung to for so long. Make-believe had been necessary because all the girls I'd known as a child could produce real fathers, whom they took for granted. To protect that empty space inside me I often talked about *my* father as though I had known him well, as though I had seen him only yesterday. Now I wanted to do more than that, and only Persis Morgan could help me.

At least reading had relaxed me, and I went to bed hoping for sleep to come quickly. But an old house talks to itself at night. This one creaked and whispered, and I found myself listening. Once I thought I heard footsteps, and once the creaking seemed so close that I sat up and turned on the light.

My door was ajar a few inches.

I knew I'd closed it when I first came into the room, and that it had been shut all the time I was reading. However, an old door could be sprung on its hinges, so that it unlatched itself. It was nothing to be alarmed about.

Nothing had come into my room.

Nevertheless, I tilted a straight chair under the doorknob before I went back to bed—and lay awake again.

Perhaps something *had* come into the room. Perhaps the word "murder" had come in, bringing with it terrible connotations to hold sleep away.

It must have been sheer exhaustion that let me doze at last, and I slept heavily through the dawn.

The moment I awakened to find sunshine flowing in the windows, I remembered the wreath that had been hung on my doorknob, with its ominous message. I wondered again why my father should not rest in peace. What was I supposed to know? I decided not to mention the wreath to anyone. Not right away. If someone wanted to startle a response from me, I would offer nothing.

As soon as I had bathed and dressed, I went downstairs, and met Gail in the lower hall. This morning she wore Levi's instead of her uniform, and a red plaid shirt. Her brown glossy hair was caught back with a red ribbon, and she looked vibrant and tanned and healthy. A nurse she might be, but I suspected that she took her duties lightly in this house.

Her greeting was sunny and cheerful. "Good morning. I hope you slept well."

Did her words once more carry a sly question? "Wonderfully well," I said. "The mountain air agrees with me."

93

"Fine. You can have breakfast anytime you like."

I told her I would take a quick walk around the house first and then join her.

Outside, I circled the house in the direction of the ranch buildings, where the valley opened out, and quickly found the spot beneath my bedroom window. No wreath lay upon the parched grass, though I found a few crumbled bits of dry leaf that must have broken off in its fall last night.

It had already been taken away, and that, too, seemed secretive and disturbing. I felt increasingly shaken by the realization that someone in this place meant me ill. Breathing deeply of the clean thin air, I gazed off toward the place where Old Desolate raised its head against a morning sky, trying to rid myself of this deep uneasiness. The sky was an amazing solid blue, with not a single cloud marking its expanse, and some remembered emotion from my childhood yearned again toward the mountain. I must go there. I must find some answer to my feeling about the mountain.

Down by the corral Jon Maddocks was currying a horse, and when he stopped for a moment and looked in my direction, I raised my hand in greeting. He nodded and went on with his work. Last night when I'd come in, Jon had been on the porch. Had he also been inside the house carrying a wreath? I shook the thought aside, not believing it for a moment. If there was disliking for me, it might stem from that direction, but it would be open and clearly stated. Somehow I knew that hurtful tricks would never be his way. For a moment I felt an urge to follow the road to the barn, so I could tell him what had happened. But I knew he wouldn't welcome me, so I'd better not. There was a soreness in me because of Jon Maddocks' treatment that wouldn't go away, and perhaps later on I would go down to see Red, and return Jon's sweater. Then perhaps I could talk to him again.

With an effort I shook off what was probably only sentimentality for the past and went inside.

Gail and Caleb were already at the dining room table. He rose to seat me, his manner grave and not particularly welcoming. This morning he still wore a proper business suit, but had added a gray turtleneck that gave him a slightly more dashing look. I felt again that this was a man who would be difficult to know, and that superficial judgments about him would not serve.

This morning, in spite of the intimidating gaze of the elk above the fireplace, the room was not as gloomy as it had seemed last night. Dark green draperies had been drawn back to allow daylight to blaze in, and though the table was still too vast in its expanse, breakfast was a cheerier meal. Edna brought my orange juice promptly, and I accepted a serving of bacon, eggs, and hashed brown potatoes done to a savory crisp. There was nothing wrong with my appetite. I ate, and wondered which one of them had hung the wreath on my door.

"You found Mr. Lange at the hotel?" Caleb asked.

"Yes, he was there," I said. "We saw Mr. Ingram too." I went on tentatively, "He has invited us to dinner with him this evening at the hotel."

Gail nodded. "He phoned and asked if Caleb and I would join you. So of course we accepted."

Caleb said, "There was no 'of course' about it. I'm not sure I want to accept, or that Laurie should go to dinner with Mark Ingram."

Gail's smile was tantalizing, and I could see that it angered him. Though he kept a tight control over anything he might feel, the betrayals were there in the tightening of his mouth, in the slight twitch of a facial muscle.

"We don't need to tell Mrs. Morgan, do we?" Gail said. "There's no point. She's so easily upset these days."

"I haven't decided whether I will accept the invitation," I told her.

Caleb picked that up quickly. "It's probably inadvisable. Stay as far away from that man as you can, Laurie, or you may cause yourself trouble."

"I rather like him." Gail seemed to take pleasure in opposing Caleb. "He's interesting and outrageous and powerful. Dangerous, too, I suspect. The problem with his leg doesn't slow him a bit."

"What's wrong with it?" I asked.

"I understand he wears a prosthesis for his right leg. That's what the Durant woman at the hotel told me. He lost his leg in a tractor accident on his Kansas farm. It's hard to imagine that man as a farmer, isn't it? But I gather that's what he's been. And a wealthy one, at that. Once I heard him say that there's more gold to come out of agriculture than from all the mines put together."

She busied herself buttering a piece of toast, and then raised her eyes to mine, that same look in them that I didn't like.

"It's always interesting, isn't it, the way life threads cross and intertwine in the most unexpected ways?"

"I don't know what you mean," I said.

"I was thinking of the roundabout way in which Mark Ingram came to Jasper."

"Gail!" There was a warning in Caleb's voice.

She chose to ignore it. "Oh, it's open knowledge, and very strange, really. If Mr. Ingram hadn't happened somewhere along the line to run into Noah Armand, he would never have heard about this place. But once he knew about it, he couldn't wait to come up here to have a look. And then, later, when he could manage it—a year or so ago—he came back, with most of his negotiations completed. Mrs. Morgan let the rest of Jasper go out of her hands years ago, so he had no trouble buying it up, as well as most of Domino. Mrs. Morgan still owns a house there, and of course the mine. The coincidence of Ingram's meeting Noah Armand is interesting, isn't it? I've always wondered how it happened. If it hadn't been for that, Ingram would probably have gone somewhere else and wouldn't be here now to upset so many applecarts."

Noah. Always Noah.

"Who told you all this?" Caleb asked, and his tone was so strange, so fraught wih emotion, that I stared at him and saw how pale he had grown.

Gail seemed not to notice. "Oh, I don't know," she said airily. "I guess it's pretty common knowledge. There's so little to do around here that I go over to the hotel sometimes when I'm off duty just to talk to someone. Or perhaps Mrs. Morgan told me. Sometimes she can run on and on, and I hardly listen."

I spoke to Caleb. "What was he like—my grandmother's second husband?"

He looked pale and upset. "I'd prefer not to talk about him."

"Then I'll ask my grandmother," I said.

"No, don't." He spoke quickly. "All she wants is to forget that man ever came here, and that she made the mistake of marrying him."

"But what was he *like*?"

Caleb considered reluctantly before he answered. "Morose. Thin and dark. Good-looking, I suppose. Women always thought so. He was an opportunist for as long as I knew him."

I hadn't thought Caleb Hawes capable of deep anger, but I could hear it now in his voice. I had roiled depths that he usually concealed.

"Why did Persis Morgan marry him?" I asked.

"I've always wondered what she saw in him. Her husband had died years before, and Noah knew his way around women. He was many years younger than Mrs. Morgan, and once he was here she couldn't see anyone else. She wouldn't listen to any of us. He'd been legally divorced—my father looked into that. Nothing we could say bothered your grandmother. All her life she's done as she pleased. So she married Noah Armand."

"Was she happy with him?"

The anger was still there. "I suppose so—for a while."

"How did the marriage end? What happened to him?"

Caleb was silent for so long that I thought he might choose not to answer. Gail was waiting too, almost avidly.

"We don't really know what became of him," he said at last. "He simply—left. Suddenly. Just the way he came, and we never heard of him again."

He wasn't telling me all of it, I knew, and I knew as well that it would be useless to probe further just now.

"It was probably a good thing that he left," Gail said. "I understand that your father never liked him, Laurie."

"How can you possibly know that?" Caleb asked sharply.

Gail's look was innocently blank. "It must have been Mrs. Morgan in one of her talkative moods. I heard it somewhere."

"Was my father here very much after my grandmother remarried? He died when I was only two, and—"

Caleb started to speak, and then was silent.

"He died in this house, Laurie," Gail said softly. "Don't you even remember that?"

"How could I when I was so small?"

Caleb found his voice. "Never mind all that! Gail, don't you think you'd better go upstairs to Mrs. Morgan now?"

"Yes, I plan to look in on her again. But when I told her we might go riding, she said to just go and leave her alone. You do want to ride up the valley this morning, don't you, Laurie?"

"I'd like to very much, but I want to wait until Hillary comes. I want him to meet my grandmother."

"You'd better make that later. She's not feeling well, and she doesn't want to see anyone. She said so. I'll run up and look in on her, and I'll ask when she wants to see you."

"I'll go with you," Caleb said. "Will you excuse us, Laurie?"

There was a determination in his manner that stopped any objection Gail might have offered in her role as nurse, and they went upstairs together. They neither liked nor trusted each other, these two, and yet they sometimes seemed allied against me.

It was a relief to finish my breakfast alone and try to forget our thoroughly unpleasant conversation. When I left the table I went searching for a telephone. Perhaps I'd better phone Hillary and let him know we were planning an early ride. Now, after what had been said about Mark Ingram, I was all the more interested in seeing Domino. But I wanted Hillary with me on the ride up the valley. The last thing I wanted was to be alone with Gail Cullen. When we returned, there would be time enough for him to visit Persis Morgan.

Except for a clatter from the kitchen, the house seemed quiet as I stepped into the hall. Perhaps the telephone was out here. I wandered the length of the hall and found myself once more before the closed door to the rear parlor. Idly I tried the knob, and this time it turned under my hand.

For just a moment I nearly panicked. Then I thrust back the feeling of fright and opened the door.

An odor of mothballs and stale air greeted me, and the only light came from the doorway. When I reached along the wall and found a switch, the crystal chandelier came to life, shedding radiance over dark furniture, over heavy, closed draperies done in a red that was almost black. The carpet was worn in several places, and there were throw rugs here and there, covering spots that must have raveled through.

I had been here before.

The recollection of a room that had seemed enormous to me as a child swept back, but now my perspective had changed. It wasn't all that large—not nearly so big as the front parlor.

From the walls dark pictures looked down, and I experienced a flash of recognition toward one in particular. It was a huge engraving—a scene from *Hamlet*—with a tragic young man in black doublet and hose, turning his back on a white-gowned, piteous Ophelia strewing flowers. I could almost recall the stirrings of imagination I had felt in studying the picture, the wondering I had done about these two tragic figures.

But on all else in the room I drew only a blank, a total lack of recall. Or was it that? Was there also an uneasiness in me, even though my conscious mind saw nothing it seemed to pick up and remember? Had a shade been drawn down sharply in my unconscious to keep me from seeing? To protect me from remembering? Was it all there underneath, waiting?

At least the room would remain safe enough as long as I could recall nothing more than a scene from *Hamlet*.

I moved about, touching a seashell that I seemed to have admired—not really a memory. A spurt of dust

99

stirred when I lifted it, and I could see that dust lay everywhere, thick on the tables, graying the satin and velvet upholstery, gathering in carved crevices of the furniture.

How utterly weird and Victorian! How fantastic to step into a room that must have been closed off for years, with everything in it left untouched. How could any sane person allow such a thing? Yet I had seen Persis Morgan, and for all her years, her faculties were obviously sharp enough. Only something so terrible that even the sane couldn't bear to face it must have happened in this room. Just as I had pulled down those shades in my mind, so Persis Morgan must have closed these doors and walked away, never to return.

Now I saw something else. Footsteps other than mine, larger than mine, had marked the dust as someone had recently moved about the room. Objects had been shifted, repatterning the dust. Here and there its gray coating had obviously been disturbed, so that a box or vase stood in a smudged patch, not returned to place exactly. Someone had moved about this room even as I was doing—searching for what?

Above me a shimmer of cobwebs draped the chandelier and grew like gray lace in every corner. Or like a fungus. The neglect was extreme and totally unhealthy. It was as if the house harbored in this room a cancerous growth that would eventually reach through every outer crack and lend its contagion of disease to the house itself. Perhaps such contagion had already reached Persis Morgan upstairs. All this must have been left untouched, sealed away, because of her abhorrence of what had happened here—because she could never again face this room, and had shut it off in an effort to wipe out its very existence.

Oddly enough, I began to feel a stirring of sympathy for her, as though terror shared made the beginning of a bond between us. Except that *she* knew the source of terror—and I didn't.

I brushed at my arms as though cobwebs touched my skin. For a moment I thought of flinging aside dusty velvet draperies, throwing open the French windows to air and sunlight—but I didn't dare. I remembered the funeral wreath hung on my door, and I was afraid.

Why shouldn't my father rest in peace? What had those words meant?

Yet I couldn't leave at once. A pedestal table, probably rosewood under the dust, held a large shallow box, mahogany-dark. Here again the dust had been disturbed, and there was a smudging of fingerprints over the surface. The box drew me and I touched its lid. It was as though I had touched hot metal, and almost of their own accord my fingers drew back.

This box I knew.

Once more the beating, tremulous feeling of dread began to spin inside me. *It* had started again—that movement toward danger that could be halted only if I almost stopped breathing, nearly stopped living—let everything go blankly away from me. Always at such times I had an instinctive dread that my heart might stop forever out of fear and this was the instant when everything would end. Yet there was no dazzle of light being struck from anything here except the dusty chandelier over my head. There was only this smudged box that almost seemed to pulse with a life of its own under my fingers.

The wave engulfed me, though I tried to fight it, tried to resist. I must get to Hillary. I must find him at once. In my present world only Hillary stood for health and confidence and an ability to face life as a whole person. Only he could help me. He must take me away from this place, help me to escape.

I ran into a hallway that seemed to stretch endlessly toward the front of the house and started down it. From the far end the sound of voices came to me—someone laughing. That was Hillary's unmistakable laughter—a lovely, mesmerizing sound that could charm any audience. Eagerly I ran down the hall to the open door of the front parlor. And saw them there. Gail and Hillary standing before a window, talking together. They had clearly just met, yet Hillary's charm was already working.

I stopped for a moment, my headlong rush halted, deflected. Slowly the spinning top in my head began to lose velocity.

Gail had tied a crimson scarf at the neck of her denim jacket, to match the ribbon that held back her hair, and she looked bright and interested. Hillary, who always wore the right, if slightly theatrical, clothes for any occasion, looked more like a dude in studded jacket and doeskin pants. All this registered superficially as the deep need in me fell away and left me standing alone. As always, he had met and captivated, and I knew I must allow him that. It was like breathing for Hillary.

Both of them heard me at the same moment and turned to look at me in surprise.

Gail said, "How dusty you are! But of course—you must have gone into the back parlor. I thought you might want to. I got the key and unlocked the room for you."

I put one grimy hand against the doorjamb beside me and steadied myself. The need to run to Hillary had evaporated, but at least I had been spared any blanking out this time. I was all right again. If Gail had unlocked that door for me, it had been done in malice and I would not let her see the effect the room had had on me.

"Do we meet the fire-breathing old dragon this morning?" Hillary asked, coming toward me. Then his look changed. I couldn't fool him, I never could. People were the raw material of his trade, and he looked at them more searchingly than most. He pulled me into his arms and held me.

"Easy now, Laurie. If you've begun to remember, let it all come through. Give it space—let it come!"

I pushed away from him. "No! Not yet. That room is a terrible place. I don't want to talk about it."

He let me go. "All right. Don't upset yourself. I won't ask questions until you feel like talking. Gail tells me we can ride over to the mountain this morning, if you like. It might be a good idea, honey. You can get out into the air and shake off the cobwebs."

Cobwebs! Literally they had been there in that room—hundreds of them, thick and gray, and somehow evil.

"Yes," I said. "Yes, I'd like that. Anything to get away, to escape the nearness of that room."

"Then let's go down to the stable and saddle up," Gail said cheerfully. "You do look a bit pale, Laurie. Some of our Colorado sunshine will do you good."

"I'll clean up and change to jeans," I told her, and moved out of Hillary's arms, resisting his concern that I'd wanted so desperately a moment before. Whatever it was had passed, and I felt braced again and ready to go on, even though a little numb. Later when we were alone, I would tell Hillary everything. But I couldn't talk now in front of Gail Cullen. That she was curious was clear, but I didn't mean to satisfy her curiosity.

I ran upstairs and changed quickly into jeans and low boots, pulled on my suede jacket. I mustn't think of that room now. Perhaps there was only one person I could really talk about it with. Persis Morgan.

When I was dressed I started for the top of the stairs and then hesitated. This morning an effort had been made to discourage me from seeing Persis, and I felt uneasy about her. I wondered if she really hadn't wanted me to come to her.

Downstairs Gail was still talking with Hillary and I could hear their voices. I ran quickly up to Persis' room.

The door stood open and I went in. Her breakfast tray rested on a table near her bed, food untouched, coffee cooling. Persis lay with her eyes closed, and her breathing was deep and regular. On the far side of the bed Caleb sat in lonely vigil, his head bent and a hand shielding his eyes.

I spoke to him softly. "Is she all right?"

He looked up, startled, then rose to his feet. "She's asleep. Miss Cullen gave her a sedative."

"Does she have a doctor who sees her regularly? Does he approve of Miss Cullen?"

His expression told me that I was interfering. "Certainly she has a doctor. It was he who recommended Miss Cullen. Believe me, it's very difficult to find a nurse who will stay in Jasper. We're fortunate to have her here."

I wanted to remark that much of the time he didn't

103

seem to like or approve of the nurse, but I asked a question instead.

"Why did she want to come here?"

"She was looking for private work, and she asked Dr. Burton if he knew of a place. We were desperate for capable help after Belle Durant left. Belle isn't a nurse, but she had all the other qualifications."

"Belle Durant worked here?" This was surprising news.

Clearly Caleb had endured enough of my questioning. "Please. Another time. We mustn't disturb her."

I didn't think the woman on the bed could be easily disturbed. Her almost colorless lashes lay on her cheeks, and when her eyes were closed there seemed no life in her face. I could easily believe, looking at her, that she might be slowly giving up her grasp on living. Guilt was suddenly sharp in my mind. Had she given up entirely after talking with me? But there was nothing I could do for her right now, and I must see Domino. The very fact that both Caleb and Persis had tried to discourage me from going there made it all the more important for me to see it for myself.

"I'm going to ride up the valley with Hillary and Gail Cullen," I told Caleb, and went quickly out of the room, lest he protest again.

They were waiting for me downstairs, and I took Jon's borrowed sweater from the rack to return it to him.

When we reached the barn I found Red tied up and eager for release, though Jon wasn't about. A young boy who helped him around the place and answered to Gail's summons of "Sam!" came to assist with the saddling.

I hung Jon's sweater on a hook and asked if it was all right for Red to run loose. Sam said, "It's okay when the gates aren't being used," and I let him free.

Gail was looking over the horses. "Jon has taken Sundance, apparently. You'd have liked him, Mr. Lange. Plenty of spirit, but a good disposition. Anyway, you can ride North Star—he'll do fine. Baby Doe should be right for you, Laurie. I don't suppose you've ridden all that much since you left the ranch."

I felt more than a little resentful of her easy familiarity.

She seemed altogether too much at home on my grand-mother's property.

Baby Doe, with her name rooted in Colorado history, was a gentle chestnut creature who took to me at once, and I felt no need to explain to Gail that I had always ridden. I stroked her nose and talked to her for a moment. Then I swung into the western saddle, with its high pommel that I'd always liked.

With assurance Gail turned Silver King, the handsome palomino she'd chosen, and started up the valley.

Red followed us to the gate, where Sam held him back and closed it after us. At first we rode three abreast up the wide valley, with Old Desolate rising straight ahead and lesser mountains following on either side, their slopes thickly wooded. These were the trees that would go if Ingram had his way.

Before long I began to drop back a little because I wanted no intrusion on this spell of mountains and rocky meadow. Something was pulling me, as it had ever since I'd determined to return to Colorado. Not the back parlor I had stepped into a little while ago, or the past that I must still discover. Something else—something that waited, knowing I would come. Strange and compelling, this feeling in me.

All about, wild flowers grew abundantly, clear to the edge of the pine forest. Their names came back to me out of memory, and a man's voice seemed to be repeating them to me. There was wild yellow parsley and mountain lupine—the bluebonnet of these higher elevations. And of course the lovely lavender and white Colorado columbine. Beside us a stream ran part of the way before it took a downhill course where the mountains parted. In the open fields, strewn with rocks, grew tall blue aspen daisies, and I seemed to remember them with their narrow lavender petals and yellow hearts. I let Baby Doe drop still farther behind the other two so that I could savor everything I saw and breathe deeply of this heady mountain air.

Every color seemed intensified in the clear light, so that beauty grew almost too painfully sharp to bear. Some of this I remembered dimly—riding up the valley through meadow and woods, with that glorious mountain coming always closer, pulling me toward its height.

Along a rocky shoulder as we began the ascent grew a stand of tall spruce trees. Now Gail rode ahead, leading the way on her golden, silver-maned beauty, and Hillary dropped back just behind me. I was glad for single file. I wanted only to see and feel, and not talk to anyone. For a little while this was surcease, and Hillary seemed to understand my need, not intruding upon me.

Ahead, over the shoulder of the mountain, the trees opened and the ground grew more rocky and barren, partly because of the mines and the debris they always left behind. In this high place we could see forever, and I reined Baby Doe to a halt. This was what I loved best—to find a high place where I could be above the world. Beyond Old Desolate the snow peaks of the Divide were visible, and mountain ranges seemed to move away endlessly against every horizon. Closer in I could look back toward the ranch, where Persis Morgan's stern-visaged house stood high and proud. Beyond it the cluster of buildings that was Jasper stood out, with mountain summits leaning over them. But up here I could forget a closed room of cobwebs and terror. For a little while I could forget.

Gail called back to us. "A little higher up you can see the Gore range. Do you want to go up?"

I hesitated, drawn as always to the heights. But now there was another pull that was greater.

"Not today," I said. All I wanted now was to reach Domino.

As we came into the open, rounding the mountain, the ruins of the old mine became visible—a few tumbled buildings rotting away, an overturned ore car, rusting tracks. Perhaps the "gallows frame" that marked the top of a mine shaft and provided the hoist had once stood up there. My father had told me its nickname.

My father. Again memory had stirred. But how could I remember?

I prodded Baby Doe with my heels and rode up beside Gail, words tumbling out in sudden urgency. "You said my father died in Morgan House. Has anyone told you when he died? Do you know how old I was when it happened?"

She turned in her saddle and looked at me coolly from eyes that held no sympathy. I would never have expected this woman's vocation to be nursing.

"I believe that you were eight when he died," she said sweetly.

"Then it must have happened just before my mother and I left Jasper. Not when I was a baby, as I've been told. How did he die? If you know, please tell me."

"I thought you didn't want to know. In any case Mrs. Morgan has asked us not to talk to you about any of this. So you'll have to let it go until she's ready to tell you. But at least I can tell you *where* he died. It was in the gloomy rear parlor of Morgan House. That's probably why the room upset you so much this morning. Because you remember his dying there."

Hillary had caught up with us, and he rode between Gail and me, putting a stop to her words. "That's enough for now. We didn't come out here to talk about Persis Morgan and her house. Let's forget it!" He reached out and touched my arm. "Over there must be the Old Desolate mine that belonged to your great-grandfathers. So now let's go down and look at Domino."

Gail turned away, clearly piqued, and I could only be grateful to Hillary for thwarting her. She had wanted to hurt me. I had felt this in her all along, and I thought again of the funeral wreath that had been hung on my door. Leaving it for me would seem entirely in character for Gail Cullen. But why? Was I only imagining, as I could do so easily, or was she being prompted to this malice? Did someone else stand behind her?

I tried to shake off such disturbing thoughts as we rode on until we came fully over the mountain. Below us lay Domino—the remains of what was left of it straggling through a gulch between steep mountainsides. At the sight a flood of warm, unexpected emotion flowed through me.

This time I didn't want to be led, but pressed Baby Doe's flanks and urged her ahead to where I had a clear view of what remained down there—bones picked almost clean by dusty winds. How utterly lonely and abandoned the little mining camp seemed, its few ancient wooden buildings left to weather into dry and tumbled sticks. Long ago someone had built here hopefully, raising a town out of a dream. A dream that had died when the last man moved away. All through the mountains of the West such ghostly remnants of mining camps had crumbled into dust—lost history, never to be recovered.

Among the broken remnants one structure seemed to have been built with a certain arrogance and pride that had stood against the years and the gales. It boasted two floors, with a gable centered over long front windows where panes of glass shone in the sun. Surely the only glass remaining in Domino! Indeed, the only window frames. I had seen this house before, I knew, and it held no terror for me, but only happy promise.

"There'll be a watchman down there," Gail said. "But he knows me by now."

"A watchman in this empty place?"

"You'd be surprised at the way these old sticks of towns have been carried away. What the storms and the deep snows haven't destroyed the tourists pick up. Mr. Ingram is trying to save what's left. Not that we're exactly on the beaten path for tourists, but they can stray into the wilds. Mr. Ingram owns most of it now—except for that house built by Malcolm Tremayne."

My own history seemed to be waiting for me, and I pressed Baby Doe with my knees, urging her down the hillside.

VIII

Gail rode down with me, and Hillary came just behind.

"Mrs. Morgan sees to it that her house is kept in repair," she said. "Though it seems silly to bother."

"It doesn't sound practical to keep up anything around here," Hillary agreed.

I descended the steep stony trail, not wanting to listen to either of them. Never in my life had I been able to sense anything of family ties. My mother and her sister had been orphaned and raised by an elderly second cousin, who had also lacked ties. Of my mother's family only Aunt Ruth was left. But now these lonely, decaying remnants of a town so long forgotten reached out to speak to me. My great-grandmother had come here as a bride with her handsome young Englishman, Malcolm Tremayne. A man who had once shot an enemy with a silver-mounted deringer—perhaps in the streets of this very town.

Even such deeds had a glamorous ring when once removed into the pages of history, and I was already excusing Malcolm for whatever he might have done—because he belonged to me. The book I had read last night had told me how beautiful they both were—my great-grandparents—and suddenly I wanted to see pictures of them. Because of those two I existed, and I wanted to reach back into the past and touch them. With a deep new longing I wanted to know my father's face. What pictures my mother had kept were only snapshots, and mostly she had hidden them from me because they were part of the silence she kept. But surely Grandmother Persis would have photographs. She would have pictures of him when he was a little boy, and then as a young man, before he married my mother. All this I must see before I went away and they were lost to me forever.

Strangely, the thought of such an exploration into the past no longer alarmed me. Perhaps because it moved into a safer, more distant time than when I was eight years old and my father died in the rear parlor of my grandmother's house. Domino drew me. I had a kinship with its very dust. Besides, I wanted to know why Caleb Hawes and Persis Morgan had not wanted me here.

As Baby Doe picked her way downward around the slabs of gray rock and past piles of mine tailings that tumbled down the hillside, I studied the ruins below. Only a handful of wreckage straggled along the single street. Here and there, with siding flapping in the wind, could be seen the remains of a brave false front. Mostly siding was splintered, shingles gone, roofs caved in. A lopsided sign that announced SALOON led nowhere, and in some places only a debris-filled indentation in the ground showed where a house had stood. Perhaps even this much would not have been left if there had not been some effort over the years to keep it from blowing away entirely. Now, however, the abandonment was clear, except for the house where my great-grandparents had lived.

Just then something moved in my line of vision—something down there among the desiccated bones. I tried to focus more sharply, but it was gone at once, whatever it had been. Some animal, perhaps, foraging in the empty place. Or the watchman Gail had mentioned.

We were silent as our horses carried us down the trail, to come out at last at the end of the street farthest from the Tremayne house. A steep hill guarded Domino on one side, while on the other rose the lower flank of Old Desolate. When we halted, the silence seemed intense. The wracked mountainside above had once been denuded of trees, and new growth had sprung up sparsely. Weeds and grass and wild flowers had taken over where they could, burying ruins under a more kindly mantling. There had never been any paving here.

Then, as one of our horses whinnied, a furious barking began and a large police dog rushed to stand in the weed-stubbled road, his bared teeth threatening us. At once a man emerged from a small shack and stood in our path.

"Good morning, Tully," Gail said. "This is Miss Morgan and Mr. Lange from New York. Do you want to call off your dog?"

The watchman had long been baked by mountain winds and sun, and he was far from young. His hair and beard were grizzled, the blue of his eyes faded, but he was capable of a lively interest, and it seemed to be directed at me. He called the dog to him and snapped on a chain. Then, holding back the animal in its attempts to leap toward us, he addressed me quizzically.

"I know your gran'maw. Knew her when she was a tyke, living right here in Domino. You don't look like you're the same stock. Not tough enough."

"I'm a city girl," I said, and smiled at him.

He shook his head. "Times're changin'. It's no good for nobody." He touched a finger to his temple and disappeared into his shack, taking the dog with him.

"I shouldn't think he'd make much of a watchman," Hillary commented.

"How many men do you think would be willing to camp here?" Gail asked. "He's an old-timer, so he's willing to stay on. Maybe he even does a little prospecting out of old habit or searches for lost mines. I've heard Mr. Ingram say he'll do well enough for now." She urged Silver King along what had once been a street, speaking over her shoulder. "Mr. Ingram says that Domino will make an ideal spot for a ski lodge."

I rode after her. "I hope he never builds it."

"We won't let him!" Hillary said with sudden heat, and I gave him a grateful look.

Somewhere ahead a horse neighed, and Gail looked around sharply. "There's someone here."

So I hadn't imagined that movement I'd seen.

She trotted toward the one house that stood out intact among all the ruins, and as she reached it and dismounted, Hillary and I joined her. A big gray stood tethered to a post at the side of the house.

"That's Sundance," Gail said indignantly. "I might have known Mrs. Morgan would do this!"

As Hillary and I dismounted and tethered our horses, a man came out the door and stood on the narrow porch, looking down at us, thumbs hooked in his worn leather belt, his battered hat set jauntily on black curls. It was Jon Maddocks, and with no volition on my part my spirits lifted at the sight of him.

"Good morning," he said. "I suppose I'm the welcoming committee. Mrs. Morgan thought you might be riding over this way today."

Standing above us, he looked brown and fit, taller than Hillary, and obviously at ease, belonging to this place.

Gail barely acknowledged his greeting, and spoke to me. "Mrs. Morgan always hates to have anyone set foot in all this dead history. Though I can't understand why. If you want to go inside, I'll stay out here and smoke a cigarette. I don't care much for dust and mice and heaven knows what."

Hillary shrugged. "Go ahead," he said to me.

I stood looking up at the house, caught by its forlorn and lonely dignity. "Perhaps there are only ghosts in there." I spoke softly, knowing very well that I must go inside. I climbed the four wooden steps to the porch, finding the boards firm under my feet and in good repair.

"Wait for me, Hillary," I said, wanting to explore alone.

Jon gestured me in. "It's open. I've already unlocked the door."

"What skeletons is she hiding?" Gail asked lightly, "If someone wanted to break in, it would be easy enough."

Whoever had set the front door in place had carved its outer panel lovingly in an effort to decorate. What seemed to be primroses grew in relief around each panel. My great-grandfather's handiwork? A memory of England? The doorknob was of cracked china, and it turned easily in my fingers. I pushed the door open upon a small dim entryway, with other doors opening off it. I chose one and stepped into what must have been the parlor. A small room compared to the one in Jasper, but with a bay window to let in light as long as it might last, deep in this slot in the mountains.

There was no furniture, and here the bare boards of the floor showed traces of the years. There were none of the fine hardwoods of Persis' house, no moldings or plaster cornices. Yet the loving touches of a builder who meant to live in his house were evident here and there. Where stairs went up at the side of the hall, the newel post also bore hand carving and the banister had a graceful curve. The ceilings were not high as they were in Jasper, but in this small place a young couple had made an effort to beautify in their own personal ways, and the result seemed less austere than their later, far grander house. I liked the young couple who had first lived here better than I did the affluent citizens they became. Here they had tried to please themselves rather than choosing an imposing frame for the sake of others.

I walked over to put my hand on the carved post at the foot of the stairs.

"Don't go up there," Jon said from the parlor door. "Some of the floors have started to rot through upstairs. Mrs. Morgan said you could look in the door—if you felt you had to—but that was all. I come over sometimes to take care of things—keep the house swept out and the roof from leaking. But she hasn't wanted to put in new floors."

"Why was she so bent on keeping me out of this house?" I asked. "*Are* there skeletons, as Gail says?"

"I've never found any." He sounded laconic again. "Though sometimes I've wondered if they might exist. Maybe she just felt you hadn't earned the right to come here and poke around."

I bristled a little. "She can't keep that right from me. I've had it since the day I was born her granddaughter. So I think I'll go to the top of the stairs, at least."

He made no effort to stop me as I went up.

How curious it seemed to put my feet on these steps, my hand on the worn banister, knowing that the feet of Sissy and Malcolm had climbed these very stairs, that their hands had touched this same rail.

113

Jon left the other two on the porch and came up behind me. At the top was a short hallway, with three open doors leading off it, the light dim because of shuttered windows in the bedrooms. The flooring at the top of the stairs seemed solid enough, and I crossed the tiny hall to a bedroom and stood in the doorway.

"You don't listen, do you?" Jon said behind me.

"Not right now," I told him.

In this room, too, the floors seemed intact and had been recently swept. Through the broken slats of a shutter a little more light filtered in and showed me the empty room. On the walls were traces of peeling wallpaper. Wallpaper in Domino! I went to touch the gold and lavender daisies with curious fingers. Mountain daisies, so faded now that only a hint of color remained. I seemed to remember—something—perhaps staying in this room on a visit?

"How old is this house?" I asked.

"Your grandmother was born here," Jon said. "So it must be well past eighty years. I don't know how long the Tremaynes lived here. This was her room when she was a little girl."

I looked around at him directly, into eyes of smoky gray. "How do you know?"

"Because she used to bring me here. I rode over with her a good many times when I was a young boy. And later too. She liked to keep in touch with Domino."

"Were you making that up—about the broken floors? Just to scare me off?"

"No. They're bad at the back of the hall and in one of the rooms. I have to get to work on them."

"*Why* didn't she want me to come up here?" I repeated.

"She didn't want you to come into the house at all, but she saw she couldn't stop you. So she told me last night to come over before you got here this morning. She told me to get you out as quickly as possible."

"But what difference can it make to her now if I visit Domino?"

"I expect that's for her to say."

114

Once more I wished there were some way to get past the prickly guard he wore against me.

Through shutter slats I could look down on the street, where Hillary and Gail were walking about. Hillary, curious as always, had stopped to look through a broken doorway across the road. I should be down there, exploring with him. Perversely, I liked it better here.

"Last night I was reading a book about the Morgan mines," I told Jon. "It mentioned an old man they called Dominoes. Did he really exist?"

"I suppose so, though legends have a habit of growing. The story is that the old fellow you read about started a tunneling operation on his own around the side of Old Desolate before Tremayne struck the main lode. He put up the first cabin here and turned the place into a mining camp. The hint of gold or silver was always like flypaper to flies, so people came in. And it took his name. They say that's what he liked to play—dominoes. I suppose he stood out among all the poker players. Let's go down now. There's nothing to see up here."

"There's this," I said, and touched the wallpaper again. "A child lived in this room and grew up to be my grandmother. I didn't ever expect to have any feeling about that, but I do." A patch of faded daisies hung from the wall near my hand and I tore off a strip. For a moment I stood staring at it. Jon was watching, and I smiled at him absently. "You have to allow me a sentimental souvenir."

"There's no time to be sentimental about wallpaper when a life is involved. She's not just a grandmother you've happened to inherit. She's a *woman*."

"But she never let *me* know her the way she used to be. So now her life doesn't involve me. This is all I can take home with me from Colorado—this bit of paper. Persis Morgan is dying, and there's no possible way for her to recover a time that's gone."

His gray eyes could be cold as a mountain stream. "She doesn't have to die yet. She's giving up—and that's something she's never done before. Not ever in her life. Why don't you stop her?"

115

"That's foolish! There's nothing I can do against Mark Ingram."

"She thinks there is."

I turned on him angrily. "Then tell me what it is—tell me!"

"I wish I could. But you'll never find out if you turn and run. That way the vultures move in."

"I thought you'd decided I was one of the vultures."

"Maybe you are. Maybe not. But you're the one she's asked to come here. You're the one she wants to trust. So you need to get back into the real world. It's okay to remember, but sometimes I think you want to live back there, making up stories about times and people that are gone. Just to comfort yourself. You don't deal with what's *now*."

His words came too close to the truth, and they made me angry. But they weren't altogether fair. I could tell him about reality if I wanted to.

"You talk so much about helping her," I said. "What are *you* doing?"

The challenge didn't embarrass him. "I'm trying. I have an idea or two, and I've been searching. There are missing pieces. You may be able to pick them up."

I didn't answer him, but stuffed the bit of paper into my jacket pocket and returned to the dimness of the hall. At the top of the stairs I paused.

"Today, just a little while ago, I went into the rear parlor at Grandmother Persis' house. Apparently that room has been shut up for years. As though something that happened there must have been so awful that she could never risk going into it again."

Jon Maddocks looked away from me out the window and said nothing. He *knew,* I thought. But I had to go on.

"There was a box on a rosewood table, and when I touched it I was so frightened that I had to run out of the room. Do you know what's in that box?"

"Why don't you open it and see?"

"Because I have a feeling that if I do something dreadful will happen."

"When you're ready you'll open it," he said, and I

116

remembered his telling me that perhaps I had to earn the right to know. His assurance made me angry. How could he possibly understand that I was trying to be my own woman, trying to fight for my life?

"I'll tell you something else," I went on. "Gail Cullen left that door unlocked for me deliberately. She knew I'd go in there. For some reason she *wants* to frighten and upset me. But I'm not going to open that box. Because if I do . . . Oh, what's the use! No one understands. I know what my husband would say if he were alive. He would tell me I can never be free until I open whatever needs to be opened. Hillary thinks that too. He thinks I should open all the boxes. But if I do, perhaps I really will go out of my mind!" I could hear my voice rising, and I hated its pitch.

"Whoa now," Jon said as though he gentled Sundance. "I think there's more of Persis Morgan in you than you know. You'll find that out when you stop fighting it."

I backed down feebly. "I didn't mean to explode like that. I'm sorry—"

"Don't be. Explode if you like. Maybe you hold in too many things. If you like, I'll go into that room with you. I'm pretty good at fighting ghosts, when I have to."

"Yes." Memory took me back. "You helped me fight them once before, didn't you? All those years since then I've had a dream of riding a pony up the valley toward Old Desolate. Everyone has always said it was only a dream, but I've known it was real. I could hear hooves pounding after me because someone was following, and a terrible fear comes through in the dream. Why did you follow me? Why was I running away, and why did I feel so desperately that I had to ride toward the mountain?"

He hesitated for a moment before he answered. "You were frightened. Terrified. You might have been hurt if you went on alone. There was no one else to ride after you just then, so I did. Though I didn't know myself what was happening at the time."

I put my hand on the post at the top of the stairs to steady myself and closed my eyes. Now I could remember being thrown. I could remember arms about me and a

117

young boy, frightened himself but holding me, trying to comfort me—the sort of comfort that I had yearned for ever since and never found again. But that child was gone, lost in the past, and so was the boy who had held her. I opened my eyes and looked into Jon Maddocks' face—the face of a stranger. I wanted to thank that boy for what he had done, but I couldn't speak such words to this man who seemed to be waiting for something more that must come from me, and that I didn't know how to give, no matter what the need of my grandmother.

"I'm going home soon," I told him woodenly.

"That's a good way to escape what's real and present."

I marched down the stairs and out of the house, not waiting to hear anything more Jon Maddocks might say to me, not daring to listen.

Hillary and Gail were coming back along the street and Hillary was gesticulating dramatically, using Domino as his stage. I was struck by the contrast between him and Jon. The one always exuberant, excited, always onstage; the other quiet, indrawn, giving little away, yet always watchful, perhaps a little arrogant—thinking what? It disturbed me that I should find myself caring, wanting to know.

As Hillary danced about, light on his feet as he would be in a stage duel, Gail followed him, entranced, the way women always did. I knew all about Hillary's fascination as an actor, though sometimes I had the curious feeling that I didn't know what he was like as a man. A new objectivity was stirring in me that I couldn't altogether welcome.

He saw me on the porch and stopped waving his arms. "What a marvelous place, Laurie! Come down here—I want to show you something. Look—this was a saloon in here. There's what's left of a sign lying there that says, *Open All Night*."

I went to him quickly, putting new uncertainties behind me. When I bent to look through a broken doorframe, I could see sagging ceiling beams and a splintered bar with shelves behind it—all fallen in upon themselves. A small pine tree thrust upward where there had once been a roof.

"Can't you see the boys from Shoot-'em-up Corral coming in here, Laurie? I'll bet they really did. I'm beginning to get a feeling for all this. For the Opera House in Jasper, and for this little ghost of a town. It might be fun to put on *Girl of the Golden West* again. Put it on right there in Jasper—when people start coming in. Or perhaps I might even write a western play of my own."

"We're leaving very soon," I reminded him.

"But why should you?" Gail put in. "You're not through yet, Laurie. You must stay a few more days—a week, at least."

I knew what she meant. Enough time to open that box. Enough time to bring everything down like a pack of cards. Why should she want that? Why should she want Mark Ingram to be home free? And why should she say this if she had put the wreath on my door to frighten me away?

"I suppose we could stay a little while longer," Hillary said. "It's not going to make all that much difference, is it, Laurie?"

I recognized his excitement over this place. It wasn't fair to bring him out here and then turn off this new eagerness that kindled him.

"All right. But, please—not for long."

"Did you find anything interesting in the house?" he asked.

I pulled out the strip of wallpaper to show him. "Just this."

His imagination caught fire as he held up the bit of paper. "Daisies—those mountain daisies! Years and years old!"

"From a room my grandmother lived in when she was a little girl."

He gave the paper back to me. "Keep it, Laurie. It will help you to remember your coming here."

Companionably he linked his arm through mine, and as we walked along the street together I felt comforted. A little. Of course Hillary and Gail would like each other. He liked everyone—exactly the way Red did. But it didn't mean anything. I'd seen women turn calf's eyes at him before, and he still came back to me. Because I fired his imagination. He'd told me so once. Because *I* was a Pandora's box full of undisclosed secrets, he'd said. Sometimes I'd wondered uneasily whether I would still interest him once he knew everything there was to know. But at least he had understood how I felt about the wallpaper, where Jon Maddocks, the pragmatist, had not. I closed my mind against the thought of Jon. I mustn't let him in at all. In that direction lay danger. The connection with the past was too strong, and I must be careful.

We picked our way past stunted pine trees that grew here and there in a street made narrow because of mountain walls on either side. Grass waved in the wind wherever it had seeded in, and clumps of columbine, lavender and white, grew in rotting debris. In one corner flaming-red Indian paintbrush made an orangey slash of color.

I tried to let all confusion and inner conflict flow away so that I could accept this place, know all of it that remained. Already I loved these lonely remnants of what had once been a thriving mining camp. I wanted to carry them back with me in memory, just as I would carry away that tangible bit of wallpaper tucked into my pocket. All this was Domino, and somehow Domino was part of my flesh and blood and bones, as I had never expected that it would be.

If it hadn't been for Domino, I wouldn't be walking this street now. Perhaps I wouldn't even be alive. Persis had said I looked like Sissy Tremayne. There was kinship for me here with my own people, with my very roots. Hillary might use Domino as a springboard for his imagination, but for me it was reality—a past to which I still belonged, yearned to belong.

I walked on to the end of what had been a street, lost in a feeling for the past that had never touched me before. My eyes misted with grief for something I had never known, and I was closer here to Persis Morgan than I had felt standing beside her bed. If I were to stay a few days more to please Hillary, perhaps there was something I could *do*. Some way in which I could help her. A new resolve began rising in me that I had never felt before.

The town had ended, running off into high grass that climbed the gulch, and we turned back toward our horses. Jon waited for us, astride Sundance. He looked right in a saddle, as a man should. He would never bother with fancy gaits in a horse, or proper posting with no saddle horn. A saddle horn was for roping, and Jon grew in his saddle, belonging to these western mountains as we did not. Even though Gail rode well, she looked a little like a dude, while Hillary and I were plainly easterners. Jon was real—a man who lived and worked in an environment he had loved and returned to. Perhaps he had never felt real in New York.

Something contrary was happening in me. Something that made me compare Hillary with Jon to Hillary's disadvantage. If this was disloyalty, it was also a clearer viewing than I'd ever had before. And if this must come, better that it should happen now, before our commitment to each other had gone too far. For Hillary as well as for me.

When we'd mounted, Jon came with us, leading the way. "Do you want to see what's left of the mine?" he asked, looking back at me. "From the outside, that is?"

"I'd like that," I told him. I might never come here again, and I was eager to see everything I could.

Gail and Hillary seemed uninterested, and rode on alone.

A switchback trail brought Jon and me to the top, where pieces of rusting machinery were strewn about, along with a few tumbledown sheds. The rusted wheels and frame of the ore car I'd noticed earlier lay on its side among twisted cables, while an equally rusted track ran into the mountain. Bare mounds of tailings fell away below us.

"Was there a smelter here?" I asked Jon.

"No. Smelters were mostly down on the plains. The ore was taken out by mule team to Jasper, where the railroad picked it up. Down there on your left is what they used to call the Glory Hole, where there was a big strike. There was a cave-in later, where a dozen men were buried under tons of earth. What's left of them is still down there."

121

I shivered as we rode on, and the narrowed way seemed even more precarious. That was what mining had always been—the threat of sudden, cruel death—yet there had always been men willing to be miners.

"Is the entrance to the mine still open?" I asked.

"I can show you where it is, but it's not open. It was boarded shut long ago and a door put in that could be locked."

Sundance picked his way delicately along the hillside, and Baby Doe followed docilely. Both were mountain horses, used to uncertain footing.

"There you are." Jon reined in, pointing. "The opening is right over there."

Timbering formed a door into the mountain, holding back its weight with strong overhead beams, framing the stout door that had been locked with a hasp and big padlock.

"Mostly old mines are nailed shut, or the openings filled in with concrete," Jon said. "But Mrs. Morgan never quite gave up on the Old Desolate. When there's silver in your blood, you don't get over it easily. She wants to hold onto it and keep access, but still bar the foolish from going in."

"She can't get many tourists back here."

"Mark Ingram means to change all that. Besides, there are old trails that lead into Domino, and sometimes backpackers find their way in even now. There's nothing more dangerous than an old mine. Tunnels are full of broken slabbing and piles of rock where there have been cave-ins. There can be shafts that go down a hundred feet or more. Most likely with deep water at the bottom. Plenty of people have been drowned in mine shafts, when they weren't killed by the fall. To say nothing of the gases that can collect inside, and the lack of oxygen. There are no snakes up this high, but there's plenty else that's not to be tampered with by the curious and ignorant."

"Are there many such mines left that people can get into?"

"Sure. Hundreds of them are scattered through these mountains, and not all of them marked. Some are just dangerous holes in the ground, overgrown and hidden, so it's impossible to locate them all. Kids and unwary backpackers fall into them and are sometimes killed."

There was nothing more to see here where my great-grandfather had found his fortune. The town itself meant more to me, and I turned Baby Doe's head. Behind me, Jon spoke.

"When you ran away on your pony that time and I found you, you kept wailing that you had to get to the mine. I've always wondered what drove you to all that urgency when you were so terrified."

Wind blew in my face, and now and then gusts howled down the gulch that held Domino far below us. I felt suddenly cold with an eerie remembrance. Terror *had* existed for me close to the mine, as well as back in my grandmother's house. If I went near those boards of a door set into the mountain, would I feel another wind on my face surging through the cracks of the planking—a wind rising from the depths of the earth? A dark wind that would carry with it the odor of death?

"Hey!" Jon said, and rode up beside me. "Don't go getting dizzy while you're in the saddle. This is rough ground for a fall, and you could tumble down the mountain."

His words braced me. "I'm all right." I urged Baby Doe on along the hillside, forcing myself to sit steady in the saddle. Hillary and Gail were well ahead by now, and the moment of dizziness passed as we rode on. I was in control again. But why had I thought of death in the mountain?

When the trail leveled, I reined in to look back—perhaps for the last time. Not at the mine, but down past it, past the tailing dumps, to the bare bones of Domino, impressing on my memory the appearance of the handful of straggling timbers that had once been a busy camp. In particular I looked for the house that had belonged to Sissy and Malcolm Tremayne, its gabled roof still raised in defiance of the years, resisting the laws of decay because it was still lovingly tended.

Jon waited for me. "You'll come back. That house

123

down there should belong to you—not to anyone else. You can't go away and never see Domino and the Old Desolate again."

"I thought you said I should live in the present. All that is the past."

"It's the present for Persis Morgan—and for you, too." His look seemed to soften as he watched me. "You'll find a way to help her. Otherwise you can't live with yourself."

"I can live with myself," I said in quick irritation.

He turned Sundance along the trail after the others, and I followed in silence.

Ahead of us a horse blew and stamped, and Jon pulled in. As I rode up beside him, a rider on a big bay emerged from the stand of pines that had concealed him. In dismay I saw that he was Mark Ingram. Apparently the loss of a right leg did not keep him from riding. His smile was amiable, and I didn't trust it at all.

"Good morning, Miss Morgan, Jon," he said. "You been down saying good-bye to the old place?"

That was exactly what I had been doing, but I couldn't accept the assumption from him. Ever since I'd come to Jasper, I'd felt about me an atmosphere of disapproval and rejection. Of more than rejection. That wreath had been a threat. And where else could threat originate except from this man?

With sudden resolve I rode over to where he sat as though he, too, had grown in a saddle. I looked straight into cold eyes that didn't match his easy smile, and knew I had to resist.

"Why should I say good-bye?" I asked.

His laughter was as easy as his smile. "Oh, come on now, little lady—you know Domino's going out of Morgan hands. All of it. And soon. I've some pretty fine plans I want to work out down there, and I expect to start building before long."

I could feel an anger rising in me that was stronger than any I'd ever experienced. It was hard to keep my voice steady.

"I don't think you'll build anything down there until you have access to the valley, Mr. Ingram."

124

"Getting that's only a matter of time, isn't it?"

"I hope a very long time. I didn't go down there just now to say good-bye," I told him, making the words up as I went along, driven only by an unfamiliar inner rage. "I went down to see what needs to be done to the property my grandmother still owns. She has some plans she wants to carry out."

Sundance stamped, and I was intensely aware of Jon sitting him a little way off, deliberately leaving all this to me.

Mark Ingram's eyes, almost a pewter color like his hair, blinked at my words. "We both know you're bluffing, young lady. But we can talk more about this at dinner tonight. I'll see you then."

He turned his bay onto the trail and rode down into Domino. I found I was shaking with reaction. I had done something I could never have conceived of ahead of time, and now that it was over I felt thoroughly shocked.

Jon came up beside me, grinning. "Good for you. I felt like cheering."

I shook my head. "Don't. He was right—I was bluffing. I just got mad and had to speak up."

Jon reached out to touch my hand on the reins. "Maybe Mrs. Morgan's found herself a fighter, after all."

"No!" I told him. "That's not true. That man frightens me. Did you see the way he looked at me?"

"Sure, I saw. From now on you aren't going to be his favorite girl. I can tell that well enough, and you're right to be afraid of him. That will make you cautious. But you can't back down now. You're in the fight."

I wanted to answer him heatedly, denying his words in order to save myself, but at that moment Hillary came galloping back along the trail, to rein in beside us dramatically, like a movie cowboy. Gail trotted more decorously along behind.

"What's kept you, Laurie?" Hillary demanded. "We thought you'd catch up. What was all that about with Ingram just now?"

I explained what had happened, and Hillary looked pleased. "Fine! Don't let that man walk all over you.

Maybe we'll give him his money's worth at dinner tonight."

I had no answer for that, and when we started toward the ranch, I managed to drop behind them all again, weary of being praised for what I was not, and for what I wasn't at all sure I wanted to do. Becoming angry with Mark Ingram for a few moments was one thing. Keeping such anger going was another, and I didn't think I had that in me. I *wasn't* like Persis Morgan. Now I wanted only to let it all go and be aware of nothing but the mountains around me. More than anything else I wanted peace.

When we went over the shoulder of Old Desolate, I could see down through pines to the wide, beautiful valley that led to the ranch and Morgan House. An unaccountable mist touched my eyes at the sight of it. Perhaps I knew why. Not because of that old woman down there, who was really a stranger to me, but because something in me wept for the long-ago child who had ridden these trails and whom I had lost for all these years. It was not the terrible day when I'd fled to the mountain that stirred me now. It was not only a young boy's arms holding and soothing me that I remembered. It was something else.

A memory I had almost lost rode again beside me. The memory of a tall, fair man who was my father. I couldn't see him or recall his face, but I could remember him—just a little. I could remember kindness and humor—the way he had laughed. I could remember his love for me, my adoration for him. These were feelings I must hold to, recover. I would ask Persis to give me a picture of him, so that I could take it home with me when I left. I would do that *now.*

I touched my heels to Baby Doe's flanks, wanting only to hurry through the flowering meadow and reach the house. Wanting to leave that angry encounter behind me so that it couldn't force me into doing anything I didn't want to do.

IX

At the ranch we left the horses in Jon's care and walked back to the house, with Red once more loping along at my side. On the porch Caleb waited for the three of us, looking severe and remote. He had never wanted anything since I'd arrived except to have me gone, and I wished I could understand what lay behind so strong an antipathy.

"Mrs. Morgan is awake, and she wishes to see you right away," he told me. "She wants to see you and the dog and the man. Those are the words she used. So you'd better go up."

Hillary laughed. "I've been wanting to meet the fabulous lady who is opposing Mark Ingram."

When we started upstairs, Caleb stopped Gail curtly. "Not you. You've been away all morning, and she doesn't need you now."

Gail lost none of her surface sweetness. "That's all right with me. I'll get back to work on those accounts I've been doing for Mrs. Morgan. Sometimes I think I'm more secretary than nurse around here. See you later at midday dinner. Around twelve-thirty?"

Accounts? I wondered. Somehow I didn't care for the idea of Gail Cullen delving so deeply into Persis Morgan's affairs.

At least I was relieved to know that the sedative had worn off. The emotion stirred by my visit to Domino was still upon me, and I could look at my grandmother with new eyes. But I must be careful now. My explosion toward Mark Ingram had made me a little distrustful of my own reactions. If I weren't careful I might find myself promising what I couldn't possibly fulfill. The brief urge to be helpful was fading.

Nevertheless, I felt a sense of uneasy anticipation. No encounter with my grandmother was likely to be static. The seeds of conflict between us were there, and eventually they would grow. Even though she meant to hold back the truth from me, the dam would not stand forever. And when it broke . . .

More than anything else I needed to control my own feelings, to resist and be strong.

She awaited us propped high on her pillows, her eyes snapping brightly, and I noted that she did not look as though she were dying.

Caleb introduced Hillary, and Red promptly placed his forepaws on the bed and gazed with limpid brown eyes into the face on the pillow. For the first time I saw my grandmother smile, and when her eyes and lips quirked up at the corners, her look was unexpectedly roguish.

She put out her own hand, permitted it to be sniffed, and then stroked his plumy coat. He accepted the caress with joy and gave her his most melting look, accompanied by little whines of happiness.

Persis snapped her fingers at him. "Over here," she said. "Come around the bed and guard me on this side."

Clearly Red was already on the same wave length. He understood gesture and command, and scampered around the bed, ears flopping, to seat himself with his chin on the coverlet. One hand on his head, she looked up at me. In spite of my resolutions I found myself warming to the tenacity for life that looked out of her eyes. There was a sympathy in me since seeing Domino that had been lacking before. A subtle bond had grown between us.

"Caleb tells me you went riding up the valley. I suppose you went over the mountain to Domino after all, even though I asked you to stay away?"

"You knew I would go," I said. "You sent Jon Maddocks there ahead of us. Anyway, I couldn't *not* go."

Caleb brought chairs for us, but I didn't want to sit down. She flicked her fingers at him in dismissal, and he gave me a look of warning before he went away. I knew it meant not to tire her, not to wear her out, but it meant something more as well that I couldn't fathom.

128

There seemed to be more energy in her now, and she didn't look in the least tired. "I expect it was foolish of me to try to keep you away," she said.

"Why should you want to?"

Heavy lids drooped and her face lost its briefly quirky look. "Never mind that. It's all ancient history by this time." Then she opened her eyes and stared straight at Hillary. "So this is your young man?"

It seemed to me that Hillary looked a little less at ease than was usual for him. As though he might be more impressed with Persis Morgan than he had meant to be. Or perhaps he found her an uncertain quantity in his range of experience.

"You might put it that she's my young lady," he said.

She shook her head at him. "Unsuitable. You're an actor. You belong to the East. Laurie belongs here."

He was ready enough to humor her, and not take offense. "You can't really know that, can you?" he asked cheerfully. "Maybe I do belong out here. Maybe I can even be on your side, if you give me a chance."

She neither accepted nor rejected. "While you're here you can be useful, at least. If you want to be."

He turned all his lovely charm upon her as he smiled. "Persis Morgan has always been able to command," he said with a slight flourish.

She regarded him from beneath half-closed eyelids, and though the look was faintly coquettish, it was not incongruous, and I found myself watching delightedly as she displayed an ability to play the old games.

"Yes, you can be useful," she went on. "I want you to stay on at the Timberline and watch him for me."

"You're talking about Mark Ingram?"

"Of course." A faint flush had come into her cheeks, and her eyes were brighter than ever. "I could put you up here at my house easily enough, but you're more useful to me over there."

"I would enjoy being useful to you," he said, sounding as though he really meant it. "I've always liked people who don't beat around the bush."

"I haven't time left for bush-beating. Ingram has to be

129

stopped. What he's doing is despicable. Laurie is going to stop him, and you can help. You're both having dinner with him tonight, aren't you? So listen to him. Find out about his immediate plans, if you can. How does he propose to get me out of this house? That's what I want to know."

I thought of my recent encounter, and was all the more doubtful that we could learn anything Mark Ingram chose not to tell us.

"Why do you consider it despicable to rejuvenate Jasper?" Hillary asked. "Isn't it a good idea to restore it to the way it used to be and bring in people who will enjoy it and draw it back into life?"

"He wants more than that. He wants to spoil the valley and wipe out Domino."

"To get people to come, he must offer something. The valley slopes will make good skiing."

"The trees will go, the wilds will go. Old Desolate won't be that anymore. And Domino—he'll erase what's left of it. Too many old mining camps have vanished."

"It's already nearly gone," Hillary said.

"Are you siding with him?"

"No!" His vehemence surprised me. "I've told you I can be on your side, but I can play Devil's Advocate either way. There's something else, isn't there, Mrs. Morgan? Something you haven't explained? If you want us to help, don't you think you'd better give us more of what we ought to know?"

She closed her eyes, and for a moment I thought it was a gesture of dismissal. I hated to see how old she looked with animation wiped from her face—old and withered and nearly finished with life. I liked her better when she was coquettish, or even domineering. I couldn't let Hillary push her too hard.

"You don't have to tell us anything you don't wish to, Grandmother," I said. "You're tired now. We'd better go, so you can rest."

That brought her eyes wide open and angry, and her words snapped. "All I do is rest! Your young man is right. I can't expect you to help me merely on trust. I can't tell you the whole story either, but I'll tell you this much. A long time ago Mark Ingram was the friend of my very worst enemy. Perhaps that abominable man is behind him now. Ingram hasn't come here merely to open a new resort. He could go anywhere for that. He has come to punish me, destroy me. And he knows he can do it. He has only to force me out of this house, make me give up the valley—and I am finished with living. But I'm not ready to die. Not yet. Not while there's an ounce of fight left in me. Not while I have a granddaughter who may be persuaded to stand by me."

Hillary spoke softly, as though he didn't want to dispel her mood of anger. "This—enemy—can you give us his name?"

For a moment she hesitated. Then she looked straight at me as though she expected some special response. "His name was Noah. Noah Armand."

Once more the familiar tremor ran through me, as though some deep, sensitive nerve responded with a quiver of dread.

"Your husband?" There was a change in Hillary's voice, though he spoke in the same low tone.

She raised a warning finger at him, her eyes upon me. "Hush. Laurie, you *do* remember something?"

I could only shake my head. "It's not really a remembering. I have an unpleasant association with that name. But I don't know why." I did not tell her that Noah had been the name I cried out in my nightmares.

"If there's something to tell, why don't you tell her, Mrs. Morgan?" Hillary asked, that new intensity in his voice, as though he might enjoy stirring everything up. His theatricality was in force again, but I couldn't forgive him if he played his stage games now.

"Don't," I said to him. "Please don't."

He touched my shoulder lightly. "I'm sorry. It's just that I feel it's way past time for you to find out the truth—whatever it is."

Grandmother Persis was shaking her head. "No, it's better not. If Laurie doesn't remember, I'd rather leave it alone. It's only what is happening now that matters, any-

131

way. Young man, if you stay at the Timberline, if you can manage to find out what Ingram means to do, you can be of service to me, and perhaps you'll help Laurie too."

"It's possible," Hillary said. "I am interested in that theater of his, and that makes a contact between us. Besides, Laurie has already agreed to stay on for a little while longer."

"A little while longer!" She gave the words an indignant ring. "Laurie has come home. She is living here with me."

I had to answer her honestly. "I haven't promised that. I can't agree to stay indefinitely."

She snorted her complete disregard for my words, my wishes, and once more I felt myself bristling toward her. To her I was an instrument to an end, and that was all. I had been trying—a little—to understand her, to sympathize. But she was entirely unwilling to understand and know me.

For a moment we stared at each other in rising antagonism while Hillary watched, not altogether amused. "How much alike you two are," he said. "I'd never have suspected it if I hadn't seen Laurie in this setting."

Persis Morgan surprised me by laughing. The sound was full and deep, making no concession to age.

"No," she countered. "Not when she looks like that—we're not. When you put on that face, Laurie, you're your father all over again."

"If I resemble my father, I'm glad," I told her. "I'd like to know a great deal more about him before I leave."

"I can tell you about him." She spoke more quietly now, her indignation drained away as quickly as it had risen. "Richard was a gentle man. My son preferred classrooms to the ranch any day. But when he got his back up—the way yours is up now—he could dig in his heels and I could never shake him. He would even fight, if he had to, for what he believed in. I loved him dearly, but I never fooled myself. He was a rather dull young man, really. That was part of the trouble."

I didn't want to think of my father as dull. He had always cut a romantic figure in my imaginings, and I would

132

accept nothing less. The fact that ranches and guns and riding had never interested him didn't mean that he had been dull—except perhaps to those who knew nothing else. But before I could protest, she went on.

"Unfortunately, he began to bore your mother. Mary-beth was part of the trouble too."

I was ready to spring to the defense of both my parents, but I didn't know how. I lacked any real knowledge of my father, and Persis' words threatened old beliefs I didn't want to lose. As for my mother—she had given her life to being loyal to his memory.

"At least you can tell me how he died," I said. "I've always believed that it was from pneumonia when I was only two. But Gail Cullen says she's been told that it happened in the back parlor downstairs—when I was eight years old. I'd like to know the truth."

"Very well." Persis looked straight at me, her words as direct and merciless as she could make them. "Your father—my son—was shot to death. He was killed right here in this house with a single bullet."

I found myself fumbling for the chair behind me. As I sat down, Hillary bent toward me, but I drew away. It was coming now—everything. I couldn't hold it off any longer. I didn't want to.

Persis went on, staring at me without blinking. "An intruder broke into the house, and Richard discovered him. So my son was shot senselessly, and he died almost at once. The police never found out who killed him, though theft seemed to be the motive. Several valuable pieces of jewelry were missing." Her voice was low, the words dry, and I knew they were uttered out of old, long-suppressed pain.

Red, who had been quiet until now, whined uneasily.

"I have to know," I said, and heard the tremor in my voice. "I was there in the room, wasn't I? I must have seen what happened. Is this what I've shut away for so long? Is this the thing I could never bear to remember?"

Her eyes closed again, and I saw a tear start down one cheek. "You were ill afterward. Your mother took you away. I was furious with her, yet I was shattered myself

133

for a long while. So I put you out of my life. I didn't want to be hurt anymore."

Strangely, the sense of revelation had faded. I felt empty, bereft. To come so close and yet have the truth withheld—as I knew she was withholding it—left me limp with the reaction of defeat.

"You haven't told it all," I said. "Not nearly all!"

She didn't answer. Her hand drew away from my touch and was hidden under the quilt.

I spoke again, urgently. "If you won't tell me, then I think I must go away soon. It's too late for anything but the truth."

In a flash her hand came out from beneath the covers and grasped mine, her grip surprisingly strong. "No! You can't go yet. You *do* owe me something—as I owe you. We can't help that, either of us. In a way you owe me life. Stay and pay your debt—as I'll try to pay mine."

I remembered walking the dusty street in Domino and thinking that if that place had never existed, I would never have existed. Yet I couldn't accept the debt she wanted to thrust upon me.

"I'll stay only a little while," I told her. "A week, perhaps. But there's one other thing I'd like of you. I want to see pictures of my father."

She turned her head away. "There are albums. Look at them if you like. If you can bear to."

I recognized dismissal, and Red seemed to sense it as well. He drew away from the bed with a faint whimper, and Hillary went without protest to open the door. I walked out feeling dazed and empty of all emotion.

In the hallway Caleb still sat on the bench waiting for us, and he stood up impatiently.

"Is she all right? I hope you haven't upset her."

I wondered at his concern, not really trusting him. In any case I had nothing to say, and after a glance at my face he went past us into her room.

Hillary put an arm about my shoulders. "There—you see! It's over now. You know what really happened and you're perfectly able to face it. You'll be fine now. You'll never have to blank out again to protect yourself from the truth."

I stiffened against his arm, knowing that for once his reassurance was of no use to me. It was facilely given—without strong reason.

"I don't think I know anything yet," I told him. "If you don't mind, I'd like to go to my room for a little while. Will you take Red outside for me, please?" I knew I sounded abrupt, ungracious, but I could manage nothing more.

"Of course, Laurie. Gail has invited me to stay for lunch, so I'll see you then."

When we reached my door, he kissed me tenderly and went off, with Red at his heels. I had the feeling that I had once more disappointed him. Strangely, I didn't seem to care.

For a moment I stood before my door, where only last night a funeral wreath had waited for me. Was that what the card on the wreath had meant—that those who died violently do not sleep in peace? Who had been trying to tell me that, and why should it matter now? If the wreath had anything to do with Noah Armand, anything to do with the room downstairs, then there was reason for me to be frightened. Yet I seemed now to be only a little numb.

I went into my room and sat in the rocking chair, tipping back and forth gently, soothingly.

Why could I feel nothing at all about what I had learned? Pandora's box had been opened at last, and some of the horrors had flown out, yet far from feeling destroyed, I didn't feel anything. My very young ears must have heard the shot that killed my father. My eyes must have looked upon something truly terrible. Perhaps I had watched my father die. Yet I could feel only empty and stupefied.

Had I been shocked into this numbness? When I grew used to the idea, would sensation return? Then might I remember fully? For the first time I looked upon remembering with less of a sense of dread. Surely it would be better to feel pain, to suffer, to feel *something,* than to experience this emptiness of all emotion.

Or was my "emptiness" due only to the fact that I didn't believe the things that Persis Morgan had told me? When I thought of that "intruder" and the tale of stolen jewels, I reacted as if to a remote fiction, and about all this I felt nothing.

But there was something else to undermine me, and suddenly a new and terrible grief surged up in me. Grief for my father's dying, for a loss that would hurt me forever—and this I could weep for. Tears were a release, washing away tension, even though I didn't know exactly why I wept. Was it only for old loss?

A sense of time passing brought my tears to an end. I hurried to wash my stained face and comb my hair. When I went down, Hillary was waiting for me at the foot of the stairs. His searching look could hardly miss the evidence of swollen eyelids.

"I'm all right," I told him quickly, before he could question me.

Gail came to meet us at the dining room door, looking trim and self-confident, having changed from her Levi's to green jumper and blouse instead of her uniform.

When she greeted me, I looked at her with no expression at all, and Hillary touched my arm. "Are you really all right, Laurie? You're entitled to fall apart a bit, you know. Don't try to be too controlled. Let go, Laurie."

"Is that what I am—controlled?"

"You do look a bit frazzled," Gail said. "Perhaps hot food will help and something to drink. Lunch—dinner, really—seems to be ready, so let's sit down." She slipped her hand easily through my arm and drew me into the dining room as though we were good friends.

Caleb was already there, looking as displeased as ever, though he pulled out my chair courteously. Hillary took the place next to me and gazed about the room in enjoyment.

"What a good stage setting this would make," he said. "I must remember that old fellow up there over the man-

136

tel. Laughing Boy. I'll bet he could tell a few stories if we got him to talk."

His light note didn't relieve my mood. For me the elk's head over the mantel seemed a thoroughly melancholy touch, and not anything I could laugh about.

While plates of thick roast beef, browned potatoes, and homegrown butter beans were passed down the table, Gail spoke again.

"It's very odd about your memory, Laurie. It seems to be so selective. Don't you remember anything about this room?"

I made an effort to behave normally. "Very little. There's a lot I can't remember. But there is something I've wanted to ask you. When I went into the back parlor today and turned on the lights, I saw something strange. Mostly the cobwebs and dust hadn't been disturbed in years. But someone had been in that room recently. There were other footprints besides mine, and I could see where a few things had been moved, as though someone had been searching. Was it you, Gail?"

Her surprise seemed genuine. "I've been in that room only once, and hardly any farther than the door. I was curious, but it gives me the creeps and I didn't stay."

"Someone searching for something, Laurie?" Caleb repeated. "How extraordinary! Mrs. Morgan closed that room off years ago, and I've looked into it rarely."

"Someone has been in there," I said. "And not long ago."

Caleb and Gail exchanged a look that seemed to carry quick suspicion of each other, but no one said anything more about the back parlor.

As we started to eat, Gail went on. "Mrs. Morgan must have held up a lot better than she usually does for you to have stayed with her that long, Laurie."

I knew how curious she was to learn what had occurred in Persis' room, but I didn't mean to satisfy her.

"I think she can hold up when she wants to," I said. "I don't think she has any intention of dying."

"Sometimes she talks about a change in her will," Gail mused.

Caleb looked at her sharply. "What does she mean by that?"

"Probably she's thinking of her granddaughter."

Caleb said nothing more, but I found myself watching him again, wondering why he seemed so much of an enigma. He was a man who waited in the background, never seeking the spotlight, but watching rather ominously. And perhaps manipulating more than I had guessed?

In any case I didn't care about my grandmother's will or Gail's casual gossip. My only regret was that when Persis Morgan was gone, whoever was left would probably sell out quickly to Mark Ingram. Perhaps that didn't really matter. Times changed, and she couldn't sit forever across the right-of-way that a man as strong as Mark Ingram coveted. Jon Maddocks' words came back to me—the thing he had said about the house Malcolm and Sissy had built in Domino. That it ought to belong to me. A curious remark. I wanted neither that house nor this one. Especially not this one. I only wanted to know those things my grandmother had skimmed over, avoided, or distorted. I was ready to open the door wide and walk through it.

"Grandmother Persis has explained what happened in the back parlor," I told Gail.

"Can't we stop talking about that?" Caleb said.

Hillary disagreed. "Perhaps now is the best of all possible times," he said quietly.

Gail gave in. "All right then. I'm sure this is a subject that is more upsetting to you, Laurie, than to the rest of us. Which of the stories did she tell you?"

So that was it—an assortment of fabrications? Was that why memory hadn't stirred in me?

"She said that my father was shot by an intruder who got away with some family jewels. I think I must have been there in that room when it happened."

"I understand that you were," Gail agreed, and threw a look at Caleb that seemed faintly challenging. "Of course that was the official story," she went on. "I grew up hearing it since my family lives not too far from Jasper. My brothers are still there. That was the story that got into the papers and was accepted by the police."

I hadn't been aware that she'd lived in these mountains as a child. Now I understood why she had so much gossipy information.

We managed to go on eating as though this were an ordinary conversation. But then this was all old history for Caleb and Gail, and no longer something that had just occurred to a living man.

"Where was Noah Armand when this happened?" I asked Caleb.

He put his fork down carefully, as though I had startled him. "Noah walked out of this house a week before your father—died. And he was never seen again. He had been quarreling with your grandmother for some time, and I think she probably told him to leave."

Gail made a small explosive sound of derision, and Caleb looked at her coldly.

"Take care," he said.

I asked another question. "My father was Noah's stepson. How did my father get along with his mother's new husband?"

"What does any of this matter now?" Caleb stared at his plate.

"Perhaps it does matter." Hillary spoke so softly that I think we were all startled, having forgotten his presence. "Perhaps it matters if, as Mrs. Morgan says, Mark Ingram was Noah's friend. So why don't you tell us, Caleb?"

"All right—if you must know, it's true that Richard Morgan, Laurie's father, never liked his mother's second choice as husband. Sons hardly ever do. Armand was a great deal younger than your grandmother, Laurie, and your father was protective of his mother and suspicious of Armand's motives in marrying her."

"Then what happened to Noah?" Hillary asked in that same soft tone that seemed somehow persuasive, so that his questions were answered.

"We don't know," Caleb said shortly. "We believe he must be dead."

Hillary pressed him further. "Why do you think that?"

"Because of the sort of man he was," Caleb answered. "Bad pennies always turn up. If he's alive, he's still Mrs. Morgan's husband. It's hard to believe he wouldn't make claims, put on some sort of pressure."

"What if he has?" Hillary asked, his tone gentle, almost amused.

We all stared at him, startled, and he laughed.

"Don't look so shocked. It's just a thought. Why don't you check with Mark Ingram?"

"Let it alone!" Caleb said sharply. "Don't go digging Noah Armand up—if it's really a grave he's in."

I wondered again what it was that had so alarmed Caleb Hawes.

"Perhaps that's a good idea, Hillary," I said. "Perhaps I will ask Mr. Ingram when we have dinner with him tonight."

Hillary's smile approved of me. Then he turned gracefully to other subjects, drawing Caleb and Gail into talk about Mrs. Morgan, Jasper, and Ingram's plans, drawing them away from more dangerous topics. Once more I was grateful for his social skills, manipulative though they sometimes seemed.

I was glad to be left to my own thoughts. An obvious suspicion was growing in my mind. Had it been Noah who returned to the house after he had left? Returned quietly, to break in, kill my father, pick up some of his wife's jewels, and disappear before he could be stopped? Had Persis, to avoid scandal, developed the lie about an intruder that everyone had believed ever since? But I could put none of this into words now.

When we'd finished our meal, Caleb said he had work to do in his office upstairs, and Hillary asked me to come with him to the Opera House, which he wanted to visit again.

I said, "Not right now, please. There's something I must do. Caleb, Grandmother Persis told me that there are albums of family pictures. I'd like to go through them before I leave. If you could help by identifying any of the faces . . . ?"

140

"I can show you the albums, Laurie," Gail offered. "I've taken them up to Mrs. Morgan often enough. Most of the pictures are marked with names underneath, so you won't need help in identifying them." She turned to Hillary. "May I go to the Opera House with you? I love that old place, and I can show you some of its secrets that you'd never find out for yourself. Mark has been showing them to me."

Hillary grinned at me a bit cockily. After all, I'd had first chance. "Don't you have some duties in the house?" he asked Gail.

"Not today. I've been banished for now."

"That won't do." Caleb spoke sharply. "You can't side-step everything like this. I'll talk to Mrs. Morgan."

"Yes, you do that," Gail said. "In the meantime I'll show Hillary the theater."

I found myself watching her, decidedly troubled. Gail was a nurse, and it seemed odd that she could take her position so lightly. It was possible that she knew Mark Ingram better than she pretended. In which case his influence in this house was much greater than I liked to think. Perhaps she held a secure if unacknowledged place here that not even my grandmother understood?

"Go ahead," I said to Hillary. "I'll look at albums for now."

Before they left, Gail set the big books out for me in the parlor, and I curled up on a plush sofa with one of them on my knees. My wish was to stay away from Ingram's Opera House because it was enemy territory. Besides, I was beginning to feel a new and enormous need to learn about my father's family. My family. This must be done in the few days left to me in this house.

Gail's small overtures to Hillary didn't really matter. In fact, perhaps that was part of what troubled me. That so much that I had believed important was ceasing to matter.

Soon I must talk again with Jon Maddocks. He knew Persis Morgan, knew what she was really like. Besides—I wanted to see him again. Perhaps of them all he was the one person I could trust. He might tell me off bluntly at

141

times when he disapproved of me, but there was also a chance that he was my friend. In this house I was badly in need of a friend.

X

The first album I opened contained not snapshots but early photographs, a little faded and stiffly posed. I found Sissy at once—the same face I'd seen in the framed picture upstairs. The face that resembled mine. Some were theatrical pictures from her Silver Circuit days, when she had entertained in the larger mining camps under her mother's chaperonage. That lady had a strong chin and a domineering look in her eyes, while the young Sissy was all curves and smiles, melting and loving, the frothy skirts of her costumes swirling flirtatiously about her. My resemblance to her was only superficial, I decided. But Persis must have inherited an autocratic strain from Sissy's mother.

The first picture I discovered of Malcolm Tremayne fascinated me, and I followed him eagerly through the pages. There seemed something romantic and rather devil-may-care and dashing about him. In the early photos he appeared as a well-dressed young man, obviously just over from England. In later pictures he grew more American in appearance, more informal in his clothes, but no less arresting. There was one of him standing before the opening to what was probably the Old Desolate mine. That same entrance that I had seen boarded over and well padlocked.

There was also one of Sissy and Malcolm outside their spanking-new house in Domino. In every picture he seemed a striking, exciting sort of man, and probably a reckless one in his younger days.

There were some marvelous pictures of Domino too, as it had once been, with the houses intact and people in old-fashioned dress in the street. What a pull that lost little town had for me—as though it had claimed me long ago and was not yet ready to let me go free. Perhaps I would ride there again before I went away.

In later pictures the posing was done before the house in Jasper—when it was the Silver Castle. It was easy to see how their fortunes had changed. Sissy was plumper, more matronly, but still smiling, while Malcolm looked handsome and successful, and perhaps a bit piratical with his flowing mustache. Apparently Sissy hadn't borne children with the prodigality of her day, for only Persis came up repeatedly, first as a little girl and then as a young woman. Not a beautiful woman, but with an arresting look about her and a poise that gave her a great deal more than beauty. She must have had great authority of manner, even as a young woman, and the resemblance to her father was evident.

She had grown up with Johnny Morgan, the son of Tyler Morgan, Malcolm's partner, and clearly he'd been a strong personality in his own right. Together they looked like a powerful pair—Persis and Johnny—well matched and content with each other's company. Their marriage must have been a good one, lasting until the time of his far too early death. There was one picture taken at his grave, with expensive floral pieces heaped about it, but my grandmother was absent from the scene. There was no mention of where he was buried.

As the years went by, fewer pictures were taken, though suddenly I came upon one of Richard Morgan when he was a young man. This I pored over, trying to recapture something lost so long ago. His seemed a good face, both strong and gentle, with dark, intelligent eyes, and it was faintly familiar to me. Following were several vacant places in the album where pictures had been removed. Pictures of my father when he was older? Of my mother? Of me? I found only one or two more marked ones of my father.

The snapshot age had long begun, and the pages grew

more crowded with smaller, more informal pictures, often unlabeled. I fancied that I could find Richard here and there—and certainly that was my mother, Marybeth, standing beside Persis in a group picture—very lovely and young. Not at all the worn, sad woman I remembered. There I was, too, as a small child, holding onto the hand of my tall father, whom I looked up at adoringly. I studied this picture with a lump in my throat, but I couldn't bring him strongly back to mind. No attempt had been made to remove all traces of us in these smaller shots. Perhaps my grandmother had given up her system of identification before she got this far.

Here, too, I found young Caleb, stiff and correct in one picture, perhaps fearful of my grandmother, who stood beside him. The snapshot of a curly-headed boy on a horse caught my attention, and I looked closely for a resemblance to Jon Maddocks. I could find it readily in the jaunty, slightly arrogant way in which he sat his saddle, filled with confidence, knowing his place to be one worth occupying. But I didn't find him again. I wondered if Persis would mind if I took this picture away with me. Just to help me recapture a memory.

And finally I came upon Noah Armand's picture—a full-length snapshot, beneath which someone had lettered his name. He had been a tall, thin man, rather handsome, perhaps with a certain appeal if he hadn't looked so lugubrious in this shot. He squinted into the sun, so that his eyes were narrowed, and heavy black brows added to the scowling look. Even in so small a picture he appeared to be an enormously dissatisfied man. He looked familiar as well, as though I had known him and feared him too.

What had he wanted in his alliance with Persis Morgan? Money, of course, perhaps position. But what had there been about him to charm her into such a marriage?

In the picture his clothes seemed well cut, and he wore them with a certain assurance. Obviously he had been an adventurer, wandering from place to place until he'd come here and Persis had recklessly taken him for a husband. Of course a single small picture couldn't give me the measure of a man, and I was reading into this some of

144

the bits of information about him that I had picked up. I knew one thing for certain. I hadn't liked him.

Persistently now, I searched for more shots of Noah, but the last of the albums came to an end with only empty pages. More than ever I wanted to know the story of his leaving a week before my father's death. That seemed altogether too fortuitous, and I wondered that the police had accepted it and made no connection with his possible return.

When I'd put the albums aside, I sat for a little while pondering my next move. If something was to be done to aid my grandmother, I had to know more than she was willing to tell me. All questions seemed to return to Noah Armand—where they stopped. Tonight I would follow up my promise to ask Mark Ingram about him, but perhaps there was someone else I could question right now.

Caleb Hawes. If I could find him alone.

I went back to the kitchen, where Bitsy, the cook—a large, rather cranky elderly woman—was washing up while Edna dried dishes. Apparently it wasn't necessary for someone to be with my grandmother at all times. After all, she had her bell.

I asked Edna where Mr. Hawes' office was, and she told me it was on the third floor, a couple of doors down from my grandmother's room.

When I'd climbed the stairs to the open door, I found Caleb sitting before an old-fashioned rolltop desk, with the anachronism of a modern calculator, battery-operated, beside him. He looked up at my step, and I sensed a wariness in his greeting.

"Will I interrupt if I come in for a little while?" I asked. "I can return later if you're busy."

He rose at once to remove a pile of books from a chair, and set it for me where sun came through an open window. There was little furniture in the room, and no effort had been made to dress it up. All was strictly utilitarian, makeshift, and temporary. As though the man who worked here expected to be elsewhere very soon.

"What happens to your law office in Denver while you're tied up here?" I asked.

"I have two senior partners." There seemed a hint of resentment in the words, but he went on quickly, "I suggested that it was wiser for me to be near your grandmother right now. Is there something I can help you with?"

"I'd like to know more about Noah Armand," I said.

For an instant Caleb appeared startled, then his normal guard came up and he busied himself rearranging papers on his desk, not meeting my eyes. I had again the feeling that Caleb Hawes might be a secretive man, and perhaps capable of behind-the-scenes scheming.

"What do you want to know about him?" he asked.

"What was Noah really like? I found a picture of him in one of those albums just now, and he didn't seem to be an especially appealing man. Why was my grandmother attracted to him?"

"I can't answer that. I wasn't here very often in those days. My father took care of Mrs. Morgan's business himself and sent me up here only occasionally. I believe he was as surprised as anyone by her marriage. Older women can be foolish sometimes, and she may have been lonely. Or perhaps it was simply the attraction of the rogue that she felt in him. Other women felt it too." He hesitated. "Does it matter now?"

It mattered to Caleb—much more than he wanted me to believe. I was sure of that. Always when Noah Armand was mentioned, an uncertainty seemed to surface—in myself as well as in Caleb.

"He must have been fairly important in Jasper, married to my grandmother. Did anyone think that Noah might have returned to the house that day my father died? That *he* could have shot my father?"

Caleb's expression did not change, but his fingers were suddenly still on the papers before him, betraying the fact that I had shaken him in some manner I didn't understand.

"I don't think anyone thought that," he told me. "Mrs. Morgan wouldn't have allowed anyone to think it. The last thing she wanted was a scandal that would involve more of her family. It was bad enough that Richard was

146

shot. No mother could have loved her son more than your grandmother loved your father, Laurie. His death almost destroyed her."

"What did she think about Noah's running off?"

This time Caleb let himself go. "Good riddance! She knew by then that she'd made a bad bargain. I think she'd been telling him to get out for some time. So if he chose to go—fine!"

That this usually controlled man should permit himself such an outburst was disturbing in itself. A smoldering beneath the surface hinted at explosive depths.

"What is it?" I asked. "What is it you're not telling me?"

For the first time since I'd stepped into his office, he met my eyes directly. "If you are wise, Laurie, you won't press to know any more than you do. Let it go. Leave while you can, before irreparable harm is done. To you as well as your grandmother."

"What do you mean—leave while I can? *What* irreparable harm?"

"That's all I have to say. If you want to know more, you'll have to go to your grandmother."

I wondered out loud. "Perhaps she *gave* him the jewels. Perhaps they were never stolen at all, but were a bribe to get him to leave. What did they consist of—the things that were taken?"

Caleb was staring at me, appalled, and again alarmed, as though I threatened him in some way. It took him a moment or two to get himself in hand.

"Really, Laurie, you ask too much. How could I possibly remember what was taken after all these years?"

I suspected that his was the sort of mind which would remember such details exactly, and that if he wanted to he could probably list every item that had disappeared.

"I suppose there's a listing somewhere? I wonder if the Denver Library would have microfilm from the newspapers of that time. Perhaps I could read about what happened here?"

He seemed relieved. "If that's what you want, Laurie, I can furnish you with those old papers myself. They have

147

been kept on file right here in this house. But first I must ask your grandmother if she wishes you to see them."

"I'll ask her myself," I said, with the strong suspicion that he might prejudice any chance of my seeing such papers.

I left him to his calculator, and just as I reached the stairs, Jon Maddocks came out of Persis' room. I felt a small rush of joy at the sight of him.

For once he seemed warmly approving as he came toward me. "You're good for her, Laurie. She's coming to life. She wanted to know all about your visit to Domino and how I thought you felt about the old place."

"What did you tell her?"

"I told her you'd fallen too much in love with the past, but that I thought there was still time for you to catch up with the present."

The tiny rush of feeling in me died. "Why must you always mock me?"

"Is that what you think I'm doing?" He stood close to me at the head of the stairs, and suddenly he reached out a finger to touch a tendril of hair that had come loose against my cheek, lifting it back. "I don't mean to mock you, Laurie. I just hope you'll wake up in time to be useful to her. You were ready to be for a while this morning."

I drew back from his touch, a little afraid of my reaction.

He came down with me, his hand on my arm. "*Will* you stay, Laurie?"

"I want to," I said. "I think I really do. But there's so much that I don't understand. Sometimes—"

"Trust yourself. Just trust yourself a little more. There's a lot of her in you."

"You said that before. But why should you think it?"

"I think it because of what you did in facing up to Ingram this morning. That took courage. And because I can remember a spunky small girl who loved her grandmother very much. A small girl who was so much like Persis Morgan that everyone around could spot it. Even a kid like me."

"It's gone now!" I cried. "I've lost a whole part of me somewhere and I don't know how to find it again."

I leaned against the stair rail, sagging a little as we reached my floor, and he put an arm about me, walked me toward my door. Behind us Gail came running up the stairs and stopped.

"Hello!" Her look questioned, faintly derisive. "I've left Hillary to explore that old theater. I needed to get back here for Mrs. Morgan's afternoon medication."

"What is that medication?" I asked.

"Only a simple sedative."

"Why does she have to be sedated? She seems fine to me."

"Perhaps you'd better ask Dr. Burton when he comes. If you'll excuse me—" She ran lightly up to the floor above and disappeared from view.

Jon hadn't dropped his arm at her appearance. For an instant it tightened around me, and then he let me go.

"There's too much of this sedation going on," he said. "It's begun since that nurse came in. When Belle Durant was here things were better. I have a feeling she talks old Doc Burton into doing what she wants. Maybe you can put a stop to it."

The moment of emotion was safely past for me.

"I'll try," I said. "I wonder if there's something you can tell me." I gestured toward my door. "Do you know why anyone would hang an old funeral wreath on my doorknob? There was one there when I came upstairs last night."

"So that's where it came from. You must have dropped it out your window. I found it when I walked around the house early this morning."

"Why would it be left there?"

"I can't even guess."

"There was a card." I'd kept it in my pocket, and I took it out to show him.

He read the words gravely and handed it back. "I don't like this. It seems a cruel and stupid thing to do."

"Where could a wreath like that come from?"

"There's an old cemetery out behind the ranch, where

149

a few Morgans and those who worked with them are buried. It could have come from there."

"Whoever wrote that card knew that my father had been murdered. Grandmother Persis told me this morning about what happened."

Jon looked away uncomfortably.

"You knew too, didn't you?"

"I knew about his death, of course. I was living here at the ranch with my mother at the time. There was a lot of excitement, and it was in all the papers."

"What do you know?"

He seemed to hesitate. "Why—that somebody broke into the house, stole some valuable jewelry, shot Richard Morgan, and got away."

"The official story."

He was silent, and I went on.

"That's what Gail Cullen calls it. Did you know she used to live around here?"

"I've heard that."

"She sounded as though something else might have happened that was never in the papers. I thought you might know what it was. And about Noah Armand's disappearance."

"Sorry," he said curtly. "I've got to get back to work now. See you later." He went quickly down the stairs to escape my questioning. Like the others, he knew more than he was telling, but since he was the one I was beginning to trust, I hated to see him turn away from me, holding onto those secrets.

I went into my room to stand before a window, where I could watch him heading toward the barn, moving with that easy lope which was characteristic, never looking back. It was good just to watch him.

I sighed and turned from the window. Everything that had happened so long ago was somehow connected to what was happening now. More and more I was convinced of this. It was connected with my presence here. Perhaps I was the catalyst who was causing old horrors, old fears, to boil toward the surface. What would happen when the truth exploded into my mind, into my life? What would happen to Persis Morgan?

What would happen to *me?*

XI

The afternoon hours stretched idly ahead, and I was restless. To be idle meant letting in my fears, letting in the conviction that something stronger than malice was operating against me. I had begun to jump nervously at unexpected sounds, and I dreaded nightfall and my room, where a door could creak open after dark.

This wouldn't do. What I needed was a plan of action, something I could take to my grandmother. Something I could announce to the world, to Mark Ingram, to whoever else threatened her. Hillary would back me, I knew, and so would Jon Maddocks if he approved. About Caleb I was not so sure. At the moment, however, there seemed to be no way in which I could take charge. Persis hadn't put that right into my hands as yet, and there was no reason why she should in the face of the unwillingness I'd shown her.

In any case was I ready to take on any sort of authority? My thoughts, my feelings seemed to be in a state of flux. Even my feeling for Hillary was undergoing a change. Not a sea change—a mountain change. Ever since that moment when I'd looked out my window toward Old Desolate, I had been changing. I didn't seem able to help it—or want to stop what was happening inside me.

Now, as I looked out that same window, my attention was caught by the old cemetery Jon had mentioned. I could see where it spread up the hillside above a stand of pine trees. The fenced-in Morgan property ended well before the burying ground, but there was a gate out there, and I knew that much of the land along the mountain and up the valley also belonged to Persis Morgan. Perhaps something could be learned from old graves. Perhaps a walk would help me to sort out my own thoughts and emotions, lead me into the plan I must make.

I picked up Red's leash and went outside. When I neared the barn, the setter came running and I clipped it on his collar, not wanting him to go free once we were outside the fence. I wasn't sure that Red would know what to do with such freedom.

We skirted the barn, the old bunkhouse, and the cabin Jon occupied. I saw that a weed-grown road started beyond the gate, and we went through to follow it. Here the rocky land began to climb in an easy slope, and when we reached the pine grove we paused in its shade.

The sky wasn't as blue as it had been this morning, and already puffs of white drifted across the tops of the mountains. We climbed again, out in the sun. The cemetery was farther than it had looked from my window in the clear air, but the road was marked in the earth, and wide enough to take a burial party, though obviously long unused. The cemetery itself had been left unfenced, its boundaries obvious where the stones ended, though a sustaining wall above the graves kept the mountain from sliding down upon them.

How very peaceful, how utterly lonely it seemed. Even Red stopped prancing about at the end of his leash, affected by the quiet. Small blue wild flowers grew among the stones, though weeds had been kept down to some extent, so that nature hadn't taken over entirely. Most of the graves were undecorated, but on several mounds lay incongruous, crumbling wreaths.

As I looked about, I caught movement as chipmunks scampered among the headstones, and Red came to life.

"Be quiet," said a voice nearby, slightly hoarse, familiar. "Don't frighten the little critters away."

I had felt so alone a moment before that I jumped and looked around. Perched on a rock in a shadow of the wall where I hadn't noticed her sat the woman from the hotel,

Belle Durant. Somehow I couldn't have been more astonished than to find her here watching the chipmunks. She
had shed her fancy dress of last evening, and once again
wore tight jeans and a green pullover. As I stared, she
raised one hand, holding up a bunch of pinkish wild flowers, nested in greens that had the look of ferns.

"Tansy asters," she informed me. "They can smell
strong, but they're pretty outdoors."

In the open, away from the Timberline atmosphere,
Belle looked and sounded more real, but she worked for
Mark Ingram and I didn't trust her. I sat on a sun-
warmed rock nearby and unclipped Red's leash. He
wouldn't go very far with me right here.

"Have you always lived in these mountains?" I asked.

She shrugged, and her red hair caught highlights from
the sun. "Now and again. Tom Durant, my husband—he
died ten years ago—was part Morgan. Of course old Mrs.
Morgan knew that, and she let me bury him here. I used
to work for her, you know."

"Yes, someone told me. You seem to be missed. Why
did you leave?"

For a moment she seemed uncomfortable. Then she
met my question with a look that dared me to criticize.

"Mark Ingram turned up. I went to work with him."
Her expression changed, as though she remembered
something that was still bittersweet. "I don't mind telling
you. Everybody knows. I knew him a long time ago, when
I was young. Before Tom. You don't forget things like
that—things that happen when you're young. So when he
needed me at the hotel, I went back to him."

"No more loyalty to Persis Morgan?"

She bristled. "I have to take care of myself. Mark will
be here when your grandmother is long gone."

"Maybe," I said, and she was silent.

I stirred myself to look about me. "Jon Maddocks says
there are Morgans buried in this place, so I thought I'd
come up to have a look."

"Sure. Do you want me to introduce you?"

She got lightly to her feet, and Red made a dash for
the chipmunks. The little creatures vanished among the

153

stones far more quickly than he could move. Belle picked her way among the grave markers to a low one of mountain granite, where she placed her small bouquet. The stone flaunted a wreath that had seen better days, and I read upon it the name of Thomas Durant.

"Is that a custom?" I asked. "I mean to leave old funeral wreaths on the stones?"

She flashed me a smile that was wide and a little mocking. "That's my idea. When I see there's been a funeral in some place I can get to and wreaths are being thrown out, I collect a few and bring them here. Sort of dresses up the place, don't you think?"

"I don't know," I said. "Wild flowers and grass do pretty well."

"But they grow here. When I bring something special in from outside, it shows them"—she waved a hand—"that they're not forgotten, that I made a special effort."

What a strangely unexpected person she was.

"Hardly anyone gets buried here anymore," she went on. "Tom's grave is pretty new, compared with most. There are a lot of these old burying grounds around in the mountains, where they sprang up near the mining camps. Sometimes they outlive the towns."

I walked among the stones, finding many of the markings nearly erased by time and mountain winters.

"Diphtheria took a lot of them in the old days, I guess," Belle said. "Though in the beginning it was mostly accidents in the mines that killed the men. Women were scarce, though a few are buried here, and of course there were the babies that never grew up. Look here at this one."

It was a small grave, a small stone, simply inscribed. The words read, *Our Darling,* and no name was given. So much pain, so long forgotten.

"I don't suppose Sissy and Malcolm Tremayne were brought here?" I asked.

"Lord, no! They'd have to be taken someplace grand. Persis Morgan wouldn't have left them here. But while they were alive they didn't feel that way. Tyler Morgan's grave is right here where they buried him. I guess you know he was Malcolm's partner in the Old Desolate, and it was his son who married Persis. Of course she wouldn't let her Johnny be buried here either. He was taken down to Denver. It always seemed kind of strange that she buried their son, Richard, here. Your father."

I looked sharply at the woman beside me. "My mother always said he was buried in Denver, near where we used to live."

"Maybe she didn't want you to know, what with all the trouble connected with that time. I guess Mrs. Morgan persuaded your mother to let her bury him here."

In spite of the sun I felt suddenly chilled in this unsheltered place. Wind blew down the valley between the peaks, and I turned up my jacket collar.

"Can you show me which grave is his?"

She pointed. "Over there in the corner—the one that's been taken care of so carefully. She sends somebody over every week with flowers. And she has Jon keep the plot clear. Of course Jon has graves of his own here to look after."

As she threaded her way among the stones, I followed, with Red coming along beside me. My father's grave was near one of the retaining walls at the top of the little cemetery, where the mountain rose above, dwarfing it still more. Again the stone was of granite, and I bent over the inscribed lettering. It was simple enough. Just my father's name, the date of his birth, and the date of his death—the year of my eighth birthday. I touched the stone and it seemed icy in this shady spot by the wall—as though it somehow rejected me.

That was being whimsical, and I turned to walk among the other graves. So many old dates and forgotten names. No one cared anymore that some distant cousin who bore the Morgan name had been born in Wales. Perhaps no one even remembered how he had died or whom he had loved and fathered. It didn't matter anymore. None of it mattered.

"Makes you think, doesn't it?" Belle said beside me. "These over here are Jon Maddocks' family. His father and mother. And his wife."

I looked down at the three graves. "I didn't know he'd been married."

"It didn't last all that long. She was a wild little thing—like one of those chipmunks—and she didn't last much longer. The baby is buried with her."

Sorrow for the younger Jon rose in me, and for my father—for all of them. I wrenched my thoughts away from death. It was life I must deal with now.

"You seemed different yesterday at Timberline," I said to Belle, drawn to her, however reluctantly.

"That's what I've grown into," she said, tipping her chin at me in slight defiance. "Mark's world. When I come out here, maybe I'm trying to find me the way I used to be. I think I had stronger feelings about everything then than I do now. But you'd better not tell Mark—he'd laugh at me. He only believes in the present and in the kind of future he wants to make happen."

"How do you feel about that? I mean about the future he plans for all this."

Under my eyes she seemed to toughen and harden a little. "I'm on his side—make no mistake. I owe him a lot, and what he tells me I'll do."

This was what I expected of her, but I pushed a little more. "I wonder what he was like as a boy."

"That's not something he talks about, and he doesn't enjoy questions."

Nevertheless, I wanted answers. "How did you happen to meet him?"

"I don't like questions much either," she said, and turned away from me.

I didn't want to let her go. She had shown me a softer side, and I wanted to know more about her—more about any of them over at the Timberline.

"I wonder why Mark Ingram bothers to fight an old woman like my grandmother. If he would just wait and let her alone, she might die quietly. Then perhaps everything would come his way. Why upset her now?"

"Mark's not given to waiting," Belle said. "He wants what he wants right away. And I can tell you he means to have it. He means to get things started up the valley soon.

He needs time to clear the slopes and put up a lodge in Domino. And he's not going to let Mrs. Morgan hold him off much longer."

"But he wants more than that, doesn't he? He wants to punish her in some way. Because a long time ago Noah Armand was his friend. What did my grandmother do to Noah Armand?"

The question didn't seem to upset her. "I don't know anything about that. I just know that Mark Ingram gets what he goes after. One way or another. And you'd better remember that. Sometimes it's just as well to be afraid."

She was entirely on his side, and her words carried a hint of threat. Just the same, an obstinacy that had its roots in anger was rising in me.

"I'm not going to let Mark Ingram scare me. It's not going to be all that easy for him to win this time. I think perhaps I'll stay and see this through." Suddenly the plan I needed was burgeoning.

Belle gaped at me. "You're crazy if you set yourself against Mark. He'll squash you like he'd squash a bug."

"Maybe not," I said. "What if the land comes to me when she's gone? I don't care about her money or any of her other property, but if she wants to leave me that house in Domino and the Jasper house as well, I might stay right here and hold out against Mark Ingram."

There! I was promising what Jon wanted. I was committing myself, and now I didn't want to turn back.

She looked a little frightened. "I don't think you're very smart."

"Why not? Why shouldn't I stay and live in Morgan House if I choose?"

"You're liable to find out why not," she told me. "If you lock horns with Mark Ingram, you're liable to find out." She started away from me, and then stopped and looked back. "How is she? Mrs. Morgan, I mean."

"Sometimes she seems fine. Sometimes not. Jon says that when you were there she wasn't kept sedated so much of the time."

"Is that what they're doing to her—Caleb and that nurse? What is that woman up to, anyway?"

157

"What do you mean?"

"Last night she came sneaking up to the hotel real late."

"I've wondered if she could be tied up with Mark Ingram in some way."

If I expected to get a rise out of her, I was disappointed. She smiled at me, and it was a smile I didn't trust—a smile that hid too much that I wanted to know.

"I wouldn't put it past her," she said.

"I'm going to get rid of Gail Cullen if I can."

"Not a bad idea."

Of course she would be pleased if I rid her of a younger rival. But her next words surprised me.

"Look, Miss Morgan, if you get in a jam anytime with your grandmother, let me know. Mark wouldn't approve, but I could fill in in a pinch. Though not for long."

"Thanks. I'll remember that," I said.

She waved a hand at me and went off down the hillside. I watched her go, more than a little puzzled. If it hadn't been for Mark Ingram, I might have liked Belle Durant. There was a natural wisdom in her, and perhaps more generosity than she was always willing to show.

For a few moments longer I stood beside the grave where my father was buried, trying to evoke some memory of him. It ought to be possible, here of all places. But nothing came to me out of the past. Nevertheless, I was experiencing an oddly euphoric feeling because I had at last committed myself. I still had no power to back up my words. I didn't even know if Persis Morgan wanted this. Yet I had taken a decisive step in my own mind. I had stopped running. I wasn't hiding, I wasn't leaning.

I wondered what Mark Ingram would do when he knew. This wasn't going to be an easy road I had chosen, and it might even be dangerous.

Red had been roving among the stones in search of wildlife, and I called him to me and clipped on his leash. As we started down the hillside I kept him close to me, lest he be tempted to run off in all directions. When I came to an outcropping of rock that offered a sweep of all the valley and enclosing mountains, with Old Desolate commanding the view, I climbed upon it and stood for a moment searching for Belle Durant.

As I studied the land below, she emerged on the far side of the pine grove, skirting Morgan property the long way around, hurrying toward home—toward Mark Ingram. I wondered how much she was his captive.

One thing I was sure about. I would have to tell Persis Morgan quickly of my stand. I would have to admit to what was now mere boasting and let her know that I thought she was right in her resistance to Mark Ingram. Even if she was wrong, she must do what she most wanted to do—hold on to her house and the valley.

Euphoria still lifted my steps as Red and I followed the downhill trail to the gate I had come through a little while ago. I walked more slowly now, trying to gather my thoughts so that I could face Persis again and sound more sensible than I felt. I went through the gate and neared Jon's small cabin, wondering idly if he had put it up himself, as seemed likely. It was no primitive cabin. The roof had a good overhang of extended logs, and the windows were wide enough to offer a view of ranch and mountains.

Had he lived here with the "wild little thing" who had been his wife, and who now slept with their baby in a mountain cemetery? Again I felt a personal grief, as though his loss were mine. Yet it was difficult to think of Jon as married, since he always seemed so much a loner.

Though the cabin door stood open, I hesitated, not sure if I wanted to see him right now. My sense of his loss, so newly fresh in me, as well as the knowledge of the step I'd just taken, blocked my way. This was what Jon wanted of me, yet it mustn't be idle boasting when I told him. I sought to accomplish something real first. Nevertheless, I might stop and speak to him for a moment. About other things.

I approached the cabin door and looked inside. Warm, earth-colored Indian rugs lay on the floor, and an ocher and red weaving hung diagonally over the stone mantelpiece. Some of the furniture looked beautifully hand-hewn, and there were two pottery jars set at either side of the door. A rather Spanish touch.

159

"Jon?" I called, and then spoke his name again, more loudly.

There was still no answer, but now I heard sounds from the direction of the barn—a man's voice raised in a shout, the neighing of a horse. As I stood watching, two men on horseback came around the corner of the barn and went galloping furiously toward the far gate of the property. It had been left open, and they went through without stopping, dust flying beneath the hooves of their horses as they pounded away up the valley. Grotesquely, incongruously, both men wore ski masks—somehow ugly and inhuman when there was no skiing.

The two hadn't looked my way, and I didn't think they had seen me. Jon was nowhere in sight, and I began to run, with Red beside me. In moments we reached the barn, and I dropped his leash. The stool where Jon had sat when I'd seen him that first time had been knocked over, and his guitar lay on the ground. I ran inside and found him there, just within the door. He had risen to his knees, and there was blood on his face, more seeping through the shoulder of his torn shirt. Shocked and frightened, I ran to bend over him.

"Can you get up? Can you stand? Let me help you to your cabin."

He seemed dazed, uncertain, and I held his arm as he struggled to his feet. He put an arm about my shoulders, leaning heavily, and we moved slowly toward the cabin. Close as it was, it seemed a mile away, but we managed to reach it. I helped him up the low step and over to the couch by the fireplace before he sagged again. There weren't many rooms, and I found the bath, caught up a towel, dampened it, and ran back to him.

A lump was rising on his head, and several lacerations were bleeding. I wiped his cut cheek and saw that he was reviving.

"I'll call the house," I said. "Gail can help. Where is Sam?"

"He's gone to bring the horses in from the corral. There's a phone over there."

I found the telephone on a low table and sat beside it,

160

dialing quickly. Caleb answered and summoned Gail. I told her that Jon had been hurt.

She wasted no time, sounding professional for once. "I'll be there right away."

"She's coming," I told Jon. I wanted to kneel beside him, put my arms about him—neither of which I'd dare to do. The shock of seeing him hurt had shaken me badly. "Can I fix you anything?" I managed.

"Coffee might help."

I left him holding the towel to his face and went into the small galley kitchen. When I'd started coffee in a percolator, I found cup and saucer and set up a small tray. Then I ran back to see how he was doing.

"I'm okay." His voice was stronger now. "Don't look so scared. If they'd meant to kill me, they could have."

"Of course I'm scared. I saw those men galloping away. Can you talk about what happened?"

He took a deep breath. "I think there were two of them. I had only a glimpse before they jumped me. Ingram's men, of course."

Belle's words up in the cemetery came back to me—that I'd better remember to be frightened. Now I was. Terribly frightened.

I went back to the kitchen for the coffee and poured him a cup, brought it to the couch where he lay, trying not to let it rattle in my hands. He sat up gingerly to sip the hot drink as I held it for him.

"Tell me what you saw," he said.

Now at least I could kneel on the floor close to him. "There were two men in Levi's and jackets. No hats, but they wore ski masks. One green and one blue. Both horses were roan, I think."

"Ingram has some of his own hands working around Jasper."

"But why would he have you beaten like this?"

"I've already been warned to stay out of your grandmother's affairs. Indirectly warned, of course. Caleb Hawes delivered a message from Ingram just recently. He likes a pretense of velvet gloves. Since I've paid no attention and have been throwing my weight against him, he

161

seems to have taken off the gloves. He means business now." Jon moved his head angrily and winced. "God! I can't think. Why wasn't I more careful? But I suppose I didn't expect much more than threats. Not right off. But you'd better follow your hunch and get away, Laurie."

"I'm not leaving." I thrust back the depleting fear. "I don't want to see my grandmother being pushed around. Now what they've done to you makes it all the worse. If it was Mark Ingram who ordered this, he can't be allowed to get away with it."

Jon managed a faint smile. "Hooray for us! But what's just happened makes a difference. This may be a lot nastier than I expected. So maybe it's better if you don't stay."

"I'm staying," I told him. I felt increasingly angry, and I was growing stubborn too, stubborn enough to overcome my fears.

The sound of a car reached us from outside, coming down the rough track from the house. I ran to the door and saw Caleb, Gail, and Hillary get out of the jeep and hurry toward the cabin. Gail ran ahead into the room, carrying a small flight bag.

"Let me see," she said, bending over Jon.

"What happened to him?" Caleb demanded.

I repeated my account of what I'd seen and what Jon had told me.

Caleb listened and nodded. "Yes, I can believe that Ingram might pull just this sort of thing. It's a threat. He's begun to put on pressure."

"You can't let him get away with it," I said.

"And just what do you think can be done?" He was frowning at me, his mouth corners turned down.

Hillary had been moving about the room, and I knew he wasn't thinking so much about Jon as he was admiring an interesting setting, a dramatic situation. But now he surprised me.

"You can throw Ingram out," he said.

Even Gail turned her head to stare at him. Jon had been lying with his eyes closed, but now he opened them and looked at me with a faint grin.

162

"The cavalry is moving in," I said. "If we all work together, perhaps we can throw him out."

Caleb had no patience with either Hillary's words or mine. "There isn't any cavalry."

"Sure there is." Jon winced under Gail's touch, and then went on. "She's standing right over there looking like Persis Morgan. Better tell them, Laurie."

I had nothing to tell, but I did my best in Jon's support. "It's just that I've decided to stay for a while and see if there is something specific that can be done to stop Mark Ingram's plans."

Hillary came to put an arm about me. "That's my girl."

I still felt surprised. I hadn't thought that Hillary was really in this fight. He had seemed a little too indifferent to Jon's injuries, and I didn't want to play dramatic games.

Caleb's words cut through our rally round the flag. "You are talking nonsense, all of you. You are young and inexperienced, Laurie, and this is becoming much too dangerous."

"Dangerous enough to call in the police," I said.

Before he could answer, the phone rang, startling us all.

"Answer it, please, Laurie," Jon said.

When I spoke into the receiver, Persis' voice sounded in my ear, strong and indignant. "Laurie, is that you? What has happened? Caleb said that Jon was hurt, and then he went rushing off. Tell him to come back here at once and let me know what is happening."

"I'll tell him," I said. "I'd like to see you myself if you'll tell me when I may—" But she had hung up with a click that expressed her displeasure and gave me neither yes nor no.

I repeated her message to Caleb, and he shook his head. "I can't leave now. Jon may have to be driven to a hospital, and I would need Hillary's help. You go and talk to her, Laurie. You're the only one we can spare right now."

"All right," I said, "I'll do what I can. But you'd better call her and tell her your plans as soon as they're made."

"Just don't upset her with your nonsense." He gave me a light push toward the door, as though he feared I might change my mind. I glanced at Jon, whose eyes were closed again, and at Gail and Hillary. No one had anything else to offer, so I went outside and whistled for Red. He didn't come, and I thought nothing of it. With all this acreage in which to run loose, my feckless dog could have followed his interests in a hundred directions by now. He would come back when it pleased him, and he couldn't get outside the fence.

Over in the direction of Old Desolate the ranch gate that opened on the trail up the valley stood wide, as the riders had left it. I was a city girl, and I didn't even glance in that direction.

XII

Persis awaited me in a chair by the window that looked out toward the barn and Jon's cabin. When I tapped at the open door she called to me to come in, still sounding vigorous and outraged. If Gail had tried to sedate her, it hadn't worked this time.

"Well?" she said when I stood beside her. "Pull up a chair and sit down. I don't like to be kept in the dark about what's going on. Why isn't Caleb here? Why you?"

I found that she alarmed me less when she was out of bed and not fading away against a pillow.

"I'm glad you've decided not to die," I said. "Getting mad suits you."

The lines between her thick dark eyebrows deepened. "Don't be impertinent, Laurie. Tell me about Jon."

"I'm sorry. Caleb sent me because Jon has been beaten, and may have to be driven to a hospital. Two men on horses came in and jumped him. They got away.

I saw them go. But they wore ski masks and I could never identify them."

Someone had helped her into a long wine-colored robe and placed a blanket over her knees. Her hands, weathered by life and marked with veins and freckles, clenched themselves upon the blanket.

"That cruel, terrible man! How is Jon?"

"Gail doesn't think it's serious. She's patching him up. Why do you believe that Ingram was behind this?"

"Because it's what he would do. He's ruthless. I've had Caleb investigate that big operation of his in Kansas. There was plenty that was unscrupulous in the way he got the land, and others always suffered. But he moved just this side of the law, or bought the law when he could. I don't think he'll stop at much to get what he wants."

"But why Jon? Even if Jon wants you to fight him, what can either of you really do?"

"He's making a threat to me through Jon. A promise of what may come if I don't give in."

I could readily believe that. "It's more than the ski resort, isn't it? Is there any real way he can hurt you, force you?"

She stared at me grimly, and I knew she wasn't going to answer. When she spoke again, the strength was draining out of her.

"I don't want anyone to be hurt," she said.

"You can't give up now. You can't let Ingram get away with this!"

Her eyes came wide open. Those deep-set eyes that could see so much and that still burned with an appetite for life. "I won't give up if you can go on sounding like that. But you could be hurt too, Laurie."

"I think we've got to try."

She held out her hand, and I felt again the force that could still surge through her weakened body.

"Maybe you'll do," she said. "I can still remember you as a little girl. You were curious about everything. I taught you to ride and shoot and play a rope. Your father was always a tenderfoot, with his nose in books, so he and your mother hated what I was doing. Maybe they

165

were right and I was wrong. But I wanted you to grow up to take over the ranch and make it the way it used to be. Now maybe you will."

"Nothing's the way it used to be," I said. "And it won't ever be again. You can't go back to those days you liked best."

"Yes, I can! I go there all the time. Even back to Domino. Whenever things get too much for me here, I go there in my mind. And when I return I don't feel so helpless anymore."

"I haven't ever thought you were helpless."

"*They* think I am. Not Jon. Caleb and that nurse. I don't need a nurse, but Dr. Burton believes she's necessary. I pack her out of my room whenever I can, and I don't always take those pills she shoves at me."

"Then let's send her away, now that I'm here."

"In a little while. I want to know what she's up to first. I don't trust her, Laurie. I'm not sure *why* she's here. I'm not sure of the real reason."

I thought of what Belle had said about Gail sneaking over to the hotel, and I began to think I knew. Ingram's machinations reached everywhere.

Persis turned her attention sharply upon me. "How is Caleb behaving about all this?"

"Caleb?" I was surprised at the question. "He seems his usual self—counseling caution, and all that."

"Has he sent for the police?"

"He hadn't at the time I left, but I suppose he will."

She was shaking her head. "Sometimes he worries me. I understand him very well. All his life he has been a projection of what others thought he should be."

"How do you mean?"

"First, his father. Always criticizing him. Never letting him breathe for himself. Not even trusting Caleb to take over the firm when his father got too old. I haven't given him an easy time either. That's why—" She hesitated, letting the words die away.

"That's why—what?"

"Never mind. I'll tell you one of these days. At least Caleb has his own ways of fighting. Sometimes they can be rather tricky ways of trying to get his own back. But he's been loyal to me for most of his life, and I think he still is. Just don't trust him completely, Laurie. I'm never quite sure anymore what he's up to."

I felt mystified by her words, and not at all reassured. "He doesn't like me. And I don't trust him at all."

"That was to be expected—his not liking you. But never mind about Caleb now. There's something else I want to talk about. I still don't like the way you went into the Domino house today when I'd asked you not to."

"If I stay, Grandmother, I may not always do exactly what you tell me to."

"I don't suppose you will. Not if you're Morgan and Tremayne. Tell me about the house. Tell me what you felt and thought when you were in it."

I was willing enough to talk about Domino. "I don't know why, but I feel a strong pull to that place. As though something in me belongs there. I loved the house, and I kept trying to imagine Malcolm and Sissy Tremayne living there. And you as a little girl. Jon says you were born there."

"I was. Go on."

"One of the rooms I went into was yours, and I brought this back with me."

I still had the bit of torn wallpaper in my jacket pocket, and I held it up for her to see. Away from the house where they belonged, the daisies that had once been bravely gold and lavender looked faded, dingy.

Nevertheless, her eyes brightened. "My mother loved those mountain daisies that grow everywhere in the summer, and she picked that wallpaper from a catalogue. I remember her telling me that she wanted to bring summer back in the long wintertime. Why did you tear that piece off the wall?"

"To remember Domino by. Perhaps to have something from a time that belongs to me too."

She closed her eyes, and I couldn't guess what she was thinking.

"Shall I come back after dinner tonight at the Timberline and tell you about whatever happens? There has to be a confrontation now."

"Yes." She spoke without opening her eyes. "I don't sleep long at a time these nights. So look in on me. I'll want to hear."

I hesitated, and then put the question that was haunting me. "Tell me one more thing, Grandmother. When my father died—did Noah Armand come back here? Caleb says he left the week before. But I wonder if that's true. Did he come back to this house, Grandmother?"

Though she was looking at me again, her eyes were lost in shadow, and I couldn't read their expression. For a little while she was still, though I saw the tightening of her hands on her lap, so that the knuckles grew white against the splotches of brown.

"He came back," she said. "I've cursed him for it a thousand times since—but yes, he did come back."

"To steal your jewels and kill my father?"

"Get me into my bed," she said. "I can't sit up a moment longer. Help me!"

She sounded frantic, and I took away the blanket, drew her to her feet so that she could stand. When I put her walking stick in her hand, she moved more strongly than I would have expected across the room to the bed and sat on the edge of it. With an arm about her shoulders I helped her to lie back upon the pillows and stretch out her legs as I drew the covers over them.

"Run along now, Laurie." She still sounded autocratic, but her voice was weak.

I plumped myself on the edge of her bed. "No! You're not going to do this to me. I think you're a fraud a good part of the time. I think you get what you want by threatening to fall apart. I'll go the minute you answer my question. Did Noah Armand steal those jewels and kill my father?"

She stared at me as though she didn't like what she saw. "You look fragile and easily intimidated, but you're not, are you?"

"I expect I am," I told her. "Most of the time. I just
168

get mad and fight against it when I'm too disgusted with myself."

"All right, I'll tell you. Noah did come back after I sent him away. He came back a week later, but he stole none of my jewels and he didn't kill your father."

"Then why did he come back?"

"To persuade your mother to run away with him. He was a miserable creature with a great attraction for women—until we found him out. The worst thing I ever did was to marry him. I've paid for it ever since."

I gaped at her. "Noah—and my mother?"

"I told you she was beginning to find Richard dull. And Noah never did care about anything but my money. That's what he married. And he knew by then that he wasn't going to get his hands on much of it. I should have known what he was up to with Marybeth, but I thought I was sending him away in time. I thought your mother would come to her senses."

She was telling me something I didn't know how to accept, and I could only wait numbly for her to go on.

"You may as well know it all," she said. "He'd promised to come back for her. She stayed home on some pretext that day when Caleb, Richard, and I went into town on business. You were supposed to be in bed with a cold, but she forgot to check. He was waiting for her in the back parlor, and she left her bags at the foot of the stairs to go tell him she was ready. That's when we all came home, earlier than expected."

I could hardly bear to speak the words, though I knew I must ask the question. "Did my father shoot him?"

"Your father never shot anyone. He hated guns."

"Then what—"

"That's enough!" She cut me off abruptly "Go away and leave me alone. Go *now*."

There was such sudden venom in the words that I felt a little sick. The truth looked out of her eyes at that moment. She detested me. I walked away from her without another word and went downstairs to my room.

There I stood looking out toward the long, spreading shadows that sealed the valley in a too early twilight. I tried to empty my mind, to reach a state of nothingness and peace. It wasn't possible.

When I closed my eyes, my mother's face was there. I thought of her often, for she was still part of my life. What she had said and done would always affect me. Yet I'd never really known her. Not as a woman in her own right, without relationship to me.

I had considered her nice-looking. After all, the way one's mother looked was *right.* Neither homely nor beautiful. Yet I had come across an old photograph of her taken in her twenties, just before she'd married my father, and she had seemed strikingly beautiful. But a stranger—not my mother.

Now I was trying to see her as a woman apart from us all. A woman with whom Noah Armand, the younger man who had married my grandmother, might have fallen in love. I could well believe that he had wanted to escape what must have become the tyranny of Morgan House and Persis Morgan. But my *mother* . . . ! How could she possibly have turned away from my father to a man like Noah Armand?

Yet, in the end, she had stayed with me. My father had died, and she had not run off with Noah, even though his shadow must have hung over her life from then on. Whether he had ever tried to get in touch with her again I would never know.

Without warning my thoughts took a new and shattering turn. Was it possible that Persis Morgan had fired the gun that killed my father? Had she aimed at Noah and killed Richard Morgan instead? If I had witnessed this, then I could understand much of what had happened afterward.

Caleb would have gone along with any story that would protect Persis. In fact, he might have helped concoct such a story. My mother and I would be sent away as quickly as possible, so we couldn't talk. That would have been easy, since I had become desperately ill. And then? Perhaps Marybeth, keeping the terrible secret, had waited helplessly for Noah to come looking for her. Or had what happened left her broken and unable to recover and make a new life for herself? What had Noah done afterward?

For the first time I was beginning to wonder how my mother had felt. Had she loved my father? She had always been reluctant to talk about him to me. If she had come down those stairs with packed bags, she must have been serious in her intent to run away with Noah. Whatever had happened, I had been so deeply and darkly affected that I had become ill and shut it all out of my consciousness ever since.

Standing before the window, I knew one thing. There had been enough of secrecy and of this shutting out of the truth. Tomorrow morning I would go into the back parlor downstairs and I would open that box which had frightened me so badly. I would face whatever had to be faced and let the memories come as they would. Gail would tell if I insisted, but I didn't want to hear it second hand from her. Persis Morgan wouldn't tell me at all if she could help it. So now I would have to do this for myself.

My eyes caught movement in the direction of Jon's cabin as Gail, Caleb, and Hillary came out the door, got into the jeep, and started toward the house. Apparently they weren't taking Jon to a hospital after all, and a sense of relief and gratitude swept through me. With the relaxing of concern for Jon, I could realize how worried I had been.

Now I had time to wonder where Red was. I'd begun to feel lonely without him, missing his excitable presence. In a little while I must get ready for this dinner at the Timberline that I dreaded. But first I would go outside and look for my wandering dog. When I went down, Hillary was nowhere in sight, and I supposed he had returned to the hotel.

Red responded to whistling or calling of his name, and as I walked about I grew increasingly uneasy. Sam was coming in with the horses, so I walked to the barn and asked if he had seen Red.

He shook his head."Lots to interest dogs around here. If I see him I'll bring him up to the house."

I thought of looking in on Jon, but if Gail had given him something quieting, it was best to let him rest. When I told Sam what had happened, alarm came into his eyes.

"I saw those men ride up the valley, and I wondered about them," he said. "But I was a long way off and I couldn't see who they were. I don't think they were wearing masks by that time. They took the trail to Domino, so they could be anywhere by now. There are a couple of roundabout trails that circle back to Jasper or turn off south. Has Mr. Hawes notified the highway patrol?"

"I suppose he has," I said. "Sam, can you look in on Jon before you go home? You live in Jasper, don't you?"

"My dad runs the livery stable. Not much doing there now, but Mr. Ingram says he'll have plenty of business for us later on, so we've moved in, and Dad helps around town where he can. Maybe I can stay with Jon tonight. I'll phone the Timberline and get word to my ma. Then I'll finish the chores and move into the cabin."

It was good to know that Jon wouldn't be spending tonight alone, and I wandered back to the house, still whistling now and then for Red. But I could give no more time to the search for him. He couldn't have gone far within the enclosure, and if he didn't show up I would look for him seriously tomorrow.

Right now I had to dress for dinner. My one short blue dress would have to do, since I didn't think a long gown was called for.

While I dressed I tried to suppress the thought about Persis Morgan that I'd been holding at bay. If she had fired that shot, killing my father, and this knowledge had lived with her all these years, it might explain her retreat, her inability to face my mother. I wondered what Caleb would say if I put this question to him.

Hillary arrived early, and as always, he was sensitive to my mood. We walked around outside to escape the forbidding presence of the house. Even the dark mountains closing us in made me less uncomfortable than the interior of the house itself. Hillary held my hand, as he'd so often done when I needed to be quiet—though that wasn't what I wanted from him now. What I needed was

172

an understanding that would help me to wisdom and courage. He could fall into any role that was required of him, and his attention was exactly right. I wanted to cry, "Where are *you*? What are *you* thinking?" Perhaps the unexpected glimpse I'd had of my mother as a woman had turned everything around in my mind, so that now I even looked at Hillary in a different way.

I tried to shrug such thoughts aside so that I could concentrate on telling him everything. About the pictures in the album. About wandering up to the cemetery and finding Belle Durant there among her withered wreaths. He whistled in surprise when I told him for the first time of the wreath hung on my door.

His reaction, however, was only to try to soothe and distract me. "Don't worry about all this, honey. Just try to stand it for a little while longer. Tomorrow you must come to the Opera House with me. I really want you to see it."

Being distracted and soothed wasn't enough at the moment, but he sounded so excited, so keyed up about the theater, that I tried to listen. Not until he had told me about his own afternoon did I voice my concern over Red.

"He'll be all right," Hillary assured me. "Tomorrow we'll ride around the fence enclosure and see if we can find him. He's probably enjoying his freedom, and he'll come in when he's hungry enough."

For the first time I found myself admitting that there might be a certain shallowness about Hillary. Something I'd never been willing to face before.

When we returned to the porch, Gail and Caleb were waiting for us. Gail look slim in something yellow and shimmery, with gold bangles forming a cuff on one arm. My raw silk dress seemed understated, and that suited me well enough. For me this evening might be more a field of battle than a social occasion.

Caleb drove us over in the jeep, left it in the empty street outside the hotel, and ushered us up the steps.

I had an increasingly unsettled feeling about the prospect of dining with Mark Ingram. Sooner or later he must be made aware of our suspicions concerning the attack upon Jon. And there were questions about Noah Armand that I wanted to ask, since once Ingram and he had been friends. Now this man was more than ever my grandmother's enemy, and he was mine too—the man I had promised her to stay and fight.

In the last half hour that we'd been together Hillary had grown a little restive. He could be marvelously considerate and sympathetic, but not for too long at a time. What worried me was that I still didn't feel concerned enough. Without any volition of my own I seemed to have turned some psychological corner, so that I was walking in a new direction. Where it led I didn't know, but only part of the time was I moving to Hillary's tune. Another part of me was back in the cabin with Jon.

When we entered the hotel lobby, Belle Durant came to greet us. She wore no Gay Nineties costume tonight, but was dressed in a generous creation that floated softly when she moved. Her own red hair was drawn back in a loose knot at the nape of her neck, and she had used makeup more adroitly than usual, so that I could see for the first time what a handsome woman she really was. The illusion of being glamorous and poised lasted until she opened her mouth. Then her rather harsh tones grated on the ear and she was the old Belle. Remembering our talk in the cemetery, I felt undecided about her. I wasn't wholly convinced that she had thrown away all loyalty to Persis Morgan because of Mark Ingram.

"Mark had to work late," she told us. "But he'll be down soon—and hungry."

An affair of masked riders that might occupy his attention? I wondered.

At least it was a relief to be away from Morgan House with all its tensions. Whatever happened tonight must be played by ear, and these tensions were different. For the moment I needed only to relax—and wait.

Gail and Hillary were obviously ready to enjoy the evening. Since their time together at the Opera House, they had lapsed into an easy, slightly flirtatious relationship that meant little or nothing. At least to Hillary. I knew it was a manner he adopted with most women. But did she? There were times when I glimpsed a certain edginess in Gail, and I continued to wonder what game she might be playing.

Besides me, Caleb was the only one to give any real evidence of uneasiness over this dinner. He had never wanted to come, and he wouldn't be here now if it had not been for Persis Morgan's insistence.

When he finally appeared, Mark Ingram seemed more of a dramatic figure than ever, with his silvery hair and his stylized Bill Cody beard and mustache. The silver-headed cane that helped to disguise his limp took nothing from the impressive effect he made. Again he wore the gray that suited him so well, with a turquoise bola tie, its black strings tipped in silver, and again he was warmly affable—the gracious host. What the affability concealed as he looked us over, there was no telling, and I found myself watching him with new eyes. We had evidence now of his being as dangerous as Belle had warned me, and I knew that I was afraid of him as I hadn't been before. There was in this man a willingness to be ruthless that would make him a formidable enemy. It would be very easy to let a growing fear of him defeat me, and I must not let that happen.

Dinner was served in one of the private dining rooms of the hotel. A small room, once more with crimson draperies, a dark red rug and red leather chairs, brightened with touches of gold and white and crystal. The linen was dazzling, the silver polished till it shone, and there were flowers on the table, as I'd once imagined. Hothouse, undoubtedly, brought up from Boulder, in an assortment of blue and gold and scarlet. All a little incongruous, all make-believe in this remote and unattended spot, but an indication of the wealth and power Mark Ingram had at his disposal.

One thing in particular I noticed, and that was his surprisingly courtly treatment of Belle Durant. His look seemed to soften and approve when it rested on her, and I wondered if this hard, powerful man was capable after all

175

of some affection. Certainly Belle seemed comfortable, and of us all the least intimidated by him.

For me, however, all this was a matter of marking time. Sooner or later something had to happen, something must be said. The curtain must go up. I steeled myself by remembering Jon kneeling on the floor of the barn with blood running down his face. That was reality, against all this pretense.

It wasn't difficult for me to observe Mark Ingram, since he was easily the center of our attention. Even Hillary seemed to watch him intently, and I sensed a barely suppressed excitement in him, as though he, too, might be waiting for the explosion that had to come.

In particular I watched Gail in her attitude toward Mark Ingram. She seemed clearly fascinated by him, and he flattered her now and then with some special attention. Perhaps Belle was the old love, of whom he was fond, but he would not be a man to overlook an attractive woman.

Only Caleb paid Ingram little attention, barely concealing his dislike. Nevertheless, he avoided any open offense.

A waiter in short white jacket and black tie—imported from where?—served us skillfully, aware of the critical eye of his employer. After smoked oysters we ate mountain trout, nicely boned, with parsley potatoes and a luscious mixture of herbed green peas and mushrooms. The salad, with its roquefort dressing, might have been just picked from the garden, and there was champagne carefully iced in a bucket. Jasper might be isolated, but Mark Ingram was already bringing in what was known as the civilized touch.

He was a considerate host, not monopolizing the talk, as he might easily have done, but drawing us out, even getting Caleb to discuss, however dryly, his father's day in the Denver law firm. All the while, an inner alarm was sounding for me. What was this pretense about? One of us had to break through into reality soon, and I knew it would have to be me. Never mind that this man frightened me—I would have to act.

Again the subject of the Forty-niners' Ball Ingram was

planning came up. He had, he told us, already informed friends in at least three states, so they could be thinking about costumes.

"Those old seats have to come out of the orchestra section of the Opera House anyway, so we'll have a ready-made ballroom. And I'm going to bring in fiddlers for the occasion."

I listened to all this with a growing sense of anger. Everyone was behaving as though nothing at all had happened today. So what was I waiting for? It was past time to ring up the curtain.

"Have you heard what happened to Jon Maddocks this afternoon?" I spoke into a startled silence. "Jon was badly beaten and left in the barn by two men who attacked him."

I sounded much too abrupt, but Ingram gave me his sober interest at once. Belle murmured, "How awful!" Gail merely stared at her plate, while Caleb regarded me with a barely concealed horror.

I wasn't here to be polite and play this absurd game of host and guest. I was here to open the battle, and I only hoped that I would find the right weapons.

"My grandmother thinks you were responsible for what happened to Jon, Mr. Ingram," I said.

Hillary put a cautioning hand upon my arm, but Ingram remained calm, regarding me sadly, almost pityingly.

"The more I hear of your grandmother's condition," he said, "the more I am coming to feel that she's not much good anymore at managing her own affairs. Why should she make such an attack upon me?"

I kept my eyes fixed upon his face, lest I miss some nuance of expression. "Perhaps you're the one who can best answer that."

Ingram sipped champagne and waited for me to go on. No one else said anything.

"This afternoon," I said, "I told my grandmother that I would like to stay and help her in any way I can. There are some of us who don't want to see Jasper and Domino and the whole valley turned into just another cheap resort. Perhaps that will come someday, but not now."

"Well, good for you!" Belle applauded.

Ingram glanced at her and then back at me. He was still controlled, outwardly unperturbed. He would have long since faced the likelihood of my alliance with Persis Morgan.

Unexpectedly, Hillary came to my support. "Of course you can't let your grandmother down." He was watching Ingram with a certain bright anger that I wouldn't have thought he could feel.

Caleb put in his own dry words. "This is hardly a wise move on your part, Laurie. You will do nothing for your grandmother's state of health if you talk like this. She needs to get away."

"I'm beginning to think that there's nothing much wrong with her health," I answered heatedly. "Nothing but loneliness and discouragement and frustration."

"Hear, hear!" Belle remained undisturbed by another look from Mark Ingram. There was a light in her eyes as though she for one might enjoy the sound of guns in the street at high noon.

"You're in no position to know anything about her health," Gail said sharply.

Before I could answer, Ingram went on, his tone still gravely courteous. "I'm sorry you feel this way, Miss Morgan. It seems a rather narrow approach. When a lot of people should be able to enjoy this place, it's a shame to hold it back for the use of a few."

"Perhaps it's for the use of the land and everything that belongs to the land," I reminded him.

"I can't allow this argument to continue." Caleb seemed to come in on cue. But whose cue? I wondered. "I have wanted Mrs. Morgan to move down to Denver for some time. There she could be properly cared for, made comfortable, and we could look after her interests more conveniently. My firm has a certain guardianship, an obligation—"

"The move would kill her," I said flatly.

Our waiter came in to clear away dishes, and for a little

178

while Belle took it upon herself to chat cheerfully in her hoarse, slightly amused tones. I watched only Mark Ingram, and at last my concentrated attention began to get through to him. He must have been well accustomed to the looks of admiring women, but I was doing something that perhaps he hadn't experienced before. When he looked straight at me, I managed to stare back, and mine was no look of admiration. His eyes shifted, then came back, to find me still staring, and to my surprise a faint flush crept over his face.

Nevertheless, when the waiter was gone, he moved to a direct attack. It was as though Hillary, Caleb, Belle, and Gail no longer mattered at the table and we two were alone.

"I want to talk with your grandmother, Miss Morgan. I want to see her soon."

"I don't believe she wants to see you," I told him.

"I think she will change her mind. Perhaps you will give her a message for me. Can you do that?"

"It depends on what it is."

"You can tell her that I'm interested in learning what became of a man named Noah Armand when he left her house twenty years ago. You will tell her this, Miss Morgan?"

I was startled. This was the question I had meant to ask him. "What do you mean—what happened to him? I understand that he went away and wasn't heard from again. So how could my grandmother know what happened to him? I thought perhaps *you* might know—since you were once his friend."

"Just give her my message," he said.

He had shaken and bested me, and I could no longer stare him down. Always the name of Noah Armand seemed to bring with it some vague and sinister threat. Something that I remembered—and didn't remember. Didn't want to remember?

When I glanced around the table, I saw that the others had each reacted in a different way. Caleb wore his usual mask of restraint, though now I knew there could be seething depths underneath. Gail seemed curiously expectant, as though she waited for something more from me. Hillary was watching Ingram with a fixed look, and he wasn't acting now. Only Belle still seemed at ease, still somewhat cynically amused, and quite sure of herself when it came to Ingram.

"You do love to drop bombshells, don't you?" she said to him.

His smile was affectionate, and he seemed not to mind her occasional barbs. As he looked at her across the table, there was an instant when their eyes caught and something leaped between them. Something strangely deep and true. Ingram might be every bit the villain we believed, yet I had a feeling that he loved Belle Durant with whatever good and sound emotion was left in him. It was there for all to see, and I couldn't help but marvel a little at how infinitely complex any human being could be.

I turned to Belle. "Did *you* ever know Noah Armand?"

"Not as well as you did," she told me.

That was unpleasantly revealing. "What do you mean?"

She glanced at Ingram before she answered, and then shrugged. "After all, he was your grandmother's second husband. There were times when you lived in the same house with him."

I didn't want to touch that at all, or think about it.

"After all, Mr. Ingram," I said, "if you were Noah Armand's friend, aren't you the one most likely to know whether he is dead or alive?"

He looked at me distantly, as though his thoughts were elsewhere. "That's something I would very much like to know. His disappearance has always seemed thoroughly mysterious to me."

A new thought intruded in my mind. A thought so disturbing that I thrust it back. When the waiter returned with fruit and cheese, I was glad for the temporary distraction. This was something I would have to think about later, when I was alone.

Ingram remained the proper host, but I sensed anger in him now, though I was not at all sure of the direction in which it was turned. Toward me? Toward Belle for being outspoken? Or only toward my absent grandmother? My newborn courage began to seep away. How could Persis and I possibly stand up to a man who might turn vindictive and dangerous in the space of a moment, even to the point of ordering a vicious attack such as had been made upon Jon?

Yet we sat at the table and toyed with grapes, drank chartreuse from fine crystal liqueur glasses, and then at last found excuses to escape a dinner party grown oppressive.

Mark Ingram stood on the hotel steps while we got into the jeep, bidding us a formal and courtly "Good night." Belle stood beside him, unperturbed. Behind the wheel, Caleb seemed lost in deep silence, and even Hillary and Gail had little to say.

When we reached the house, Gail left us quickly and ran inside, to go to my grandmother.

Caleb said he would take the jeep around and come in the back way, and he, too, took himself off hastily. I was eager now to run upstairs to report to Persis, as I had promised to do, but Hillary lingered on the steps.

"You showed a lot of courage tonight, Laurie," he said, the sober mood still upon him. "The fight's been opened now. So don't back down. You'll need to get your grandmother to change her will in your favor. As soon as that's been done, you can take charge and Ingram will be helpless to move any further."

I knew all these things were true, yet I didn't like his choice of words, and he quickly sensed my hesitation.

"I'm sorry," he said. "I didn't mean that the way it sounds."

"I didn't think you wanted to take sides."

"I didn't. And I do want a chance at that theater. I could really do the job of fixing it up. Just the same, I don't like what Ingram is doing. If he comes to see your grandmother, I'd like to be there."

"Of course," I said, and let it go at that.

"What will you do tomorrow?"

I didn't mention the back parlor. That was something I must face alone.

"I'll have to look for Red if he hasn't turned up. He's been gone now since this afternoon."

"I'll come over when I can and we'll search for him together."

For a moment longer we faced each other, and there was a new uncertainty between us. Then Hillary kissed me lightly and went away. I watched him go, feeling both regretful and relieved.

Inside the house I climbed the stairs slowly. I had a promise to keep to my grandmother. But now the question that I'd been holding off ever since that moment in the dining room when it had come to me returned full force to torment me.

If Persis Morgan had shot her son, this surely would have been an accident. But if she had then killed Noah Armand—that was murder. Had his body been spirited away in order to hide a crime that my grandmother had committed?

I mounted the last steps reluctantly, not knowing how I could face her with this question in my mind.

XIII

When I reached the door, Edna was coming out of Persis Morgan's room with a tray and empty milk glass. I was glad to see that Gail wasn't there.

"She's waiting for you, miss," Edna said, and I went in.

Once more Persis sat propped against her pillows, a crocheted bed jacket about her shoulders and a lively look of anticipation in her eyes.

"Good!" she said. "I'm glad that dinner didn't last forever. I've been waiting. Tell me everything. Tell me right away!"

With an effort I thrust back the dark thoughts for

which I had no real foundation. Drawing a chair beside the bed, I reached for one cold hand and held it between my warm ones. I had to get the worst over with at once—Ingram's words.

"Mr. Ingram sent you a message, Grandmother."

"All right. Deliver it."

"He said to tell you that he would like to know what became of Noah Armand when he left this house twenty years ago."

Whatever she might have expected, it wasn't this. She stared at me in a mingling of surprise and alarm.

"He wants to know *what?*"

I repeated the words, and she turned her head from side to side despairingly. "How can he ask a question like that? What can I possibly know?"

"He seems to think you may know something."

"But I haven't heard from that man since he left this house, and I hope I never hear from him again."

She didn't sound as though she were lying, but I didn't always trust her.

"Mr. Ingram wants to see you," I said.

"No! I've seen him once, and that was enough. I let him come here when he first arrived in Jasper. I know what he intends, and I don't ever want to see him again."

"I've told him you won't see him, but I don't think he takes 'no' very easily."

"Never mind. Let it go for now. I'll have to think. I'll have to think quietly when I'm alone. I'll have to discuss this with Caleb. How did Caleb answer him when Ingram brought this up?"

"I don't think he did. I don't think Caleb said anything."

She seemed to sink a little lower against her pillows, and withered lids came over great dark eyes, where all the life that was in her still lived.

"Grandmother," I said, "is there anything more I should know about Noah Armand? How can I help you when I understand so little?"

"I've told you all I can. Laurie, did that man ever show up again in your mother's life?"

183

The way she put the question relieved my mind, and I let ugly suspicion go.

"Not that I know of. But then—how could I know if she chose to keep it from me? All I can tell you is that if he did, he didn't stay."

"What else came up tonight at dinner?"

"I talked about the attack on Jon," I told her, "but Ingram seemed to shrug it off. Just the same, I think more than ever that he was involved."

"Of course he was involved."

"But why—why?"

"I'm so tired. I don't want to talk anymore tonight, Laurie. Is there anything else you have to tell me?"

"Nothing, Grandmother." Questions were of no use now when she was using her familiar method of escaping from them.

When I pulled the comforter up and checked to make sure her bell was within reach on the table, I bent to kiss her lightly on the cheek. It was the first time I had touched her that way, and I was startled by my own emotion.

She opened her eyes. "Thank you for that, Laurie. It's more than I deserve. You've already suffered enough at my hands, but now you'll manage. You have to manage."

I left the lamp burning beside her bed and went downstairs.

Ever since the wreath had been left on the door, I'd found myself approaching my room with a certain uneasiness—as though anything that was meanly vindictive might await me here. But the doorknob was bare, and when I went in the room stood empty. I wished again for Red's comforting presence and dared not think that anything serious might have happened to him. Tomorrow I would find him, I was sure.

My thoughts were turning unhappily as I undressed and got between cold sheets. Something in this house was terribly wrong, and I could only believe that it stemmed back to the happening I had so long rejected in my memory. My father and mother had been a part of it, and so had Noah Armand. I had been there too, and tomorrow I must find the answers to all that troubled me. Only when I knew everything could I find the proper means of fighting Mark Ingram. If I were to take a stand against him at Persis Morgan's side, I would need all the strength I could muster.

But I must not think about any of this now or I'd never go to sleep. I let myself drift into thoughts of Jon instead, let him come warmly into my mind. Was I falling in love with him? It was not an altogether happy thought.

What about Hillary if this happened? What about me and my ability to love?

When I finally slept, I dreamed again of riding up a mountain meadow, knowing I must reach the mine. Knowing that if my father was to live I must reach it. Once more the sound of hooves followed behind, only they didn't frighten me because now I knew it was Jon coming after me. I woke up when the pony shied and I went sailing into the air, never to reach the ground. But this time, awake, I was aware of something new the dream had given me. I had been riding to save my father—at the mine. And of this I could make nothing at all.

My watch told me it was past two o'clock. I got out of bed and went to the window, where I could see the cone of Old Desolate rising black against a lighter backdrop of sky and stars. Close in, among the ranch buildings, a light burned in a window of Jon's cabin. Did that mean pain and sleeplessness? I was glad that Sam had arranged to stay with him. What had happened still seemed too terrible to be believed. Not in this peaceful setting. Yet it was a setting that had known times of fear and violence in the past, and there might be more to come. More to threaten my grandmother and Jon and me—all stemming from Mark Ingram.

Nevertheless, I must stay. I knew that now without any doubt I must try to see Persis Morgan through whatever was to come. Looking out toward that lighted window, I knew how much I needed to talk with Jon. But I must wait until he felt a good deal better. In the meantime I would face that room downstairs tomorrow morning, without fail.

As I turned back to my bed, I heard light footsteps in the hall and wondered who could be up at this hour. Curious to know, I opened my door a crack and was in time to see Gail slipping into her room down the hall. She was fully clothed—not in her shimmery dress, but in jeans and jacket.

I remembered what Belle had said, and guessed that she must be coming home from a rendezvous with Mark Ingram. What had been only a suspicion that he had deliberately planted an enemy within the house grew into conviction. I wondered how much Belle knew, and what she thought about this. In any case something must be done about Gail.

So why not now? I put on my robe and slippers and went down the hall to tap on her door. There was a moment's silence, and then she came to open it a crack.

"We're both awake," I said, "so perhaps this is as good a time as any to talk."

If she could have closed the door in my face, I think she would have, but she didn't quite dare. Instead she opened it and let me into her room. She had started to undress, unbuttoning her blouse. Her dair hair was loose, falling tousled about her face, and what makeup she had worn was smudged, so that her mouth had a well-kissed look. She stared at me with eyes that were still languorous with love.

"What do you want?" she said.

I glanced about a room that was not much different from my own, except that it had been lived in longer and there were more personal possessions lying about. Gail might be antiseptic enough as a nurse, but she wasn't a particularly tidy person.

"Do you mind if I sit down?" I asked.

"I don't think this is the time—" she began.

"It's the perfect time. You've just come from the hotel, haven't you?"

The languorous look was vanishing, and she seemed faintly alarmed. "So what if I have?"

186

"Your personal life is your own affair," I said. "But when it involves Mark Ingram, then that becomes my affair. And my grandmother's."

She stared at me, admitting nothing.

"How long have you known Mark Ingram," I asked bluntly.

"I don't know him at all . . ." she began, and then shrugged. "Have it your way, if you must. But I'm not going to tell you anything."

"It's pretty clear that you're in his hire," I said. "He planted you in this house, didn't he?"

Coolly, insolently, she finished undoing her blouse and took it off. She wore no bra, and she reached without hurry for a pajama top, slipped into the sleeves, and began to button up the front. All the while she watched me with that sly, faintly triumphant look that I'd seen her wear before.

"Mr. Hawes employed me," she said. "Through Dr. Burton. You know that."

"Because Mark Ingram wanted you here. Because that is where your loyalties lie. Isn't that right?"

I wasn't alarming her in the least now, and she had begun to smile. "You don't really think I'm going to answer your questions, do you? Why don't you just go back to your own room? You have enough troubles of your own, Laurie Morgan."

"It doesn't matter whether you answer or not," I said. "I just wanted to know what you might have to say in your own defense. My grandmother will be letting you go very soon, and Mr. Hawes won't have anything to say about it."

This time my words stung through her pose of mocking indifference, and again she looked a little uneasy. After all, her real employer might not be pleased to have Persis Morgan let her go.

"I'm sorry," she said. "Let's talk about this again tomorrow, when we're not both tired and apt to say things that don't make much sense."

"I'm making very good sense," I assured her. "But we will talk again tomorrow. I think as a nurse that you

187

ought to be on call all night in this house. It's rather serious if you've been running out."

I left her and went back to my room, not at all sorry that I had flung down a glove. Things were coming into the open and that was all to the good. I didn't have to play this game of pretense with Gail Cullen any longer.

My bed was cold, but I had let out a few of my emotions, and I fell asleep more quickly than I might have expected.

The next morning I slept late, and when I went downstairs the others were finishing breakfast. I asked about Jon, and Gail, behaving as though nothing had happened between us last night, said cheerfully that she had been down to see him.

"He was up and wouldn't stay in bed, though he let me fix breakfast for him and Sam. He's bruised and a bit sore, but he seems all right."

I would visit him as soon as I could, but now there were two immediate projects ahead. First I would go into the back parlor and open the mahogany box, come what might. Then I would go outside and search seriously for Red.

Gail was in uniform again, and when she left the table she went upstairs to my grandmother. Caleb sat for a while, lost in his own unhappy thoughts, whatever they were. I didn't want to open the subject of Gail just then, but I tried one question.

"What did you think about Ingram's message to my grandmother last night?" I asked him.

"I have no idea what to make of it," Caleb said.

"Do you know what became of Noah Armand?"

"I hope he's dead. I hope very much that he is dead."

When I finished my coffee and toast and rose from the table, he nodded to me and went off upstairs, eager, I think, to escape any further need to talk to me.

There could be no more postponement.

No one seemed to be around when I went down the hallway to the rear parlor and turned the knob. Gail had not locked the room again. Perhaps she wanted to tempt me into doing exactly what I was doing now, though I wasn't sure why.

The room was as dark and stuffy as I remembered, but this time I didn't mean to rely on dim wall lights. I went to a French door that opened onto the porch. Its dark red draperies hung almost solid with dust and cobwebs, and I held my breath and closed my eyes as I pulled them open. The prickle of dust touched my face, and I sneezed twice.

Flooded with sunlight, the room seemed less grim, less threatening, and it also seemed a great deal more dingy and dirty. Now I could see those footprints in the dust more clearly, and knew that some of them were mine. The others that I had noted earlier were still there, but they didn't matter to me now. Only one thing mattered—the box that waited for me on the rosewood table.

Until this moment I had moved with a fine deliberation, allowing no hesitation, no delay. But now my steps slowed as I approached the table and stood before it, unable to bring myself to the point of raising the lid. Which, I told myself, was ridiculous. What could the contents of a box seen through the eyes of a child matter to me now? Certainly I mustn't allow my own imagination to frighten me into inaction. Not when I had come this far.

Nevertheless, I managed one more delay for myself. The light from the window, from the wall sconces, didn't seem enough. I wanted to banish every last shadow, and I crossed the room to touch another switch. The chandelier, less elaborate than the one in the front parlor, blazed on, its lights shimmering through cobweb lace, driving all traces of haunted darkness from the room. The radiance was disturbing, but I knew I must face down my own fear of light that dazzled.

I reached for the dusty mahogany box that bore several fingerprints someone else had recently left on the wood and raised the brass catches. The lid came up easily, revealing red velvet within. Red velvet, against which a single silvery object shone in the electric light. It was a small blunt-nosed gun, embossed in silver that had not completely tarnished, closed away as it had been from the air. The gun was still bright enough to catch the light and

189

reflect it. There were other small objects in the box as well, each in its own nested compartment: a leather powder flask, a small collection of bullets, a box for percussion caps. And there was one larger, empty compartment, twin to the one that held the gun. All this I seemed to recognize in a flash, because I knew the interior of this box very well.

A trembling had begun deep inside me as the old sense of spinning started in my brain. I was whirling, whirling into oblivion, being tossed into a place where I could not think or feel or remember. But this time I fought the sensation, refused to give way to it, resisted with all the will left in me. There was a terrible moment when everything seemed to fly apart inside my head.

It was as though I could hear the amplified explosion of a gun going off in this room, echoing down through time. I could hear the dreadful impact of a bullet on flesh, see the dazzle of light on the gun. And the blood—spurting.

A voice belonging to the present reached me from the doorway. Dimly I recognized that Gail was speaking to me.

"You remember now, don't you, Laurie? Why not pick up that deringer? Pick it up and hold it the way you did that other time. Put your finger on the trigger and pull. Go ahead—fire it. You want to, don't you?"

There was no reality for me in the present. I was back in another time, and I reached for the small gun as though I couldn't help myself. I could hear the screaming, hear someone shouting. And I could still see the blood. Because *I* had fired the gun. It was I who had picked up this shining deadly little weapon and pointed it, firing.

My hand held the real gun now, and my forefinger was on its trigger, ready to pull.

"You're remembering, aren't you?" Gail was close beside me, whispering almost in my ear. "What they've told me is true. It was you who fired that gun. *You* killed your father, didn't you?"

Someone else came in behind us, someone spoke to me. I knew it was Hillary, but he belonged to a future time, and I was in the past and could make no contact with him. I raised the small weapon at shadowy figures that struggled in the room, and I would have pulled the trigger, but Hillary took the gun quickly from my hand.

The floor seemed to heave and rise toward me, and he caught me when I fell. This time there was a true blanking out, and I was conscious of nothing until I opened my eyes to find that I lay on the sofa in the front parlor and Gail was holding ammonia salts to my nose. Hillary stood behind her, concerned and visibly shaken.

Caleb had come in too, and his voice penetrated my haze. "Lie still, Laurie. Don't try to get up. You should never have gone in there. Gail, you should have stopped her."

I gasped for breath from the fumes, and Gail corked the little bottle and stood up. "How could I possibly stop her? I didn't know she was there until—"

"You knew," Caleb said.

"I'm all right," I told him. "Don't fuss."

"Lie still," he repeated as I tried to sit up, but I heard no sympathy in his voice.

Dizziness shook me again, and Hillary propped another cushion under my head. "You're all right now," he assured me. "Take it easy, Laurie. It's over, so just rest and collect yourself."

I paid no attention. "I can remember firing that gun! I remember someone screaming. And most of all, I remember the blood."

Caleb spoke sharply to Gail. "Can't you do something? Make her some hot tea. Anything!"

As she went off, he thrust Hillary aside and drew a chair near my sofa. He looked a little gray as he spoke to me.

"Your grandmother and I both hoped that you might never remember, never need to know."

"Just tell me all of it," I pleaded. "Don't hold anything back." I could control my voice a little better now, and in spite of the horror it was as though I had walked through a dark curtain into daylight. No matter how terrible the scenes were in this new place, I must find the strength to

191

face them. Daylight was better than dark. I repeated my words. "Please tell me."

Caleb left his chair abruptly, moving about the room, driven by his own inner tensions, not responding to mine.

Hillary came and took my hand. "It's all right," he assured me again. "Just rest now. You've had a shock." His voice, too, sounded strained. Because he was seeing me with new eyes?

I spoke to Caleb. "I must know the rest. You have to tell me all of it now."

He stopped his pacing and sat down again, making up his mind. "Very well. If that's the way you want it. I'll tell you what little I know. I came into the room just after it happened. Only the day before, your grandmother had been telling you for the dozenth time the story of those two deringers, and how they had belonged to your great-grandfather, Malcolm Tremayne. That he was supposed to have shot a man with one of them. For honor and chivalry, of course. She always made those stories romantic when she told them."

"There is only one gun in the box," I said dully.

"Wait—just let me go on. For some time Mrs. Morgan had been teaching you to shoot with modern guns, in spite of your parents' objections. She felt that any girl who grew up on a ranch should understand about guns. So she taught you when you were very young, just as her father had taught her. Richard and Marybeth didn't like it at all, but they could never do a thing with Persis Morgan. Of course she didn't teach you with the deringers. You were forbidden to touch them unless she was present. However, because they were curiosities, with their old-fashioned muzzle-loading, she showed you how it was done, never dreaming you might experiment for yourself."

I drew my hand from Hillary's. I could remember much more clearly now—remember the forbidden excitement of trying to load the little guns. There *had* been two of them in the box. I knew how to use the powder from the flask, ram in the bullet that I'd wadded in a bit of cloth so it wouldn't roll out, and set the percussion cap. I could remember hiding behind the sofa in the back parlor

192

with one of the guns I'd loaded in my hand. I was supposed to be upstairs in bed with a cold, but it had been more interesting to hide in the back parlor and watch my mother with that man I didn't like. And then my father had come in and the men had started to fight.

Caleb's voice jarred me back into the present again as he went on bluntly, not sparing me now. "You must have been sitting on the floor behind the sofa, playing with those guns. Apparently you'd managed to load one of them yourself, and when Noah Armand came into the room you stood up to see what was happening. That was when Richard and your grandmother and I came home ahead of time. Mrs. Morgan stopped on the porch to talk with me, but Richard went inside. I suppose he saw Marybeth's suitcases at the foot of the stairs and he heard voices in the back parlor.

"He rushed in and attacked Noah with his fists. You must have thought that your father was in danger, and you pointed the gun and pulled the trigger. It was Richard who fell, fatally shot. Deringers were never any good at a distance, but pointblank they killed."

I was sitting up now, listening tensely, and I covered my face with my hands. Caleb's voice went on.

"Mrs. Morgan got there before I did. In fact, I was out in the yard at the time I heard the shot and rushed back into the house. She was in time to see Noah go out one of those French doors. Marybeth was kneeling beside Richard, sobbing, while you stood there with that deringer in your hand and black powder all over you."

Horror seemed to flow through me in a burning tide. Hillary put an arm about me, and I tried to steady myself. I still had to hear the rest.

"Go on," I said.

Caleb sighed. "There's not much more. Mrs. Morgan took charge of the gun that had been fired and she washed you free of black traces. She never spoke to Marybeth again, except to tell her what she must say to the police. Between us we concocted the story of the intruder, and she took several pieces of jewelry from her case and put them into a box to be hidden away. No one must ever know that Noah came back to the house, or that you, Laurie, fired that gun. No one must guess that Noah came back to run off with Marybeth."

"What did Noah do?"

"He took off at once, and he's not been heard from since. Before Mrs. Morgan called the police, I remember we stood at the foot of the stairs, away from the horror in the parlor. I remember her thinking out loud. Once she suggested that I take Richard's body to the mine in order to pretend that he'd had a fall that might have killed him. But of course she knew that wouldn't work—the wound was too evident. There was only one servant in the house at the time, and she was old and deaf, and had been upstairs in her room lying down. So she knew nothing. She was roused only to take care of Marybeth and put her to bed. From the beginning your grandmother insisted that you were to be protected at all costs, and that no scandal was to touch the Morgan name."

His dry, controlled tones told me that he spoke out of old abhorrence for that child, Laurie Morgan. For what a long time he must have detested me, and how much he must have hated my return!

I lay back on the couch and closed my eyes, shutting both men away. I knew now why I felt that front hall was a place that frightened me. I remembered where I had been—sitting at the top of the stairs, listening and terrified, while they stood in the hallway below and my grandmother planned aloud. I must not have understood much of what was happening. Their talk about riding out to the mine with my father meant only one thing to me. For some reason my imagination made a leap into the belief that they were taking him there to die. This idea had totally possessed me, and had given me something I must do. Later I had understood well enough that he was dead—but not then.

I must have gone out to the barn for my pony. I rode him bareback up the valley, driven by a need to get to the mine to my father. Jon saw me go and came after me. He found me when I fell off my pony, and he brought me back. I had a vague memory of my mother pushing everyone aside and getting up to nurse me. And after that—nothing. Only delirium that mercifully shut out reality and kept me from remembering what I had done.

Until now.

Gail came with a tray and a pot of tea and offered me a sedative. I shook my head. I didn't want to weaken myself with any more oblivion. The honeyed tea was hot and strengthening, and I tried to pull myself together. I must begin living again, moment by moment. My mind was working now, turning over details that were safe to think about, sidestepping the rest until I could face all of it. I wasn't quite ready to face the full, terrible reality yet.

"What became of the other deringer?"

Caleb was tiring of my questions. "We don't know. It disappeared at the time. Perhaps your grandmother knows."

It didn't matter. Only the one that fired the shot mattered. The one I had held. But I had to go on questioning.

"What about the jewels?"

"I disposed of them as your grandmother directed," Caleb said. "They had to be put where the police wouldn't find them. They had to be missing."

"Where did you hide them?" Gail asked.

"That's for Mrs. Morgan to say."

Hillary turned from the window, and I saw how shaken he still looked. Perhaps I could understand why. In real life Hillary was always the spectator. On a stage he might live vicariously, with the intensity of an actor. He could step into someone else's skin and pretend another's emotions while he played a role. But he wasn't accustomed to the raw primary colors of what must now involve him through me. Life had been thrown at him, and he found himself suddenly without a role to play.

"You needn't stay with me, Hillary," I said. "I'll be all right now."

"Of course I'll stay. I'll stay as long as you need me."

The strange and not altogether welcome fact was that right now I didn't seem to need him at all. After that first moment of realization I had been fighting to recover my own strength.

195

By the time I finished the tea, the world had steadied around me. I was no longer dizzy and trembling. The old sense of spinning wildly into oblivion was gone. The cure for that had been effected—but at what cost! To live for the rest of my life with the knowledge that *I* had killed my father! How was I to live with that knowledge? I hadn't been able to live with it, of course. All my life up to this point had been spent in trying to escape this very fact.

Caleb, having opened the sluice gates, was running on in his careful voice that must have so long hidden his own anger and pain. He was hardly the unemotional man I had imagined, but only strongly in control of his feelings.

"When everything had died down and the police were through, your grandmother closed the back parlor and kept it locked. I think if she could have burned it out of the house, that's what she would have done. It was never to be touched, and she grew almost superstitious about that. As though all the lies that had been told for the sake of preventing scandal and further damage to your mother and you, and of course to the Morgan name, could be locked into the room and never allowed to escape."

"Damage to the Morgan name," I repeated. "That was important, wasn't it?"

"It still is. That's what she has held onto with all her might, along with the land and the house here and in Domino."

Yes. I'd seen that in her—the ironclad pride.

"She has protected you, Laurie."

"But now it's all escaped, hasn't it? It's all gotten out of hand!"

"Nothing is out of hand yet."

"Perhaps it is if Mark Ingram knows. Do you think this is what he's holding over my grandmother's head?"

"I don't know," Caleb said dully. "But I do know that he's dangerous and vindictive. He's carrying some sort of grudge. That's why I've wanted your grandmother to move out and not try to fight him. Your coming here hasn't helped."

My brief suspicion that Persis Morgan might have done

the shooting had been exploded. Guilt was in the open now—where it belonged. A child's guilt, but guilt nevertheless.

What was I to say to my grandmother when next I saw her? What could I say, now that I knew everything? It no longer seemed strange or cruel that she had never written letters, never claimed me as her granddaughter. Until she needed me badly. I felt increasingly devastated by all the ramifications that were still coming clear. There was too much for me to grasp all at once, yet somehow I must find the courage to face what had happened.

For one thing, I must face the memory of my mother. If she had blamed me—as she must often have done through the years—I, too, could blame her. I could still remember occasions when she had looked at me strangely, waiting perhaps to see what I could recall. No wonder she had wept, no wonder she had been sad. Had she waited, hoping for Noah's return? It might have been better for us both if she had tried to make a new life for herself, leaving Jasper behind. Instead Jasper and its terrible events must always have been with her, and most of all her own guilt, her betrayal of my father, which had precipitated the tragedy. I was the product of those years.

With an effort I stood up and found that I was steady enough on my feet. All I wanted now was to escape from this house for a little while—escape them all. I needed to get away where I could lick my new wounds and try to recover my bearings, find my way.

Caleb had apparently endured enough, and he had quietly left the room. Gail was still there, and she had listened almost avidly. Now that I stood up, she started toward the door.

"If I'm not needed, I'll get back upstairs to Mrs. Morgan. She's not feeling well this morning, and she shouldn't be left alone."

I remembered vaguely that something should be done about Gail, but this was not the time. Now I must ask her something else.

"Wait," I said, and she turned. "Please don't tell her

197

what has happened. I'd like to tell her myself when she's able to see me."

Gail shrugged and went off. Only Hillary was left.

He came quickly to put his arms about me. "I'll stay with you until you're feeling better."

I didn't want him here with me now, and I couldn't help that.

"I need to be by myself for a little while," I told him.

He touched my cheek lightly. "You must forgive yourself. Others who were older brought this about. They are the ones who should be punished. Not you."

I could only remember that my hand had held the gun, my finger had pulled the trigger.

"Laurie," he said, and there was a slightly grim note in his voice, "I do understand what you're feeling—a little. Remember, I lost my father too."

But I had no pity in me now for anyone else's loss.

"I'll be all right," I said.

He walked with me to the foot of the stairs and let me go when I started up. I had the feeling that in spite of his protestations he wanted to get away. When his high moods evaporated, I knew he could become extremely depressed. Just now we both needed to be apart.

In my room I lay on the bed with my eyes closed and tried to let everything slip away. What had happened couldn't be easily assimilated and accepted in all its terrible reality. The word Gail had flung at me on my first day in this house was still ringing through my mind. Too large a word for me to face and understand: Murder. *Murder directed at my father. By me.*

I don't know how long I lay there trying only to empty my mind. When the knock came on my door, it startled me. Before I could answer, Caleb called to me.

"Laurie, I have word of your dog."

That brought me up from the bed at once, and I went to open the door. "What have you heard?"

"A man from town telephoned to report that when he was out on a chore for Mark Ingram, he heard a dog barking over near the mine. He didn't investigate, but when he got back to the hotel and mentioned it, Belle Durant said it might be your dog. So he called to tell us."

I made up my mind quickly. "I'll ride over there and look for him. I need to get out anyway. I need something to do."

Caleb seemed uneasy with me, as though bringing everything out in the open had made him even more uncomfortable about me than before. Until now he had veiled his dislike a little. Now it looked hotly out of his eyes, and he made no attempt to dissuade me.

"As you please," he said, and went away.

I changed quickly into jeans, shirt, and jacket, and started for the barn. As I followed the path, I looked off toward Old Desolate and saw—consciously this time—the gate that led away from the ranch. Now I remembered. Those men who had ridden off yesterday after the attack on Jon had gone through that gate without stopping on their gallop up the valley. The gate had been left open behind them, and no one had gone to close it for some time. I had been thinking only of Jon's injuries and the need to get help for him. Red could easily have dashed through that opening. The dog that had been heard near the mine must be Red. He was a town dog, and not used to free spaces. He might not know how to get back to the ranch.

I was glad to have a strong purpose in this hour when I needed something important to do. It never occurred to me to question Caleb's message.

XIV

Sam was in the barn, and he helped me saddle Baby Doe. In answer to my question he said that Jon was feeling better, but was still sore from the beating and was taking it a bit easy today. I thought of stopping in to see him, but if

Jon knew what I meant to do he might insist on coming with me, no matter how he felt. I didn't want that. Let him rest.

"Somebody heard a dog barking over near the mine," I told the boy. "So I'm going to ride up there to see if I can find Red."

"Want me to go with you?" Sam asked.

I shook my head. I still needed to be alone. I had to figure out, among other things, what I was going to say before I saw Jon. I wanted very much to talk with him, but first I must try to find my direction.

"Better take this with you," Sam said when I was in the saddle, and he handed up a flashlight. I thrust it into a pocket and turned Baby Doe's head up the valley.

The high cone of Old Desolate beckoned me, as it had since I was a child, and I found the mountain stillness comforting. Human problems grew small in the face of all this vastness, and I needed that sort of perspective now.

How unreal were the lives we had been leading, I thought as I rode along. If only I could recapture the essence of that little girl who had once ridden up this valley on a pony beside her father. But that had disappeared forever. It had vanished in the sound of a single shot that had gone echoing through Morgan House.

That was when all the lies had begun that changed our lives. My grandmother's first of all, in the deceptive trail she had built to fool the world. Caleb had gone along, doing her bidding. But not, I thought, quite as willingly as she supposed. My mother's whole life from that time on had been a lie. She had given herself to concealing the truth, even from me, and if she had suffered over my father's death, or longed for the return of her lover, she had never let anyone know.

I had a strong feeling that Noah must never have returned. Surely if he had, if only to get in touch with her, I would have been aware of some change in Marybeth Morgan. But for as long as I could remember, she had been the same—a sad woman, gentle and loving, but somehow hopeless. It was difficult to imagine her with the

200

sort of spirit it must have taken to be willing to leave her husband and her child and run away with Noah Armand.

Why had he never turned up again? If he had cared enough to come back to the house for her, if they had planned to run off together, leaving my grandmother's fortune behind, why had he never been heard from since? There was a strange mystery here that troubled me. Was there more to what had occurred than Caleb had told me?

Could something have happened to Noah in that house? Could there really have been some quick vengeance? But at whose hands? Caleb's? Persis Morgan's, as I'd thought earlier? Persis was her father's daughter. And there was a missing deringer that might have been fired and had to be concealed.

I didn't care for these thoughts that had begun to haunt me, and I tried to give myself to an awareness of the beauty of mountains and valley all around me, and that vault of blue overhead. I had enough horrors to make my peace with now without dreaming up new and terrifying problems.

Baby Doe carried me along at a moderate pace, and from time to time I gazed off toward the high shoulder of the mountain, where the trail led toward Domino. Suddenly a tiny movement up there caught my eye. As my sight adjusted from sunny meadow to darker spruce, I made out a figure almost lost in the shadow of the trees. A man on a horse. His face showed as a white patch, watching my progress up the valley. He was too far off for me to identify, and he could have been anyone at all—man or woman.

The watching presence worried me after what had happened to Jon, but I didn't want to turn back. Riding on, I whistled now and then, and called Red's name, but there was no sign of my dog anywhere. When I next looked up at the stand of spruce trees, the rider was gone. I was not particularly afraid. Perhaps my mind was too full of all that I had learned, all the puzzles that still faced me, for there to be any room for fear. I had lived through too much today to be able to fear anything more.

Baby Doe's pace slowed as she started up the slope.

201

She picked her way over stony ground, her hooves clattering on rock, the sound echoing from the peaks. Once as we followed the trail, I seemed to hear a faint, distant whining, and I reined in at once to listen. But when the horse was still, I could hear only the wind in the trees and the noise of a dislodged stone rolling down the path. Again I called Red's name, but there was no response, so I rode on. I didn't know until later how close to him I was, and that the mountain itself and his own thrashing must have kept him from hearing me.

Near the tall spruce trees I found the area empty of human presence. The only movement was among mountain jays, and the chipmunks that played among the rocks below the trail. Only a few hoof marks in the earth betrayed the presence of the rider who had sat in this spot watching my journey up the valley.

When I came out along the far side, I paused again and gave myself to the impact of the view. Even with all this new desolation inside me—a desolation that matched that of the mountain itself—I felt the same surge of emotion that I had experienced the last time I saw Domino.

Those few broken houses, the single dusty street far below, caught at my heart. It was as if I were being pulled back into my childhood, back into lives I had never known that still affected me. Back, perhaps, to a safer time, before I, too, had begun to live a lie, deceiving myself most of all.

In the gulch below me straggled the timbers of what had once been the thriving mining camp, and I found again the one house that had been preserved and that still belonged to Persis Morgan. As I sat my horse, studying it, something seemed to move down there—as it had before. Had my mysterious horseman gone down into Domino, and was he perhaps watching me from amid the wreckage? No matter if he was. Undoubtedly there were riders up the valley from time to time, doing Ingram's bidding, but they needn't threaten me. What had happened to Jon had been deliberate, planned, and no one except Caleb and Sam knew I was here.

In any case it was not down into Domino that I would

ride today. The mine ruins lay over on my right, with the remnants of the trail leading toward them. I followed the curve of the hill past ugly tailing mounds, still calling for my dog.

I had no answer, and I was afraid my search was hopeless. But before I turned back, I would ride a little closer to the entrance and try shouting for Red again. I knew that if he could hear me he would respond with an ecstasy of barking.

Baby Doe picked her way gingerly along the slope. Now, as I neared the entrance, I saw something surprising. The door to the mine stood open. The entry was a gaping black hole in the side of the mountain, with the wooden door standing open on its hinges, the padlock hanging loose. I felt hair stir at the nape of my neck, and I knew that an eerie fear of this place was part of my childhood. A fear that reason could not quiet.

Here in this high spot the sun was hot on my face, reflecting from the tailings, where nothing grew, yet at the same time a wind moaned around the shoulder of Old Desolate, cold at the back of my neck. As cold as the valley wind had been yesterday in the cemetery. I wanted nothing more than to wheel my horse about and escape from this haunted place as quickly as I could.

But reason held me there. With the mine open Red could have wandered inside. He could be helplessly trapped, and the least I could do was to go to the entrance and call to him.

Near the square black opening, framed in supporting timbers, I dismounted and peered in. Past the doorway there was nothing to be seen but blackness. A cold musty odor seemed to flow out from the depths of the mountain.

Again I shouted for Red, and this time, faintly and from a distance, but more distinctly than before, I heard the high whining of a dog. I called out loudly, and there was a wild barking and yelping in response. I knew a cry for help when I heard it. Red was in the mine and trapped in some way so that he couldn't get out.

I checked myself from rushing headlong through that open door, remembering the things Jon had told me about old mines. I would take no chances. Perhaps I could ride down into Domino and get old Tully, the watchman, to help me find my dog.

The barking grew more frantic. I looped Baby Doe's reins through the rusty iron handle of the open door and took out my flashlight. Before I went for help I would see if I could locate the direction of Red's barking. The slim pencil of light helped very little in cutting the black wall of darkness, but at least it showed a flat expanse of earth that hadn't been choked with debris. I went in a few steps, listening to the explosions of sound Red was making. Because of the echoing inside the mine it was difficult to find the exact direction, but it seemed to come from a tunnel that branched off on my right. I moved a few cautious steps more toward the sound, shouting again to keep him barking. My voice roused further echoes that seemed to crash through the rocky tunnels of the mine.

I tried speaking more quietly, telling him to "Stay," assuring him that I would be back for him soon. Then I turned toward the welcome square of sunlight that marked the opening. If Tully was of no use to me, then I must ride back to the ranch and get Sam.

I had gone inside farther than I'd intended, and as I moved toward the door, something terrifying happened. Without warning the sunlit square of the opening was no longer square. A wedge of blackness had cut across it, and the yellow band was swiftly narrowing. Even as I flung myself toward the opening, the wooden door slammed shut and I heard the click of the padlock that secured it. Outside, Baby Doe whinnied and stamped.

I called out frantically. "Wait, wait! Don't go away! I'm in here—don't shut me in!"

But whoever had closed that door had seen my horse and must know where I was. So the closing of the door had been deliberate.

Outside I heard Baby Doe whinny again, heard another horse answer, followed by the sound of hooves moving away. I shouted again in desperation so that the echoes crashed and Red began to yelp piteously—at some distance away.

The noise was awful, and I made myself be still, listening. Beyond the door there was only silence. The horses were gone. It was not by any mistake that I had been shut in here and my horse led away.

Panic surfaced and I threw myself against the wooden door, hoping the hinges might give, or the wood splinter. But though the boards shuddered, my only reward was a bruised shoulder. I stopped my assault quickly.

Darkness—blackness!—the worst thing of all. The beam of my flashlight was strong enough for only a limited area, and I hoped the batteries were new. I mustn't lose my head. All I had to do was wait for help to come. Both Caleb and Sam knew where I had ridden. However, it might be a long while before one of them decided that I'd been away an unreasonable length of time.

Black silence seemed to have a pressure of its own on my eardrums. I moved the beam of light about me cautiously. A false step in any direction might plunge me into some unseen shaft. Yet to sit down and wait in patient surrender was beyond me at that moment. If I moved, if I took some action, perhaps I could hold off a terror that waited for me, just beyond the edge of reason. As a child I knew I'd been horribly afraid of this mine—perhaps only because it was a black pit in the mountain that my father must have shown me. Later it had become the place in which I feared that he had died. But these were thoughts that I must not let in.

At least I wasn't in total ignorance of how the mine lay as it tunneled into the mountain. The book on Morgan mines that I'd studied had shown a diagram of the Old Desolate, its upper passages like veins striking out from the top of a main artery that thrust its way deeply into the earth. There had been brief descriptions of mining operations in the pages I read, and the writer had used the terms of miners. Knowledge that I'd never expected to need.

My flashlight beam picked out the narrow entrance passage where I stood, sloping straight into the mountain. The floor was strewn with debris as I moved farther in, seeking for a way to reach Red. He was quiet now, probably losing hope as I didn't come to him. There were chunks of fallen rock, rotting timbers, an old pickax and other discarded tools left along the way.

Ahead the blackness seemed complete, and I could smell danger in the very odor of dampness and rotting wood, though here near the entrance the air wasn't especially bad. Not yet. Somewhere ahead I knew there would be a deep shaft dropping to the next levels, and down there, deep in the total blackness of the mountain's heart, there would be catwalks along the connecting winzes—the passages—as the book had indicated. At the lowest levels there would probably be water. All of the mine was a honeycomb under my feet, perhaps ready to collapse at any point, to crumble in upon itself. I remembered Jon pointing out the Glory Hole, where men had died in such a collapse, and wondered if that would be my fate. Ladders down the shafts would be rotten now, unless they were of metal, and I could only hope that Red hadn't fallen down there.

The flash beam suddenly cut into an emptiness of space, and I realized that the narrow entrance tunnel I followed had suddenly opened into a vast room with rock walls and high ceiling.

I knew what this was. The main shaft of the mine had not been sunk from outside, with the A-frame and hoist placed over it outdoors, as was usually the custom. Here it must have been necessary to tunnel in for a distance before the shaft was sunk, so that a huge room must be hollowed out to accommodate the hoist that would pull up the big ore buckets and the cage that would take men up and down.

In the tiny piercing light I could use against the black dark, I made out the rotting frame and the pit that opened beneath it, almost at my feet. I stepped back in sudden terror and bit my lip, tasting blood.

This time my voice cracked as I shouted, "Red! Red, are you down there?"

My blessed dog answered mournfully from another direction, and I stepped well away from the edge of the pit. I mustn't let panic take over in this horrible place.

206

Somehow I needed to find the right tunnel in order to reach Red. With his furry body in my arms we could console each other until help came. We weren't in here forever. This I must believe in defiance of voices that whispered in my mind, *Forever, forever!*

I played my light ahead and called to Red until I could feel sure I had located the passage that would lead me to him. It was disturbing that his barking still seemed so far away. A dog might penetrate into a cluttered passageway a great deal farther than I could possibly go. But at least I must try.

The light beam told me that slabbing had been done to some extent in here. I could see what the word meant now—the shoring up of walls and ceiling with supporting timbers, so that the core of rock that held the ore could be removed without the tunnel collapsing. But the book had told me more than I wanted to know. When slabbing failed, as sometimes happened, those beneath could be buried under tons of earth and rock. The manic voices of terror whispered in my mind again.

Dampness and old rot had surely taken their toll, and the slightest disturbance might cause everything to fall in upon me, burying me here in this mountain tomb. Forever. Forever.

"Stop it!" I told myself, but I didn't speak the words aloud because terror lay in the very sound of harsh echoes. I knew the direction now, and I could let the echoes sleep.

This was the way. A small, more crowded passage than the others. A passage whose opening was partially blocked. Red could have squeezed through, but not I. Yet I had to reach him.

I stuck my flashlight in my pocket, and working carefully in the dark, I began to pull away fallen rock and litter from the opening. My hands were quickly cut, but that didn't matter. All that mattered was to reach Red, so that we could comfort each other. To be alone in this place, with nothing alive near me, was the most terrible threat of all. Or at least nothing alive that I wanted to be near.

There hadn't been a real cave-in at the entrance to the

passage, and in a little while I'd made a way I could get through. I used my flash again and saw that the way beyond was not entirely blocked. Blackness stretched ahead into limbo, and I wondered what creeping things might hide away in here. Snakes, Jon had said. And surely rats. But to sit still and wait would be worse than trying to reach my dog.

Now the ceiling was fairly low, as though the tunneling here had not been completed, and I would have to crawl. I dropped to my hands and knees, doing without light again, though the absence of it was always frightening. The walls seemed to close in on me as I crept along, cold and hard and even more alien in the dark.

Once, when I'd turned on the light, something skittered out of my way. No more than a black shadow, but a shadow that would have sharp teeth, I was sure. For a few moments of shuddering I couldn't go on. But I must.

Crawling was more difficult than walking. There was no mud, but there were still clumps of fallen rock and fragments of splintered wood. The cold of deep earth seemed even more penetrating now, and the air was growing stale and unpleasant—a dirty smell, but at least untainted by the odor of gas. There was still oxygen to breathe. Perhaps the opening of the door had filled the tunnels with fresh air for a little while.

I was still fearful of every shadow that might move when my light was on, and even more terrified of what I might put my hand upon in the dark. Both my hands and knees hurt, but that didn't matter. In my own mind lay the greater dangers. If death came from rock above me, it would be quick. Only in my imagination, in the thought of not being found, lay utter horror.

Red's whimpering seemed closer now. I spoke to him softly, told him I was coming, and again I moved on, reaching one cautious hand along the passage floor and then another. I used my light only now and then, conserving its battery being all-important now. There might be hours ahead for me in this place. One glimpse from the beam showed that the walls had moved apart a little, as though a more complete job had been done at this point.

Obviously this hadn't been a large operation, like the rest of the mine. Perhaps this vein had run out quickly and been soon abandoned. I came to a spot where supporting timbers were falling into decay, and I knew they might crash down upon me if they were jarred. I thought again of all those who had been buried in mines during the years of the gold and silver madness.

But still I must move ahead. Gingerly I made my way past the place of danger, and the going became easier. The smell was all-pervading now, smothering me in its thick, earthy odor. I could understand about claustrophobia.

My hand, testing the ground ahead, touched something different, something hard and rounded, with sharp-edged hollows in it. Not a rock. My flesh knew and recognized and recoiled in horror. It was time for light.

The beam played over what was left of what had once been a man. The white skull, the rib cage, the long leg bones and folded arms—all laid out in orderly fashion where he had been left, here in the mine. *Left,* not trapped.

Suddenly I was sure, without any doubt. I *knew* who this man had been. It had to be Noah Armand. More had happened at Morgan House than they had wanted me to guess. Noah, too, must have died, and they had brought him here, left him to the tomb of the mountain. Perhaps it hadn't been my father they meant after all when they had stood in the hallway talking about the mine.

Red barked faintly, questioning, pleading.

"I'm coming," I called.

With the light turned off, I moved carefully, clinging to the side of the tunnel farthest from what lay there, working my way past horror. Only when I was safely beyond did I turn on the light again. Ahead the tunnel took a turn, and as I followed the bend around, my flash showed me Red, lying on his side, his leash caught beneath a chunk of broken rock.

At the sight of me he thrashed and yelped and tried again to free himself. I crept to him and wrapped my arms about his wriggling body while he reached for my face with an ecstatic tongue and shivered with joy.

The air was better now, and I breathed more deeply. Perhaps there was a way out. Perhaps Red hadn't come in through the main door of the mine, but had found another opening in the hillside. Hope took the place of terror, and I let the flashlight burn while I tried to free Red's leash. Now I saw what had been done. No accident has caused this securing of the leather strap. It had been drawn under the big chunk of rock so that only fingers could release it.

Someone had found Red in his wandering. Someone had placed him in this passage and seen to it that he could never extricate himself. Then the message had been sent to me, the mine door left open, knowing that Red's barking would lead me in. I held him tightly and pressed my face against his head that was no longer silky and clean.

"We've got to get out of here," I told him, wincing a little as I looped the leash around my wrist. I didn't know how much more laceration my hands and knees could take, but I had to go on. Then, as I started to crawl again, the sound of shouting reached us from a distance—from outside the mine. Red barked furiously, and I shouted back, recognizing the voice.

"Jon! We're in here! Jon, come and help us out!"

His next shout was much closer. "Keep on yelling so I can locate you, Laurie."

We filled the tunnel with sound, and the echoes no longer mattered. In a few moments Jon was crawling through the far passage.

By the time he reached us, I was weeping in relief. He sat on the floor of the tunnel, drew my head against his shoulder, and let me cry. His arms were around me and his cheek was against my hair. It was wonderful to just let go and stop struggling for my life. And most of all it was wonderful to have Jon hold me. I had come to my own moment of truth.

I'd loved him since I was a little girl, and I loved him now. I had been looking for him in other men through all

210

my years as a woman, yet I wouldn't have dared to tell him this. I could only cling to him and weep in relief.

"That's enough," he said after a moment. "You can finish your bawling outside. Are you all right, Laurie? Can you crawl a little farther?"

I could have crawled anywhere, and Red and I crept after him as he led the way out. Around the next bend we could see daylight, and the air was fresh. Weed growth and the gnarled roots of a fallen pine tree almost blocked the entrance, but Jon squeezed past and pulled us both after him into the sunshine.

The sight of Sundance tethered nearby was very welcome, and the high thin air had never tasted so sweet. I flung myself on the grass with Red beside me. For these few moments I wanted only to know that I was safe and with my love. This intensity of feeling was all I could bear for now. Horror lay just beyond, where reason started, but I still held it away.

"Do you see where you are?" Jon asked after I'd rested for a few minutes.

He was sitting on the grass beside me, not touching me now, but waiting for me to recover with more patience than I might have expected.

I opened my eyes and looked around. The tunnel had wound through the shoulder of the mountain, to come out near the stand of spruce where a lone horseman had sat earlier, watching my progress up the valley. It was that rider who must have waited, knowing I would come, who must have knotted Red's leash and locked me into the mine.

I looked at Jon and saw that his head bandage showed the seeping of fresh blood.

"You've started to bleed again," I said. "You should never have come out. But how lucky for me that you did."

"I'm all right," he assured me. "I scraped myself on the rock in there. When Sam told me you'd ridden out here looking for Red, I came as fast as I could. It's a good thing I kept shouting for you along the way. This old tunnel's been lost for as far back as I can remember. I knew

211

it was supposed to be around here somewhere, but no-body recalled any longer where the opening was. This is where old Dominoes gophered his way to silver."

He was giving me the time I needed by talking.

"The old man started to take out ore before Tremayne and Morgan came along and bought the claim from him. Those old hard-rockers could put in an operation all on their own, or with a partner or two. Most mining was just hard labor anyway. Drilling, picking their way into the rock, planting explosives, and shoveling out blast waste and ore rock—all that was done by hand."

I still wanted to postpone what must be talked about, and I knew Jon was humoring me.

"Why did they work that hard for so little?" I asked, to keep him talking.

"Lure of the treasure hunt, I suppose. Over the years brush swallowed the opening and that tree fell across it. Red must have found his way in, perhaps chasing a chipmunk. Then I suppose he couldn't get out."

"He couldn't get out because someone put him there," I said.

Jon didn't seem surprised. "Can you talk about it now?"

"I have to talk about it. Someone phoned the house and told Caleb he'd heard a dog barking out near the mine. So I rode up here to see for myself. When I reached this spot, I thought I heard Red whining, but I wasn't sure, so I went on to the mine. The door was open and—"

"Open?" Jon broke in. "Smashed open?"

"No. The padlock must have been opened with a key. I went just inside the entrance and started to call for Red. When he answered me, I went in a little farther to locate the direction. I remembered what you said about mines, and I wasn't going to explore. But someone shut the door behind me and closed the padlock."

"God!" Jon said, and the word had an angry sound. He reached for me again and put both arms around me as we sat on the ground.

I had to know more. "Who would have a key to the mine?"

"Your grandmother, of course. And I have one that she had made for me. It's hanging right where I keep it. Her key is at the house."

"Gail," I said. "She must have taken it. She's working with Ingram, and I suppose she could have given the key to him. When I rode out from the ranch, a man on a horse was watching me from right about here. Too far away for me to recognize."

"Tell me the rest," Jon said, and I heard the grim note in his voice.

I told him as best I could. About having a flashlight, thanks to Sam. About finding the right tunnel and starting my long crawl through it toward the sound of Red's frantic response. I was trying to sound matter-of-fact and keep the memory of panic out of my voice, but Jon heard.

"Never mind," he said. "You don't have to suffer through it again. You found Red and I found you."

"First I found Noah Armand," I told him.

He put me at arm's length so he could look into my face, questioning.

"There's always been a mystery about what happened to Noah," I said. "I had a feeling that they'd never told me the whole truth. I still don't know what happened. But his bones are back there in the mine. I had to crawl past them."

As I spoke I could remember that moment all too vividly.

Jon gave me a small shake. "Hang on, Laurie. Don't jump to conclusions. Old bones in a lost mine could belong to anyone. Nothing points to Noah Armand for sure, does it?"

"I suppose an identification could be made, if it came to that. I suppose there would be bits of clothing or jewelry. All I know is that he is part of whatever happened. Jon, I went into the back parlor today, and I opened that box. I remembered. *You* know what I did, don't you? You know that I loaded one of those deringers that my

213

grandmother had kept, and I shot and killed my own father."

He held me tightly. "I only know rumors. Hints my mother dropped. Take it easy, Laurie."

I could talk now, with my head against his chest, though words came out starkly.

"I remembered some of it. I remembered firing the gun. And Caleb told me the rest. Persis had told me some of it, too—earlier. That my mother was going to run away with Noah Armand. My father came home in time to find his wife in the back parlor, probably in Noah's arms. I was there behind a sofa, playing with those deringers. So when I thought Noah was going to hurt my father, I must have shot, meaning to stop him. Instead it was my father who died." My words faded sickly away.

Jon held me, and there was a deep tenderness in him. For a moment I clung to him. Then he sat me up away from him.

"We'd better start back soon." My face was still wet with tears, and he touched a finger to my cheek. "Don't look like that. *You* didn't kill Richard Morgan. A child did. A child who couldn't possibly know what she was doing. Someone from a long time ago. If you'd grown up with the knowledge, you'd feel easier now. It's come too suddenly, and that can be shattering. Just give yourself time."

He drew me up and I stood close to him. "Jon, last night at that awful dinner I told Mark Ingram that I'm going to stay here with my grandmother. So perhaps that's why he had me locked in the mine."

"Could be. Let's get back to the ranch now, so you can tell your grandmother the whole thing."

"But that will worry her—and she's helpless."

"Not so helpless now that you're here. She'll want to know."

"Even about those bones?"

"Everything. Though she may already know about them. If she hasn't always acted wisely in the past, then she needs everything you can tell her so that she can deal with the present now."

"Must it be reported?"

"It should be, I suppose, but let's wait until you've told Persis."

"What are you going to do now?"

I'd never seen him look so grim. "I mean to have a talk with Ingram as soon as possible. Up you go on Sundance. Give me your foot."

I didn't want to take his horse. He had been hurt far more seriously than I. Except for a few cuts and scrapes, all my hurts were inner. But I knew there was no use arguing with Jon Maddocks, and when I was in the saddle, holding the reins gingerly, he walked beside me, a hand on the bridle, quieting Sundance, who was feeling mettlesome. I'd unclipped Red's leash, but he had no wish to stray from me again, and he came along willingly when I called him.

As we started down the valley, I thought of an old question that still troubled me. We were closer now, Jon and I, and I could ask him.

"What did you mean when you said I had to earn the right to know?"

He looked up at me, and again there was a tenderness in him that I yearned toward. "You're earning your way just fine, Laurie. I'm sorry it's had to be so rough. When you come out on the other side you'll know for sure what you're made of."

Would I? Would I ever know for sure? I certainly didn't know right now.

Jon pointed ahead, and I saw that Baby Doe had been tethered near a few cottonwoods by the stream below the trail. She stamped and whinnied her impatience at the sight of us.

"The mare was left far enough away from the mine," Jon said, "so that when she was found it would look as though you'd tied her here and wandered off. Yet she couldn't get home on her own. A delaying tactic."

"Do you suppose I'd have been left in the mine? I mean—"

"Don't think about that. You're out. Come on down and I'll put you on your own horse."

215

This time when I dropped into his arms, he let me go quickly, his manner turned brusque, as though his thoughts were already moving ahead, gathering anger for an encounter in which I could take no part. I trusted him to act wisely, but at the same time I was a little afraid. Mark Ingram was more a power than a man, and I didn't know whether Jon could stand up against him.

We rode down the valley together, and when we reached the barn we said nothing in the face of Sam's surprise at our appearance. Jon was only a little less dirt-smeared than I, but this was no time for explanations.

"Better go clean up, Laurie," Jon said, "before you see your grandmother."

I looked into smoky gray eyes and saw kindness there, and a concern for me that almost brought the tears, but I didn't find what I most wanted. I turned Red over to Sam and walked away quickly.

At the house the same look of surprise that Sam had shown met me in Caleb's eyes as he came downstairs from my grandmother's room.

"What has happened to you?" he asked.

I explained briefly. "I went looking for Red and I was shut into the mine on Old Desolate. It was lucky that Jon Maddocks came looking for me and helped me to get out."

"Shut in?" He continued to stare at me.

"Yes, and the padlock closed. Who was it that phoned you about hearing Red on the mountain?"

"I have no idea. He didn't give his name, though he said he'd talked to Belle. But, Laurie, how could you possibly—"

"It was a trick." I broke in on his disbelieving words. "Someone tied Red inside an old tunnel, and when I took the bait the door was shut on me. And locked."

He looked genuinely dismayed, but I couldn't trust him now. I couldn't trust anyone.

"How did you get into the mine?" he asked.

"The door was left open. On purpose, I suppose. Where does my grandmother keep the key?"

He moved to a small table in the hall. "Keys not often

in use are képt in this drawer. Here you are. You can see that the key is tagged."

I took the ordinary padlock key from him and read the name *Old Desolate* on the tag. The key had either been replaced quickly or another one existed besides Jon's. I gave it back.

"Nevertheless," I said, "the door was open when I went in, and it was shut on me and locked." I didn't like his air of skepticism, and I started past him up the stairs. "As soon as I've showered and changed my clothes, I'll want to see my grandmother. She must be told about what has happened."

"I'm afraid that won't be possible," he said.

I paused on the stairs to look down at him. "What do you mean—it won't be possible?"

His expression was as disapproving of me as ever. "I mean that Mrs. Morgan has been unconscious for several hours. We've sent for Dr. Burton, but it may take a while for him to arrive."

For a moment longer I stood staring down at him. Then I ran up to Persis Morgan's room. Gail waited in the doorway, and she didn't mean to let me in.

XV

"I want to see my grandmother," I said to Gail.

Caleb had come up the stairs behind me, and he put a hand on my arm. "Let her be, Laurie. She won't know you now."

He had aligned himself with the nurse, and neither of them wanted me in that room.

"Just let me by," I said.

Gail shrugged and stepped out of my way.

From downstairs I heard Hillary's voice. "Laurie, are you there? Is anybody home?"

I called down to him, glad for an ally of my own. "I'm up here. Come upstairs, Hillary."

I didn't wait for him, but walked into the darkened room. Hillary must have heard the tension in my voice, for he came up the stairs two at a time.

"What's going on?" he said as he joined me, dropping his voice.

"Persis is unconscious," I told him. "And Gail and Caleb don't want me in her room."

His eyebrows raised expressively and he looked around at them. Neither spoke or offered further objections.

Heavy draperies of an oppressive brown had been pulled across the windows to shut out the light, and the room seemed airless, its very atmosphere stifling. From the bed I could hear Persis Morgan's heavy breathing. I ran to the window and pulled aside all that dark weight, raised the sashes to let in air and sunshine. Looking out, I glimpsed the town, bustling with activity as it did all day, the mountains rising austerely behind. Then I went to the bed and bent over my grandmother's still figure.

She lay on her back, her mouth slightly open, her breathing stertorous. One hand lay outside the covers, and I touched it.

"Grandmother, can you hear me?"

"Of course she can't hear you," Caleb said from the doorway, but he kept his voice low.

"I don't think she's asleep," I said. "And I don't think she's unconscious because she's ill. I think she's been drugged. There was too much sedation this time, wasn't there?"

Gail came into the room, crisply in charge. "She's had no more than her usual pills," she assured me.

I doubted that, and I stood beside the bed, trying to think what to do.

Hillary put an arm about me. "I don't know what's happened to you, Laurie, but you'd better go and clean up. Then you're coming with me. There's no way you can help your grandmother right now."

That wasn't true. I must think of something. But about one thing he was right. I needed to shower and bathe my cuts. Then, when I felt better, I would know what to do.

"When will the doctor be here?" I asked.

"It will probably take him an hour or more," Gail said. "In the meantime you look as though you need food."

"I don't want anything to eat," I told her, and Hillary said he'd had lunch at the hotel, and he would wait for me downstairs.

I hurried down to my room to get out of my clothes. When I stood before the mirror in the bathroom I saw dirt streaking my face, with bits of wood and earth caught in my hair. In an instant I was back in the mine, remembering, trapped and frightened, with that smooth skull under my hand.

Hastily I splashed water on my face, shed my clothes, and stepped under the shower. For a moment all I wanted was to wash memory away, to stop being afraid. But my escape from the mine hadn't freed either Jon Maddocks or me from the danger that threatened us, and threatened Persis Morgan as well. I must talk to Jon as soon as possible. And there was one other thing I would do. I would go to the hotel and find Belle Durant, remind her of her promise to help if she was needed.

When I went downstairs I found Hillary in the parlor, looking through Morgan albums, absorbed in old pictures. He had stopped at the snapshot I had found of Noah Armand.

I could feel myself freezing at the sight of it, and Hillary saw my face. "What's the matter, Laurie?"

I didn't want to talk about those bones in the tunnel. Not now. There was too much I needed to do.

"I want to go over to the hotel," I said.

He smiled at me. "That's just where I plan to take you. There's something I want you to see. A little distraction won't hurt right now, and you can come back here quickly before the doctor arrives."

I knew he was going to put his arms around me, but when I stepped back he let me go. "Something's been

219

happening since we came here, hasn't it, Laurie? You've turned into a woman I don't entirely know."

I tried not to hear his words as dialogue from a play. He must have feelings—deep feelings— but I was beginning to realize that I didn't know what they were.

"We have to talk, Hillary. But not now. Not while my grandmother—"

"I know," he said gently. "Come along with me now, and I promise I'll get you back here quickly. I do want to show you something."

"All right," I said. "But first I have a phone call to make."

He waited for me in the parlor. Jon's number was in the small book by the hall telephone, and I dialed it quickly. But though I let the ringing go on for some time, he didn't answer. Probably because he had already gone to his meeting with Ingram? Perhaps I would find him at the hotel too. An increasing sense of anxiety was rising in me.

Hillary's mood seemed cheerful enough, and I knew he didn't really believe anything was seriously wrong between us. But I couldn't convince him now. We crossed the yard together, and at the gate I stopped and looked back at the house. Once more brown draperies had been drawn in Persis Morgan's room and the windows closed. I was sorrier than ever that I hadn't urged more strongly for Gail Cullen's dismissal while I had the chance.

Along the street we walked beneath scaffolding, dodged workmen, picked our way past debris that was being cleared out of one of the false-front buildings. When we reached the Timberline, we found Belle at the desk, looking rather distant and unwelcoming. It wasn't going to be easy to approach her, but I must say what I'd come to say. I must remind her of a half promise she had made me that time in the cemetery.

Mark Ingram was there as well, large and benevolent and assured. A benevolence I trusted even less than before. Impeccable in his gray cords, the silver-topped cane in one large hand, he beamed at us. There was no sign of

220

Jon, to my relief. I must tell Hillary all that had happened, but when we were alone—not here.

I spoke directly to Belle. "My grandmother needs you. She's been oversedated and she's unconscious. The doctor has been sent for, but she ought to have better care than she's getting. More trustworthy care." I flicked a quick look at Ingram, but he was impassive, merely listening. "Belle, will you come?" I pleaded.

She hesitated, obviously uncomfortable. Then she glanced at Ingram. "Sorry, my job is here."

I would have to get her alone, I thought. I would give my words time to soak in, and come back to the attack later. Belle, I suspected, was not one to act impulsively. However, I had another question to ask her. "Caleb received a phone call from a man who said he'd heard a dog barking over near the mine on Old Desolate. The man told him he'd spoken to you and you said the dog probably belonged to me. Can you tell me who he was?"

"Nobody talked to me about any dog," she said.

I stared at Ingram, but his expression still exuded that benevolence I didn't trust, and I knew he would admit to nothing.

Hillary sensed an impasse and broke in, speaking to Ingram. "I'd like to show Laurie the Opera House. We won't be long."

Ingram's expansive mood reached out to all of us in an excess of goodwill that I didn't believe in for one moment.

"A fine idea," he said. "In fact, I'd like to show it to Miss Morgan myself. Belle, come along with us. You're not needed here right now."

Moving with obvious reluctance, she came from behind the desk.

I didn't want to spend time sight-seeing, but this might be my one chance to have a further word with Belle. I tried to relax and not fidget.

As we crossed the street, I sensed that a hint of something electric was stirring in Hillary. He was planning some moment of drama that I didn't welcome at this time. I would have to deal with it when it came and try to get this visit to the Opera House over as quickly as possible.

The double doors stood open, and the lighting system had already been repaired and connected inside, so that illumination flared when Ingram touched a switch. Moving ahead of us, Hillary went eagerly to pull open the door to the orchestra, and I stood at the head of a dark aisle, waiting for the house lights to come on.

It was Belle who went to find the switch, and the dull glitter of a chandelier, dusty wih disuse, bloomed overhead, along with tulip-shaped lights along the side walls. Someone had at least swept out the orchestra pit, and the floor and spaces between dilapidated seats were clean enough. Ahead and below us the stage stood dark and shadowy, the curtain—what was left of it—raised into the proscenium arch, its edges frayed by age.

"Isn't it beautiful?" Hillary whispered, as though reluctant to disturb old ghosts.

I knew he was seeing it as it could be, and I nodded.

"Red and gold, of course," he went on. "Lots of velvet. The two tiers of boxes on either side of the stage are jewels in themselves. Their brass rails should be restored, and all the seats must be red. It can be a beautifully rich little house!"

He had forgotten my grandmother, forgotten all our problems, in his rapture over this theater.

Mark Ingram smiled blandly. "You're right, of course. I've been thinking of bringing out an expert from New York to do the theater over. So I'm glad to have your impression."

I looked quickly at Hillary and saw a flash of very real anger in his face. He didn't like this man any better than I did, but he coveted this theater.

Ingram must have seen the look too, but it only amused him. He had a talent for stirring up emotion, playing with it. All this was rather a game to him. Destroying my grandmother was a game. Had shutting me into a mine tunnel also been a rather deadly game?

Now he laughed. "I *had* been thinking of sending for an expert, but perhaps I won't need to. The job is yours, Hillary, if you want it."

His anger didn't die out at once, and this time the real

222

Hillary was coming through. For an instant I glimpsed his passion for the theater—all aspects of the theater. Then he was his charming self again and laughing with Ingram. But I didn't think he had liked being manipulated, even though he might be willing to work for Mark Ingram because of the theater.

Belle had rejoined us and was listening, still looking uncomfortable. "When you refurbish it, Mark, who's to come? There are a dozen more easily accessible old towns in Colorado that have more to offer than this one."

Ingram's soft chuckle wasn't particularly pleasant to hear. He was enjoying every movement of his chessmen. "Belle is our local pessimist. She lacks vision, I'm afraid. But you and I can see the future, can't we, Hillary?"

Hillary was no longer listening. He'd started off by himself, lost in his own fantasy of what this theater would one day be, caught up in his own excitement.

"Come look here, sir," he called out, and I winced at the "sir." Hillary was playing his own game too, erasing that moment of open anger, presenting the role of a young man, extremely respectful toward one who was older and wiser.

"I suppose your friend will be writing and acting in his own plays?" That was Belle's whisper rasping in my ear.

I looked at her more carefully in the dusty light. She hadn't bothered with makeup today, and her wide cheekbones were more prominent than ever, her untinted mouth large and a bit rebellious.

I asked a question that was not entirely idle. "Do you know if Mr. Ingram was out on a horse this morning?"

She turned and started down the aisle because Ingram was beckoning to her. "I wouldn't know," she said over her shoulder. "I had a hangover this morning, and I didn't get up until a little while ago. He's still peeved with me about that."

I followed her down the aisle to the edge of the stage, where Ingram and Hillary were conferring. The older man was gesturing toward a rickety wooden gallery that could be reached by stairs backstage. A catwalk ran above ropes and pulleys, controlling the flats that made up what

223

was left of stage scenery. I felt an odd sense of recognition, though I didn't know why.

"All that trash will have to come down," Ingram said. "There are a couple of old dressing rooms in the loft up there—too small and inconvenient. We'll clean it all out and build some decent rooms backstage, even if we have to add an annex. Will you go up and have a look, Hillary? I don't think you've been up there. Belle can show you the way. Those stairs are a bit too steep for me—harder to get down than up."

"Of course," Hillary agreed cheerfully. "Come along, Laurie. Let's explore."

He went ahead of me toward the door at the left of the stage, and ran up the few steps.

Belle came after us more slowly, still reluctant. "This place gives me the creeps. I'm not much for ghosts, but I can believe in them back here."

I could too. It was dim backstage, and the air seemed cold and musty. There was a smell of dust as we moved about. I stood between wings that seemed to represent a street scene beneath ancient grime, and looked across the stage. By New York standards it was small, but any empty stage can seem large.

"Look up there," Belle said, pointing to the gallery that ran across the back above the flats. "One young soubrette is supposed to have thrown herself down from there, breaking her neck when she hit the stage."

I shivered, but Hillary was calling to me. "This is the way up. Come on, Laurie. I want you to see the theater from up here."

Belle gave me a little push. "Go ahead. I've been up before. Just watch yourselves, you two."

Hillary climbed first, light and graceful as a cat, and I took hold of the unsteady rail and went after him. As always, I was ready to climb anything. I would choose heights over depths any day, but something else was pulling me now. I had been up here before. The steps reached a landing and then climbed again, and I looked down at Belle, her wide face upturned, watching us, her look anxious.

"Be careful!" she called.

Hillary paid no attention. I knew his imagination was leaping ahead to how it was all going to be, and he began explaining to me how perfect, how beautiful, how comfortable for both the theater's patrons and for the actors backstage everything could be made.

"Look at this," he said, poking into a tiny dressing room that boasted a cracked mirror on the wall and a sagging makeup shelf. "Imagine all the itinerant actors who have occupied this room, dressing and making up in front of that very mirror. And then going out to the cheers and jeers of an audience of miners. Maybe that's what I'll do a play about—one of those actors. And of course the miner's daughter who loved him. It can be beautifully corny, Laurie, and today's audiences will love the nostalgia."

I hardly heard him, because it was not the shabby little dressing room that drew me but the long gallery that stretched high above the stage. I could almost hear my father's voice echoing in this high place.

All right, my little mountain goat! We'll have a look if you must. Wait till I see if it's safe.

That remembered voice drew me. I knew we had gone out there together. I left Hillary to his make-believe and stepped carefully onto what was hardly more than a catwalk. The railing was steady enough, and the wood underfoot seemed firm. I moved cautiously, drawn by the spell of memory that was so strong in me, and by a sense of long-lost companionship. Always I had loved to stand in high places where I could see what no one else could see, and my father had understood my compulsion.

If I went just a little farther out I would be able to view the whole theater, as I had seen it long ago with him.

I inched toward the middle of the stage, where I could look down from what seemed a vast height above the bare boards, to where Mark Ingram stood before the row of old-fashioned footlights, staring up at me. Beyond him lay the entire dim and dusty theater, clear to a dark row of back seats. It was as exhilarating as standing on a moun-

225

tain, and I could almost feel my hand in my father's strong clasp, protecting me.

Had Sissy Tremayne ever danced and sung on this stage in the days before she married her Englishman and went to live in the mining camp of Domino? It was possible.

"Come back, Laurie," Hillary called. "It can't be safe out there."

I took one more tentative step toward the center of the walk and heard the cracking of rotten wood. Not the railing that I clung to with my lacerated hands, but the boards under my feet. Before I could recover and draw back, one foot was going through a widening crack. The stage below me showed through jagged splinters—a drop that could break every bone in my body. My scream sounded thin and high, and I clung with all my strength to a railing that had begun to shake.

Hillary was there in an instant behind me, moving lightly, surely. "Hang on," he said. "I can get you."

His arm came about my body with wiry strength just as my leg went through, and he pulled me back slowly from the widening crack.

"Let go, Laurie, It's all right now."

When I managed to uncurl my fingers from about the rail and he'd drawn me to safety, he led me down the stairs to where Belle waited, her face white with shock.

"My God!" she said. "I thought you were a goner for sure. Like that actress I was telling you about. Come on back to the hotel, hon, and I'll get you a good stiff brandy."

Mark Ingram joined us backstage, looking like a gray lion, and not at all pleased with me. "Are you all right, Miss Morgan? Can you walk? I must say that was a stupid thing to do."

I had a feeling that my shin was bleeding, and I sat on the steps to the orchestra, to pull up my pants leg. New scratches ran down the leg—and they had begun to burn.

Ingram took charge, leading the way back to the hotel, while I walked with Hillary's arm around me on one side

226

and Belle supporting me on the other. I could have walked alone. Mostly I was just shaky from my fright.

In Ingram's office behind the hotel desk I was seated on a sofa, with my leg outstretched, while Belle busied herself sponging blood away.

"What have you been doing?" she asked, looking at the raw patch on my knee.

I didn't answer. Oddly enough, now that my first moments of fright were over, I wasn't particularly upset. In a way that I couldn't explain I had again made contact with my childhood. Besides, anything that happened to me from now on, however disastrous, would pale when I compared it to that tunnel in the mine. To die was to die, but there were some ways more horrible than others. Or perhaps I was just getting too numb to feel anything at all anymore. The only active need I had was to get back to Morgan House to see my grandmother, and to talk to Jon Maddocks.

Hillary tried to reassure me. "Don't look so stricken, Laurie. You held on fine, and everything's okay. You weren't ever in any real danger because I was right there."

"I don't agree," Ingram said. "There was plenty of danger."

Belle, busy with her ministering, looked up, and I turned my head so that I could see Mark Ingram sitting behind the wide expanse of mahogany desk in his office.

"It begins to seem, Miss Morgan," he went on, "that you are accident-prone. I knew that old story of the deringer. Miss Cullen has told me. And I know about your memory returning, so you're aware of what happened in the past. Then there's the escapade in the mine this morning, with the door blowing shut—or whatever happened—so that you were almost trapped inside. Now, finally, this. You could have been killed if you'd dropped to the stage. Enough is enough. I don't want anything more happening to you."

Belle spoke slyly. "It will give Jasper a bad name if you get yourself killed around here, Laurie. Mark wouldn't like that."

"What's this about the mine?" Hillary asked, and I remembered that I still hadn't told him. I only shook my head.

Ingram scowled at Belle and she subsided. When he looked like that, his benevolence was gone and he resembled a buccaneer, I thought—completely ruthless and without mercy. He was trying to frighten me off. If I wouldn't leave any other way.

"What about the mine?" Hillary insisted, but I cut in on him.

"How did you know about what happened?" I asked Ingram.

"Maddocks has been here. With some pretty strong words. I don't like what has happened any more than he does, but all this is something we can deal with among ourselves."

"You mean you didn't send those men to beat Jon up yesterday?" I demanded.

Hillary pressed a hand on my shoulder. "Take it easy, Laurie."

"You're in no position to make accusations—either you or Maddocks," Ingram said coolly. "Not if you want your grandmother to stay in her house for whatever time is left to her. But that's not what I want to talk about now. Hillary, this morning Miss Morgan went in search of her dog on Old Desolate and managed to get herself trapped in the mine. Or thought she did. It was lucky for her that Maddocks was able to bring her out. Now I would like you to take her back to New York. When she has safely returned to where she belongs, you can come back here and get to work on the theater. With fewer worries to distract you. I'm going to commission you for the entire job."

Obviously Jon hadn't told him about my finding bones in the mine, or he would have mentioned it.

"If the wind blew the door to the mine shut," I said, ignoring his outrageous words, "how did it manage to fasten the padlock?"

He smiled at me—a pirate's smile. "I don't know what you're talking about, but did you examine the door after
228

you got out to learn whether the padlock really closed it or the door just happened to jam? Isn't the latter more likely?"

Jon and I had not gone back to look at the door, and I felt an edge of uncertainty crowding in. Something I didn't want to accept. It would be too late now to go back and check. By this time, I suspected, the padlock would hang open and the door would really be jammed.

Hillary was silent, listening in amazement.

"In any case," I said, "I'm not leaving for New York. I'm staying right here, and I want to get back to my grandmother as soon as I can."

"I understand she has gone into a coma," he said. "This may be serious."

"She's been drugged," I told him. "I'm going back to her now. I want to be there when the doctor comes."

"You may as well start packing at the same time. I'll have Belle make reservations for a plane from Denver tomorrow. Hillary, you can borrow my car for the drive down. I'll send one of my men with you."

Hillary came suddenly to life. "Sorry, Mr. Ingram, but Laurie isn't leaving. She doesn't want to go, and I want her here with me. We're planning to be married anyway, and we may as well make it now as later. Then, if her grandmother will permit, we could move in temporarily and keep an eye on what is happening. What do you think, Laurie?"

His words left me speechless. We'd never talked seriously about marriage—by Hillary's choice. Not even in the days when I'd believed that Hillary Lange was the only possible man in the world for me. Now I was beginning to distrust myself, to wonder about my own judgment, my tendency to waver in my emotions. He was waiting for a response, his eyes bright with a new exhilaration, as though his enormous self-confidence could carry him through in whatever he proposed. It occurred to me in that moment of astonishment that Hillary Lange had never been conditioned to failure. He had never had to fail.

Before I could find anything to say, however, Ingram

began to laugh. I didn't think he was tuned in to failure either, and when he gave in quite gracefully, my misgivings increased.

"All right," he said. "If that's what you want, Hillary. If you're willing to take over the risk of having this danger-prone young lady on the premises, I wash my hands of all responsibility."

There was something both challenging and a little wicked in the look Hillary turned upon me, as though he dared me to deny his words. What role was this? Machiavelli, perhaps? Whatever he was doing, whatever his motive, I couldn't let him go on.

"I'm not getting married," I said, and then continued in a rush before he could speak. "I want to go back to my grandmother right now. I want to talk with her when I can and find out what she wants me to do. Certainly I'm not leaving Jasper."

"I'm sorry to be so sudden, Laurie," Hillary said, not believing me in the least. "I do get carried away sometimes."

I wasn't getting through to him, I thought helplessly, but now wasn't the right moment to try—not with Belle and Ingram there.

"It may already be too late to talk to your grandmother," Ingram said. "But go on back to the house and see if you can stay out of trouble for a while. Better take care of that leg while you're about it. Belle will drive you over in my car. I expect you'll want to go along, Hillary."

He was still managing us, and I didn't like his words about my grandmother, but this was royal dismissal, and I knew he was displeased with all of us. At least I could escape now, without further argument.

Hillary helped me out to Ingram's station wagon, and I sat with my leg outstretched while Belle took the wheel. Hillary was being considerate and careful, and for once completely oblivious of my feelings. Perhaps he was choosing to be oblivious.

I spoke to Belle. "Are you sure you won't change your mind and help with my grandmother? We need you badly, if only for a little while."

She shook her head, her lips pressed tight.

When we reached the fence across Morgan property, we found a strange car parked near the gate.

"The doctor must have arrived," I said. "Hillary, you needn't come in with me. My leg isn't that bad, and I can manage fine."

Hillary came around to help me out of the car, but before I took his hand I turned back to Belle.

"Just come in for a moment," I urged. "Just come in and see her, Belle."

Perhaps I was exerting a greater strength of will than I'd known I possessed, because her resistance began to crumble. I gave her a little push and she got of the car.

I smiled at Hillary. "It will be all right now. It has to be."

"Of course," he said. "But I need to talk to you, Laurie."

"Not now, please. Later. Persis has to come first."

"All right," he said. "You needn't hurry, Belle. I'll walk back to the hotel."

As he strolled away I heard him whistling. It was a cheerful sound, unmarked by worry. Belle and I went down the walk together and into the house. She didn't look at me, and her lips were still pressed tightly together in resistance. But now that I had her this far, I wouldn't let her go.

Upstairs, we found the door to Persis' room open. Caleb glanced around at Belle in surprise, and then beckoned us in. Bending over my grandmother, with Gail beside him, crisply the nurse again, the doctor was examining his patient with a stethoscope, then raising an eyelid to see the pupil.

Someone had once more opened the draperies to let air into the big room, and I was thankful for that. In the brighter light I could see that Persis had been turned on her side, and her breathing seemed to have quieted, so that she slept more peacefully.

When the doctor stepped back from the bed, Caleb introduced me to him, and he nodded to Belle. Dr. Burton was a small, plump man, with shrewd eyes that were not unsympathetic. He wasted little time on the amenities.

"She's sedated," he said. "But she's not too deeply unconscious. Miss Cullen must watch her for any changes, but her state isn't dangerous, considering the few pills Miss Cullen thinks she has taken. She still responds to pain—a good sign. She'll sleep her way out of this and be drowsy for a while."

"How did it happen?" I asked.

Gail spoke quickly. "I've already explained to Dr. Burton. Mrs. Morgan always wants her sleeping capsules near her bed—so she can take them or not as she chooses. There's been no need to ration them since she's seldom willing to use them. But this time a few are missing. Not enough to be serious."

"I'm relieved," Caleb said, and I wondered if he really was. I would wonder that until I had a chance to talk with my grandmother and ask why she had taken those capsules. *If* she really had taken them herself.

Belle spoke for the first time. "How long do you think she'll sleep?"

Dr. Burton was putting away his instruments. "She's been sleeping for a number of hours, so it may not be too much longer. Give her plenty of liquids when she wakes and anything she wants to eat. I'll try to get back this way later."

When we went out of the room, I followed and stopped him at the head of the stairs. "Dr. Burton, how did you happen to find Gail Cullen for this post?"

"Why—she came to me looking for private work. I've known her since she was a little girl. She didn't mind coming up here, so the arrangement was very suitable."

"I don't think my grandmother took those capsules on her own," I said.

He blinked at me uncomfortably. "Come now, Miss Morgan. Gail Cullen is a capable nurse. And of course Caleb Hawes is an old friend. Just what are you suggesting?"

"Nothing," I said, and turned away.

He paused at the top of the stairs. "I know your grandmother well. You have to remember that old people get absentminded sometimes. She's been failing in the last months, and she may not have remembered what she'd taken."

"That's possible. Anyway, I hope I can persuade Belle Durant to stay here for a while now and look after her."

"But Miss Cullen is—"

"We'll see about Miss Cullen," I told him, and went back to the bedroom.

For a moment I stood in the doorway, trying to summon the courage I knew I was going to need. Belle was bending over Persis while Gail watched, clearly indignant.

Caleb came toward me. "Why have you brought that woman here?" he demanded.

"Because I mean to let Miss Cullen go," I told him. "I want Belle Durant to stay with my grandmother, if she will."

"You have no authority—" Caleb began.

I didn't let him finish. "I'm her granddaughter. I have the authority of blood. I don't think you are going to put me out, are you?" I walked past Gail to Belle. "What do you think?"

Belle shrugged. "Doc Burton's probably right. Nothing to be done till she wakes up. Wish I'd caught her sooner, got some coffee down her, stopped this from happening."

"Will you stay?" I said. "Not for me, Belle. For her."

Gail stepped forward. "I won't have this interference with a patient. I don't know how she came to take those extra capsules, and I can't be held responsible—" She threw a helpless look at Caleb, who said nothing at all.

"I'm taking the responsibility out of your hands," I said. "You've already failed at your post, and it's best if you leave as soon as possible. I'll see that arrangements are made to take you where you want to go."

Her mouth dropped open and her stare was one of astonishment. A small, warm feeling of triumph spread through me. I hadn't known I could sound like this. I hadn't ever tried to take charge of anything before. Yet now neither Caleb nor Gail was standing up to me. With Belle's help perhaps I could do the right thing for Persis

Morgan. With Belle's help and Jon's. I still had to talk to Jon.

"Belle," I said, "you'll stay?"

She gave in. "All right. I'll stay. For a while, anyway. I'll need to go over to the hotel and talk to Mark, pick up a few things. That can wait until she begins to come out of this. But you don't have much of an army to stand against what Mark Ingram wants."

"Jon Maddocks will help," I said. "If you'll stay with my grandmother until I get back, I'll go and talk to him now."

I knew by her look that I had her promise. She drew a chair near the bed and sat down. When I went out the door I found Gail and Caleb talking in the hall, and I passed them without speaking.

The scratch on my leg was superficial, and so were my cuts and bruises from the mine. I could walk well enough, and once outdoors, I found the clear air bracing. For a long while it was as if I had been swimming under water, moving in some element that was strange to me, in which I couldn't think clearly, or be entirely sure of who I was. Now, at least, I was making a stand. I had taken hold of something.

Red came to meet me with his usual uninhibited joy, and I bent to fondle him before I went to the open door of Jon's cabin and looked in. At a wide table near the galley kitchen Jon sat with a loaf of dark bread on a board and a piece of cheese before him.

"I'm hungry," I said. "I seem to have skipped lunch. May I come in?"

XVI

Jon's smile held nothing back. He was my friend and I could trust him. He looked more jaunty than ever with a clean patch of bandage on his head—like a wounded hero. Which he was. Red came in with me and lay down on the hearth. He felt at home here too.

"Help yourself," Jon said, pushing the loaf of bread toward me.

I wanted a lot more than food. I wanted to talk openly and honestly—about everything. No—not quite everything. But at least about what had happened since I'd seen him.

I brought a plate and mug from the cupboard near the sink and sat across from him. The bread was home-baked—his mother's recipe, he said—and I covered a slice with a chunk of longhorn.

He was waiting. "Go ahead," he invited. "Tell me."

"Grandmother Persis is unconscious because of too many sleeping pills, but she'll be all right. Burton thinks she may have taken them absentmindedly. I don't. I think she was given them on purpose. I've brought Belle Durant over from the hotel to stay with her, and I think I've fired Gail Cullen."

Jon's eyes were bright with approval. "Good for you! I always thought there was something fishy about that woman coming here."

"Now she can go back to her employer—Mark Ingram—if that's what he is. He seems to be getting stronger and more sure of himself all the time, and he wants to come over and talk to my grandmother when it's possible. If she doesn't want to see him, I'll try to keep him away. Jon, have you done anything about what happened to you yesterday, and about the mine this morning?"

"After the attack on me I listened to Caleb's advice and didn't report it."

"Why didn't he want it reported?"

"He said it was pointless and nothing could be done. He said it would only upset Mrs. Morgan to have the police coming around again, and unless I had some means of identifying the attackers I'd better let it go."

"I wonder what Caleb is up to."

"Anyway, after you were shut in the mine, I phoned and a couple of officers from the highway patrol were reached by radio and came over right away. As Caleb said, there's not much they can do. They'll want to talk to you, and they'll keep an eye open, but there's no one to arrest, no proof I can give them, except that I was beaten up. At least they've been put on notice. They borrowed horses and rode over to the mine to have a look."

"Where I suppose they found the padlock hanging open and the door firmly jammed?"

"Who suggested that?"

"Mr. Ingram didn't think I'd really been locked in the mine. I expect the door was taken care of right away."

"Too bad we didn't go back and have a look."

"I checked for the key to the mine, and Caleb said it was in the drawer where it's always kept. But Gail could have put it back if she was in on this."

"What else has been happening?"

I chewed for a while on bread and cheese, and then I told him everything at once.

"I nearly fell through the high gallery above the stage at the Opera House. Hillary rescued me. Ingram tried to get him to take me back to Denver, but I said I wouldn't go." I hesitated.

"And . . . ?"

"And I've had a proposal of marriage."

"A busy day. Have you accepted?"

I shook my head, and Jon grinned at me. "Well, don't. Not for a while."

"Not ever from Hillary," I said. "I know that now."

"That's good. Because you're Laurie Morgan and you belong here. And because you're not in love with him."

"I thought I was. I always seem to be thinking that. And then it goes away."

"Fevers pass."

"But I don't like that. I don't like to feel that I can't trust my own emotions. I really thought I was in love with Hillary."

"So? We've all been there a few times—falling in love with something that isn't there, something we only want to believe is real. Then finding out that it isn't."

His words were not entirely comforting, because what if the way I felt about Jon was only another mirage?

I ate my bread and cheese, finished every crumb. And then everything seemed to hit me at once. I did something that astonished me. I put my head down on the table and began to cry. So much had been happening that I hadn't been allowed a quiet time to sit down and think about it, yet the moment when I'd opened a box and picked up a silver-mounted deringer was always with me at the back of my mind. The knowledge of what I had done was like an undertow in the ocean, ready to suck me down. Now, quite suddenly, it had.

Jon left the table and brought back a box of tissues. When I'd mopped my face and blown my nose, I stared at him angrily, though the anger was for myself, not for him.

"I don't know why I did that."

"Of course you do. And I suppose it will keep on hitting you for a while. But somewhere along the line what I've already told you still holds true. You have to accept the fact that it wasn't you, Laurie Morgan, who fired that shot. Not the you who is living now. If you learned this about any other child, wouldn't you understand and forgive?"

"I don't know. It's too awful. And how could I forgive if it was my son who died? I keep thinking about my grandmother and what a terrible time I put her through. And about what I did to my mother." What I had done to my father didn't bear thinking about.

"Your grandmother's over it now. She's had more time than you've had to get used to it, and she's fond of you."

"All these years she's been protecting me from having the truth known. I suppose if it all came out there could be an investigation, even now. I wish I could read what the newspapers said at the time, even if the story wasn't true. I was going to ask Persis to let me see those papers, but there's been no time."

Jon left the table and went to his desk. From a bottom drawer he took a folder and brought it to me.

"There you are. My mother clipped everything. If you really want to read about it."

While he finished his lunch, I ate an apple and read through the clippings. There was a picture of my mother and me as the bereaved. I looked as though I detested the photographer, and my mother seemed to be shielding me. I tried to read her face in the blurry reproduction. What an awful time that must have been for her to live through. Had she really cared about Noah? She must have, to be ready to go off with him. Yet she could well have loved my father too, hating to hurt him. And then to have her child—

I put the picture aside. In still another, Persis Morgan faced the camera indignantly, a younger Caleb at her side. There was a rather handsome picture of Noah too, taken earlier, and some speculation in the account as to his leaving Jasper. No one seemed to suggest, however, that he might have returned, and there seemed to be no suspicion of his death. The probable "intruder" was discussed at length, and the articles he had stolen were listed.

My grandmother had sacrificed three valuable pieces to support her story of a murderer-thief. One was described as a gold plume brooch set with diamonds. There was also a topaz and diamond filigree necklace, and a necklace of cabochon garnets—all beautiful, valuable old pieces that had probably belonged to Sissy Tremayne as she came up in the world.

It was safer to think of the missing jewels than to dwell on tragedy.

"I wonder where Persis had them hidden," I said.

238

Jon began to stack dishes and carry them to the sink. "There are two likely places. In the mine, or in the Tremayne house in Domino. The house seems the most reasonable choice, judging by the way your grandmother doesn't want anyone wandering around in there. Though I've done a lot of work in that house and I've never turned anything up."

Having slept quietly for a while, Red ambled to the door, and Jon let him out. I got up and washed our few dishes, taking my time because I didn't want to leave. Belle was with my grandmother, and there would be little change for a while.

"Do you have work to do?" I asked. "Is it all right if I just sit here quietly for a little while?"

"Sam's taking care of things. Stay as long as you like. I'll get back to work shortly."

"I don't know why, but I feel safer here. The minute I go out that door everything can get at me again. I know I have to go out and face it—but not right away."

Outside it was clouding up as though it might rain, and the air had grown colder. Jon busied himself lighting the fire, and I stretched stomach down on the sofa, with my chin in my hands.

"Belle showed me your wife's grave up in the Morgan cemetery," I said. "What was she like?"

For a few moments he worked at the hearth with his back to me, and I hoped I hadn't offended him. The question seemed a natural one because I wanted to know all that had happened to Jon in those years since he had ridden up the valley to rescue me.

"She was a pixie," he said at last. "Oh, she could do all sorts of practical things. Sew and cook and weave. And feed chickens. But she had an imagination that ran away with her. She was fun to be with, yet I couldn't always tell what she might be thinking. I'm not sure she belonged in the real world. She just lent herself to it at times. If I hadn't brought her here to the ranch, perhaps she'd be alive now, and so would the child. The snow came before I could get her to a hospital. Belle Durant was working for Mrs. Morgan then, and she knew what to do. If it had

239

been a normal birth, we'd have pulled them both through. It wasn't."

Flames roared up the chimney as he built the fire high, and I turned to its warmth, seeking comfort. When the fire suited him, Jon looked around and saw my face.

"Don't be sorry for me, Laurie. Your grandmother helped me through that time. She'd experienced even worse, and she kept me busy—worked my tail off, listened when I wanted to talk, and kept me fighting to live. She made me understand that blame is a waste of time. Any kind of blame. Of oneself or others. Or of fate—whatever you want to call it. What matters is what you do with yourself and your life afterward. That's when we started our scheme to bring Jasper back to life. She wanted to restore it, and we'd begun some of the work before Mark Ingram turned up. She had let too much of it go out of her hands a while back, but she was going to buy it up again and make it into a live town, a working town."

"But what work could there be without tourists?"

"We were going to stock the ranch with grass-fed cattle. There's a growing demand around the country. All natural feed, with no pesticides or hormones used. The men we'd hire would come here to live with their families, and the old services for one another would begin again. There would be tourists too, of course, but they would come to see a mountain town that was alive, and not just make-believe. Then Ingram arrived and started turning the screws. He's only interested in a showplace to bring in money. Since he came, your grandmother has grown weaker. I can't get her to fight anymore, though I hoped you could."

"I think she wants to fight now," I said. "She was showing signs of coming to life when this was done to her. The sleeping pills, I mean. It's a delaying tactic, I think. Perhaps because she was going to change her will. Together we'll manage somehow, and find a way to block Mark Ingram."

"I had a feeling that you were a fighter too," he said. "You had to wake up to what was needed."

240

"How could you know what I didn't know myself?"

"Because I remember how spunky you were as a little girl. No horse could scare you. None of the things your grandmother taught you made you quit, no matter how hard they were. I couldn't believe all that was gone forever."

"I can't have it both ways," I said. "If I'm not the child who fired the gun, in the same way I'm not even a grown-up version of the child you remember. I lost her somewhere along the way."

"No! What happened with the gun was superimposed—an accident. You responded to a frightening situation with a courage that you were too young to handle. That's what you must forgive. The rest hasn't been lost. You don't lose *character*. Maybe you just miss out for a while in developing it."

Was that what had happened to me? I wanted to believe in his words.

Jon's look was warm and kind—that of a loving friend. Which wasn't what I wanted him to be. "You'll be fine, Laurie. Just give yourself a little time."

There was an ache in me, a longing for what I couldn't have, yet at the same time new resolution seemed to rise in me from some unexpected source. I sat up on the couch so I could feel braver.

"Thank you, Jon. I always seem to be thanking you for rescuing me. I always seem to be leaning on you."

He sat down beside me and put an arm about my shoulders. "Leaning's not all that bad, Laurie. Providing it can be done both ways. You have to be willing to be leaned on too. That's what I'm doing now, what Persis Morgan is doing. So why not get started?"

For just a moment I clung to him. Clung physically to his strength and emotionally to his wisdom—both greater than my own. Then I stood up.

"I'll go back to the house now," I told him. "That's where I need to begin."

He came with me to the door, gave me a quick, affectionate hug, and watched me walk away. Red romped at my side on the path to the house. As I hurried into the

241

wind, the longing in me that I couldn't help was stronger than ever. I'd never known before that loving could be so exquisite a pain. Was this the way my mother had felt about Noah Armand? And as hopelessly?

Outside, the world had turned gray and chill, with clouds racing overhead. This time it was really going to storm, and the air had a feeling of electricity to it. Red was ready enough to race me to the house, but he was becoming addicted to the outdoors and made no attempt to follow me inside when I reached the steps. As I crossed the porch to the open front door, the sight that met my eyes was so astonishing that I stood still to stare. Dressed once more in her long red gown, Grandmother Persis was on her feet and being helped down the stairs by Belle Durant. With one hand she clung to the rail, and Belle's strong arm was around her, supporting. Behind them, Caleb exclaimed in horrified protest, while Gail looked down, disapproving, from the floor above.

When Belle saw me, she grinned. "This is your grandmother's idea—not mine. Come and lend a hand, Laurie. I can use some help."

I ran to offer support as Persis came down the last few steps.

"Let's get her into the parlor. Then you can go tell Bitsy to fix her some soup," Belle directed. "And coffee will help too."

When Persis had been helped to the sofa, where she insisted on sitting up, drowsy as she was, I hurried off to the kitchen. No one was there, and I opened the refrigerator. A jar of soup, left over from yesterday, and made with beef and beans and barley, was what I wanted. I heated it, started coffee. Then I carried bowl and cup back to the parlor on a tray.

Caleb and Gail were still in the room. Persis, sitting up against pillows, smiled faintly as I came in.

"How did you manage this?" I asked Belle as she began to spoon the soup for my grandmother.

"She started to wake up soon after you left. I told her about the dose of sleeping pills, and she started to fight

242

her way back. She said it was time to get up and get downstairs. So here she is."

"Stop talking past me!" Persis said. "There's a lot to do."

"You need time to recover," I said. "Just rest for a while."

She took another mouthful of soup and then reached for the coffee cup and held it in both hands. "There's no time for resting. We have to stop that man. First I have to make a new will. Caleb?"

Her words still blurred a little, but she was growing stronger by the moment. He crossed the room to her at once.

"Caleb, have you drawn up a new will, as I asked you to do?"

As always, he held himself in check, but I sensed seething indignation just below the surface of his guard. "There's been no time. And I'm not sure——"

"You can go to work on it right now," Persis told him. "In the meantime, Laurie, bring pencil and paper, and I'll dictate an informal will this minute. Belle and Caleb can witness it, and this will serve until the details are worked out."

Caleb protested. "If I am still a beneficiary, I can't be a witness."

"You won't be the main beneficiary now," she said bluntly. "I've already told you of the change I must make. But you are an old and trusted friend and you will be considered, of course. So you'd better phone Jon. Tell him I want him right away."

Caleb went into the hall to telephone, and I watched him go thoughtfully. I hadn't known until this moment that Caleb would have been the one to benefit most.

Gail had been listening in silence, but now she hurried to a desk to find writing materials and bring them to me. As though she really wanted to help, though I wondered why. Clearly she hadn't taken my "firing" seriously.

Persis regarded her indignantly. "What are you doing here? I told you to go. I told you I didn't need you in this house any longer."

I was beginning to understand. Gail had already been dismissed before I had told her to go. And she had struck back in her own way, trying to stay as long as she could. For whatever reasons prompted her.

Caleb came back. "Jon will be here right away."

"Is this true, Gail?" I asked.

She made a last attempt to stand her ground. "Of course it's not true. Mrs. Morgan is confused. She's not remembering properly. Perhaps she heard you telling me to go, but you have no authority, Laurie."

"I remember perfectly well," Persis said. "I remember that odd tasting glass of milk Edna brought up to me."

"Milk?" Gail said.

"Yes, of course. Edna had been told to bring it up."

"I didn't order any milk for you. Not this time." But she knew she had lost. We were all staring at her, and she gave me a single savage look and then whirled out of the room. I could hear her running up the stairs.

"Let her go and report to Ingram," Persis said. "I'll be glad to have her out of the house. She was a mistake from the first, Caleb."

Caleb said nothing, and there was no telling what he might be thinking.

"Laurie," Persis said, "sit here beside me and we'll get started."

I sat on the sofa beside her with my pen poised, but she found it difficult at first because the fogs of unnatural sleep still clouded her mind. Spells of drowsiness still interfered. Belle fed her more soup and coffee, and finally she began to state what she wanted, so that I could set it down. Jon appeared before she had finished her slow sentences, and he stood in the doorway listening, until Caleb beckoned him in. Once or twice she turned to Caleb for assistance in the wording, and he helped her stiffly. How could he be happy about a will that was taking a great deal away from him? And how lonely Persis Morgan must have been to feel that Caleb was the only friend to whom she could entrust her fortune.

When it was done at last, and Belle and Jon had

244

witnessed her signature, she looked around the parlor with an air of growing satisfaction.

"I feel better now. It's time I came to life again. Laurie, we must talk."

"Yes," I said. "There's a lot to tell you. I haven't had any chance until now. This morning I went into the back parlor, and everything returned to me. I know what I did, and I know what you did to save us all from the consequences."

"This isn't the time," Caleb began, but she waved him to silence.

"Go on, Laurie," she said.

I threw Jon a quick look and found him watching me, his expression kind, encouraging. I stumbled on.

"Grandmother, I think I came upon Noah's bones in the mine this morning. That's another long story. I went searching for Red, and found him where he'd been tied up inside the mine. Someone locked me in, but Jon came looking for me and rescued me. But before he came I found those bones in the mine."

"That's enough, Laurie," Caleb said. "You shouldn't be telling Mrs. Morgan all this now." He looked rather white about the mouth, and his eyes didn't meet mine.

Persis was quiet, lost in her own thoughts, and I didn't try to go on. After a moment she seemed to rouse herself and sat a little higher against the sofa pillows.

"Bones in the mine?" she questioned. "But they could belong to anyone at all. Any unfortunate. There's no reason to think that Noah—"

"Certainly not," Caleb broke in. "More than one man was lost in that mine in the old days."

Gail surprised us all by speaking from the doorway. I didn't know how long she'd been there, listening.

"Bones in the Old Desolate? How fascinating! Perhaps Mr. Ingram will be interested to learn about those bones, Laurie. Especially since he told us that Noah Armand was an old friend of his. I know he's interested in the mystery of that disappearance."

Persis looked at her with the haughty air she could summon on occasion. "I expected you to be upstairs packing, Miss Cullen. You can go back to your employer now."

Gail smiled at her brightly. "Maybe I'll do just that. And you can count on my being out of this house as quickly as I can go. Caleb, will you take me over to the hotel with my things?"

"I'll take you," Jon said, and followed her out of the room.

"Finish your soup," Belle ordered, and Persis looked up, smiling.

"I'm glad you're here. Will you stay with me now?"

For a moment Belle seemed undecided, reluctant, and then she gave in. "I'll stay for a while. But I think you should get back to your bed now. You've been up long enough."

Persis nodded agreement. "Yes. I want to be quiet. I need to be alone to think. Caleb, will you put this will away safely, please? It will serve until your office draws up a proper one. Why don't you start working on a draft for me now?"

Caleb took the paper, bowing to her wishes. I could understand why he had been against my coming here from the first. Although he would still be remembered generously, a fortune had just gone out of his hands. And more than that. I recalled what Persis had told me about Caleb Hawes always being a projection of what others had thought he should be. Perhaps for once real power had been within his grasp, only to be snatched away because of my coming to Jasper.

When he looked at me openly for the first time since I'd entered the room, I saw a blaze in his eyes that shocked me. But it was quickly veiled as he and Belle went to help Persis up the stairs.

I ran ahead to smooth out her bed and plump the pillows. When she lay back against them, with the comforter pulled over her, she reached for my hand and held it tightly.

"One more thing, Laurie. While I still have the strength. Go downstairs and fetch that box with the deringer in it. Bring it to me. Now."

Caleb started to object, but she dismissed him with a wave of her hand. "Go and work on my will. Let me be."

He hesitated in the doorway, and for once I thought he might refuse to do as she directed.

She spoke to him sharply. "No more plotting, no more schemes. I'll do what I must do."

He bowed slightly and went out of the room, his shoulders held stiffly, the tension inside him almost visible.

"What do you mean by plotting and schemes?" I asked when he was gone.

"Oh, don't think I haven't guessed how much he's counted on my will to free him from the bondage he's lived under most of his life. I know he has schemed to influence me."

Her words made me uneasy. "Yet you put your temporary will right into his hands? You trusted him with it?"

"In his own way he's loyal to me. His scheming won't carry him far enough to destroy what I've trusted to him. He might cut himself out entirely that way. But enough about Caleb. Go and get me that box, Laurie."

I stood uncertainly beside her bed. The thought of doing what she asked filled me with dismay. I had no wish ever to touch that fateful box again.

"Better get it for her," Belle said. "I'll stay right here with your grandmother."

Moved by a will that was stronger than any of ours, I went downstairs. At the door of the back parlor I paused with my hand on the knob. I had never wanted to step into this room again, yet now I must.

When I pushed open the door and walked in, I found that nothing had been changed or touched. No one had closed the heavy draperies that I'd flung open. This afternoon no sun poured in the windows, and the lights were still burning as I had left them. As I looked about the room thunder went reverberating along the peaks and a spate of rain streaked the glass.

This room must be cleaned now, I thought. Perhaps refurnished. Its ghosts must be laid and old tragedy thrown off. But old tragedy was still new to me, and I felt a little sick as I followed my own footsteps through the dust to

247

the rosewood table. When I touched the lid of the flat mahogany box, my skin seemed to shrink. Yet no reverberations ran through me. All that was over. My dread was different now—it grew out of knowledge of my own act. I was able to pick up the box and take it out of the room.

Gail was coming down the stairs, with Jon behind her, carrying her bags. She had packed her belongings in haste, and was ready to leave.

Jon went to the door. "Wait here," he told her, "and I'll bring the jeep around. It's started to rain." He looked at the box in my hands. "You'll be fine, Laurie," he said, and went outside. Strangely, I knew I would be.

Gail sat down on one of her bags and regarded me mockingly. "I wish you luck. I'll be glad to move on to another patient."

"Are you going back to Denver?"

"I don't know yet."

There seemed nothing more to say, and I didn't want to go on making idle conversation. I started past her up the stairs.

"You've been terribly foolish, you know," she said, looking up at me. "You had a lot when you came here. Now what do you have? Only the knowledge of what you've done, of what you really are. How are you going to live with that for the rest of your life?"

"I've already begun to live with it," I said, and hurried away from the tormenting sound of her voice.

At my grandmother's door I braced myself before entering the room.

She was still sitting up against her pillows, with only a bedside lamp holding away the gray afternoon. Draperies had been left open upon rain-swept mountains, and Persis was staring out through streaming panes. Belle watched as I carried the box to a table, and as I set it down Persis glanced at it briefly, then looked away. She, too, must find it hard to face what this box held, but she permitted herself no weakness.

"We will open it together," she said. And then, irrelevantly, perhaps postponing the moment, she asked, "Do you like the rain, Laurie?"

"Mostly I'm used to city rain," I told her. "Suburban rain. A storm seems more threatening here."

She went on, musing almost absently, "I've always loved storms in the mountains. They're much too tame down below. Rain can drive and blow with real fury up here, and it takes sturdy building to stand against the storms year after year. And sturdy men and women."

The first spate had turned into slanting sheets of water flung against the glass of every window, so that the closed room whispered with rain and wind sounds. Lightning flashed and a clap of thunder followed quickly, reverberating. I could imagine every gully, every canyon running with water, sweeping down in its sudden, dangerous course.

Belle motioned me toward a chair near the bed. "I'm not all that crazy about storms, so I think I'll stay awhile before I go after my things. Laurie, let me wipe off that box before you open it."

I was grateful for her solid presence, even though whatever came now must lie between my grandmother and me. At best Belle belonged in the real world. Her very presence made nightmare unreal.

When the smudged dust had been wiped from the lid, Persis reached out to touch one of the brass clasps, but she didn't release it.

"Open it, Laurie."

I tried not to hesitate. This time I knew how the clasps worked, and I raised the lid upon the single small gun within. Its silver mounting shone dully in the muted light, and though I no longer feared the flash of silver, I drew my hand back quickly.

"Deringers always came in pairs," Persis said. "There were two of these originally, and they had a history."

In spite of the graceful silver decorations the small gun seemed ugly, blunt-nosed, chopped off. I still couldn't look at it without shivering.

"Hand it to me," she said.

I had wanted never to touch that bit of murderous metal again, but her tone of voice was not to be disobeyed. I lifted the deringer from the box by its stubby barrel and gave it to her, butt first, surprised, now that I was paying attention, to find it so light in my hand.

She took it firmly, clearly familiar with the feel of it in her own hand. Yet I knew this was costing her something too. What she held lay at the heart of all she had tried to close away in that room downstairs. Why she was putting us both through this ordeal, I didn't know, and I could only wait.

"This is a .41," she said. "That's a fairly large caliber for so small a gun. It can fire only one shot. That's why there were always two in a set. Malcolm Tremayne bought the real thing, as you can see. Henry Deringer's own markings are on it, and that pineapple design he used for the finial ornament is his as well. Of course his name is on the plate, too. Look."

I made myself read the lettering.

DERINGER   PHILADELPHIa

"Just one *r* in his name," Persis pointed out. "They didn't add another *r* until counterfeits and imitations became common. By that time 'derringer' was a generic term for this type of pistol. This one is a muzzle-loader because Henry Deringer was stubborn about switching to the breech-loader for this particular gun."

Such history meant little to me, even though I listened. I only knew that this was the weapon that had killed my father. A weapon that *I* had fired. I began to feel a little sick, and Belle noticed, going quickly to bring me a glass of water.

"Drink this," she said. "Did you know that deringers were the guns the forty-niners carried? Along with their short-handled spades and their washing pans. A gun like that took up so little room, but it could be devastating at close range."

I knew all about that.

Persis was watching me. "They were handy for gamblers, as well as prostitutes and bartenders. Southern ladies used to hide them in their bodices for protection when they went riding in lonely places. But better handguns came in and they went out of style. My father was proud of his pair. The original trim was German silver, but he had additional decoration put on over the iron. Silver from the Old Desolate. That's why this one is so extensively silvered. They weren't made of steel, you know. Iron barrels were used. The steel imitations were often better guns, but this was one of those rare early ones. When I was small, Father still carried them both loaded for quick use, because, like the rest of the West, Jasper saw some rough times in the early days."

Her voice droned on—almost a monotone—and at last I understood what she was doing. She was giving this small gun historic life apart from me. It and its twin had existed and been used before I was born. They had been carried by my great-grandfather, Malcolm Tremayne. This pistol in itself was no more than a curiosity now— lifeless and harmless. Slowly I began to relax. I could stop shuddering at the sight of it now. I might as well shudder at the sight of my own two hands—which were no longer the hands of a frightened child.

Now I could even remember an old engraving I had seen—a representation of John Wilkes Booth in the box behind Lincoln, firing a strange-looking pistol. I'd always thought the artist must have been faulty in his drawing, but a deringer was just such a tiny gun as that.

"What became of the other one?" I asked.

"I've never known," Persis said, and I thought again of my suspicion that she might have fired one of those guns herself, killing Noah Armand. I had to know.

"Those bones I found in the tunnel—" I began.

There was wry understanding in her eyes. "No, Laurie. They don't belong to Noah, and I didn't shoot him, though I might have wanted to. I'm afraid they date from a long-ago escapade of my father's. No one ever told me outright, since I was a child when it happened. But he was supposed to have shot a man who probably deserved it in the lights of that day. The body was undoubtedly hidden in that old tunnel Dominoes dug into the mountain. A tunnel that was conveniently allowed to be lost after that. Those bones you found, Laurie, were probably

251

his victim's. I only wish they could belong to Noah Armand."

She closed her eyes and Belle moved quickly to her side. Relief washed through me in a tide that left me a little giddy. It was better to have Noah alive and still dangerous than to believe that my grandmother had killed him.

But for now I'd had enough of guns.

"Let's clean out the back parlor soon," I urged. "Let's get rid of all the ghosts and make it into a new room."

Persis heard the relief in my voice, and she opened her eyes and smiled at me. For just an instant I glimpsed the handsome woman she must have been in her prime. For that moment of sudden intensity it was as though age had evaporated and she and I were the same. Years meant nothing to the inner youth that had never left her. She held out her hand to me and I took it with a new recognition.

"When will you start?" she asked me.

"Perhaps tomorrow morning. Could Edna help me? You've never seen so much dust, so many cobwebs!"

"Let it wait a little. Tomorrow morning I want Mark Ingram to come to see me, and I want you here. I'm ready to talk to him now. Will you tell him for me, Belle, when you go for your things?"

"I'll tell him. And I expect he'll come running. But he won't give up, you know. Not just because of the signing of a new will. He knows how to harass and threaten. He'll go right on trying to drive you out. And Laurie too. I must say I was surprised, though, when Hillary Lange turned things around and wouldn't let Mark pack Laurie off to New York. He had to swallow that. Of course if she marries Hillary and they stay, perhaps you'll have another soldier for your army, Mrs. Morgan."

"I'm not going to marry him," I said. "I'm not going to marry anyone."

"Just testing," Belle said, and grinned at me. "Sure, I'll tell Mark you want to see him, Mrs. Morgan. And then I may be out of a job. He's not too pleased with me as it is."

252

"You'll come back here to work," Persis said. "You don't have to be loyal to that man forever. I need you now."

"I don't have to be loyal to him at all. It's just that old habit dies hard. Maybe for him too. Maybe there's still a tie between us. Maybe he's even fond of me—in his way. But could be it will do him good if I make a break on my own. Soon as this storm's over, I'll go have a talk with him. Though not for a while, I think. Laurie, you're looking frazzled. Why don't you put that gun back where it belongs and go lie down in your room for a while? I'll stay with your grandmother."

Suddenly I knew how tired I was. And besides, there were so many things I needed to be alone to think about, to begin to digest.

When I'd put the deringer back in its box beside the empty mold that should have held its twin, I bent to kiss Persis' cheek and caught the scent of verbena. She was really coming to life, consenting to a touch of vanity. I loved her for it.

When I went downstairs I moved with a lighter step, for all my weariness. The back parlor still made me uneasy, but I was not afraid of it anymore. I returned the box to its table and finally, I could rest in this house and feel wholly safe.

For a little while longer I could feel safe.

XVII

I undressed and got into bed, expecting to lie awake. Instead I fell asleep almost at once, and slept for the rest of the afternoon.

When I opened my eyes to the sight of continuing rain at the windows, I thought of Domino being churned into mud, its crumbling timbers soggy-wet and gray, as they had lain disintegrating under countless rains and snows. And I thought of the mine tunnels, where outdoor sounds of storm would scarcely penetrate, where water might collect deep in the earth, but old, white bones would lie entombed, protected and dry. But they were only bones that belonged to history, and they needn't make me afraid.

I turned my thoughts instead to rain drumming on the roof of Jon's cabin, and after a moment I got out of bed and went barefoot to the window. The pathway to the ranch buildings shone wet and muddy, but I could barely see the shapes of the nearest mountains. Old Desolate had vanished. Closer in, the cabin stood with its outline blurred and brown, a light in one of the windows. Jon would have taken Red inside, I knew, and I could imagine them both stretched before a roaring fire. Jon would lie on the sofa, reading perhaps, while Red slept on the hearth with his head on his paws. I wanted to be with them.

Someone tapped on my door, and I threw on a robe and went to open it. Caleb looked worn, driven—and no more friendly than before.

"Do you want to come down to supper?" he asked. "It will be ready in a little while. Belle is still here, and she'll join us."

"I'll come as soon as I can dress," I said. "I've been sleeping."

"I know." His tone was dry. "Your friend Lange has phoned twice. I came to your door and you didn't answer, so I thought it best to let you sleep."

I thanked him and he went away. I wasn't ready to face Hillary. I didn't know how to make him understand the change in me when I didn't understand it fully myself. Nor did I want to hurt him. Today at the Opera House he had pulled me back from terrible danger. There were some people in the world who believed that the acceptance of a favor acknowledged debt to the giver. Debt in proportion to the favor done. I didn't want to owe Hillary my life, but the fact remained that I did.

I pulled on navy slacks and a white sweater, swirled my

254

hair on top of my head and pinned it in place. My face in the mirror looked wan and hollow of eye, and I added lipstick, but left off eye shadow. My eyes were shadowed enough.

When I went downstairs, Belle and Caleb were going into the dining room. Belle took Gail's place and gave me her cheerful grin.

"I've been fired," she said. "I phoned Mark to tell him that Mrs. Morgan needs me, now that Gail has left, and he said I might as well stay on. I gather that Gail has offered to help out at the hotel for a while, without her uniform. Though I'm afraid all those costumes of mine aren't likely to fit her."

I met Belle's look across the table and smiled, glad that she was here, with her good sense, her capability, and her wry, realistic outlook. I wondered what she would think of the debt of a life.

"Anyway, Mark wants me to keep an eye on things over here," she went on casually. Caleb choked on a piece of bread and she smiled at him kindly. "Don't worry. I'm not much good as either a spy or counterspy. I'm too much given to telling people what I think."

"What have you told Ingram?" I asked.

"That he ought to pull out and leave your grandmother alone. Then your young man came on the phone and asked about you, Laurie. I'm afraid you've upset him badly."

"I don't think it will last," I said, and knew that was probably true. Hillary's real love was his profession.

Caleb said little through most of the meal, and I asked no questions. If he was working on the draft for Persis Morgan's new will, that was for her to follow. Belle, at least, was talkative enough for the three of us.

Mostly my attention wandered. I was still haunted by an unsettled feeling, by something restless that drove me—though I could find no real direction in which I felt I must go. I ought to make plans, confer with Persis about the coming confrontation with Ingram, but I felt at sea, not knowing how to begin.

When we left the table, Caleb returned to his work and

Belle said she would look in on my grandmother and then go over to the hotel for some of her things since the rain had about stopped.

I had paused uncertainly at the foot of the stairs, and when I looked out the front door I saw Hillary coming up the walk. He moved with his usual lively, eager step, and his face lighted when he saw me. It was disconcerting to realize how little I'd gotten through to him.

"We need to talk, Laurie," he said as he ran up the steps.

I opened the door. "Yes, of course. We can go into the parlor if you like. There's no one around right now."

He made no attempt to kiss me, his manner matter-of-fact as he sat in one corner of the red plush sofa. I sat in the other, and he began to speak at once.

"You'd better know what Mark is up to, Laurie. I don't much like something he did this afternoon. It may mean real trouble for your grandmother."

"Tell me."

"Not even the storm stopped him. I heard all about it later. He put on a poncho, took two men with him, and rode up to the mine. They removed the door from its hinges and went in. Mark couldn't go into the tunnels very well, with all that uncertain footing, but he directed the other two with their lanterns and flashlights. They found the passage old Dominoes dug—the one from which Jon rescued you—and they located those bones. I heard all about it when they got back."

"So?" I said, thrusting away my memory of that passage. "What does it matter? The bones have been there a long time."

"They knew what they were looking for, and they found it. The .41-caliber bullet that came from that deringer, Laurie. The bullet that killed Noah Armand."

Somehow Ingram had inoculated Hillary with a rather dreadful excitement, and for him excitement was the essence of drama.

"I'm sorry to deflate Mr. Ingram's balloon," I said, "but Persis has already told me about the bones I found in the mine. They probably belong to a man my great-grandfather shot in the bad old days. The deringers were his. So of course a .41 bullet would be found."

"And you believe her?"

"Of course I believe her. But I'm sure that Mark Ingram will make something of nothing if he can. It doesn't matter. My grandmother can stand against him, and she's not going to stand alone."

"I don't know, Laurie. Ingram is much too pleased about this. He was laughing when he showed me the bullet. I don't like it that he's coming to see your grandmother tomorrow."

"She wants him to come. I'm sure that whatever is there in the mine can be identified in other ways."

"Nevertheless, you'd better warn her. I wonder if she's strong enough to endure what he may do."

"If she's not, I am."

My words surprised me a little, and they surprised Hillary too. He was still watching me rather strangely, as though I had turned into someone he didn't know, someone who didn't entirely please him. Which was, perhaps, what had really happened.

He edged near me on the sofa and took my hand. "This isn't the right moment for romantic speeches, but I meant what I said this afternoon, Laurie. I'd like us to be married. Then I can stand with you too."

It was difficult to explain something I didn't understand myself. Nevertheless, I had to try.

"Something has happened to me since I came to Jasper. I don't seem to want the same things I used to want. Or perhaps I've just begun to find a way back to what is really me and to give it a chance to surface. I know I don't want to be married right now. I can't go on pretending that I still feel the way I did. It's hard to say this, Hillary, but I must."

For a moment or two he sat very still, studying me, his expression revealing nothing. Then to my dismay, he turned my hand and kissed the palm gently.

"You've been badly shaken, and there are psychic wounds that need time to heal. You can't be sure how you feel about anything right now. Isn't that true?"

257

I drew my hand from his. "No, I don't think it is, Hillary."

I could sense the sudden tension in him, but he made an effort to control whatever he was feeling.

"Listen to me, Laurie. I'm going to stay on at the Timberline and start this work on the Opera House. Perhaps there may even be some compromise eventually between your grandmother and Mark Ingram. She doesn't have to be driven out if she doesn't want to go."

"No, she doesn't," I said.

Now he was angry with me. "I'm going now," he said stiffly. "I'll see you later—when you've had time to think everything over."

I went with him to the door and watched him go striding off toward the Timberline with the same swinging walk that used to thrill me. Now it seemed a shade too theatrical. Perhaps he was releasing his own annoyance with me into that swinging stride.

Feeling a little shaken, I went upstairs to take Belle's place, freeing her to go to the Timberline for her things. My grandmother was out of bed again, sitting beside one of the long windows.

"Good!" she said, turning her head to stare at me. "You look a lot more rested. We'll need our wits about us when Ingram comes to see me tomorrow."

There was no use trying to hold anything back. It was better to have it come from me than from Ingram.

"Grandmother, Mark Ingram has gone to the mine and his men have found the bullet from the deringer. I think he means to make something of this if he can."

She listened calmly. "Nothing is changed. No one can prove that was Noah Armand in the mine, no matter what Ingram would like to believe. The whole thing is ridiculous, and we can forget it."

"But he may bring out—other things."

"By now that doesn't matter either. Oh, I realize there may be a three-ring circus for a while. Once I thought I could never face that. I know better now. It will all die down, as scandals always do when something juicier comes along. Will you mind terribly, Laurie? All they can do is stir things up. You were a child when it happened."

She reached out to me, and I took her hand in both of mine. We'll get through whatever comes together," I said. "And nothing at all may happen. There's nothing Ingram can fight us with but intimidation. And that can't beat us down if we don't let it."

She nodded. "Will you telephone Jon for me, please? Ask him to come up here right away."

I went to the extension in her room, and when Jon said he would come my spirits lifted. He was the knight of my childhood, riding a cow pony.

How foolish could I get?

In his worn Levi's he didn't look much like a knight when he came into the room, but my grandmother had confidence in him and so had I. He listened to what Hillary had just told me about the bullet being found in the mine tunnel, and he agreed that Ingram was bluffing and had no strong hand to play from.

"Except for his willingness to fight dirty," Jon said. "We have to be on guard against that."

I loved seeing these two together. Jon didn't play the game of flirting with her, of playing up to her as Hillary did. He simply treated her as a woman whom he respected and listened to, talking with her easily. He made no concession to her age, and just the way he treated her made her grow a little stronger.

Why, I wondered, had she left so much of her wealth to Caleb Hawes in that earlier will when she might have made Jon her heir? But I knew the answer well enough. Caleb was the logical manager of her money affairs. Jon would have wanted none of that, and if she had ever broached the matter to him, I knew very well that he would have refused.

When he left, I went downstairs with him, and there was a moment when we stood on the porch together. A moment of sharp physical awareness, each of the other. He made no sudden move, but put a hand on my arm, drawing me to him. I went gladly, eagerly, but he held me lightly, kissed me, and let me go.

259

"This is crazy, Laurie. You know that," he said, and went away from me before I could protest. I was left shaken and a little angry with the stubborn man he was. When he was out of sight, I went into the kitchen to heat milk for Persis, doing busy things to quiet my indignation and my longing.

I wanted to shout, *"Why* is it crazy? How can it be crazy when I love you?" But he had gone away too quickly, and I was left to nurse my own heavy disappointment.

As I was about to take Persis' milk upstairs, I saw Belle coming along the walk. One of Ingram's men had brought her over in a car, and he carried her bags up the steps and left them inside the door. Her grin was as cheerful as ever. If she had felt any pangs about parting from Mark Ingram, she didn't show it.

"There'll be a trunk coming tomorrow," she said. "I'll take care of these bags later. Want to give me that milk to take up to Mrs. Morgan, Laurie?"

I gave her the tray and went out on the porch again, looking out at the scattered lights of Jasper and the massive shadow of the peaks rising to block the sky. The Timberline was alight, as usual, and I saw nearer lights as well. Someone must be working inside the church tonight, and I wondered what was being done in there.

So far I'd not had time to look inside the little church that had been freshly painted and restored, and now I started toward it. I was too restless and distraught to go to my room, and I needed some purpose to use up my energy.

How quiet the town seemed at night. Except for someone singing a bit raucously down at the Timberline, a hush lay over the street. I knew my way by this time, and I didn't mind the dark. Where there were lights, a sheen of wetness lay over everything, and I stepped carefully to avoid puddles. The night air was fresh and clean and briskly cold, and my courage began to return. We would work together against Mark Ingram, Persis and Jon and I. Between Jon and me the last word hadn't been said yet. There was more to come. He had wanted to hold me.

260

The church was only a block away, and as I walked toward it I saw the light move in the windows. Whoever was inside carried a lantern and was moving about. The double doors stood open, and I went up the few newly painted steps and stood in the vestibule.

The entrance space was narrow and filled with shadows, the doors to the church proper opening across it. I went to stand where I could see in.

The interior had not yet been restored, and it was hardly a church anymore, except for the vaulted beams of the ceiling and the round window ahead, above what had once been an altar. The pews—perhaps they had been only benches—were gone, and the bare, shadowy space was unfurnished except for several straight chairs and a wooden table on which the storm lantern now rested.

One of the chairs was occupied by a woman who sat in a posture of utter grief, her head upon arms that had been flung across the table. Her shoulders moved as I stood watching, and if the woman had been anyone else, I would have gone silently away. But it was Gail Cullen who sat weeping in this deserted place, and perhaps it would be good to know why.

I moved toward her without trying to be quiet, and she heard me. Her head came up from her arms, and she stared at me, startled, her eyes swollen, her face wet with tears. I had never before seen her in a state of distress, with all the hospital starch gone out of her. It seemed a little unreal that she could weep like other women.

"Is there anything I can do?" I asked.

"Just go away!" she said. "I thought I could be alone here." And she sat staring at me with an anger that must be all the stronger because it was I who had caught her in this weak moment.

I crossed the bare, splintery floor, where the church congregation had once sat in their rows, pulled another chair toward the table, and sat down.

"Perhaps this is a good time to talk," I said, and remembered that I had said this to her once before.

She pulled a wad of tissue from a box on the table and dried her eyes, blew her nose, offering nothing.

I went on. "Perhaps this is as good a time as any to ask why you left that wreath on my door, with its cruel note about my father."

Her tears had ceased to flow. "I don't know what you're talking about."

"Let's not play games," I said. "Who else at Morgan House would retrieve one of Belle's funeral wreaths and hang it on my doorknob? With a card which hinted that my father would never sleep in peace."

She seemed to be considering this. "I should think it would be someone who wanted to frighten you away from Jasper and Morgan House."

"I believe that too. You left it there, didn't you? You disliked me from the moment that I arrived, though I don't understand why. Why did you so want me to leave?"

"I didn't want that!" She was emphatic. "Not in the beginning. I thought the old woman needed you."

Her words were hard to believe. "Then why the wreath? Who else—"

"Perhaps that's what someone wanted you to think. So I would be the one you'd blame."

"You mean it wasn't you?"

"Of course it wasn't. Not that I might not think that sort of thing a good trick—if I wanted to start frightening you. But I never did. I never liked you, but I didn't do that."

She sounded as though she was telling the truth.

"But then who—" I began.

"Take your pick. You've got this whole enormous metropolis to choose from. Nobody around here ever locks a door at night, so whoever wanted to could walk into that house. Perhaps someone acting on instruction. Perhaps someone you don't even know."

I was trying to digest this. Her manner, her earnestness almost convinced me. Besides, I rather suspected that she would admit it easily enough if she had been guilty. I began to feel a new uneasiness. Being sure it was Gail had enabled me to dismiss the trick as something of no consequence—the act of a malicious woman. If someone else was behind it, there could be a more ominous implication.

"Maybe *you* can cry a little now," she said. "I've got a whole box of tissues with me."

I wasn't ready to let her off altogether.

"Have you any plans?" I asked her. "What will you do now?"

"Plans? Oh sure, I'm full of plans!"

"Why did you drug my grandmother?"

She stood up, rocking the small table, looking scornful again, and no longer tearful. "I didn't! You don't need to believe me, but I didn't drug her. I do have some professional ethics."

It was difficult to believe in her ethics, professional or otherwise. "Then who could possibly have—"

"Why don't you try asking Caleb?"

"That's absurd. It's not the sort of thing a man like that would do."

"Isn't it? When he was pretty sure you would blame me? It must have seemed a good way to scare you off. And the drugging would postpone her making a new will. After all, he's the one who would have most benefited in the old will. Then, eventually, when she was gone, he could make a further profit by selling out to Mark Ingram. Only you came along to spoil everything."

This was the first time she had ever been open with me, yet all her old antagonism was still there, and I didn't know whether anything she said could be believed.

Her look changed suddenly as she stared past me, and I turned to see Caleb standing in the doorway, regarding us in chilly disapproval. Perhaps he would think this meeting between Gail and me conspiratorial. Perhaps that was what he would want to think.

"Well," he said, "this is surprising. I didn't know you two were such good friends."

I sat at the table waiting, trying to see Caleb Hawes in the further light Gail had shed on him. He came toward us doubtfully, as though finding us here together had disturbed him. As perhaps it would if any of the things she had told me were true.

"Your grandmother saw the light from her room, Laurie, and she sent me to find out who was here. Even though she doesn't own the church anymore, she feels a proprietary interest, since her parents built it."

"I saw the light too," I told him. "And when I came in Gail was sitting here crying. She tells me that she never left that wreath on my door, and that she didn't drug my grandmother."

He came across the room. "You can believe very little of what Miss Cullen says."

"Any more than I can believe what you say!" Gail picked up her box of tissues and walked past him out of the church.

I looked up at the round window above the altar space, its colors hardly visible in the dim light from the lantern. "Perhaps this is a place for the truth. Perhaps that's the game Gail and I were playing just now. Maybe not all the truth, but perhaps little trickles of it. It is true that you were to inherit most of Persis Morgan's wealth. That's no secret now."

"I was one of the few close friends she had left. Until you came here, she didn't expect to leave anything to you."

There was so much cold venom in the words that I began to feel uncomfortable with him here in this place. Perhaps the things Gail had told me explained a great deal.

Uncharacteristically, he moved quickly, suddenly, and came to sit at the table in the chair Gail had left.

"There's no need for us to be antagonistic," he said. "There are worse enemies than we need to make of each other."

"I've never wanted to be anyone's enemy."

"I know. I'll admit that I've disapproved of you and resented your coming. But now we have a common foe to face."

"Mark Ingram?"

"Partly. But I've always had a feeling that someone else was pulling hidden strings. Someone whose very name makes your grandmother cringe."

264

There was one name that made me cringe too.

"Noah?" I said. "Noah Armand? Do you think he's alive?"

"I don't know. For some years I kept track of him. But eventually my sources lost the trail and were never able to find him again. I know very well, however, the machinations that man was capable of. Laurie, I was the one who brought him here originally. I was the one who was to blame from the first for Noah coming to Jasper."

He turned his face from the direct light of the lantern and shaded it with one hand.

"You'd better tell me," I said.

After a moment he went on. "I knew him when I was away in college. Maybe we were opposite poles attracting. He had wild, crazy qualities that I didn't have—didn't want to have. But he made life exciting, wherever he was. He was full of schemes—miraculous schemes—most of them for getting rich without working very hard.

"After college we kept in touch with occasional letters. I knew he'd married and wasn't happy. I knew when he got his divorce. He wrote that he'd like to see Denver and the Jasper that I'd written him about. So he came. And like a fool, I brought him up to the house to meet Mrs. Morgan. You know the rest. It was all my fault. I made it possible for him to marry Persis Morgan. All those years older than he, she was intrigued at first. But Persis got onto him soon enough, and would have cut him off without a dime. Your pretty little mother never stood a chance. She was like a rabbit charmed by a cobra. He thought it was amusing to have both Persis *and* her young daughter-in-law. He should have died instead of your father. You don't know how many times I've wished your aim had been better."

Everything swept back as I listened to Caleb. The thought of the man who had caused all our loss and sorrow swept over me, weighing me down. I had no spare pity for Caleb, no longer any blame for him, no matter what he had done. But I just couldn't stay here with him a moment longer.

I jumped up and ran out of the church and back along

the road toward Morgan House, sometimes stumbling in the dark, until the light from the door and from my grandmother's high window fell across my path and brought me in.

I ran up the stairs and straight to my room. I couldn't bear to see Persis now, or face Belle's good cheer.

As I undressed, the face of the man I could remember only from a snapshot was clear in my mind. And the thought of my mother, my tragic, doomed father. How I'd hated and feared Noah Armand, even as a child. If he were alive now—as Caleb had seemed to think was possible—what further horrors lay in store for us? If he allied himself with Ingram, whom he already knew— Oh, the possibilities were endless and frightening. As Persis' husband he might still be able to make claims upon her.

When I got into bed, I couldn't sleep. Night thoughts are always the worst. Threats are magnified, problems become insoluble, and depression deepens. Worst of all, when I closed my eyes, all the terrible pictures returned. The memory of that scene in the parlor was gone over and over vividly in all its terror. Perhaps the very fact that I had blocked it out for so long made it return all the more insistently and horribly now.

Finally I gave up and got out of bed, to see that it was well past midnight. In slippers and robe I went softly upstairs to Grandmother Persis' open door and looked in. Moonlight shone at the windows. Belle snored lightly on her couch on the far side of the room, and I could hear my grandmother's deep, steady breathing. All was well.

Back on my own floor, I listened again to the uncanny groanings of an old house. Caleb's door was closed on silence. I'd heard him when he came home. The stairs were dark, but I didn't want to turn on lights. I could probably feel my way down to where a patch of moonlight fell through the front door. Perhaps I would try the hot milk treatment myself.

Then, as I hesitated at the top of the stairs, I heard a faint creaking of hinges as the front door opened. It was never locked, as Gail had pointed out. Anyone could enter or leave, and I wondered if Caleb was still up. The patch of moonlight changed its shape and spread to the foot of the stairs, but for a moment no one came in. I held my breath, waiting, not daring to call out.

After a moment a shadow moved into the lower hall, cast by moonlight. Whoever it was moved softly along the hall toward the rear, and I heard the door of the back parlor open. Quickly I went down a few steps and leaned over the banister. No light shone down the hall, and the door to the parlor had closed. Because of high, old-fashioned door sills there was no line of light to reveal whether whoever had entered the room had turned on a lamp.

I had to know who it was, but I mustn't take risks alone. Walking lightly, so that as few boards as possible would creak, I hurried to Caleb's door. A knock would sound through the house, so I turned the knob softly and opened it a crack.

"Caleb?" I whispered. "Caleb, are you there?"

The silence had an empty ring to it, and there was no sound of a sleeper. I touched the switch beside the door so that light flashed on and then off immediately. Caleb's bed was empty. Unslept in. I knew he had come upstairs earlier, so he must have gone out again.

I thought of rousing Belle, getting her to go downstairs with me, but that would take too long. I needn't actually confront the person in that room. There was a better way.

This time I left my slippers at the top of the stairs and went down softly in my bare feet. Hardly a step creaked. Moonlight from the open front door lighted the hall, and a chill breeze blew in. I hurried across to the front parlor and tiptoed to the double doors at the rear. These were locked, as they had always been, and I didn't want to go through anyway. I pressed my ear to the wood, listening.

Beyond the double doors I could hear movement. The sound of furniture being shifted, of someone moving stealthily. I had to know who it was, but how could I find out safely? After what had happened to Jon, and after my being shut into the mine, I knew very well that whoever played this game was dangerous, and that I might well be a target. Whether I liked it or not, I had better go back upstairs and summon Belle.

A cloud engulfed the moon, and the dim light that had come through the windows faded, leaving me in blackness. I felt my way cautiously, but it was not an easy room to cross because of Victorian taborets and all the bric-a-brac. I struck the corner of something my reaching hand had missed, and a vase teetered and fell on the carpet. It didn't break, but there was sound—and beyond the double doors a sudden silence.

Then movement, swift and heedless now. I heard the opening of a door to the porch and the sound of running feet. I rushed to a side window, trying to see out. Only mountain shapes stood against a lighter sky, and the grounds near the house were lost in inky shadow. Though I stepped onto the porch, I could see nothing, hear nothing but the normal rustlings of a mountain night. The intruder could have gone in any direction, and he was already out of my sight and hearing.

Now there was nothing to keep me from going into the back parlor. The door opened at my touch, but no lights were burning. A flashlight must have been used. When I touched the switch by the door, the wall bulbs came on and showed me an empty room. A table in one corner appeared to have been moved and a chair set in its place. Otherwise the room seemed untouched. Except for one thing.

The mahogany box lay open on its table. Startled, I went to look more closely. Everything was in place and every molded compartment filled. Instead of only one deringer, the twin space was now taken. Two identical pistols lay in the box, their silver mountings shining in the light.

XVIII

I hardly slept. Nothing made sense, and the very lack of reason set fearful questions rising to keep me awake. Questions to which I could find no answers.

In the morning, because of the coming meeting with Mark Ingram, I had no time to do anything about my discovery of the missing deringer. Caleb seemed to have disappeared during the night, Belle had breakfasted earlier, so I ate alone. By the time I reached Persis' room, she was up and dressed, thanks to Belle.

"Come in, Laurie," Belle invited. "We're getting ready to go downstairs."

I kissed Persis' cheek and caught again that brave whiff of verbena.

"You look wonderful," I said. "I like that gown. It reminds me of the wallpaper in your room in Domino."

"That's why I bought it. Years ago. My closet is full of things I haven't been wearing. Time I changed all that. I'm going downstairs before Ingram gets here. I want to be ready for him."

"Aren't the stairs difficult for you?"

"I have to manage. Once I've settled with Ingram, I plan to move downstairs to the back parlor. It's a perfectly good room, and I ought to be down there, where it will be easier for everyone."

Her look met mine defiantly, as though she expected opposition.

"Good for you," I said. But I didn't feel as brave as Persis Morgan looked.

Jon arrived while we were still upstairs. The bruise on his cheek bone was changing color, and he had removed the patch of bandage from his head.

"I see you're ready for battle, Mrs. Morgan," he said.

"I am, as far as I'm able. I'm glad you're here to help me downstairs. Though I'm not feeble, you know. I've made myself get up nearly every day and walk about my room—even while Gail and Caleb were trying to turn me into a cabbage. Where is Caleb?"

Belle knew. "He took the jeep and drove down to Denver late last night. He stopped in to say he'd get back as quickly as possible. You were asleep, so we didn't wake you, Mrs. Morgan. He wanted to deliver your will to the office himself and have it put into proper form."

"That's fine. I'll report that much to Mark Ingram."

I still felt uneasy about Caleb Hawes.

When Jon had helped Persis down the two flights of stairs, she seated herself in a high-backed wing chair, with windows behind her, so that morning light wouldn't fall directly upon her face. Sitting there, she looked more like royalty than ever. The daughter of a silver king!

Jon posted himself behind her, and he, too, seemed braced for battle, his black hair crisp and curly from a wet comb, his chinos and blue shirt fresh from the laundry, and his best boots polished and unscuffed.

How very much I had loved him as a little girl. Perhaps I had never stopped loving him. Perhaps I had been searching for him ever since leaving Jasper.

I found a chair near the hearth and turned it about so that I could be a spectator to whatever happened. I would join in if I were needed, but I knew Persis would want to handle this herself, with Jon ready to help her, if need be.

Ingram arrived promptly, and Hillary was with him, but not Gail. I don't know why I had expected that she might show up, but that thought had crossed my mind.

Belle brought them into the parlor, and there was a moment when she and Mark Ingram stood together in the doorway and I sensed again the bond between them. Belle had gone away from him, yet he knew she would come back. His confidence in her looked out of his eyes, and her smile of greeting was warm. Sudden doubt rose in my mind. How clever were we to harbor Belle Durant in our midst? Yet, strangely, like Mark Ingram, I trusted her.

270

Belle stayed near the door, while Ingram went straight to my grandmother and took her hand. It was as though she were an old friend whom he was delighted to see again—no matter that we all knew him for the powerful and dangerous man that he was.

When Hillary smiled at me brightly and pulled a hassock close to my chair, it was evident that his earlier anger had subsided. Again I sensed his state of barely suppressed excitement. This was a performance he wouldn't want to miss.

"Good morning, Mrs. Morgan," Ingram said. "I'm glad you've finally consented to see me."

"Sit down, please." She had not relinquished command. "No—over there in the light, where I can see you. My eyes aren't as good as they used to be."

His smile was easy and amused as he obeyed, allowing her the privilege of shadow. Hillary, Belle, and I seemed to fade into the background, with the central focus of the room on the two antagonists, while Jon Maddocks stood alert and watchful behind my grandmother's chair.

Persis continued to dominate the scene, and for the time being Ingram permitted her this.

"There is very little you and I have to say to each other," she told him, and I was pleased to hear such strength and resonance in her voice. This was the Persis Morgan of whom others had told me. This was a *woman*.

"I agree," Ingram said. "But it's time we said it to each other instead of using other people's wits and mouths."

"I intend to stay in this house," Grandmother went on. "I intend to continue holding the valley land and this house and the one in Domino. I would like to buy back from you those portions of Jasper and Domino that you've already purchased. So you need suffer no loss. Jon Maddocks and I have plans of our own for the area. I'm sorry that Mr. Hawes isn't here to make you an offer. But that can be taken care of later."

For once Mark Ingram was taken by surprise. Whatever he had expected in this encounter, it was not an offer on her part to buy him out. After a pause he began to

271

laugh. The sound had an easy, confident ring, but he cut it short quickly.

"I'm sorry, Mrs. Morgan. It just struck my funny bone to see a lady who hasn't even a gun in a holster, let alone one in her hand, trying to outdraw me. That's a pretty good trick."

"It's hardly a trick. I own the land you want, and I don't mean to sell it. I've made my granddaughter my heir in a temporary will, and Caleb Hawes has gone to Denver to draw it up formally. I can stay here as long as necessary to block you, and when I am gone, Laurie will stay in my place. The authorities will be warned that you have tried to threaten us, and have perhaps even harmed my friends in order to drive me out. So you will be watched from now on."

There was a visible stiffening beneath his easy manner that showed an edge of steel. He turned to stare at me across the room, and I was startled to see not merely dislike in his eyes, but something far stronger and more deadly. If this was what he felt toward me, he had hidden it well until now.

He spoke again to my grandmother. "I've always admired guts. And I'm sure that's a word you understand. But this time you're being foolish, Mrs. Morgan. There's no way you can stand against me and keep me from what I want to do."

"I don't know what you mean," she said haughtily. "We have all the time there is to sit here and wait you out. I don't think you have that kind of time. If your investment here turns out to be a loss, then you can't afford to wait for a decision in your favor that will never come. You'll have to pull out."

He reached into a pocket of his jacket and took something from it, rolling it in his fingers, holding it up for us to see, and I watched, hypnotized. I knew it was the bullet from the deringer that Hillary had told us about. So small a thing to kill a man, to turn him into a heap of bones in a mine tunnel.

"Laurie!" Hillary said in warning, and I realized that I had made a move as if to rise.

272

"I'm all right," I told him, and was aware of Jon watching me from across the room, his concern for me evident.

Persis paid no attention, her proud look still upon Mark Ingram. "What do you expect to prove with that bullet?" she asked.

His smile was gentle—that dangerous smile that I didn't trust. "Why—that Noah Armand died in this house, and that his body was carried to the mine and left there. The police are going to be interested, and an investigation may open up a lot of other things too." He glanced briefly at me.

"Don't believe him," Hillary whispered.

Persis didn't believe him either. Before he finished speaking, she was shaking her head. "I'm sorry to disappoint you. The man in the mine died violently, yes. But he isn't Noah Armand. Those bones have been there since my father's day. I know about them."

Jon put a hand on her shoulder in support. "Good try, Mr. Ingram, but it isn't going to work."

With as casual a gesture as though he were taking out a pack of cigarettes, Ingram dipped a hand once more into his pocket. When he drew it out he held a small square of tarnished metal that might be silver.

"Perhaps you've seen this before, Mrs. Morgan?"

She took it from him and held it up to the light. Her gasp was soft and quickly stifled. "Where did you get this?"

"From the same place the bullet came from—those bones in the mine."

"I don't believe that."

"The police will believe it. I have witnesses who will swear to its being found there. And it won't look good for you that this body was never reported."

"What is it?" I cried. "What is it he's found?"

Persis turned the square of silver about in her fingers and then dropped it into the hand Ingram held out for it. She looked haggard as she answered me.

"It's a belt buckle that I had made for Noah one

Christmas, soon after we were married. His initials are on it, and he was wearing it the last time I saw him."

Ingram nodded. "Yes, I'm sure he was. That was the time when he returned to run off with Laurie's mother, wasn't it? And was murdered—here in this house."

"That's not true!" Persis cried. "Not a word of what you are saying is true."

Hillary tried to stop me when I rose, but I pushed his hand away and walked over to stand beside my grandmother.

"Of course it's not true. In fact, Noah Armand may still be alive. There isn't any way you can prove those bones in the mine are his, no matter what sleight-of-hand tricks you play with that buckle—however you came by it."

They were all staring at me now, and I hurried on.

"I talked to Caleb Hawes last night. He told me that he had made a search for Noah after he left this house, and that he was able to keep track of him for a while. Then the man he had on the investigation lost the trail—so there's no telling whether he is dead or alive. But he certainly lived for several years after he left this house. There will be proof of that."

"Caleb never told me that," Persis said softly. "I would never have allowed him to track that man. I never wanted to see or hear of Noah Armand again."

Someone across the room released a deep breath, and I realized that it was Belle Durant, still at her place by the door.

Mark Ingram had not been shaken in the least. He turned a mock-kindly look upon me. "Has it occurred to you, Miss Morgan, that Mr. Hawes might have a very good reason for lying, and that this supposed tracking down of Noah Armand could be a complete fabrication? In fact, I'm pretty sure that's what it is."

He dropped both belt buckle and bullet back into a pocket of his jacket and returned to his chair. He crossed his knees with an air of having all the time in the world, lighting a cigarette, while we watched him in stunned silence, waiting for whatever would come next. Not one of us had any doubt, I think, that more would come from this man.

Ingram's smile had turned a little grim when he began to speak again. "You forget that Noah was at one time my very good friend. I knew him as well as anyone could. And I was more or less in his confidence. It cost you a small fortune to get rid of him, didn't it, Mrs. Morgan? All that money you paid him, before he played you the dirty trick of coming back! You wanted him gone pretty badly. You thought you could save your son's marriage by paying him off handsomely and sending him away. Perhaps you thought you might even prevent Richard Morgan from killing him. Have you ever wondered what became of all the money you paid him after he disappeared?"

Persis stared at him without speaking, and I saw the tightening of lips grown thin with age.

"He was my partner as well as my friend," Ingram went on. "Everything would have gone fine for him if it hadn't been for his stupid infatuation for your daughter-in-law. And hers for him! I warned him against it. But he had to come back, didn't he? He had to make a last try for her. But not before that money was safely in my hands. I told him I would wait for him in Denver and we would go back to Kansas together. Only he never showed up, and I had to start out alone. The money was all I needed. Ironic, isn't it, Mrs. Morgan, that I'm where I am today because of that nest egg in cash that you paid over to Noah Armand? You don't think he wouldn't have come after that if he was able—yet I never saw him again."

I felt a little sick. As sick as my grandmother looked. Jon bent over her, and Belle came a few steps into the room. Only Hillary didn't move. He sat where he was, on the hassock beside me, his hands about his knees—a frozen spectator.

Jon said, "If you were waiting in Denver, Mr. Ingram, why didn't you come to Jasper to investigate when your partner didn't show up. Why did you let it all go until now?"

275

"I did come—quietly. The place was in an uproar and swarming with reporters and police. But no trace of Noah turned up, though I made a few discreet inquiries. No one even seemed to know that he'd come back. I knew because he'd told me on the phone that he meant to."

"Why didn't you bring up what you knew with the police?"

"There'd been a murder, and I didn't know any of the details. I didn't want to become involved. So I went off to Kansas alone, knowing Noah could find me when he wanted to. If he stayed away, there must have been a reason. Over the years I've put together a few suspicions. So when Gail told me about the bones in the mine, I had my final clue. I can't be patient forever, Mrs. Morgan. If I can't have what I want because you choose to block me, then perhaps I owe it to Noah to go to the police now."

Persis managed to rouse herself. "You can do as you like. The man in the mine wasn't Noah Armand. There's no way for you to prove what isn't so."

"It may not be necessary to prove it, Mrs. Morgan," Ingram said smoothly. "It may only be necessary to stir up the past a bit and let the investigation take its course. Will you enjoy the publicity that follows? It's sure to make headlines, and how will that be for your granddaughter? How will it affect her for the rest of her life?"

"Mark!" That was Belle's stricken cry. "Mark, you can't do this!"

"Get out of my house!" Persis' voice cracked as she shouted at him, her proud poise gone.

He went straight to Belle and took both her hands in his. "I'm sorry. This is what I have to do."

Then he was gone, out the door, and an odd mutual releasing of breath seemed to sigh around the room. But before we could recover, he was back, smiling at us as outrageously, as though no controversy had ever existed.

"Of course I'll do nothing about this until after my Forty-niners' Ball," he announced. "Too much has gone into that. It's to be held this coming Saturday night, you know."

I think we all gaped at him, unable to make the switch

that Mark Ingram had made so easily. He went right on in the face of our astonishment.

"Gail is helping me by phoning friends in Boulder and Denver and other parts of the country. There's no time for formal invitations. But they'll come. I want to hold it right away, in order to celebrate the opening up of Jasper to the world. I'll have the press here, of course, and various people from the media. Maybe a congressman or two. Naturally, I hope you will all come. That dress you're wearing, Mrs. Morgan, will do very well as a costume. I'll hope to see you then."

He was entirely confident as he made a sweeping gesture with his broad-brimmed hat. Then he was really gone.

"Don't worry," Belle said cheerfully. "All that stuff he's been carrying on about—it's just bluff. He always thinks he can pull things off in a big way, even when he's losing. But there's nothing he can do if you just hold on."

"I don't believe he's losing," Persis said. In the last few moments all her courage and eagerness for battle had drained away. "Perhaps there's nothing else to do but give in and let him have his way."

"Don't do that!" Hillary's words were unexpected as he left his place and came to where we stood around Persis. "Don't worry, Mrs. Morgan. Belle's right. Ingram was lying. I could tell. You and Laurie can stand against him if you don't let his bluffing beat you down."

I hoped he was right. I knew, as the others could not, that Hillary had a keen eye for reading character, for discerning the gesture or the look that betrayed.

"What's more," he went on, "I think we should all go to that ball of Ingram's. Mrs. Morgan, you can do some bluff-calling of your own if you're there. If you don't go, he'll think you're afraid of him."

Belle laughed. "Why not? That's the very way to confound him." Then she caught my grandmother's look. "Never mind—you don't have to decide now. Jon, help me get Mrs. Morgan upstairs to her room. There's been enough excitement for one day."

Persis gave in, her energy drained, and Belle and Jon

277

helped her up the stairs. The return of the missing deringer was still on my mind, but I couldn't add another worry for Persis at this time.

At the front door Hillary gave me a quick hug and then went jauntily off toward the Timberline. It was as though his anger with me had never existed. He was still refusing to accept any break between us, and for me he was a problem that still had to be solved.

Jon came down while I was there on the porch, and we sat on the front steps together while I related all that had happened last night. I told him of my curious meeting with Gail and Caleb in the empty church, and about what had happened later when someone at the house went into the back parlor.

"Now there are two deringers in the box," I told him. "The one that was missing has been returned. What can this possibly mean?"

Jon got up at once and went with me down the hall. In the rear parlor the French door to the side porch stood open, as the intruder had left it, and the room wasn't as dark as usual. Jon noted the table that had been moved and the chair that was set in its place near the wall.

"To stand on?" Jon puzzled.

He climbed on the straight chair and reached toward the wall above his head. A small patch of wallpaper up near the black walnut molding had been torn, and when he pulled, it hung down to show cracked plaster. But there was nothing to tell him whatever he wanted to know.

"I wonder," he said as he got down from the chair. "In fact, I've always wondered."

"What? What do you wonder?"

"Nothing. Nothing that makes any sense. When your father died, the police picked this room clean. There would be nothing left for anyone to look for now. But whoever came in last night must have thought there might be."

"And whoever came in had that deringer in his possession," I said. "But who could it have been?"

Jon shook his head and went to the box on the small

278

table. I had closed it last night after I found what was in it, and he raised the lid. The two blunt-nosed little guns were there. The twin pistols that had been reunited.

"I wonder what time Caleb left Jasper last night," I said. "I wonder if he could have come into this room before he went off."

Jon was silent, and another question rose in my mind. What if it had been Persis herself who had kept the second pistol? What if she had asked Caleb to replace it last night?

"You'll have to tell your grandmother," Jon said.

"No—not now! It's better not to!"

My vehemence alerted him, and he must have guessed what I was thinking, for he let the matter go.

Further speculation was futile, and we returned to stand for a few moments longer on the porch.

"How are you?" I asked, not wanting to let him go.

"Never felt better." But if there might have been a moment of intimacy between us he turned it aside. "Hillary may have a good idea about attending Ingram's ball and calling his bluff. Maybe we can show a united front if we go."

"In costume?"

Jon's mood had lightened. "It's not hard to look like a forty-niner. Save me a dance, Laurie. Or don't you dance with cowboys?"

"I dance with cowboys every chance I get," I told him.

But already he was looking away from me, off up the valley toward Old Desolate.

"I'm itching to get started out there," he said. "We need to be ready for next year."

"Can you really graze cattle in the valley?"

"Sure. It's big enough, and there's plenty of grass. In the summertime, anyway. We'll need to do some planting, and we'll need more land down on the flats during the winter, and that can be managed. The cows that are held back for breeding and not sent to market can be fed with our own hay. We can swing it if your grandmother holds onto her courage. Are you going to be a partner in this, Laurie?"

"I am if you'll have me."

I couldn't hold back what I felt any longer. It was there in my eyes, on my lips, whether I wanted it to be or not. He couldn't help seeing it. He pulled me into his arms, kissed me almost roughly, and then set me away from him.

"The heiress and the cowboy!" he said. "That's not what I'm after, Laurie."

I watched him move away with that easy lope that covered ground so quickly. My heart was thudding, and my thoughts were angry. Now I knew what stubborn pride I would have to confront. Somehow I would have to manage that. How very few times in my life had I ever been determined about anything. But I was determined now. I had my directions finally, and I knew where I was going. No more fantasy and make-believe and escape, but only the reality of Jon Maddocks and the life I wanted to spend with him.

When I whistled for Red, he came bounding around a corner of the house, and I took him for a run that we both needed. More than ever I knew that Mark Ingram had to be defeated. Really stopped. Sent away, once and for all. Jon had to have his chance at the valley, and Persis and I had to have our chances too.

But as I returned to the house, I found myself wishing that there weren't times when I still felt afraid. Something faceless always seemed to be working against us, and I would have to look past Mark Ingram to find it. He was involved, but there was something more.

Two days later this feeling in me was reinforced when an attempt was made upon Ingram's life. The whole thing was common knowledge in Jasper within an hour of when it happened. Belle learned about it and brought the news to us.

One of the few sports Ingram could enjoy was riding, and he was often out on the mettlesome gray that was his favorite mount. On this morning he was riding over to Domino when he was fired upon from behind a clump of rocks. The first two shots missed, but the third cut through his jacket and resulted in a slight flesh wound in his upper arm. He had the good sense to get out of there as fast as he could, and he rode Juniper back to town at a gallop. While his arm was being bandaged, he ordered his men out to search the area from which the shots had come. A rifle was missing—the hunting rifle that had always stood behind the bar at the Timberline, and anyone could have picked it up.

At Morgan House we talked over the shooting, and Belle showed how much it had upset her. If it hadn't been for Persis' need, I think she might have returned to him then. But not even Belle, who knew Ingram so well, could guess what had happened. Caleb was home by that time, and he had no suggestions to offer either.

"Sure, Mark has enemies," Belle said. "He's always made plenty of them along the way. He can be dangerous, and dangerous men draw lightning. But who knows which enemy has turned up again to try to get rid of him now?"

Whatever his private suspicions might have been, Mark Ingram shrugged off the incident. The wound was slight and to be ignored. Though it was noted that he never rode out alone after that. Always two or three of his men rode with him wherever he went, and they looked a grim lot when they followed the trails around Jasper together. Like something out of the old West.

The remaining days before the Forty-niners' Ball went by without any further event. And that was just as well. Even the mysterious attack upon Mark Ingram, which seemed to indicate that someone was on our side, had been disturbing. We needed a spell of calm to rest us and to give us a chance to be braced for whatever was to come.

Persis ate her meals with a new appetite, and she even exercised a little, and slept better at night. She began to come downstairs more often, and even walked about outside. Pretty soon, she said, she would be up on a horse again. Belle was delighted with her improvement, but afraid she would overdo.

Caleb had returned from Denver looking subdued, but with the new will in hand, and it had now been properly executed. I was Persis Morgan's main heir. If that fact served only to increase my uneasiness and my sense that I might be in even greater danger than before, I told no one how I felt.

There was one uncomfortable moment when I met Caleb alone in the hall near my room and told him about the deringer that had appeared with its twin in the mahogany box in the back parlor. I watched for his reaction, and even in the hall light that was always so dim, I could see how shaken he was. He took me by the arm and led me quickly back to his room.

"Who knows about this?" he asked.

"Only Jon. No one else."

"Sit down for a minute," he directed, and I sat in a worn leather chair and looked about a room that had been kept almost bare of decoration. This was the room he must stay in whenever he stopped in this house, and right now he was living here. Yet apparently he had never set any stamp of his own personality upon it, and it was as coldly austere as I had once thought him to be. I wondered what Caleb would be like if he ever really let himself go to the point of explosion.

While I sat waiting for him to speak, he stood at a window and stared unseeingly out at Jasper.

"Who do you think placed the gun in that box?" I asked him finally.

"I think I know," he said. "But I'm not going to talk about it. I'm not going to guess. I just want to suggest that you should not mention this to your grandmother. Can I ask for your word on that?"

I wondered if he suspected what I suspected.

"I won't promise anything unless I understand why."

"I think you've come to love her. That's why. You won't want to damage her in any way."

"But she has only to walk into that room to see for herself that two guns are there."

"I don't think she'll do that. But it's a good thing you told me about this."

"I thought *you* might have put it there."

Dislike for me showed in his eyes, and our interview

282

was over. Whatever he could have told me, he had no intention of putting it into words. I left him feeling more frustrated than ever and defeated by the secrets that were still being held all around me.

During those days before the ball I saw nothing of Hillary, since he had gone to Denver. He phoned before he left to tell me that he wanted to buy materials in order to decorate the Opera House for Ingram's party. I was just as relieved not to see him for a little while.

Jon was being especially wary with me. It was as though he wore a sign to hold off anyone who might come close to him.

Nor did we see Mark Ingram during this period, but Belle, who lived with us now, warned us not to be optimistic. She had a feeling that he meant to spring something unexpected at the ball.

As my state of anxiety grew, I began to wish that Persis would change her mind about attending the party. I wasn't sure whether she could stand up to whatever he might be planning. Her strength wasn't as great as she was trying to pretend.

Of Gail we saw nothing, but Belle reported scornfully that she continued to ingratiate herself with Mark Ingram and that something was definitely going on there.

In spite of Belle's defection I knew there was still a bond between her and Mark Ingram, growing out of a long relationship. They were still fond of each other, and there were moments when I even wondered if Belle Durant was to be trusted.

Once Jon came to see my grandmother when she was sitting in the downstairs parlor, and this time I was present.

"I'd like an answer to something," he told her. "I want to know where you and Caleb put the jewels that were sacrificed in the cause of that story you cooked up for the press. Caleb won't tell me."

"He's under orders from me not to. Bringing them out again won't help, though I know it's been in your mind for a long time. It could be dangerous, so don't ask me again."

"I won't ask you, but I'll look," he said. "As I've already been doing for a while—with no result."

"What do you think you can learn from them?"

"I'm not sure I'd learn anything. But I don't think you've played fair with us, and I'm wondering why."

She would say nothing, and the exchange ended there.

Hillary, too, troubled me during those few days. When he got back from Denver, he came to see me, behaving as naturally as though I had never tried to tell him that everything was over between us. I had the feeling that he, too, was up to something and that it concerned Mark Ingram. He hinted at the mysterious and wondrous, and sometimes got carried away with his own playacting. Certainly he was busy working on the Opera House. All construction in Jasper had ceased while the men gave full effort to the theater. Hillary reported that progress was considerable. Of course complete refurbishing wasn't possible in this short time, but at least it would be clean and some painting would have been done. All those ratty old seats were being cleared out, and the orchestra floor would be fine for dancing. Only reels and square dancing would be permitted, and several mountain fiddlers were coming in to call the dances.

It was going to be quite a party, Hillary said, and I knew he was excited about it. Too excited.

Once I tried to pin him down. "What about Mark Ingram? What is he really planning?"

Hillary looked as though he hadn't been really focusing on me. But now he concentrated, though not by answering my question.

"I'll wait for you, Laurie. All this will wear off, you know. I'll be there when you need me. Remember that."

I made no attempt to answer because I didn't know what he was talking about and I didn't believe there would ever again be a time when I would turn to Hillary Lange for anything. We had grown away from each other, though he hadn't really accepted that as yet. Only once, in a moment of anger, had he believed, and he had clearly talked himself out of that.

Persis insisted that I wear one of the old dresses from a

trunk full of clothes dating back to before the turn of the century. No one in her family had ever thrown anything away, apparently. One could live like that in a house that came down through the generations. I brought out a pile of old garments, and she selected for me a dress that her mother had worn in the early 1900s. It was of black lace over nile green satin, cut straight, with a little train. All the bustles and flounces and hoops of the last century had been abandoned by that time. The neck was low and square, and Grandmother loaned me an emerald necklace to wear with it. The black pumps that I'd brought would serve, being well hidden by the length of the gown.

On the night of this party that I had no wish to attend, Belle came to my room and dressed my hair in an upswept, puffy style that was not unbecoming. She had put on one of her green hourglass gowns and a red wig she had adopted for use at the Timberline, and she looked perfectly in character.

"I'm not sure what I represent," I said.

She considered me in the mirror. "You're a lady from the East who wears the latest Paris fashions and is visiting a quaint mining town. Wait till you see your grandmother!"

Persis Morgan was not wearing the daisy-sprigged dress, but was decidedly the grande dame in gleaming black satin. About her throat sparkled a diamond dog collar that had once belonged to Sissy, and a diamond crescent of Sissy's shone in her beautiful gray hair.

As we went downstairs, Jon came through the door and stared at the three of us. "Resplendent! I'll hardly dare to be seen in your company."

He had managed a minimum of costume in a miner's rough clothes, with a coil of rope over one shoulder and a pan for washing dust under his arm. All he needed to look authentic was a beard.

Caleb was the real surprise, having unearthed a long frock coat and stovepipe hat. Thus garbed in lugubrious black, he looked the sober old-time lawyer—which perhaps he really was. A throwback from another age. An even less scrupulous age?

Earlier Mark Ingram had phoned that he was sending his station wagon for us, so we needn't come in the jeep. While Belle and Caleb helped Grandmother Persis down the front steps and into the car, Jon held me back for a moment.

"Try to stay near her as much as possible tonight," he warned me. "I don't know what may happen, but she may need you."

"Where will you be?"

"Around. Don't worry about me." And then, almost absently, "Laurie, you look beautiful. Who are you—Sissy Tremayne?"

"I think I'm trying to be Laurie Morgan," I said.

For just an instant his eyes warmed with approval, and then he looked away. I really didn't know what to do about Jon Maddocks.

We all went down the steps together and toward whatever this uncertain night might hold for us all. Mainly I was aware of Jon's hand over mine for a moment as I took his arm. So small a thing to take comfort from.

XIX

The Timberline was ablaze with lights as we drove toward it, and a spotlight had been set up to shine upon the white face of the Opera House. Not exactly a forty-niner's touch, but then the jeeps and other four-wheel-drives that had poured into town belonged to a later era too. The upper street had been cleared to use for parking, but as guests of honor we were brought straight to the theater.

Ingram's informal summons must have been considered as a great lark, for the foyer was filled with men and women dressed in hastily conceived costumes and ready for adventure.

The press was there with cameras and reporters, and at once my grandmother was besieged. Mark Ingram himself strode through the lobby to rescue her from the flash-bulbs, leading her into the theater grandly on his arm. The rest of us trailed after them. I noted that Ingram, of all the crowd, had not troubled to wear a costume, but then for him costume wasn't necessary. He was already a dramatic, always costumed figure in his gray cords. He seemed to belong to a Jasper that no longer existed, and his manner of total assurance worried me. But if Mark Ingram seemed confident, Grandmother Persis could carry the charade still further because *she* was the real thing. Her own air of aristocratic poise could put him to shame. It was an American aristocracy she represented—from mining camp child to grande dame in one lifetime.

Belle and Caleb, Jon and I followed the conspicuous two with a bit of jostling because of the group that for-ever gathered around Ingram. Once we were inside, Jon gave my arm a reassuring squeeze and slipped away into the crowd, I watchd his tall figure disappear and wished that he had stayed with us. With me.

Hillary found us quickly, looking handsome and dramatic in a trapper's fringed jacket that he must have found in Denver. He, too, was a costume man. It was his natural habit.

These details of what we wore and how we looked I can still remember with a strange clarity. Much of the rest is a blur because of what happened that night to wipe out trivial detail and leave only the stark and tragic.

I know that at first I tried to stay close to my grand-mother, as Jon had suggested. But when a fiddler struck up his first tune and the calling of the dances began, I was swept away to be partnered by strangers, swept into reels and do-si-dos, and other unfamiliar steps. Not knowing what I was doing didn't really matter. The few who knew carried the rest of us along on an exciting outpouring of energy, and we caught on quickly. At least I knew that Belle was with Persis. Caleb was with her too, usually standing against the wall, not far from her chair, looking as though he thoroughly disapproved of all these festivities. Looking somehow watchful as well, as though he waited—for what? Like Caleb, Ingram was not dancing either, this being one of the things he couldn't manage gracefully, but I glimpsed him now and then, always with a lady on his arm and an air of triumph about him that made me uneasy.

In the beginning I was swept along on a flow of energy. Even the sparkle of light spilling from the great center chandelier added to my state of excitement, and I was entranced by the color from great swaths of crimson and gold materials that Hillary had draped over dusty boxes to give an illusion of richness and drama. The slanted floor of the orchestra sometimes lent unexpected speed to our steps, and sometimes made it an effort to dance uphill. Spare fiddlers sat on the stage, taking turns to music that never ended—an integral part of the total exhilaration.

Later, Ingram had said, refreshments would be served at the Timberline, but in the meantime a bar had been set up in the theater lobby, and it was already well patronized. All this ran by in reels of color and light and sound, borne on waves of that vitality and excitement that Mark Ingram could generate.

Once I danced with Hillary and saw that he was in his element, caught up by an excitement that was really his norm. Once I saw him dancing with Gail and thought what a handsome pair they made—he with the fringe on his trapper's jacket making a blur of graceful movement; she dressed as if for a rodeo in frontier pants and embroidered jacket, a Stetson set jauntily atilt on her head, with a thong under her chin to hold it in place. The time was when I might have felt a pang of jealousy, but now I only wished happiness for Hillary—away from me.

I even danced once, briefly, joyfully, with Jon. The music had changed to a sentimental waltz, and he whirled me around the room, laughing a little, though his eyes were grave. After that he disappeared again, and I didn't see him until later that evening, when it was all over.

One impression has stayed with me especially. As I danced, a sense of unreality grew in me. I seemed to have lost touch with everything that was familiar. Grandmother Persis was sitting somewhere across the floor and Belle was with her. Probably Caleb too. But for me they existed on a distant plane. None of this was real—none of it existed. If I closed my eyes, all the make-believe would vanish in a flash. I was sure of that.

As the first intoxication died, I began to feel oddly frightened of what was happening to me. The chandelier shone with too dazzling a light, the fabric draped over the boxes was too richly scarlet, too metallically gold, the noise and the music and the laughter—all were too shrill, too artificial.

What I was feeling was a little like that intensity of sensation that can come just before a storm, to be dissipated only when the crash of thunder follows the slash of lightning. I found that I feared the storm, the sense of imminent disaster, and I knew that I had to escape the crowd. I had to find a quiet space where I could breathe more easily, and where I would be out of reach of the thunderbolt when it came.

I fought my way around to the steps at one side of the proscenium. I ran up them and through dusty curtains into the hush of a backstage world. The playing of the fiddler seemed to be thrown outward, as was intended by the acoustics, and while I could hear and see from the wings, some of the tumult quieted. I found a stool that had been left near the curtain pulleys, and sat down to put my hands over my ears and close my eyes, to let a semblance of quiet flow through me.

Where was Jon? I hadn't seen him since we danced. I didn't know until later that he was no longer in the building.

Voices reached me from overhead, and I realized that someone else had found the stairs to the old dressing room loft. I hated that place after what had happened to me up there, but it was anyone's privilege to explore. Though perhaps I'd better warn whoever it was about the splintered catwalk, in case it hadn't been blocked off.

I stepped to the foot of the stairs to call out, and then, abruptly, as if at a signal—which Ingram had indeed given—the fiddling stopped. My attention was distracted to the stage. When the crowd paused in the middle of a promenade to look up toward the footlights, Mark Ingram strode out from the opposite wings, carrying a microphone in his hand. He walked with scarcely a limp tonight, handsome and powerful of build, his gray hair growing thickly back from his forehead and an air of command in every line of his body.

I stepped into the nearest wing, where I could better see and hear him. My heart began to beat rapidly, as if with some dreadful anticipation. The sense of danger had quickened in me. What, exactly, he meant to do I wasn't sure, but I had a feeling that it would be outrageous and dramatic, and that it would be intended to crush and defeat my grandmother. I must try to get back to her as soon as I could, but for now I could only stand arrested, along with all the others who stared at the man on the stage.

As I looked across the boards—empty now except for the current fiddler on his stool, and for Ingram standing before the footlights—I saw that Gail Cullen had come into the opposite wing, resplendent in her rodeo outfit, all her attention upon the man who occupied stage center.

The theater quieted, all the myriad faces upturned toward Ingram as he began to speak. When I glanced across the stage again, Gail had disappeared. Perhaps she had stepped out of sight behind another wing.

At first Ingram's words were quiet—a welcome to his guests, a promise of more festivity to come. Then he went on.

"I have an announcement to make that may interest a number of you. Some of you already know about my plans for Jasper. It will be opened to the public about a year from now, and it is going to be one of the finest year-round resorts in the Rockies. I can promise you that the skiing will be superb and that the town will have a great deal to offer to those who want to visit us and see what the old West was like."

The crowd cheered. No one contradicted him. No one spoke up to say that he didn't own the valley, that he didn't own all of Domino, or all of Jasper, for that matter. I edged forward in the wings. Someone had to answer him. He was making something come about through his sheer, overpowering arrogance and the conviction that he could make happen whatever he willed. I was growing angry now, and anger overcame my fears. I ceased to dread the thunderbolt. He had to be stopped, and I moved toward the stage.

He must have caught movement from the corner of his eye, for he turned his head and looked at me.

"Ah," he said, "here is Laurie Morgan now. I'd like to introduce her to you. And I want to introduce her grandmother, Persis Morgan, as well, since she is part of Jasper's history."

There was scattered applause from the crowd, and Ingram beckoned to me. "Won't you come out, Miss Morgan?"

What plan he might be concocting to embarrass me and humiliate Persis, I would never know. At just that moment a ringing cry of terror stopped him. The sound came from the back of the stage, high above it. Ingram turned to stare upward, and a sigh of horror whispered through the crowd.

Over our heads Belle Durant clung with both hands to the rail of the catwalk that led across the stage above the flats. A hush fell over the entire theater, and with the strange fatality of slow movement we watched as the railing began to crumble in her grasp, breaking away. Then the action speeded up dreadfully, and she fell through the broken boards of the catwalk, crashing to the stage.

The sound of her fall echoed sickly for a moment in the crowd's stunned silence. I rushed toward her, reaching her before Ingram could recover, since he moved less easily than I. Belle's satin dress made a pool of green on the floor of the stage, and I dropped to my knees beside her.

She opened her eyes and looked up at me. "See— Tully," she said, and closed them again.

Then Ingram was there, pushing me aside. He knelt, checking for a pulse in her neck, shouting for medical help. I got to my feet, stunned and helpless, making no sense of her last whispered words.

A woman dressed incongruously as a dance hall girl came out of the crowd in response to Ingram's call for a doctor and mounted the steps to the stage. There were others crowding around now—Caleb and Gail and Hillary, among all the strangers.

My grandmother would be alone, I thought. I must go to her at once, but I found it hard to move in my state of shock. The thunderbolt had indeed fallen from the sky.

It was Hillary who drew me away gently and took me through the crowd to where Persis sat alone near the lobby entrance. Her face was white, her mouth drawn and grim, but when she held out her hand to me it did not tremble.

"It was Belle, wasn't it? Is she—do you know?"

I shook my head, still feeling numb. "A doctor is with her. And Mr. Ingram."

"Him! Why was she up there? How did it happen?"

"I don't know. That catwalk was already splintered. Why she would go out on it—" I broke off, afraid to think about possibilities.

"She wouldn't," Persis said. "She didn't like that gallery. I doubt that her fall was an accident."

Caleb had fought his way through the crowd to Persis' side, and he spoke sharply. "You don't know that it wasn't an accident."

"Belle spoke to me," I said. "She told me to see Tully. He's the caretaker in Domino, isn't he? But why would she tell me to see him?"

No one answered me.

"Go and find out how she is," Persis said to Caleb.

He hurried away, and she sat with her eyes closed. I shook my head at Hillary when he would have spoken. I wished that Jon were here, wished for his capability and good sense. We needed him badly now, and where was he?

By the time much of the crowd was spilling out of the theater, chattering excitedly, speculating. The floor was less crowded than before, and Caleb came back to us quickly.

"I'm afraid she's dying. It will take too long for an ambulance to get here and move her to a hospital. Ingram's talking about flying her out by helicopter. But he can't do that until daylight."

"Here they come," Hillary said.

Ingram himself was carrying her, and when I saw his stricken face I knew how much that hard man cared about Belle Durant.

Her red wig had fallen off, and her own vividly tinted hair hung loose. I could see blood streaking her face, see how pale she looked above the green décolletage. The doctor walked beside her, spangles glittering, but no longer seeming incongruous. I felt reassured by the look of concern on the woman's face.

"Will you go with them, Hillary?" I pleaded. "Maybe he'll let you be there."

Hillary pressed my shoulder and went away.

It was Caleb who took charge. He gave Persis his arm to lean on, and I walked on her other side. We forced our way through the foyer and onto the street, crowded now with all those costumed visitors, looking strangely as though they belonged. As though they had all been here before on the streets of Jasper.

"We'll never get a car through this jam," Caleb said.

Persis ceased to lean so heavily on my arm and drew herself tall. "I can walk. Just help me a little."

Somehow we got her through. Before we turned our back on the Opera House, I looked again toward the Timberline, where Ingram was carrying Belle into the lobby. Gail Cullen stood near the entrance. She had lost or discarded her hat, and she was staring wide-eyed at the woman in Ingram's arms, the sequins glittering on her jacket in the Timberline's lights. Hillary ran up the steps behind them as I watched. Then Caleb pushed a way along the street for us, and we walked on toward Morgan House.

I thought of that moment when I'd heard voices in the dressing room loft. The words had been soft, whispered, and I couldn't tell whether they had belonged to a man or woman, or both. If only I had—but that sort of regret was a waste. The thing was done.

Sharp in my memory, nevertheless, was the sight of Mark Ingram standing arrogantly on the stage, ready to carry out some dreadful plan that would have humiliated my grandmother. His ingenuity would have taken care of that, I knew, and only Belle's fall had stopped him. Now we might never know what he intended, and that was certainly just as well.

Away from the glare of light and the sound there were few stragglers. My long skirts hampered me on the rough walk, and once when I stepped on the hem I heard a rip. Persis moved slowly, but steadily and surely, pausing now and then to lean on Caleb's arm and rest. I still wondered where Jon could be and why he wasn't with us. A high, full moon lighted our way to Morgan House.

When we reached it, the porch light was on, and there was Jon, sitting comfortably on the steps, with a beer can in his hand.

"Why didn't you stay?" I cried. "We needed you!"

"You're home early," he said. "I was going to join you again in a little while. It sounds as though the festivities have moved outdoors. What do you mean—you needed me?"

"It's too late now," I told him. "Belle—" But I couldn't get the words past the choke in my throat.

Caleb helped Persis up the steps to where she could sit in the swing. Then in dry, unemotional terms he explained what had happened, and Jon listened grimly.

"Belle was pushed out on that catwalk," Persis said when Caleb finished. "She *must* have been pushed."

"You can't say that," Caleb reproached her. "We don't know any such thing."

I broke in to tell Jon what Belle had whispered to me.

"Tully?" he said. "I wonder why Tully. Maybe I'd better ride over to Domino in the morning and see what I can find out from the old man. I came back to the house so I could have it to myself and make a search that I've wanted to make for a long time. You'd better come inside and see what I've done, Mrs. Morgan. You won't like it, but I had to try, and I wasn't sure you'd agree if I asked permission."

She let Caleb help her up from the swing. "First I want to know how Belle is. Laurie, will you call the hotel?"

I went into the hall to the telephone, and a stranger answered. "Belle is dead," he said shortly. I hung up, feeling ill. Ill and surrounded by evil, by the constant threat of an evil that could strike any of us down at any time. Belle, so warmly outspoken, had drawn fire. We would all miss her terribly.

The others saw my face when I came back.

"She's gone?" Persis said.

I nodded, and Caleb bent toward her.

She pushed him away. "I'm all right. Just angry for now. I'll cry later. Belle was my friend, and this has happened because of me. We've got to fight that man, punish whoever did this. You must go to Domino as soon as you can, Jon."

"I'll go," he said. "But right now come into the back parlor, Mrs. Morgan, so you can see the mess I've made."

He led the way to the open door and reached in to turn on lights. Persis closed her eyes, and I remembered that she hadn't set foot in this room for twenty years. Lights flashed on, and she opened her eyes and looked about the room. It had obviously been searched, for old dust and cobwebs had been disturbed, a rug thrown back at one corner, furniture moved about, one of the draperies down in a heap by the window. Persis said nothing, her eyes searching, remembering.

"What were you looking for?" Caleb asked, his voice oddly harsh.

"For something I didn't find," Jon said. "Though I think someone else did. Not the police, or it would have come out in the papers. I always wondered about that missing deringer."

"Let it go, Jon," Caleb said. "Just let it all go. It can't possibly matter now."

"It can matter a lot if we find a way to prove that Laurie never killed her father."

The hush was suddenly intense, and I found that my knees wouldn't hold me. I went shakily to the old horsehair sofa and sat down on its slippery surface. Persis followed me carefully into the room, ignoring Caleb's offer of his arm, and sat in a chair. How strange we all looked in our costumes for the ball. Strange and somehow appropriate in this old room.

"Go on," Persis said. "What are you talking about?"

"One of those guns was missing, wasn't it? So it might have been fired when the other one was fired. Perhaps at the same time, so that only one shot seemed to be heard. In that case there ought to be another .41-gauge bullet around somewhere. There were no traces of blood found at the time to show that Noah might have been wounded when he left. So the second bullet, if there was one, should be here in this room. But no one ever reported finding such a bullet, though I understand the police went over the room thoroughly."

Both Persis and Caleb were staring fixedly, and he went on.

"Tonight I decided to come in here while you were all away and make a real search myself. Of course I didn't find anything. But I think the second gun *was* fired—not the one that killed Richard Morgan, but a second deringer in Laurie's hands. The bullet could have gone astray—and I'm pretty sure that's what happened. I think it must have struck up there near the corner of the ceiling, so that it cut the wallpaper and cracked the plaster, but its force must have been spent, so that it ricocheted to the carpet, or some other part of the room."

I found myself shaken by a mingling of hope and anxiety and disbelief. "But—but then who—"

"Found the bullet? That's what I'd like to know. Was it you, Mrs. Morgan?"

She looked both shocked and confused, and her face told us the truth. "No, of course not, Jon," she said. "I never thought of such a thing. What are you getting at?"

"Mr. Hawes?" Jon questioned.

The creases that ran down Caleb Hawes' cheeks looked

deeper than ever, and his color was a pasty gray. He came to stand beside Persis' chair, beseeching her.

"Yes, I found the bullet. It's with those jewels that were hidden away. I searched before the police came and I found it, just as Jon had said." He broke off for a moment, seeking control, then went on. "Will you forgive me for what I thought? I believed that you fired the gun that killed Richard, Mrs. Morgan. And if that was what you'd done, I had to protect you."

"I? Kill my son?"

He stumbled on, all his careful control crumbling. "I thought you'd picked up the second gun that Laurie had loaded and you'd tried to shoot Noah Armand. But in the struggle Richard must have stepped in the way and you shot him instead. I always thought that was why you concocted the story of an intruder, faked the theft of the jewelry. I thought you had hidden the gun, and all I wanted was to see that your secret was kept."

For a long moment no one said anything. Then Persis spoke sadly. "My old friend! But what a fool you've been. Of course it was Laurie. She was the one I was protecting. And her mother. From all the scandal that would have made the newspapers and the investigation a circus."

But Jon was already contradicting her. "No—I doubt that it was Laurie. The spent bullet must have come from Laurie's wildly fired gun. But it would have been Noah Armand who shot and killed your son, Mrs. Morgan. Then it was he who took away the second deringer that he had used."

I still couldn't believe or understand, and I was shaking my head. "Even if what you say is true, Jon, how can we ever know which gun killed my father?"

"Noah wouldn't have missed. Not when they were so close."

"But then my mother must have seen it all. My mother was here in this room, and she would have known that Noah killed my father. Yet she never said anything." Tears came into my eyes, and I looked at my grandmother. "She let me believe—"

"Stop that!" Persis said. "You didn't believe anything.

You didn't remember, and you can't start judging her now. Love does crazy things to people. I know. I loved that man once, and it took a long while for me to come to my senses and face my mistake. Just be glad. Be grateful to Jon for working this out, and let everything else go—including any blame you may want to heap on Caleb."

I roused myself to stare at Caleb Hawes. "That was why you hated to have me come here, wasn't it? Because you wanted to protect my grandmother."

His look was still unforgiving—of me. "I owe Mrs. Morgan a great deal. She was kinder to me than my own family. I *wanted* to do what I did."

Jon came to sit on the sofa beside me, taking my hand. "Just hang in there, Laurie. Don't try to sort it all out right away. Just try to believe. That's all you need to do."

"I wish I could," I said. "But I don't think we'll ever really know."

Grudgingly Caleb had arrived at a moment of total confession. "There's more. Mrs. Morgan, I was the one who put the sleeping capsules in your milk."

"You?" Persis made a despairing gesture. "But why—why?"

He stumbled on desperately—a man I could hardly recognize. "I thought if I could stop you from making a new will—just for a little while—you might fall out with Laurie. Or she might leave. That was why I hung that wreath on her door." He turned to me. "And that's why I opened your door the first night you were here. I wanted to frighten you so that you wouldn't stay. I hoped you'd go back to New York before you could further damage your grandmother. I knew you would think it the sort of trick that Gail would play. You'd never have blamed me."

To my surprise, Persis had recovered from her first astonishment and was nodding her head thoughtfully. "Yes. Perhaps I can understand—a little. None of us ever gave you a chance to use your own talents, did we, Caleb? And desperation always gives bad advice."

I wished that I could be as generous, but there was nothing I could say to this man now. Perhaps I would never really know the truth about Caleb Hawes. Whether it was my grandmother's well-being he protected or his own interest in her will—how could anyone tell? Perhaps he didn't know himself by this time.

"At least this would explain Noah Armand's disappearance," Jon said. "He knew he'd murdered Richard Morgan, and he took himself off as fast as he could, and was never heard from again."

My hand tightened on Jon's. There was something that Persis still didn't know.

"The second deringer!" I cried. "Someone put that second gun back in the box with the other one. It's there right now."

Persis gasped, and Caleb scowled at me. But he went to the mahogany box and opened it, displaying both pistols, one more tarnished than the other, which had stayed in its case all these years.

Caleb spoke in apology. "When Laurie told me this second gun had turned up, I thought you'd put it there for some reason of your own, Mrs. Morgan."

"Of course I didn't!"

"I realize that now. But if you didn't put it there, then what does its reappearance mean?"

"I think we all know what it means," Persis said softly. "It means that Noah Armand has come back."

"Maybe," Jon said. "Anyway, I'm not going to wait for morning to ride to Domino and talk to old Tully. There's a full moon, and I'll go there tonight. Mrs. Morgan— those pieces of jewelry that you pretended were stolen— are they in the house in Domino?"

"Yes, they are there. Caleb can tell you where the box is hidden, since he placed it there for me. You may as well retrieve the box and bring it back. You want that bullet, don't you?"

Dully Caleb explained where he had hidden the tin box that contained Persis' jewels, and Jon started for the door.

I stood up, making the quickest decision of my life. "I'll go with you. I want to hear what Tully says."

Caleb said, "That's absurd," and Jon looked at me uncertainly.

"If I were your age, I would go," Persis said, and I dropped a kiss on her cheek.

"I won't try to argue with two Morgans," Jon said. "Go get out of that fancy dress, Laurie. I'll saddle up and wait for you."

I ran for the stairs, pulling up my long skirts so as not to stumble. In my room I changed quickly to jeans and low boots. My hair was tumbling from its coil on top of my head, and I pulled out the pins and let it hang free. No time to do anything about it now, and I'd cope with tangles later.

Persis had returned to the parlor with Caleb, and she held out a hand to me. "Be careful, Laurie. You're all I've got now. And that man is dangerous."

This time I knew she didn't mean Mark Ingram.

"I'll be with Jon," I told her, and we went outside together.

The ranch seemed quiet, with only the underlying night sounds busy with their whispering. The moon was bright, but it had started to dip down the sky toward the mountains. Over near the Timberline voices still sounded, carrying in the mountain stillness. Lights were ablaze down there, and pain returned as I thought of Belle. Anger as well. Then I turned my back and started for the glow of the barn.

Wind blew cold down the valley, and Old Desolate stood high and black against the sky, with moonlight shining on its rocky head. I held back my tumbling thoughts. I couldn't wholly accept as yet, or understand. Time enough for all that later. Now I was going to Domino again, and once more I was riding there with Jon.

XX

The horses stamped and snorted over being disturbed from their sleep, but the cool night made them step out briskly and we rode up the valley at a good pace. My hair blew free in the wind, and it felt good to have it loose from its pins.

Jon wore his revolver this time, and he had thrust a few tools into his jacket pockets. Mostly we rode in silence, with Sundance leading the way. My senses were keyed to the night, so that I was aware of the smallest detail, aware most of all of Jon riding ahead of me.

Both valley and rimming mountains seemed unfamiliar by moonlight, and deep night shadows filled the pine forests and cast patterns that I had never seen before. Down by the stream thickly crowding bushes shimmered like silver in the pale light. Riding with me, as always, was that memory of my terrified gallop up the valley as a child, when I was driven by the mistaken fear that my father had been trapped in the mine and would die there if I didn't reach him.

For the first time that full realization that I had been holding away, not daring to believe, swept through me. Perhaps I had not been responsible for his death, after all. Perhaps it hadn't been my hand that fired the shot that killed him. Perhaps I could remember him more safely now. With the barriers of pain and fright fading, old and loving memories could come through. Sometime I would talk to Jon about him. Jon would remember him.

As we turned up the shoulder of the mountain, the horses slowed, picking their way on the narrow stony trail. Up ahead, Jon reined Sundance and waited for me to ride up beside him.

"When we come into view of the mine and Domino, we'll tether the horses and go down on foot. The dog will probably announce us, but we can at least be close before he knows we're coming. I don't want to give too much warning, in case the old man doesn't want to see us."

"Will you talk to Tully first or go first to the house?"

"The house first, if we can make it without too much disturbance. I'd like to be sure the box is there before I tackle Tully."

"What could Belle possibly have known concerning him?"

"He was here at the time of the shooting, and he wasn't always Ingram's man. So who knows?"

As we sat our horses, speaking softly, a sudden crack of sound came from a distance, echoing and crashing against the peaks.

"That was a rifle shot!" Jon said. "It came from the direction of Domino. Come along, but quietly."

Again we rode through the darkness of the pines, pushing our horses a little. My heart was thumping hard, and I didn't dare think of the implications of that shot, or of who might be waiting for us among Domino's ghosts. Always I had been afraid of Noah, even as a child. I had grown up fearing his name, and I was still afraid.

As we passed below the place where Jon and I had crawled out the entrance to the old tunnel, he spoke to me over his shoulder.

"Yesterday I came up here and filled in the opening with cement. Those old mines are a temptation to kids who want to adventure, or for tourists exploring. Nobody can get in or out of it now."

Nothing would ever make me go into the place again. I was through with mines forever.

We rode out along the moonlit hillside above the shadowy bones of the little town. Patches of ruin gleamed like silver in the pale light. More like silver than the ore that had come out of the mine.

"This is far enough," Jon said, and dismounted.

He tethered Sundance to a sapling, and then secured Baby Doe. Together we started down the steepening trail into the gulch. Domino lay sleeping in its black and silver world, and the night was utterly still. The dog hadn't heard or scented us yet, and to look at the peaceful scene, no one would guess that a shot had rung out a little while before.

"It's too quiet," Jon whispered.

We continued down the path, expecting to hear at any moment the barking of the dog, and to have Tully challenge us. Or someone else? But nothing stirred. As Jon said, it was all too quiet.

The trail ran past the way to the Old Desolate mine, and glancing toward it, I saw that the entrance stood dark and open, with the door still removed, as Ingram's men must have left it when they went in to find a bullet my great-grandfather had fired so long ago. And to fake the finding of that silver buckle.

Jon took my arm as we went down the last steep pitch of rocky path and stepped into the street that cut through Domino's silver bones. Almost at once we had the answer to part of the silence that greeted us. Ahead, in the middle of the road, lay a black shadow that was not a shadow.

Jon bent over the sprawled body of the dog. "This was the shot we heard." He caught me by the arm and pulled me to the side of the road. "I don't like this. Where can old Tully be?"

Scattered timbers offered us slight shelter, but we clung to them, avoiding the center of the street, where the moon shone brightly and any movement would be clear to the watchers. If there were watchers—or a watcher. If horses had come in, they'd been left elsewhere, like our own.

Quietly, keeping near the ruins, we walked the short street. The Tremayne house loomed close, and I was grateful for the shadows of its porch as we ran up the steps. Jon went first, gun in hand, watching for trouble. The door of the house stood open, as it should not have, and inside, the stillness was eerie. As though the house watched us and listened. Or as though someone inside watched and listened?

"Stay near the door till I look through the place," Jon said softly. I paused just across the sill.

He took a flashlight from his jacket and cast its beam through the downstairs rooms, then ran up to the floor above. I heard his light footsteps moving to the front, and then into each room in turn, before he came down to join me at the door.

"There's no one in the house. Let's see if we can find what we came for, and then we'll search for Tully."

"Why hasn't he come out to challenge us? Or to investigate the dog?"

"I don't like it. Come on back to the dining room with me."

We went into the empty room beyond the parlor, and Jon went at once to the far corner and shone the flashlight across the floor.

"Someone's had these boards up," he said. "Maybe we're already too late."

He slipped the gun into its holster and gave me the flashlight. Then, with one of the tools he had brought with him, he pried up a loose board, and then another. I moved the light so that it would shine into the hollow under the floor. There was nothing there.

From behind us there was suddenly a brighter illumination in the room, and as I whirled about, Jon sprang to his feet. Gail Cullen stood in the doorway, holding a lantern high. She wore tan slacks, a brown jacket with the collar turned up, and a scarf tied around her hair. She, too, had made the night ride from Jasper.

"Thank God you're here!" she cried. "Hillary needs help! He's fallen in the mine, and you've got to rescue him. But first—there's the old man, outside. We need to get him into the house, out of the cold wind."

Hillary in the mine? But there was no time for astonishment or questions. We followed her to the front of the house and found old Tully lying below the porch, where Gail had left him. Blood streaked his face from a gash on his forehead.

"Who did this?" Jon demanded. "And who shot the dog?"

304

Already he was gathering up the old man's slight body in his arms, carrying him into the house without waiting for her answers. Gail and I followed. She looked pale in the dim light—and desperate.

"Leave him here," she said. "It's Hillary who needs help."

Jon lowered Tully gently to the floor of what had been the parlor. At once he tried to get up. "Don't go with her! Don't go to the mine! He's got a gun. Killed my dog. Shot 'im."

"Lange killed your dog?" Jon said.

Gail burst in a little wildly. "He had to! This crazy old coot sicced his dog on Hillary. He had to shoot. And then Tully tried to attack him. So Hillary hit him. There was nothing else to do. But don't waste time here. You've got to hurry."

"Noah started it all," Tully mumbled. "Noah and that Ingram feller."

Jon kneeled beside him. "Tell us," he said. "We'll try to help, but first we need to know what's going on."

Gail made a sound of impatience. "Let it wait till later."

"I keep some stuff here when I'm working," Jon said to me. "There's a bottle of water and some cloths in the kitchen. Get them, Laurie."

I felt torn, anguished. Hillary helpless in the mine? I knew what that was like. But Hillary shooting a dog, striking down an old man? I let it all go and ran back to the kitchen, where I found a thermos bottle of water and a pile of cloths in the galvanized iron sink. In a moment I was back in the room.

Jon gestured to Gail, and she stopped her protesting to kneel beside him. Gently she began to wash the blood from Tully's face and forehead, though her hands were shaking.

"Can you talk?" Jon asked the old man.

Again he made an effort. "Noah—down in the mine. Wasn' dead that time. Twenty years or more ago, I reckon. I heard him down the shaft, yellin' and screechin'.

305

But when I went inside, there warn't no way I could get 'im out."

"We can't stay and listen to this," Gail cried, sitting back on her heels.

"Why is Hillary in the mine?" I asked her.

"Oh, I don't know!" Her vagueness made me uneasy. "I suppose because he's got a thing about that awful place. He's been there before. I suppose it's natural that it should haunt him."

"I don't know what you're talking about. What has Hillary to do with the Old Desolate?"

"Plenty. I suppose I may as well tell you. It doesn't matter now. That time when your dog was lost, Hillary found him over near the mine chasing chipmunks. So he put him inside that end of the tunnel the dog had dug open and phoned Caleb to give him a story for you. You know how Hillary can change his voice when he wants to. You did what he expected and went looking for Red. So then he shut you into the mine too. Just to give you a taste of what it's like. He meant to play the hero later and rescue you. Only Jon beat him to it."

"But why would he do a thing like that?" I cried in disbelief. Something was missing—the key to all this.

"Because— Oh, how can I tell? You know how he is! You know how excited he gets. Too excited."

I still didn't know what she was talking about. Of course Hillary got keyed up and excited. That was part of whatever genius drove him. But he couldn't—wouldn't— have shut me into the mine!

"He's an extreme manic-depressive and getting much worse," Gail said. "Do you understand what that is?"

Jon broke in. "Hush a minute, both of you. Tully wants to talk."

The old man was struggling again to put his thoughts into words, and we were quiet, listening. His story went back twenty years, to the day that Noah Armand had fled from Jasper, expecting pursuit because he'd killed a man. He had meant to hide temporarily inside the Old Desolate, Tully said.

"When I couldn't help, he told me to go git somebody. But not from Jasper. So I went off on my own."

While he was gone, Ingram had come searching for Noah and had heard him shouting from the mine. Noah had fallen down the main shaft in the dark and was badly hurt. When Ingram tried to rescue him, he fell too, and smashed his leg. They were stuck there for a day or more, until Tully brought back a couple of squatters he'd been seeking.

Between them they managed to get Ingram out, though his leg had turned pretty bad by that time. He was taken by muleback to a doctor, and Tully lost track of him after that. Until a year or so ago, when he turned up pretty flashy-rich, and with a new leg. He'd hired Tully as a watchman for Domino, and that had been fine. Even got a dog for him.

I pressed the old man to tell us what had happened to Noah Armand, and he mumbled out what little he knew. They'd all thought Noah dead when Ingram was brought out of the mine. Couldn't blame Ingram for that—he was mostly out of his head himself. But Tully and his pals went back for the body and found Noah alive and delirious. So they got him out too. By the time he mended a bit—nursed right here in the old Tremayne house—he wasn't altogether right in his head. Though he was strong enough to go off on his own eventually, and Tully never heard a word about him again.

Tully had gotten smart to Ingram right away, he told us. "A big grudge that feller is carrying. Blames everybody for losing his leg—but mostly old Mrs. Morgan, because she drove her husband out and made everything happen. Said he was going to pay her off if it was the last thing he ever did. Maybe he'll think different after what's happened to Belle."

Gail had apparently told him about that, and a tear streaked incongruously down Tully's stained face. Nevertheless, he struggled on again.

"Belle was okay. Real good to me. She never deserved what happened to her. It was that crazy kid of Noah Armand's coming back here to mess everything up!"

307

"What's he talking about?" I asked Gail, and Jon put a hand on my arm.

"Hillary," Gail said. "But of course you wouldn't know, would you? He didn't want you to find out until he was ready. He's always used his stage name. He came out to Colorado nearly a year ago, though of course he didn't show his face in Jasper. He didn't want to be recognized later. But he was all around here in the mountains, and in Denver and Boulder, finding out what he could. That's when I met him and he told me some of what he planned. I guess I *wanted* to help him. It wasn't hard to get a nursing job at Morgan House, where I could be on the inside. You never suspected, did you, how well Hillary and I knew each other?"

All along I had thought Gail was going to the Timberline to see Mark Ingram. I felt a little sick over my gullibility, but totally bewildered as well.

Somehow I managed the words. "Hillary is—Noah Armand's son?"

"He'll tell you himself. Just get up there to the mine. I'll stay here with Tully if you'll just go."

I looked at Jon, but he was shaking his head. "Not right away. Not until you've told us a few more things, Gail. What about Belle Durant?"

Gail covered her face with her hands. "That was awful. I don't think Hillary intended what happened. He'd gone to Domino and talked to Tully. By that time Tully knew who Hillary was, and he'd told Belle. I guess at the ball she wanted to give Hillary a chance to explain before she blew everything into the open. Hillary said he took her up to those gallery dressing rooms, where they could be away from the crowd. But after he knew, he had to stop her talking. Whatever he did must have frightened her, because she ran out on the catwalk to get away from him, and then fell through. That's what he told me."

I felt increasingly ill and I must have looked it, for Jon came to put his arm around me, though he didn't let up with Gail.

"Then you've been helping him all along?" he said. "Even when it came to murder?"

308

She shrank away from the words.

Apparently Tully had been listening, for now he managed to prop himself up on one elbow. "Lange tried to kill Ingram too. Shot at 'im and missed. City boy!"

Gail pushed Tully down. "Hush! You've got to lie still." Then she looked up at us. "Will you go to the mine now? Just go up there and help him." She seemed more distraught than I'd ever seen her.

"I'll see if I can find out what's happening," Jon said. "Are you all right, Laurie? You'd better stay here."

I wasn't all right. Maybe I never would be all right again, but I wouldn't stay behind with Gail for anything. Nevertheless, there was one last question I had to ask her. Not a trivial question, because I had the feeling that it tied in with everything else.

"What became of my grandmother's jewelry, Gail?"

She answered listlessly. "I've got it right here in my bag. Hillary gave it to me to keep for him a little while ago. Tully knew where Caleb Hawes had hidden it, and Hillary got that out of him."

Jon took the box from her and opened it. The bullet was there.

"We'll need a lantern," Jon said.

"There's another one at the mine," Gail told him. "I'll keep this one here."

We went out into cold and windy moonlight. This time we didn't take the horses. Jon led the way up a steep path, past the tailing dumps, and I scrambled after him up to the narrow road that had once serviced mine equipment. I still felt numb with horror and disbelief.

The opening to the Old Desolate loomed ahead of us, a black gash into the mountain, the door still off its hinges.

"Wait here," Jon whispered. "We can't trust him for a moment." He took his gun from its holster and held it ready in his hand.

Inside the mine I could see faint light. As Gail had said, one of Tully's lanterns burned far into the tunnel.

"Lange?" Jon called. "Where are you, Lange?"

I remembered how a voice could echo in there, and

309

found myself tensing. But there was no answer—only a deep, vast silence, once the echoes had died away.

"Stay here," Jon said over his shoulder. "I'll go in as far as the shaft."

Even the moonlight at my back carried menace with it now, and I wouldn't wait anywhere without Jon. The thought of Hillary terrified me, but I followed close on Jon's heels. Lantern light lay ahead, and he turned his strong flashlight on the rough rock walls of the passage. Underfoot there was rubble, and once I stumbled.

Neither of us called out again. If Hillary was able to hear, if he wanted to hear, he would know we had come.

As we went deeper into the mountain, the dark earth smells of the mine seemed to rush out of the depths toward us—frighteningly familiar. This was a place where I didn't want to be, but there was nothing else to do except move quietly after Jon. Quietly, so that the rocks wouldn't hear my footsteps.

"Here we are," Jon said, heedless of sound, and I saw that we'd reached the big room where the main shaft had been sunk into the heart of the mountain. Ahead yawned black emptiness.

From behind us a voice spoke—Hillary's voice, high-pitched with excitement. "Stay right there! And drop that gun you're holding, Maddocks."

I swung around and saw him standing half shadowed in the lantern light, a rifle in his hands. That same rifle that had stood behind the bar at the Timberline? The one that had been used in the attempt on Ingram's life? I felt sick again with shock and despair.

Jon dropped his revolver, and Hillary stepped forward to prod him with the rifle.

"I saw you going down into Domino," Hillary said. "So I told Gail to make it good about my being trapped. She's scared enough by this time to do as I say."

"But why?" I pleaded. "Hillary, tell me why all this has happened?"

Light from the lantern on the rocky floor threw shadows eerily up his face. "You were such a pushover, Laurie. I knew I had to meet you if I was going to pay off your grandmother, and Ingram too. I had to get you out to Jasper. I'd found out about your aunt in Dillon, and I meant to look her up, maybe meet you if you were around. You saved me a lot of trouble by walking into the theater that day. Then your grandmother sent for you, and all I had to do was tag along."

"For the money?" I said. "Was that it?"

His voice came down from its strung-up pitch, sounding almost gentle. "In a way I fell for you, Laurie. For a while you needed me, and maybe I'll put you into a play yet."

Jon's arm tightened about me. "Why do you want us here, Lange? What game are you playing now?"

Again Hillary's voice changed, turning rough—that marvelous stage voice that knew so well how to play on the emotions. Only this was no longer playacting.

"Playing? A game? No, it's not that anymore. You're going to suffer a little now. The way my father suffered, because of Persis Morgan. Because of Mark Ingram. You're going to help me pay off a debt."

"Gail told us," I said. "Is it true? Are you really Noah Armand's son?"

The pressure was rising in him now, keying him up to a dangerous pitch. Yet somehow he managed to hold himself in check. He *wanted* me to know every bit of it—so the debt he spoke of would be paid.

"Of course it's true! Though I never knew the story until a year ago, when my father died. In a mental institution. Think about that, Laurie. I was with him at the end, and his mind cleared for a little while, so he could tell me the story. About how badly Persis Morgan had treated him. About how Ingram had left him to die here in the mine, and then had gone off with all that money from Persis Morgan."

"Did he also tell you that he killed my father?" I asked.

"That too!" Hillary was driven now by a stronger passion than I had ever sensed in him before. A passion of strange and twisted devotion for a father he had hardly known. "Your mother played with him, led him on! He

311

had to kill your father in self-defense. He picked up that extra deringer you'd loaded and used it—as he had to. I found that gun in his things at my mother's house after he died, and I brought it out here with me. I wish I could have seen your face, Laurie, when you discovered the two guns back in their case. I hunted for your spent bullet too, but I never found it."

"Does your mother know all of this?"

He brushed my words aside carelessly. "We were never close. And she let him down too. Oh, I'd have told you some of it after we were married, Laurie. I wouldn't have let you go on thinking what you did about yourself. But now I know you're one of the cheaters too—running out on me for this cowboy! And for what you did to my father—just by loading those guns! You and your grandmother were to blame."

I held onto Jon's arm, weak with horror. Hillary would see only what he chose to see, what he chose to believe, and he had clearly idealized his father out of all resemblance to the real man.

"It's time now," he said, picking up the lantern. "You're going down the shaft—both of you. There's an old ladder there, though it's broken in places. If you fall, it's a pretty long drop. Like the one my father had to take. You won't have to stay forever, but it will give Gail and me time to get away. And at least we have that jewelry of your grandmother's to take along."

Jon said, "We're not going down that shaft. Just shut us in here, if you must, and get yourself away."

Hillary had picked up Jon's revolver, setting the rifle aside. "You'll do what I tell you to."

"No," Jon said.

The gun was pointed at Jon, and Hillary's nervous finger was on the trigger. There was one chance, and I had to take it. I flung myself against Hillary's arm, knocking it up, so that the shot went wild, roaring and reverberating through the tunnels, making the very walls tremble. Jon threw himself to the side into darkness, and Hillary fired again and again, wildly, so that the roaring increased and I could hear bullets striking rock, ricocheting, bringing down slabbing over our heads. He wasn't aiming at anything now—just firing wildly, out of control.

It didn't stop until the gun was empty. The lantern had fallen on its side, and I couldn't see Jon, couldn't tell if he had been hurt. I wasn't even sure about myself. All the roaring had confused and frightened me.

When the echoes shivered away, the sounds didn't die out with them. There was a new cracking and creaking all about us, as though ceilings and walls might crumble in and crush us. Jon was on his feet, catching me by the arm, pulling me along.

"Quick!" he shouted.

Hillary had seen what was happening too, and he was ahead of us. Already rock was crumbling into the doorway. The overhead beam had cracked, and timbers and rock were coming down. The crash sent up a great roar of its own, and even as we stared in dim lantern light, the mountain seemed to move. For an instant Hillary stood silhouetted against the moonlight. Then he was gone.

The entire wall, the ceiling, the beams over the doorway—all crashed in, filling the space that had made an opening into the mountain. For what seemed a long time afterward, chunks of rock fell. We could hear some of them rolling down the slope outside.

Finally it was quiet again—almost quiet. I stood very still in my terrible fright, while Jon picked up the lantern, still burning, and held it high. The opening had been blocked with rock. And Hillary was in there. What was left of Hillary.

When there was nothing more to fall, Jon went to the mound of broken timbers and crumbled rock. But there was nothing that could be done. Hillary could never have escaped alive. So much rock had crashed in that a small mountain closed the door and not even a crack of moonlight shone through.

"There's nothing to do but wait," Jon said. "There may be a long night ahead until someone from the house comes looking for us."

"There's Gail," I said. "Maybe she'll have heard."

313

"If we can expect anything from her. She's going to save her own skin first."

"But we've got to do something . . ." My teeth had begun to chatter from the reaction, from the shock of Hillary's death—the shock of everything he had told us that was now beginning to come through to me. Even Belle's tragic, pointless death.

I must have sagged against the wall, for Jon reached out to steady me. "Hang on, Laurie. We'll wait for a while and see what happens. If no one comes, we'll try the tunnel I sealed up, to see if there's any way of digging past the cement. I saw an old shovel back there. In the meantime let's see if we can get some rest. It may be morning before they come for us."

In the lantern light I looked at my watch. It was already the morning of a new day, but it would be hours until dawn. Jon drew me down and we sat together against a rock wall. The floor was infinitely cold and hard, and so was the wall at our backs, but we held each other for warmth and I took comfort in his arms. He smoothed the tangle of my hair, and his touch was tender, as it had been so long ago.

It was something to have the lantern for as long as it burned. It would be worse when total darkness came. As it had come for Noah Armand down in that shaft, and for Mark Ingram, who had tried to rescue his friend, losing his leg in the effort, then somehow blaming my grandmother all these years for sending them both into disaster.

I pressed my head against Jon's shoulder.

"It's nearly over, Laurie," he said. "Just a little while more."

For all those early morning hours we huddled together, and time went by. I tried not to think of Hillary. I tried not to think of the Glory Hole out there—where all those men had died. I thought about the future. There had to be one—with Jon. If ever we got out of here, I would make it happen.

I must have slept a little in Jon's arms. But when I woke with a start, I found myself lying on the rock floor

314

while he moved toward the blocked entrance, lantern in hand.

"There's someone out there," he said.

I could hear the voices now, the shouting. One voice seemed to be giving orders, sharply and clearly.

"That's Mark Ingram!" I cried, and Jon shouted back to him.

"We'll get you out!" Ingram called, and I heard the vigor and determination in his voice. "I've got some of my men here to start the digging. So just hold on."

XXI

It took what seemed forever to accomplish, but the rock had fallen in a limited area around the doorway and it was still loose enough to move when there were many hands with shovels. We knew when Hillary's body was found and carried away.

The task was done at last, and welcome daylight poured into the mouth of the tunnel, where we waited. When Jon pushed me out ahead of him, a cheer went up from the men standing around with shovels and pickaxes. Then Jon was out beside me, and what we saw was more heartening than anything we could have imagined.

Beyond the workmen, yet close enough to be in command if necessary, Persis Morgan sat proudly in the front seat of a Land Rover. She was dressed as I had never seen her, in Levi's and jacket, and Caleb Hawes sat glumly beside her, behind the wheel.

I ran toward them and hung onto the door next to her, unable to find words.

"Don't sputter, Laurie," she said. "I can't get up on a horse yet, but they couldn't stop me from coming. I thought I'd better supervise this job."

Her words were jaunty, but her eyes told me how worried she had been. I hugged whatever I could reach of her.

Mark Ingram, astride his horse, regarded us ruefully, but with a reluctant gleam of respect for my grandmother. He wasn't the same man I remembered. Loss and pain had shaken and beaten him, dispelling the cocky benevolence. This was a grim but far less driven man. More than ever I knew that he had loved Belle Durant.

We weren't able to put together all the details of what had happened until some time after when we were back at Morgan House.

Gail had indeed heard the crash and rumble of falling rock. She had ridden her horse up the trail and seen that the door to the mine had been closed by the mountain itself. She was already afraid of Hillary, not knowing how to escape what she had started. I remembered her weeping that night in the church. When she saw the rockfall, she rode straight back to Morgan House, roused my grandmother, and returned her jewels. Persis had then phoned Ingram for help, and he'd gathered his men and headed for Domino, with Persis insisting that she must come too.

Gail had not gone with them. She didn't want to see Hillary again, alive or dead, and was going home to her family for a while. If anyone wanted her, that was where she would be.

On the way to the Old Desolate, Ingram rode along beside Persis in the Land Rover, and he had admitted without shame the bluff he'd tried to pull when it came to those bones in the mine. The buckle, for instance.

All those years before, when he had tried to get Noah out of the shaft, he had used Noah's belt in a futile effort to pull him up the ladder. But he had fallen himself, injuring his leg so badly that it had been removed later. When Tully had rescued him, before they took Noah out, Ingram still had that belt in his hands, and he'd kept the buckle all this time. To remind him of a debt of vengeance he meant to pay. But since Belle's death he wanted that no longer. All he wanted now was to

316

away from this cursed place. After what had happened to Belle, he couldn't stay on.

As I listened to all this, I thought again of human complexity and marveled at the old mingling of good and evil—in all of us.

"You can buy me out if you want," he told Persis. "I'll charge you a good price. But I never want to see any of this again."

In Domino someone went first to minister to Tully, and he had been taken back to Jasper and was safe in bed at the Timberline recovering.

While we talked of these things over breakfast in Persis' room, she sat against her pillows, sipping milk laced with brandy. She looked weary, but pleased with herself.

"Now then," she said when the telling was over, "what about you two?"

That was a good question, but I didn't look at Jon, nor he at me.

She snorted indignantly. "Go away then, both of you, and *talk!* I was never so backward when I was your age!"

Jon smiled at her, but his look was sober when he turned to me. "Do you want to go for a walk, Laurie?"

I was in a mood to go anywhere he led me, no matter how tired I felt.

Persis held out a hand to each of us, and I bent to kiss her cheek. Caleb came into the hall as we left and held out his own hand, a bit hesitantly, as though he weren't sure I would take it. But I could forgive him now. I understood a little better.

Outdoors, we found the sun climbing high above the mountains, and I stood for a moment looking off toward Old Desolate.

Jon watched me quizzically. "Maybe we'd better do as she says and talk a bit."

I nodded, determination growing in me. Together, but not touching by so much as a finger—as though we'd never spent those frightening, tender hours in the mine—we followed the path to Jon's cabin. Red came with us joyfully, more sure than I was that we three belonged together.

Inside, when the fire leaped in the grate to Jon's satisfaction, throwing a rosy flicker over the room, we sat a bit stiffly on the couch, watching the flames. What a stubborn, impossible man he was!

"I'm sorry about Hillary," he said at last. "Sorry about all you must be feeling. Sorry if you loved him."

"I thought I loved him. At first. But then I met a cowboy I've known all my life. A stubborn, impossible cowboy."

"Don't, Laurie," he said.

I'd had enough, and being a Morgan, I went right on. "If you won't, then I must. It's hard to believe that you, of all people, would put money ahead of life."

"Shut up," he told me, but there was no sting in the words. "I'll do my own talking—if you'll just listen. I don't like all that Morgan money behind you. I'm not all that liberated. But I love you, Laurie, no matter what. And I think maybe you'll fit in out here, after all, though I didn't expect that at first."

"But I *belong* here—" I began to protest.

"Wait! You don't really know that yet. You haven't had a chance to live here under normal circumstances. There are all sorts of objections I could give you."

I suppressed a desire to sputter out some objections of my own. Men could be so terribly slow. They came to conclusions through careful steps of logic—yet they were the same conclusions a woman flew to surely and instinctively, leaving the man behind with his plodding good sense. Now I must be careful and submit to logic.

He went on. "I don't want a wife to wash my socks and cook my meals. I can do those things just fine for myself. And I don't want a big house with servants and all the possessions that go with that sort of life. I don't want to be owned by possessions. So—what will *you* do, Laurie Morgan, if you make your life out here?"

I didn't need a moment's time to think. "I want a job I'd like to help on the plan you and Persis have going. That's where money can be spent. And I can help if you'll teach me. I want to find a way to use *me*."

"That's what I want for you," he said, and kissed me.

318

There was a mingling in me of happiness and sorrow. It would be a long time before the effects of what had happened would wear off. But now, with Jon's arms warm and comforting about me, I knew that this was a beginning. Perhaps the beginning of the very first day of my life.

NEW FROM FAWCETT CREST

DOMINO by Phyllis A. Whitney	24350	$2.75
CLOSE TO HOME by Ellen Goodman	24351	$2.50
THE DROWNING SEASON by Alice Hoffman	24352	$2.50
OUT OF ORDER by Barbara Raskin	24353	$2.25
A FRIEND OF KAFKA by Isaac Bashevis Singer	24354	$2.50
ALICE by Sandra Wilson	24355	$1.95
MASK OF TREASON by Anne Stevenson	24356	$1.95
POSTMARKED THE STARS by Andre Norton	24357	$2.25

Buy them at your local bookstore or use this handy coupon for ordering.

This offer expires 1 September 81   8096